#9 Grundpark Road

Randy K. Wallace

#9 Grundpark Road

ISBN: 978-0-9846517-8-8

Library of Congress Control Number: 201193975

Cover design by All Things That Matter Press

For my wife Wendy, whose confidence in my writing has been un-wavering, and for my daughters Alexandra and Suzanna who encourage and inspire me.

BOOK I

CHAPTER 1

Daniel slept while, outside his bedroom door, the cogs of fate tumbled.

***

"Honey, he's just a boy. The foster care people trust us," said Hilda. She was two years younger than her forty-year-old husband Leonard, but even a skilled carny would guess she was ten years older. The ads claimed that fostering was a job for warm caring families, but successful foster parents, as Hilda well knew, often learned to cut off their emotional ties to avoid the pain of watching the unfortunate children come and go. It was easier to care less. Caring foster parent, an interesting oxymoron, she thought.

"Don't worry. His new family will give him a home. They'll want him and they'll love him. He'll have a life. Wouldn't you love a child you were willing to pay for? I tell you, Hilda, he's going to be fine," Leonard said.

It didn't matter if it was true or not, her husband had made the deal and it was too late for regrets. It eased her conscience to hear him rehearse it once more. "What will we tell the authorities?" she said.

"He's thirteen. We tell them he ran away. It happens all the time. We just say, 'He was a hard child to deal with. He had all kinds of problems. Officer, we woke up this morning, the window was open, and his bed was empty. He's been having troubles for months. We did everything we could.'"

Hilda sighed. The buyer had assured them he'd ship the merchandise out of province. The most the boy would ever be was an unsolved missing person case. Still, referring to Daniel as merchandise struck her as cold.

Hilda hadn't slept. She had promised Leonard that she wouldn't. Three a.m. drew near. Lights in adjacent homes had been out for several hours, but the sky had already begun to brighten. She wandered to the end of the counter where numerous kitchen calendars hung on the wall. She had always wanted to keep a journal, but these charts were as close to a diary as she would likely ever get. More than appointments, they represented her family's life; every up and down over the past five years were marked there, and they were the reason she ignored Leonard every time he demanded she throw them out.

She lifted the current calendar, revealing last year's. Jumbles of scribbles covered nearly every square. A bright pink sunburst drew her eye. It was the first birthday Daniel had spent with them and had been his thirteenth. Pink hadn't impressed him, though. Hilda smiled remembering how she had paraded him to the calendar so that she could show him she hadn't forgotten his very important day. She had been surprised to see his reaction, but she should have known, after all, he was a teenager. She had focused on making the star bright and eye catching. Pink was the only highlighter she had.

The sound of a slowing vehicle drew her attention to the window and she watched a limo roll up to the driveway and back into the open garage bay. She didn't have to look at the clock to know that the driver was on time. How could she have let it get this far? Her gut gurgled. The taste of vomit rose in her mouth and she forced it back down while her husband brushed by on his way to the garage.

***

Leonard stepped into the garage. His goose-bumps felt like sandpaper. A man stepped out wearing what looked to be a once perfectly creased double-breasted jacket and matching trousers, now wrinkled by long hours in the driver seat. His muscular build was easy enough to discern, while his deep tan created a startling contrast between his face and his light blond, almost white hair.

"The boy's just in here," said Leonard, ushering the man through the living room. He hoped the driver wouldn't notice the dilapidated furniture, but when he glanced back the man's face was expressionless. It hadn't occurred to him that his guest didn't care.

Light from the hall illuminated the bedroom. A smallish boy with a slight frame lay on a ratty homemade bed beneath a haphazard jumble of moth eaten sheets and blankets. The stranger slid his hand into his inside breast pocket producing a small brown bottle and a syringe. His intent was obvious and the method of sedation he planned to use was of no concern to Leonard.

The boy slept, his eyes flickering beneath his lids.

CHAPTER 2

Daniel dreamed. He stood in the school gymnasium, watching boys warm up playing Twenty-one or shooting free throws. There were some good players. Daniel knew he was small for a thirteen year old, but Tim Brindle was smaller, a broomstick of a kid everyone teased about staying out of the wind. No problem beating him out for a spot, he thought.

The whistle blew. "Everybody over here!" the coach bellowed. Daniel wanted to run too, but his dream legs wouldn't move and the other boys left him behind.

"Sterling!" the coach yelled, "You want to play on this team or not?"

Oh, great start, Daniel thought, pushing forward, but there was no room to squeeze between the boys and none of them budged.

"Pair off and shoot fifty free-throws each."

Kids peeled off in pairs and began shooting baskets with flawless precision, leaving Daniel alone.

The coach strode in Daniel's direction. *Damn.*

"Let's go, Sterling. I'll rebound for you," he called out, passing the ball.

It spun through the air, hurling toward him; he willed his hands to catch it but he couldn't move them fast enough. He watched helplessly as the ball slammed into his chest knocking the wind out of him.

Daniel jerked awake. A heavy weight pressed into his ribcage. He blinked to focus in the dim light and struggled to rise, but a stranger's knee bore down on him preventing it.

Daniel thrashed under the heavy mass. He tried to scream, but a hand snaked out and cupped his mouth. He achieved nothing more than a muffled snarl.

Daniel realized it was Leonard who held him down while a big man inserted the needle into an inverted container and exchanged the space inside the syringe with liquid. The giant tapped out the air bubbles and stabbed the needle through cotton pajamas into Daniel's thigh. Daniel's head began to reel and his vision tunneled.

***

After a few moments, Leonard felt the boy's rigid frame relax as he slipped into unconsciousness. The buyer returned the spent syringe to his pocket, saying, "Pick him up." Leonard snapped to like a recruit in training.

He carried the limp body through the house to the waiting car. What Leonard first thought to be a limousine was a hearse, its cargo a makeshift coffin made of plywood and painted black. Numerous holes along the sides provided ventilation. The man flipped open the top revealing a padded interior, dimpled randomly with staple heads.

He took the boy from Leonard and placed the body in the box, secured the lid, and pushed the casket far into the back of the car. The driver slammed the tailgate closed and hopped into the driver seat. He retrieved an old briefcase from the passenger seat that looked like it may have come from a garage sale or the Salvation Army and passed it through the window to Leonard. After waiting long enough to see the money counted, the driver threw the car into gear and disappeared into the early morning.

***

The dashboard lit Dexter's face like a fireside storyteller. He flicked on high beams and drove out of the small Albertan suburb. His mind leapfrogged from one thought to another starting with his new home on the Mexican coast, financed by a dozen trips a year just like this one.

I should be making the lion's share, he thought and his lip rose into an involuntary sneer.

The world had changed, but business hadn't. The front for his illicit trade was a legitimate worldwide adoption organization supplying families who were otherwise ineligible or unwilling to risk adopting a 'less-than-perfect' child.

What a charade. Adoption? Yeah right. We sell people! The only difference is that legal sales come with documentation and have less of a profit margin. I make them the real money.

Greed and envy burned inside him, fueling his long drive west. He glanced at a piece of paper tucked into the visor with the address scribbled across it. Where the hell is Vanderhoof anyway?

CHAPTER 3

Terrance McMaster sat in discussion with his wife while expecting the hearse that was by now winding its way toward them. A stack of pages, each covered in painstakingly printed notations, lay in the middle of the table. Hours of contemplation had left the curled corner of each leaf darkened from use. He sat scrutinizing his calculations in excited anticipation for the coming day.

A full beard camouflaged a chin too long for his round face. His large head and close-set eyes made it impossible to find glasses that fit. No matter which frames he chose, the arms stretched around his face making him look like he wore child's rims and giving him a beady-eyed appearance.

His wife stood watching over his shoulder, sucking food from her teeth and working her pin-straight hair into a bun with practiced precision.

McMaster's chest expanded. "Matilda!" he yelled, letting out a disgusted breath.

"Sorry," she whispered, clasping her hands.

He continued. "We'll have to call him by some other name."

"Why?"

McMaster rolled his eyes and cocked his head slightly in her direction. Sarcasm dripping from each word, he said, "What will happen if someone finds out he's staying with us?" Her slack, bovine look never seemed to leave her face and he hated her for it. What had he ever seen in her? He couldn't tell if she was stupid or just didn't care. Neither of these scenarios inspired his respect. He went on, "If police are looking for him, they'll have a hard time connecting our 'nephew' with some missing kid." He turned back to his documents.

Although the projected benefits were hard to predict, he listed them nonetheless. Against those, he subtracted the cost of the acquisition's living space, its food, clothing and occasional downtime for poor health. There was always the possibility of total loss, but the risk seemed acceptable. Hell, he couldn't even guarantee his investment in his livestock. But in less than a decade, he was sure to recoup this expense and begin reaping his dividends. The boy would still be in his prime. Contemplation ended with the sound of tires churning gravel at the end of a long driveway.

***

The driver noted the old-fashioned red barn standing beside the small, quaint country cottage, its roofline accented with dormer windows. A wraparound covered porch completed the portrait. Fences and outbuildings dotted the area north of the main house. He slowed to a stop beside the barn. In the yard, a mangy German shepherd cowered uncharacteristically on its chain, wandering aimlessly back and forth, disinterested in the crow that squawked from the top of the doghouse.

***

McMaster took one last sip of coffee before rising. His belly hung over his belt like a half filled water sack and bounced with every stride. He slowed before passing through the door in an effort to compose himself. The driver greeted him through the open window with a nod and casual rising of his index finger from the steering wheel—casual considering the nature of his visit.

"I've made preparations in the barn," McMaster said.

Dual doors swung on rustic hand-forged hinges. The barn was a classic design, the roof reminiscent of a little Dutch girl's hat. McMaster lifted the board from the metal brackets. He pulled the drop pin from the ground, and yarded both doors open exposing an immaculate space inside. The smell of fresh paint still lingered. He waited for the driver to back in so he could close the big doors behind it.

The driver opened the rear door revealing a small black casket. The low-grade plywood used in the coffin's construction gave it the appearance of having gone through several exhumations, and the flat black paint failed to hide the imperfections in the wood. He grabbed one end and pulled it most of the way out of the vehicle.

McMaster rushed to do his share of the work. The weight of the box took him by surprise. It slipped from his grip and tumbled to the ground. The sudden jerk wrenched the opposite end from the driver's hands. The coffin hit the ground hard on one edge and teetered there before settling right side up.

The driver grunted. His disgust was almost tangible.

Although the unconventional crate had sustained some damage—the seam along the bottom gaped while the lid was askew—it remained intact. McMaster felt mortified and could only offer a sheepish grin and shrug his shoulders.

The driver retrieved his end of the box. McMaster could feel his revulsion. He scrambled to do his part, never allowing their eyes to meet. They moved it carefully to a nearby set of sawhorses set out for the purpose. After fumbling with bent latches, McMaster opened the casket. Inside lay the figure of a boy, dressed in flannel drawstring pants and a tee shirt. McMaster's thin smile drooped, revealing his more common expressionless façade. "He's smaller than I expected."

"He'll grow."

McMaster raised a finger and hurried away. He returned with a tattered satchel. The man took it, flipped it open to ensure the contents, and tossed it into the empty cargo space. By the time the man had buckled his seatbelt, McMaster had the barn doors open. Minutes after its arrival, the hearse retraced its path along the gravel driveway, leaving the barnyard empty and silent.

The smuggled goods awaited closer inspection. The padded coffin looked like it had provided a comfortable enough ride for its occupant. McMaster stood over his purchase appreciating the care taken to ensure its safe arrival. No one would have suspected a hearse of carrying this kind of contraband.

McMaster gazed into the crate with a look that, under other circumstances, could have been mistaken for pride. The color of the boy's face was a healthy pink and the man had been right, he would grow. Satisfied, McMaster closed and fastened the lid, leaving the boy and casket, a morbid spectacle in the gloomy half-light.

CHAPTER 4

Daniel's dreams swam with images spawned by what little his starved senses could glean. His subconscious mind struggled against invisible attackers. Somewhere beyond his view, a door slammed shut. His imagination provided a kitchen chair wedged under the doorknob by a vindictive foster parent. He struggled to awaken, but could not force his eyelids open. His relentless nightmare swept him along at its whim.

***

Inside the house, McMaster sat in front of the television. His hand moved instinctively to the remote and he selected his favorite program. Lit only by the fluctuating light, he sat disinterested. *The deliveryman said the boy would sleep until morning, but he could wake up at any time. What would happen then?* He'd better check on him.

McMaster stood and walked away leaving the TV on, a sin he reprimanded his wife for at every opportunity but, since he paid the bills, waste was his prerogative. He went to the liquor cabinet, poured himself a double shot, slammed it back and slid the empty glass onto the table. He stopped on the front porch long enough to throw on a light jacket. He tramped to the barn, flashlight in hand, its beam bouncing along the ground.

He approached the casket and lifted its lid. The boy rested, his face slack and vacant, his shirt collar visibly damp from drool that still oozed from the corner of his mouth. McMaster ogled his new toy. The boy's chest rose and fell in slow rhythm giving no reason to think he would wake any time in the near future.

McMaster closed the lid and returned to the house and his favorite chair. He bathed in the glimmer of the television, watching a program he couldn't care less about, let alone remember.

***

Daniel opened his eyes to the black. He felt sick to his stomach. Groggy and disoriented, he clasped his arms across his chest to try to keep the warmth inside. The moisture from his breath, combined with the cool night air, had turned his confines into a refrigerator. He shivered.

The last thing he remembered was brushing his teeth and going to bed. With fall approaching, Leonard had agreed he could try out for the basketball team. He had dreamt about that, now this.

Darkness was absolute. Dread seeped into him. He sat up and slammed his face into something soft, but at the same time unyielding. Every tensed muscle strained from the unexpected impedance and he fell back, bewildered. Stiff and sore, he was desperate to stretch and move. He tried to roll to one side but his knees came to a stop against the same surface his face had met. Fear took hold as he realized that he was in inside some sort of enclosure. Frantically he explored his prison, reaching, pushing, and twisting. He was in a crate of some sort, but it was not square. The box narrowed near his head. He screamed, but it was as though he were screaming into a pillow. Writhing arms and legs had no leverage. He stopped, gasping through a tightened throat, overpowered by a sense of futility and growing claustrophobia. He struggled to quell his fear, his sense of place in the world lost.

Succumbing to panic, he threw himself to one side of his prison walls with all of his might. He could feel movement and took advantage of the momentum. All at once the box slid to one side. There was a brief calm before it crashed to the ground. The enclosure collapsed from the impact. The top came down on his face.

Daniel thrashed inside the broken box. With each bone-jarring drive, he could feel the fasteners loosen more. It spurred him on. In a final effort, the top and sides of the crate separated from the bottom. He pushed himself up and felt something bite into his left hand. He felt metal sliding into his flesh, puncturing his palm. He pulled away, ignoring the resistance as what he guessed to be nails retraced their path. He rolled from the wreckage, clutching his hand to his chest. He knew he was hurt, but in the dark he had no idea how bad. His fingertips pulsated.

He hobbled away from the box using his three good limbs, only to collide head-first into a wall. Tears welled in his eyes. He sat up and leaned against the wall, his aching chest heaving, his throbbing hand cradled in his lap and his free hand clutching his smarting head.

Exhausted, confused and groggy, his eyelids grew heavy. Daniel wondered if this was what it was like to have a drug overdose as he drifted into unconsciousness.

CHAPTER 5

The stars slipped across the night sky, chased by the rising sun. The interior of the barn shifted from black to grey until the world warmed with color once more. Dust particles danced in streams of sunlight.

McMaster slept on the verge of wakefulness, turning and twisting in his sleep. Mrs. McMaster took no notice. She lay with her knees crooked and her face hanging over the edge of the bed. He rarely disturbed her unless he came too close. It was enough that her husband provided for her. She had no urges for the man other than that. She rose and went into the kitchen. He'd be up soon and he'd want to eat.

***

McMaster came to the table to a waiting meal, as he expected and demanded. He rushed through breakfast and, between mouthfuls, reiterated to his wife, "Matilda, he has to know who the boss is. You've got to be firm all the time. He's not our child and he's not our friend." His elation grew as he restated every detail he could think of. His monologue ended with the meal. He tossed his napkin in the general direction of the table on his way out. The screen door slammed behind him, bouncing against the frame once before settling onto the latch.

He reached the barn feeling excited about the day that lay ahead, and eager to put his newly acquired asset to work. But when the doors swung open, the smile on his face vanished. His mouth dropped in disbelief at the sight that awaited him. The shattered casket and broken sawhorses lay in ruins on the floor. McMaster ran to the debris, his heart sinking with every step. With my luck, he thought, he'll be laying dead in the dirt.

His eyes widened in disbelief. The boy was gone. Comprehension slapped his face. The boy had planned all of this and was now escaping. Had he slipped out while my back was turned? McMaster ran to the gaping doors and locked them behind him. He scanned the open area between the barn and the house—no movement. He stood in motionless panic, his heart thumping in his chest. If the boy had managed to get outside, he could disappear and be gone forever. McMaster cursed. Why hadn't I been more careful?

With his ears cocked and his head bobbing like a chicken's from side to side, he inched to the house, scanning the yard, bushes and buildings.

He reached the porch and spun toward the barn. He called to his wife in the house, "Matilda, I need you out here!" His voice reverberated with urgency; veins protruded from his forehead.

"I'm in the middle of putting bread in the oven," his wife called from inside.

His veins doubled in size. "Shut up *woman* and get out here. This is important!"

She cringed, familiar with his tone. An old bruise on her face had faded enough that her makeup now covered it. She scrambled through the door and arrived at her husband's side, panting.

Without acknowledging her, McMaster continued to scan the yard and in a low conspirator's tone he said, "He could be anywhere. He broke out of the box. I left the door open for just a moment, but he could have slipped out. You keep your eyes open out here and I'll double-check inside."

He slipped across the driveway with his knees bent and his head doing a chicken-bob. He nudged the door open and, like a character in a movie, slid his wide frame through and then closed it behind him. The only thing missing to make it a scene from an action film was a dramatic roll in the dirt. Even before he completed his first sweep, his eyes came to rest on his captive leaning against the far wall. McMaster called over his shoulder, "Never mind. He's here." Mrs. McMaster nodded in the direction of his voice and returned to her bread.

The boy slouched with his head drooping forward. Dried blood matted his hair. A congealed drop hung from the end of his nose. Was he breathing? McMaster was still too far away to tell. He felt nauseated at the thought that something horrible may have befallen the boy. The impact on his financial outlook would be disastrous. It wasn't until he stood over the body and could see the regular movements of his chest that a sigh of relief escaped him.

A cursory examination was all that was necessary to see that the head wound was superficial. The bleeding had stopped some time ago. What blood was there was brown and crusty. He reached out with one finger and prodded the boy as if afraid to catch some infectious disease.

"Hey, wake up." He waited for a response. "You! Boy! Wake up!"

Daniel's eyes turned into narrow slits and he tilted his head toward McMaster.

"Get up!" McMaster ordered, and added with barely a pause, "Come with me."

Daniel's eyes closed.

With a disgusted grunt, McMaster reached forward hooking his hand under Daniel's armpit. He hardly weighs more than a sack of grain, McMaster thought. He hefted him to his feet and dragged him toward the house.

***

Daniel winced as pain shot up his arm. He stumbled once, regained his footing, and ran a few steps to catch up to the big man's stride, his only desire to stop the agony. He attempted to identify his surroundings, but his eyes would not focus under their sudden exposure to bright sunlight. He managed only fleeting glances of the ground, green trees, and unfamiliar buildings.

The step up to the front porch came as a painful surprise. His foot slammed against the first riser while his body flew ahead, caught by the steel shackle of McMaster's grip. His arms hung limp, fingers brushing the wooden surface of the porch before McMaster hoisted him up and set him up straight on his feet like a stumbling two-year-old. There was a brief pause at the door before they burst into the kitchen. McMaster plopped him into a dining room chair and loomed over him.

Snapping his fingers in front of Daniel's face, McMaster said, "Boy, do you understand me?"

Daniel did not respond.

McMaster placed both palms on the table and leaned forward. Then, speaking as if to someone hard of hearing, with long pauses between each word, he said, "Do, you, understand, what … I am, saying, to you?"

A weak nod indicated affirmative.

"You can call me Mister McMaster. This is Missus McMaster." His hand swept in Matilda's direction. "We own you."

Daniel's eyes widened. "No you don't."

He felt the wind from McMaster's hand a fraction of a second before it crashed into the back of his head. The joints in his neck cracked as he snapped forward, his face stopping mere inches from the table.

"I own you," McMaster repeated.

Daniel focused on the tabletop and warm fury rose in his face. With pursed lips, he said, mimicking McMaster's insulting tone, "One person cannot own another person. You can't own me." There was no time to add another thought. McMaster's hand flew, this time rocking him to the side, but Daniel ignored the pain that exploded in his ear. "One person cannot own another person," he said again.

McMaster yanked him to his feet and hauled him through the kitchen door, never slowing enough to allow the boy to gain his footing. Thrown off balance by McMaster's sudden step off the porch, Daniel stumbled after him, tripping in his effort to keep up. He landed on the side of his foot and twisted onto his back. Flailing, he tried to right himself. He fought to twist his arm from his captor's grasp, but McMaster's grip was like iron. McMaster dragged him as he thrashed all the way to the woodshed.

The shed was a minimal post and beam construction designed to keep wood dry. The floor was made of rough sawn lumber, covered in a layer of wood debris Daniel imagined had been left over from years of firewood storage.

McMaster released his grip, sending Daniel toward the back of the building. It was then that his eyes fell upon Daniel's puncture wounds for the first time.

"What happened to you, boy?"

"I hurt myself," Daniel said, his voice thick with mockery. The skin on his hand was already turning red in the places where each nail had entered. A fleeting thought occurred to him — the sting hadn't come right away, much like a slice from a sharp knife, the pain dawns on you later.

McMaster became furious. "A warm and comfortable bed is a luxury. When you start giving me the respect I demand, I'll consider upgrading your quarters. Until then, you've got a new life to get used to. I *will* have your respect boy, one way, or another." McMaster turned and left.

When McMaster slammed the door and clicked the lock closed, it felt like a punctuation of his harsh reality. Daniel followed McMaster's departure from inside the woodshed, looking out through the cracks in the walls. He could see the haphazard gouges left in the dirt from his passage moments earlier, but focused his stare at McMaster. Maybe he could light him on fire with his anger and hatred. McMaster seemed oblivious.

My name is Daniel, not boy!

CHAPTER 6

That night Daniel slept deeply, his body too fatigued to care where he was or why strangers had taken him from Leonard and Hilda's home.

He opened his dreaming eyes to find himself looking through the eyes of another—a fly on the wall, as Hilda might have said. He knew these new eyes belonged to a man called Grundpark. There was no reason to know, but he knew the name was right and true just the same.

Daniel looked down to see his wrinkled and callused hands grasping old leather straps—reins, he knew immediately. Rain poured from the evening sky and in the same way he knew that he was Grundpark he also knew he was in a time long passed and that it had been raining for weeks.

The clay was sticky glue and the shallow ditch beside the road ran swollen with water. Mud caked the horse's hooves and tugged at the steel encased wooden spoked wheels. Grundpark's head turned skyward ignoring droplets that splashed into his squinting eyes. He heard himself say, in Grundpark's deeper voice, a *thank you* that he had had the good sense not to load the wagon heavily for this particular trip home. The water that had pooled on his brim trickled over his collar and down the back of his slicker. With an effortless flick, the reins rolled toward the horse's shoulders and rapped them. He clucked to the animal, but if it picked up speed it was imperceptible. Hunkered against the downpour, Daniel sat, a stoic hump swaying to the rhythm of potholes and protruding rocks, no longer the skinny thirteen year old sleeping in a pile of woodchips.

Hidden amongst spruce and pine, the stable appeared: a lean-to made of logs. Recognizing that it was almost home, the horse shook its head and livened up its step. Daniel guided the steed inside and pulled the rig to a halt with familiar ease. He dropped the reins across the seat and jumped to the ground, experiencing none of the limitations of aging that he would have expected from a frame as old as Grundpark's. There was none of the stiffness in his joints or even a hint of curvature in his back. Either I have become the old man and kept my youth or I'm pretty spry for a geezer, he thought, and just as quickly it came to him—he knew the latter was true.

Moments later, the horse was feeding at its trough in a stall at the back of the building. Leaving the animal, he walked to what appeared to be a well. He put his back to the hole and climbed into the darkness. At the bottom, he stepped into several inches of water. The darkness was suffocating. He reached to a familiar spot and plucked a lamp from a nail that he'd bent into a hook.

He slipped a match from his pocket and popped it into a flame with the tip of his thumbnail. In one fluid movement he lit the lantern waved the match out and tossed the stub away. He returned the lamp to the nail and turned his attention to the hand pump at the bottom of the shaft. As he pushed and pulled the pump handle, the water level dropped around his feet. With a final thrust, he took up the lantern and turned to the tunnel.

Wooden supports lined the passage that was once a mineshaft, which he had dug with his own hands. He tramped along the narrow path, at the center of the halo. Although the air was dank, the floor of the cave was dry enough. Somewhere far below his feet, water flowed over bedrock in underground lakes and streams. Porous rock kept moisture from collecting during the storms, but he kept the entry pumped out nonetheless.

The passage opened into a large homey chamber. Being devoid of dividing walls as it was, furniture delineated each living space. Rich décor contradicted the underground haven making the cave curiously welcoming.

The space was set apart further by an extraordinary stone door adorning the farthest wall. Three-dimensional carvings inlaid with gold and amethyst surrounded a central design depicting colorfully clad figures kneeling around a giant cross-sectioned egg. Two concentric rings formed the oval. The first ring, carved from the bright yellow stone, was a simple pattern of rhombus shaped dimples. Thousands of gemstones, that could only be diamonds, created the second, more striking inner band. At the center of the door, chest high, an intricately engraved bronze plate completed the artwork.

Daniel-slash-Grundpark stood in front of the door admiring the craftsmanship of a society long extinct. For a time, he stood as a statue, contemplating the strange dissimilitude between himself and the door. On one hand, his skin was ancient parchment covering a youth he mourned. On the other hand, the door stood in its original glory, hiding ancient secrets. He wondered at the significance of his revelation and decided there was none, just an interesting observation. He reminisced how the cavern had drawn him inexplicably to this place. Years had passed since he made the discovery and still it amazed him. He had even moved his belongings from his house so he could live next to it. Grundpark ran his fingers along the stone, satisfied that his treasure was secret and safe, then he went about his evening tasks.

He stirred heat into his meal in a silence broken only by the sound of the crackling fire in the woodstove. He took the hot dish and set it on a pad in the center of the kitchen table. From a nearby hutch, he removed good china and silver cutlery. He added a crystal glass and a bottle of wine then sat down with a cloth on his lap and enjoyed both food and wine. The sound of rushing water from somewhere up the passage was mildly annoying. What could it be now? He dipped his bread in the thick broth amongst chunks of carrots, potatoes, and meat, and savored the taste and texture.

After raking his bowl clean with the last morsel of bread, he extinguished the lamps until only one remained which lit his path to the stone door. From his pocket, he produced a small leather pouch. From inside that he pulled a short wooden rod, admiring it while running his fingers over his fine workmanship. It was nothing compared to the artwork of the door, but still, very good if he said so himself. Had it been ten or twelve years since he first whittled it? The carving of the key had been especially difficult since Indian Rosewood was nearly as hard as stone.

Grasping it in the middle, he twisted it and the cylinder divided, revealing a star shaped pattern in the middle of one end, which he slid into a hole in the door at the center of the bronze plate. His key was merely a replica. What did the original look like? It didn't matter; his creation functioned perfectly. He turned it. Somewhere inside the door, primitive workings clicked in smooth precision, a testament to the amazing ingenuity of its creator.

He dimmed the light before pivoting the door on its central focal that acted as a single hinge. Light flooded from the room, a phenomenon as entrancing as it had been when he first witnessed it. He doused the flame and fully opened the door.

Grundpark stepped into the radiance, shielding his eyes from the glow emanating from thousands of crystals, the reality of the amazing depiction on the door. He had stepped into a giant geode, unique in its size and composition. Unlike diamonds, these crystals emitted their own light, gathered from the lantern and then amplified. Beautiful, he thought.

As much as he wanted to, he could not ignore the sound of the running water. Fed up, he donned his coat and made his way toward the sound. He paused periodically to examine the integrity of the passage. It was a routine he performed ritually like so many other aspects of his life. His eyes wandered upward to a huge boulder that served as a sort of threshold to his home. He felt safe beneath its unshakable mass.

He sloshed through watery mud. A thick oozing sound made him turn in time to see sludge flow into the passage behind him. Damn, now I'll have to deal with that too. He reached the entrance. Water flowed over the rim above as if the world had become a pitcher and his cavern had become the cup. Grundpark climbed to the surface and trudged through the downpour to the barn where he stored his hand tools. He'd need a shovel to redirect the floodwaters.

Several hours later, drenched and exhausted, he descended the ladder only to discover knee-deep water at the bottom. With a weary series of sighs, he pumped out the excess and then soaked with sweat and rain he trudged toward his underground haven. The slosh of each footfall echoed from the darkness. He halted at the mudflow, forgotten in the wake of the flood. Unnatural warmth wafted toward him from the cavern, beckoning him to his bed. To hell with it, he thought. The mud will have to wait.

He waded forward, the thick and sticky muck like gauntlets grasping his legs, pulling him down. His thighs and calves ached and he hadn't yet passed the halfway mark. He rested then trudged onward. Midway, he stopped to catch his breath and noticed then that his steps were disappearing in the mire. Liquid clay and gravel dripped from the ceiling and walls. The passage was in danger of collapse at any moment. Home would not be safe until the ground dried and he added more beams for support. Cold and disappointed, he waded in the direction of the dark and the rain.

The earth shifted around him.

Fluid earth flowed in from all sides, rising up his legs. He struggled, but the thick sludge held him like an ever-tightening vise. Panicked, he pulled hard at his boots, lost his balance and fell forward. Mud continued to rise. Above, the ground sagged imperceptibly, and the sky poured down its mourning.

**

Daniel woke to bright light with the feeling he had stepped from one very real world to another. His gut told him that his dream was important, but already the events were slipping into that grey unreachable place between sleep and consciousness. The real world took solid hold and he remembered where he was.

One thing about his dream remained, though. The cold that had seeped into his bones was genuine. His body ached and his palm stung, but he allowed his anger toward McMaster to cloud the pain. His was a world without love. It had always been that way. It was all he could remember. Why should he ever think that it might change? Maybe Leonard and Hilda had already called the police. They might try to find him.

He thought about times from the past. Back then, there had been hope that one day somebody would tell him about his real mother and father, but no one ever had. What was the longest he'd spent in one place? Two years? Probably.

He missed his counselor and their bi-weekly visits. He'd started visiting with Pete when he was five. There was no one he had known longer. Pete would listen and try to help him understand. Poor guy, he was the one who could never understand. Instead of trying to explain, Pete should have said, "It sucks, Daniel. Your life is hell and it probably won't get any better." Daniel could have believed that.

Few of the foster homes had been warm and welcoming. One foster dad beat him up and he told Pete about it. That day, he waited at the Children Services office, sitting on the hard sterile bench next to a garbage bag full of his clothes. He was there when the office closed. One of the social workers stayed behind, making a series of frantic calls, trying to find someone to take him. The social worker eventually did, but there were five other children in that house and, within the week, they bounced him. Was there an official term for it? 'Bouncing' was as good as any. It described the way he felt. At least that time he knew why. He knew when he piled out of the van at ten o'clock that night he'd only be there a day or two. Maybe tomorrow they'll bounce me again.

There were good days, too. Images of friendly faces washed over him. He struggled to remember names, but couldn't. Tears, outstretched arms, and screaming filled his memories. Sometimes the tears belonged to others, but the screaming and outstretched arms were always his alone.

Even those who swore their love proved to be liars. If they loved him, they would have found a way to keep him. They would have made good on their word. Then their names would have been worth remembering. He was over that now and he'd be damned if a pig like McMaster would get the better of him.

CHAPTER 7

Matilda followed Terrance to the shed. Daniel was asleep with his knees pulled up to his chest and his hands clasped between his legs. He had made a makeshift blanket by pulling bark up around him. There were streaks of clean on his face where, she could only surmise, rivulets of his tears had washed away the grime.

The horror of seeing Daniel lying in the dirt shocked Mrs. McMaster. She turned to her husband and was sickened to see a thin satisfied smile stretched across his face.

"I've got some things to do. Check on him every half hour or so. Make sure he gets something to eat," McMaster said on his way out.

Daniel woke as she slathered the cream on the palm and back of his hand. When she was done, she rose.

"Why are you doing this to me?" he said.

"We bought you," she replied and turned to walk away, adding, "Better get some rest."

CHAPTER 8

A sharp stab in his side woke him with a start. He looked up to see the hulking pig glaring down and realized McMaster had kicked him.

"You remember me? You remember that I own you?"

Daniel nodded, no point arguing.

"I am a man of my word, boy. So help me, if you attempt to escape … ever … I will kill you with my bare hands. Do not doubt me!"

Daniel held his gaze in defiance.

McMaster waited only seconds before sending the boy's head sideways with a quick slap.

In a slow monotone Daniel said, "I got it."

"Good. There are a few things you need to understand. The first is this: if you want to eat, you'll have to work. You'll eat what's in front of you because that's all you're going to get. There won't be seconds. You're nothing more than livestock as far as I'm concerned." He placed a bowl of cereal on the floor.

Daniel fought the urge to bring the bowl to his lips and drink, but he waited in the hopes that McMaster would leave him alone. When he showed no sign of going, Daniel ate, forcing himself to take slow measured mouthfuls.

"From now on you will be called Justin."

"But my name is Daniel."

McMaster's reply was blistering. "You are Justin and that is all you will be called from now on! Justin!"

The boy looked down in resignation.

"You will be given a place to sleep and three meals a day. There will be no days of rest and no holidays of any kind. The only time you will not be working is when you are eating, sleeping, or using the bathroom. Do you understand?"

Daniel acknowledged, but inside he raged.

"Good." The orientation droned on until finally McMaster threw a couple of old blankets in his direction. "This is your new home."

Hours and days crawled by, and Daniel's hand healed. For the first few days he was happy with his solitude. But after he regained his strength, he became bored and began to wake with the hope that today would be the day McMaster would put him to work. It would mean an end to the nothingness. And as long as he remained in the shed, there would be no chance of escape.

The morning that McMaster arrived to collect him came at last. He marched him to an entry at the back of the house. The mudroom was equipped with a deep laundry basin and he washed while McMaster towered over him. They hadn't given him an opportunity to bathe or have a clean set of clothes since he had arrived, and now they were letting him wash his hands. At least some part of him was clean.

McMaster hauled him through the house. He whipped passed rooms with little time to observe their purpose. They didn't pause until they reached the kitchen where McMaster dropped him into a chair made of steel pipe and plywood that appeared to have been at one time covered in vinyl. It stood mismatched with the set of solid hardwood chairs surrounding the table.

If trust meant clean clothes, a table to sit at and more freedom, Daniel vowed to be trustworthy. After all, 'trustworthiness' was no more than a series of actions.

Daniel ate. He was still eating when without warning Mrs. McMaster began to clear the table. There was still a half a slice of toast on the plate and Daniel held the half-full glass of milk in one hand. As McMaster instructed her, the woman pulled away the silverware, bowl, and plate with the toast still on it. He had just enough time to snatch the last of his meal. The woman made a second trip for the glass and Daniel downed the milk with a single gulp before she took it. McMaster hoisted him up and hauled him to the door. He chewed and swallowed as he rushed to keep up. Mrs. McMaster gathered a jug and a paper bag from the kitchen counter and followed the two outside.

McMaster led him to the back of the barn. The soil there was muddy. Midway along the back wall a long thin cable was coiled and attached to a heavy concrete block. He's going to chain me up like a dog, thought Daniel. Secured on stakes at each end, a long nylon cord stretched parallel to the back of the building. "Dig a trench the full length of the barn along this string. I want the ditch as straight as the line. You'll have dinner when you're done. The water and the lunch in the bag is all you'll get till then." McMaster clasped the cable around Daniel's wrist, snapped the lock in place, then walked away with Mrs. McMaster trailing behind.

Daniel picked up the shovel, hefting it in two hands like a baseball bat, aiming it in McMaster's direction. He brought it part way through a swing, his look telling all. In despair, he stood wondering—not at the task, but at the life the McMasters expected him to accept. Accept it? No. *To hell with that.*

Using the shovel like an axe, he hacked at the cable next to the metal ring. It was made of a tougher material than he first imagined, but a dozen strokes managed to dent it and sever several strands. Fifty or sixty more of the same would cut the cable in two. Ignoring the loud ringing, he chopped, oblivious to McMaster's heavy footfalls growing nearer. More strands parted. Daniel hammered harder.

McMaster appeared around the edge of the building. His eyes flew wide. He clenched his fists in rage and broke into a lumbering run, heaps of flab rocking above his waistband.

Daniel looked up. He took a final swipe at the cable then dropped the spade and ran. The distance between them grew rapidly until he came to the end of his tether. The cuff bit into his arm, yanking him to a stop. His legs flew out from under him and he paused, suspended like an action figure, outstretched in midair. He slammed into the ground and the line snapped in two. He scrambled to his feet, but McMaster was upon him. He ran, ducking beneath the massive swinging arms.

McMaster grabbed hold of the trailing cable.

Daniel felt it tighten. Though his hand threatened to part from his wrist, he leaned forward and scrambled for every inch. He dug into the soil with both feet and his one free hand. Pain tore into his arm, but he pulled harder. Suddenly, he was free. He pitched forward, caught himself from falling, and ran.

McMaster took up the chase, stopping long enough to scoop up the shovel.

Daniel rounded the corner of the barn and loped toward the driveway. Twenty feet of steel line slithered around the building behind him. Suddenly it caught. He whipped the cord to try to release it. The arc raced toward the barn and snapped against the wall, but did not come free. *Time—need time.* There was none. He whipped the line again, but to no avail. He raced back.

He looked up in time to see the flat side of the shovel sweep through the air at him. There was a brief explosion in his skull and the world disappeared.

CHAPTER 9

Consciousness came paired with a searing pain emanating from his head. He opened his eyes, then realized he could see through only one. The floor spun. He closed his good eye and vomited. Yellow bile spewed and dribbled from his chin. He spat to clear his mouth and retched again at the acrid taste of his own vomit. The muscles in his stomach tightened and his head threatened to burst. Stars circulated behind his eyelids and his body contracted. He willed it to settle, opened his eyes to see that the room had not ceased spinning, and then drifted back into merciful unconsciousness.

***

McMaster went to the woodshed pushing a gurney. He arrived to find Daniel curled in a ball. The left side of his face was swollen and misshapen; his eye was a fat slit. He pulled the lids apart revealing the bloodshot orb and a fully dilated pupil. Maybe it was blind. Serves you right if it is, he thought. He hoisted the kid onto the gurney and wheeled it to the barn. Mrs. McMaster stood next to a bed near the centre of the building. She helped transfer the boy. Dried blood caked his shirt and the stench from his rotting old clothes and fresh vomit was unbearable. Once she saw that he was breathing she took quick strides from the building.

In the farmhouse, Mrs. McMaster busied herself with lunch and brought it to the table minutes before her husband was due to walk through the door. Her hands rifled through the flatware searching for appropriate utensils. Her hand fell upon the carving knife, fingers caressing it for a moment longer than necessary. Then she let it fall into the drawer … no more than an impotent desire. She pulled out a butter knife and fork. Waiting for food was intolerable for Terence. Her fingers rose to her face finding their way to a crescent scar that coursed around her right eye, yet another blunt reminder of her husband's temper. She quickened her pace.

McMaster sat without paying a second's heed to her and waited while she filled his plate with his favorite fare. A tall glass of iced tea waited for him, which he guzzled before picking up his fork. He finished half of what was on his plate then lifted his empty glass, rocked it in the air and put it back onto the table.

Mrs. McMaster recognized the gesture and moved without hesitation to refill his cup.

He finished his lunch, consulted his watch, and retired to his favorite chair in the living room. With a small clicking sound the TV came to life.

He chose one of his preferred channels and watched as a gap-toothed, overweight woman beat on a smaller, retarded looking man on the *Jerry Springer Show*. He chuckled at that—his first utterance since entering the house.

Mrs. McMaster waited in the kitchen until she heard a blaring commercial, signaling it was safe to interrupt. She padded mouse-like into the archway, stopping short of entering the room. "Should I take lunch out to the boy?"

He emitted a moan. "It's not enough that I have to think for myself; I have to think for you too?"

Without responding, she left to see to the boy. His stench seemed to have worsened. She gagged and covered her nose before approaching, then placed the cup and plate on the ground beside the bed.

"Get up and eat. It won't be here very long," she said, regretting her sharp tone immediately. *If only I had the guts to direct my anger at the one who deserves it most.*

A sharp pain shot through her eye and it began to water, as it sometimes did. Her fingers migrated there and massaged the scar until the stinging subsided. She wiped the moisture on her sleeve and contemplated the boy. *Would his eye heal any better than hers had? Would her husband come after her the way he'd promised the boy he'd come after him? He probably would.* She winced as another pain stabbed her head like a ninja's saber. They occurred more frequently these days. *Maybe it was God's way of reminding her she was going to hell, and … maybe that's what she deserved.* She wiped her eye and returned to the house.

***

Several hours passed before McMaster appeared in the frame of the barn door.

"Get up."

Delirious, Daniel rolled to his side. Tears seeped from beneath his eyelids to add stains to the ancient yellowed pillowcase that could not hide the old, paper-thin excuse of a pillow inside. He rose and followed McMaster across the yard to the house.

"In here," McMaster said, pointing into the bathroom. A towel and clothes waited on the back of the toilet. "Clean yourself up. It's going to be a hard day's work for you tomorrow." He left the room. The sound of his footfalls faded down the hall.

Daniel's head throbbed and the scent of some cheap flowery air freshener served to accentuate the unpleasant smell radiating from his filthy body. He turned on the water and stripped. Steam rose from the shower. He tested the temperature then stepped inside. Warm water poured over him, soothing his aching body.

The door creaked open. Daniel stiffened, eyes blinking through a mask of soap bubbles. Through the translucent plastic curtain, he could see that the shape belonged to Mrs. McMaster. He peeked as she shook air into a garbage bag. She picked up his clothes and slid them gingerly inside giving no indication that it mattered that he stood naked just a thin sheet of plastic away.

The shower had turned out to be the highlight of his day. Tomorrow, they promised him, he would work in earnest. Once back in the barn, he fell asleep to visions of escape.

Later that night he woke, but not to warm sunlight or the harsh sound of McMaster's angry voice. He woke to a stabbing pain from the mashed side of his head and stinging pain from the side of his face. Wide awake now, a feeling of hopelessness washed over him. He wished for nothing more than to be back at Leonard and Hilda's.

"It's all just a bad dream," he repeated under his breath. "If I believe hard enough then maybe I can make it untrue. I could make it... unhappen. Please God, tell me I'm right." Another tear rolled down his cheek and dripped onto his soaked pillow. "Please," he begged. "Make it unhappen."

CHAPTER 10

Once again, Daniel followed McMaster to the back of the building where the stakes delineated the ditch. A heavy metal chain had replaced the thin cable. The final link was attached to a makeshift shackle fashioned from a short piece of large diameter pipe.

Dismayed, Daniel waited, afraid of the weight he'd have to pull around throughout the day.

"Sit down."

He sat.

McMaster tossed the end of the chain into his lap. "Put this around your ankle." McMaster tossed him a lock and Daniel snapped it closed.

"Show me it's secure."

Daniel gave it a yank.

"Get to it." McMaster walked away.

Daniel's lunch and a supply of water waited for him next to the block. He picked up the shovel and pushed it into the ground. Probably the cheapest one McMaster could find, thought Daniel. He could feel the folded metal ridge through the flimsy sole of his running shoe, the kind you could buy for a few dollars at the department store, the ones displayed next to the rubber boots. It was the only place anyone had ever taken him to try on new shoes. The scent of rubber and vinyl were the only 'new shoe' smells he knew. Several of the shoelace eyes had already come out of their holes and dangled loosely on the lace, but no one would replace them until their soles flopped like gaping mouths and were more like flip-flops than shoes. By such standards, these ones were still in excellent condition.

His thin socks did nothing to protect his inside ankle from rubbing on the haft each time he stood down on the spade. He was surprised that it was his hands and not his feet that were the first to give out. Large blisters formed on his thumbs and index fingers. They felt squishy and hurt each time he put pressure on them. He took a break to drink some water, but his cramped fingers formed permanent C's that would not grip the bottle. He worked at the stiffness until he could flex each finger. When I get out of here, I'm never gonna be a ditch digger.

Soon after, two of the blisters burst. They stung like a bad burn. By the time the sun told him it was noon, pressure on the shovel handle had squeezed all of the blisters flat, stripping out the moisture. The pain was so intense he could hardly hold on to the shovel.

It was an unexpected relief when McMaster wandered over to check on him; a moment to rest.

Infuriated by Daniel's new injuries, he said, "Kid, you look like you've never had a callous in your life. Your leg's not looking so good either. Were you some kind of mommy's boy? I'll bet you didn't even have chores." He took a moment to switch the shackle from one ankle to the other. "Take a break. I'll be right back." When he returned, he brought an old pair of leather gloves with him.

Daniel ate his lunch, balancing his sandwich between his aching fingers. Half the day was gone and he still had two thirds of the ditch left to dig. If McMaster's word was good, and so far it had been, he wouldn't be finished until after dark.

Thankfully, the sustenance helped. He sat on his concrete stump and rested. The stinging in his hands eased some, but he wondered how he was going to be able to carry on, even with leather gloves. Just trying to put them on nearly brought him to tears, the crusty old leather abrading his sores, but ... once in place it turned out they did make a difference. He began to make steady progress and, sooner than he had expected, his goal was in sight.

Part of his increased speed was due to softer soil, but he knew that he had also developed some skill during the day and was making better progress with less effort. Digging with his back to his destination allowed him to sink the shovel in and break off clean spadefuls the depth of the trench.

As daylight waned, his eyes adjusted to the darkness. With the white line of the string as his guide, he pretended to be a machine. As his mind disengaged from his body, the pain in his hands and legs faded to a dull ache. Repeatedly he pushed the shovel in, pried it back, lifted it and plopped the dirt onto the pile beside the hole. His motions became automatic and the ditch grew in front of him.

He halted at the sound of McMaster's stern voice. "That's enough!"

He tramped down on the spade one last time burying the blade in the ground, an unconscious exclamation point at the end of his progress. He slumped, glassy eyed and exhausted, but grateful the day had come to an end. McMaster removed his shackle, exposing a skinless patch that somehow found enough light to shimmer, and led the husk of a boy to the barn. Daniel inched up the ladder into the loft using his forearms instead of his hands to balance precariously on each rung. He dragged himself into bed.

***

In the morning, he woke with no memories of pulling his covers to his chin, nor dreams to mark the passing night. Bright light streamed through every crack. The sun had reached its peak. Why had McMaster allowed him to sleep in? He rolled to the edge of the bed and winced at the soreness. Every muscle and every joint ached. He did what he could to ignore the pain.

A tray waited on the floor next to the bed containing more food than he had seen at any one time since his arrival on the cursed farm. He blinked, convinced he had not yet woken and drowsily crawled out of bed to retrieve it. Both palms burned; the night of rest had not helped. His fingers were too stiff to bend. With trembling hands, he placed the tray in his cot next to him. Ah, breakfast in bed, he thought with a wry chuckle to himself and crawled in with it.

Mrs. McMaster arrived with some bandages. He held out his hands, patiently helping her in whatever way he could. She turned his hands over and examined them. "These aren't nearly as bad as they look. In a few days you won't need gloves. You'll have calluses, but don't let this happen again." She paused. "I can't help you, if you don't tell me what you need."

"I need to leave this place," said Daniel.

"You could choose to like it here. You would see that it isn't so bad," she said.

Liar.

McMaster appeared in the doorway and her face became a scowl. "You try to take care of yourself from now on. I don't plan on going out of my way like this all the time," she scolded as she descended the ladder.

"Thank you," he mouthed, before she disappeared below.

CHAPTER 11

McMaster led Daniel to an old rusted pickup truck and pushed him inside. He tossed a pair of antique work boots into Daniel's lap. "We're going for a little drive." A pair of handcuffs dangled from the passenger side door-handle. "Snap the free end on to your wrist."

"I won't run, Mister McMaster. I promise."

The man loomed until Daniel dropped the metal clasp over his wrist and fastened it securely, then waddled over and into the driver seat where he pumped life into the decrepit farm truck. It seemed to Daniel that he pounded the accelerator more than he pumped it. The engine coughed and then, as if responding to each swift kick, reluctantly came to life.

McMaster left the yard in a cloud of dust. He followed back roads, weaving past swamps and through groves toward a remote area at the north end of the property. The ruts pounded McMaster's voice into an involuntary staccato. "I have a new excavation project for you. It's going to be your new home for quite some time."

Daniel held on tight. The truck jerked from side to side, shooting up rooster-tails in watery holes and hopping across ruts like a psychotic rabbit. An unexpected pothole and subsequent jolt sent his head into the roof. If he hadn't been so scared, it might have been fun.

McMaster came to a halt in a small clearing containing the remnants of several ancient log buildings that time had reduced to five or six rounds of rotten timbers. To the left, a poplar tree stood sentry over an old hand dug well. A twinge of recognition flashed in Daniel's mind, but he dismissed it as fast as it came as impossible.

He waited while McMaster pulled an extension ladder from the back and slid it into the well. Familiarity itched. McMaster released Daniel and escorted him to the muck hole; the only evidence that it might be something more was the rotten timbers surrounding it, preserving its rectangular shape.

McMaster provided buckets, rope and a shovel, as well as a forklift load of lumber which included some large beams. Other equipment included a gas motor of some kind and a coil of hose.

"Boy, we're going to pump this hole dry. Then you're going to dig it out and shore up the sides as you go."

Daniel stood for a moment peering into the dark. It was much deeper than it first appeared. More than half the length of the ladder disappeared below the water. He lowered himself onto the top rung then slowly worked his way down, all feelings of déjà vu pushed aside by fear. When he reached the surface of the water, McMaster lowered the large flexible hose. It had a metal attachment at the end, allowing more than one pipe to be connected as needed.

"Justin!" McMaster hollered, "Keep the end in the water ... and don't suck up any mud. You got that?"

I am Daniel, he wanted to shout, but all he could muster was, "Yes."

McMaster started the small gas engine. The pipe grew taut and heavy as it began to suck up the water. Daniel was surprised to see how fast the level in the well dropped. In moments, it was necessary to step down the ladder in order to keep the hose submerged. When he could pull it no further and the end was close to coming out, he called up, "Mister McMaster, I need more hose."

The sound of the gas engine ceased and a brief clanging of metal against metal ensued. The few gallons of water that were in the hose suddenly poured back into the well. The wire ribbed plastic pipe recoiled as if surprised by the sudden lack of resistance. Then it sagged; a lifeless worm.

McMaster's face appeared over the edge. "Here take this," he ordered, passing down a piece of chalk and a small cloth. "Dry the ladder off near the waterline and put a mark where the water level is."

Daniel obeyed and passed the items back up to McMaster who took them and disappeared from view.

Daniel waited with the understanding that he was not to do anything unless directed. McMaster had made that perfectly clear. After a painfully long twenty minutes Daniel shifted his weight on the ladder to ease cramps that were beginning to live in his legs. Tingles shot through his toes as the blood coursed back into them, filling his boots with sharp needles of pain.

At his wits end, he started up the ladder, but stopped short when McMaster's unshaven face appeared over the edge. "What the hell do you think you're doing? Did I say anything about coming out of there?" Daniel scrambled down the ladder narrowly avoiding a swipe from McMaster's open hand. "I want to know if the water level down there is rising."

Daniel glanced at the mark, but if there was a change, it was imperceptible. "It seems like the water level is the same as it was," he called back.

The sound of the gas engine echoed in the well and the water level began to drop once more. A few moments later Daniel yelled, "Mister McMaster, I think you'll want to see this."

McMaster peered over the edge. "What is it?"

Daniel moved to one side to avoid blocking the view.

McMaster strained, but could see nothing in the dark. His frustration was instant. "Speak up boy! Just tell me what you've found."

"It looks like there is a ladder attached to the side of the well."

Now there was audible excitement in McMaster's voice. "Keep the hose in the water. We're going down as far as we can today. Do not stop working or do anything without my orders. I have some work to do up here."

Daniel worked as ordered. A considerable amount of time had passed, longer than normal between the old fat bastard's haranguing checkups on him, when he finally heard, "Boy, come up from there!"

Daniel crawled out of the hole and McMaster pointed his eyes in the direction of a newly erected high meshed fence with several strands of barbed wire across the top. McMaster explained, "This fence is electrified with enough juice to kick a steer on its ass and fry it for supper. See over there?" He made an emphatic gesture to a generator, which had a heavy electrical cord running from it to one end of the fence.

You're leaving me alone, Daniel thought, but his hopes diminished when McMaster brought Brute, the lethargic German shepherd, from the back of the pickup and released him to roam outside the area. With no word of explanation, McMaster produced one of Daniel's few shirts and tossed it to the dog. It leapt on it, tearing at it until it was no more than tattered shreds.

Daniel stared, surprised by the apparent shift in the dog's disposition.

"You can see I keep Brute chained for a reason. He'd prefer to have you for supper over Alpo, so take whatever chances you want. You'd better think twice before you go up against Brute, though. He's less forgiving than I am."

Maybe you've thought of everything, maybe you haven't. Go ahead and leave me alone.

CHAPTER 12

Agonizing days passed in the damp, cramped space. At first, Daniel hauled slopping buckets filled with watery muck. Later, he pulled up sticky sludge that would not pour. At the base of the ladder he began to drag up drier mud, but still saturated and as heavy as a pail of rocks.

Mornings were refrigerator cold, temperatures barely above freezing. But Daniel was thankful for that. By the second trip up the ladder, he was hot. By the fourth or fifth trip, sweat poured from his brow. Clunky steel-toed boots rang off aluminum rungs in monotonous regularity. Each step was a snitch, calling out his tempo, tattling should his pace slow. Now and again, a gruff voice came from above, "Boy! I've got a size ten boot that's going to find a home up your size two ass. Get moving!"

Even though his legs grew stronger and he was able to keep a good pace for longer, his work never seemed to satisfy McMaster. Oh, he had tried moving faster, but it didn't help. It only meant that exhaustion set in earlier, which in turn increased the frequency of McMaster's blaring criticism. Apathy replaced fear and, before long, Daniel worked mechanically, ignoring McMaster's shallow ravings and the occasional sweep of a giant mitt.

Anticipating the yelling and hitting became a kind of game; a way to measure time. McMaster's phrases were repetitive and predictable. "I've got a size ten boot, boy!" he'd scream. And Daniel would mimic, *I've got a size ten boot, boy,* even scrunching his face to match.

If you want me to move dirt faster then maybe you aught to find a *better* way for me to work, Daniel thought, knowing he could never make the suggestion aloud. He smiled at the thought of how stupid saying such a thing would be. It would be an invitation to a beating and McMaster had never needed one in the past.

The ladder was no guarantee that the hole was anything but a well, but McMaster was like a child waiting for Christmas morning, worse even. Days earlier, after Daniel had completed dredging the shaft, the hole had shared some of its secrets: delicious secrets that were his to keep. No point giving unnecessary satisfaction to a man that deserved none, Daniel thought, reveling in his deceptiveness. He wouldn't tell McMaster until he had dumped the dirt from the last bucket.

At the bottom of the well on the west face there seemed to be evidence of an old shaft that had long since caved in. The unnatural circular stratum delineated the old dig and reminded Daniel of a cross section of a giant candy. The sooner he told McMaster, the sooner he would have to begin the excavation.

He surveyed his completed work. He had cut his corners squarely at the bottom and the base was as flat and hard as it must have been when the original artisan had completed it. Unexpected familiarity washed over him. Impossible, he thought. I could never have been here before. He shook the feeling off like a shiver and climbed out of the hole.

McMaster met him, glaring. "What's with the half empty bucket? Get down there and fill it to the top," he bellowed.

"I'm done. There's nothing left to bring up."

McMaster's shoulders dropped. "You didn't notice anything out of the ordinary down there?"

"Nothing that I could tell," he said, avoiding McMaster's eyes.

"You're definitely at the bottom?"

"It's as hard as rock down there. Check it out for yourself."

Daniel half expected the blow that followed, but McMaster's speed caught him off guard. His head rocked to the side.

"Don't test me, boy." He grabbed Daniel by the shirt collar. The journey to the truck was short. McMaster clapped on the cuffs and left Daniel attached to the tailgate while he went back to the well.

The wallop had been worth it just to see the look on McMaster's face as he stood next to the well looking down into the darkness, his fear and consternation unmistakable. The hole was dark and Daniel knew that no amount of squinting would allow McMaster to discern the subtle color and texture changes in the soil below. McMaster circled the well, peering into the darkness. Eventually, he came back to the truck and rifled through the glove box until he found a small flashlight. He returned to the well and tried again.

After a half an hour of pacing and thinking, McMaster gave up. He put his back to the ladder and stepped onto the first rung. It was a comical display. First, he stood with one foot and tested the ladder's stability by lunging side to side. Then he bounced a little to make sure he had seated it. Dissatisfied still, he repeated the entire farce using the other foot. When he had exhausted all manner of analysis, McMaster lowered his full weight onto the first step.

After McMaster disappeared from view, it was a long wait before he reappeared, sweating and out of breath, his broad smile telling volumes.

"Get in," he said, as he transferred the cuffs to the door handle.

***

Everything changed at the site after that. McMaster didn't go back to the well until several large deliveries had been made, supplies they'd need for what McMaster called 'Phase Two'.

"These are plans for my new elevator. He seemed to accentuate the word 'my' and Daniel hated him for it. McMaster instructed him on how to read the plans and explained how the elevator would work. The finished contraption replaced the need for a ladder. Once the lift was complete, Daniel would return to digging.

Daniel stood at the bottom of the well while McMaster worked above, sending timbers down and providing instructions for each step of the way. The new framework replaced the ancient lumber and fortified the equally aged walls. Daniel attached heavy angle iron to the lattice of beams that would guide the platform on its journey up and down the shaft. Rollers that he secured to the platform would keep it centered and traveling smoothly.

When Daniel had completed his work, McMaster refused to try the contraption, which suited him just fine. He couldn't help grinning as he rode it to the bottom of the well. Could any other boy have done something so amazing? Without me, none of this would have been possible, Daniel thought, but his enjoyment was short-lived. McMaster immediately replaced the bucket with a barrow and scaled the progress he expected from Daniel accordingly.

Weeks passed. Daniel continued to trudge along the passage under ten times the weight of the pail. You bulky bastard, he thought. I can't dig any faster than I am already and you won't listen, will you. No. You won't accept that I can't go faster until I can't do it anymore or until you've beaten me half to death. While he cursed the tyrant, he hurried from one end of the tunnel to the other, working as fast as he could.

His boots soon became waterlogged and his shirt became a sopping rag. Whenever he paused, the moisture in his clothes cooled, leaching the heat from his body. Without thought of self-preservation, Daniel's temper exploded. To hell with this, he thought, throwing his wheelbarrow to the ground and storming his way to the lift. He stepped onto the conveyance and reached for the control box. The electric motors spun.

Rising from the hole, Daniel's face was aglow with sweat and hatred, his mouth was a twisted snarl and every sinew strained over muscles that rippled beneath threadbare clothes. As the elevator climbed, timbers passed like wooden arms raised in a chorus of solidarity. The platform reached ground level and jerked to a halt.

McMaster stood waiting, as Daniel had come to expect; always hovering to ensure there was never a chance to escape. Was that a hint of surprise, Daniel wondered, when the fat man saw the spade raised high in Daniel's hands?

Although unarmed, McMaster barred the way. "Is this what it comes down to then, boy? Do you think you're man enough to use that?" There was a pause as if he waited for a response to his rhetorical questions. "I didn't think so," he said, and reached out to take the shovel.

If Daniel had been thinking straight, he may never come out of the shaft with weapon in hand and murder on his mind, but he was far beyond logic. Adrenaline overload had turned him into a different kind of machine—one designed for annihilation. The fat thing's mouth had moved, but the sounds did not make sense in Daniel's flaming ears. Was it some kind of threat?

Suddenly, the thing lurched forward with outstretched hand. Like a dancer following the lead, Daniel stepped back, raising the shovel higher. The arm snaked out again, but Daniel's heightened awareness made him faster this time. He swung the spade downward in a smooth arc, all the force of his weight and strength behind it. The world around him dematerialized. The only thing left was the contact point where wooden shaft and flabby flesh would meet. The handle slammed into McMaster's forearm and for a split second Daniel thought the breaking sound came from the shovel.

Things happened fast. Daniel could not keep up. McMaster roared a thunderous blast. There was no opportunity for thought. While Daniel had focused on his target, McMaster found one of his own. McMaster's right arm snapped in two, but his left hand clamped on the back of Daniel's neck. Massive fingers dug into Daniel's flesh, finding nerves that shot daggers down his back right into his fingertips. He forced Daniel's face toward the ground.

Darkness again.

CHAPTER 13

Daniel's recovery was slow. For weeks afterward, sharp spasms accompanied every breath. And though it was McMaster who nursed a broken arm, it was Daniel who struggled to get out of bed. He'd never know for certain the extent of McMaster's wrath after the incident. He wondered how many times McMaster may have kicked him while he lay unconscious.

In the months after Daniel's recovery, the mine became more of a home and a refuge than a prison. At first, the dim light and closed space were terrifying, but Daniel had eventually grown comfortable with the fact the ceiling could cave in at any moment, so much so that each morning his arrival underground felt like a homecoming. The mundane and repetitive mine work was a fair price to pay for sanctuary from McMaster's frequent thrashings.

It was the dull, mind-numbing task that allowed his thoughts to drift far away. Old timbers marked the original passage, making it a simple matter of removing rock and dirt then shoring up the walls and ceilings as he progressed. Maybe the broken arm had been worth it. McMaster kept more of a distance and no longer hounded him about his progress. The occasional snide remark was easy enough to ignore.

More months passed, marked only by the changing seasons above ground and Daniel's steady progress below. His physical strength and hatred continued to grow as if one somehow depended on the other. Daniel's shovel slammed into stone and snapped him out of his most recent wrathful thought. Ramming his shovel into the dirt, he searched for an edge, but found none. Too big to move, he cleared dirt until there was none left to clear. The passage ended abruptly as if some giant had deposited a great stone for a door, blocking his passage.

McMaster didn't flinch at the news, nor did he hesitate. In a tone that called that called him stupid, McMaster said, "Dig around it then."

The only way to continue was to cut a new passage through earth and rock that had never been disturbed. Daniel worked hard, but when fewer loads came to the surface McMaster was infuriated. "Don't try and feed me your crap, boy! I didn't put you down there so you could waste my time. I don't care if you're grinding through solid rock; you'd better keep your ass moving." McMaster raised his hand high, rage ripening his face. He stood, elbow cocked while Daniel braced himself for a blow that never came. "Get down there and get to work. I want to be on the other side in two days tops."

Daniel added another abhorrent thought to the infinite others he already harbored toward McMaster as he rode the elevator into the abyss.

Each time he rammed his shovel into the hard ground he imagined cutting into McMaster's dense scull. The earth gave way and Daniel progressed.

CHAPTER 14

A year had slipped by and the boulder lay yards behind, a mere memory of an obstacle overcome. A short section of tunnel behind the rock had been intact, resulting in a giant leap forward. Even though the progress pleased McMaster, Daniel knew that only time lay between him and McMaster's next raging fit. Daniel allowed his mind to wander.

This time it will be different. McMaster will raise his fist, but instead of cowering, I'll catch him off guard again. I'll cut through his flesh like Jell-O. The pig will die in a pool of his own blood. Then he'll be sorry. He'll be sorry and it will be too late.

Daniel jammed his shovel angrily into the dirt. It struck something, not rock this time. The spade skipped to one side making a hollow, nonmetallic sound. He dropped to his knees and scraped away the dirt with his hands, revealing a smooth, grey object. Strange, it was like nothing he'd seen before. He pulled at loose dirt. In minutes he had cleared enough soil to identify it—a human skull. He sat back on his haunches, afraid to continue, yet simultaneously intrigued. His face glowed in the dim light. My discovery and mine alone. To steal a thing that McMaster would kill for was calculated revenge that tasted warm and sweet. He sat in his gloomy retreat, the coolness of the cavern seeping into him while he savored the moment.

Whatever the circumstances of its death, the corpse was buried face up. Gaping eye sockets stared at Daniel. The body lay intact, but it would take days, perhaps weeks, before he would have moved enough soil to reveal each piece of the human puzzle without destroying it.

***

As he expected, it did take weeks. Though the earth had done little to preserve the flesh of the man, Daniel was surprised to see that the skeleton and clothing were in good condition. Daniel worked around the gravesite by carving a narrow path beside it. When he dug into the shaft seven or eight feet he began to remove material above the corpse. Soon, a mound of dirt formed a long high step adjacent to the wall. He would have to work carefully during the final stages of excavation to preserve the remains and that, unfortunately, would slow him down too much. McMaster would certainly become suspicious.

In his bed that night a solution occurred to him. *A ratio. Five to one should to do it.* For every five wheelbarrows full of dirt from the tunnel, he would haul one from where the body lay. He would lose a little time, but maybe not so much that McMaster would detect a delay.

Five weeks after his work began, Daniel stood over the corpse, it frozen in the position in which it had died. He had long since ceased to think of the corpse as a man. 'He' had become an 'it' or 'the skeleton', sometimes even 'the fossil'; just something else to dig up. But when he brushed the dirt away from the full-length leather jacket that had somehow managed to preserve most of what lay beneath it, recognition unexpectedly flooded in. His dream that had lain dormant for years suddenly revisited him like an old memory rather than the vision it had been. He knew without searching its pockets that the man he'd found was Grundpark. More than that, he remembered everything. He remembered the passage, the cavern and the door that lay ahead, somewhere beyond, through countless tons of rubble. He wondered if McMaster had had the same dream. If he had, Daniel could only hope he would not also make a connection to its strange reality.

McMaster's bellowing voice echoed from above, wonderfully muted by distance and darkness. The day was over. Daniel gathered his lunch pail and, with some regret, left his find for yet another day. He rose out of the tunnel to a clarity and surety that he'd never experienced before. In some alien way, his mind felt open.

That night Daniel lay staring at the rafters. He didn't have to guess what McMaster would do if he found out he'd been lied to. It didn't matter. Daniel felt invincible. He could accomplish anything. He could solve any problem that came his way. In all likelihood he would have to rebury the body or tell McMaster what he'd found. He could engineer that easily enough, though. In the meantime, Grundpark was his secret and there was inestimable pleasure in that knowledge.

CHAPTER 15

During his morning shift, Daniel avoided spending time uncovering his new discovery. Nothing would have been more gratifying than to take the time to play archeologist and painstakingly exhume the body. But if McMaster grew suspicious, life would become colossally difficult. Grundpark would have to wait.

During lunch, rather than sit in the dim light of the well, Daniel took his meal to where the body lay. In the half hour McMaster allotted, Daniel worked furiously; food could come later. He could take bites between wheelbarrow loads. It required only a few minutes to clear away most of the debris around Grundpark. Fortunately, the woolen material of the skeleton's clothes was still largely intact. He worked it free and, taking the fabric in hand, pulled the corpse from its grave. He would have to move it to an alternate location as soon as he had time so he could continue his work unhindered. He must never allow McMaster to discover it. He had used the word 'allow' and considered the power it suggested. If he ever allowed McMaster to discover his treasure, it would need to be intact.

Later, using a makeshift sled constructed from remnants of lumber, he transported the body along the passage to the front side of the boulder that still partially blocked the tunnel. He recognized it now as the unshakable mass that had served as Grundpark's threshold. Daniel mused that time is slave to no one. His eyes grew large recognizing that it was a rather lofty thought for a boy who had never paid much attention in class when he had the chance—a fact he now regretted. Too bad he couldn't be as powerful as time, a slave to no man. There was a sweet poetic sound to the phrase, as if someone else had said it and now he merely dredged it up from the cobwebbed corners of his mind. Never mind. Wherever it came from, he liked it anyway.

Lying on its debris, the body was out of the way of his regular path. McMaster's call from above interrupted him. His break was over.

He worked silently in the gloom; glancing warily in the direction of his silent companion each time he passed by. The corpse's hollow eyes stared at him accusingly, scolding him for taking it from the warm earth. Daniel would have turned its head toward the wall, but he was afraid it might break in the process, so he left it.

McMaster was as constant as the dead man's stare. At the end of each day, before climbing into the pickup he'd ask, "How far did you get today, Justin?" or "Is there anything interesting to report?" And each day, Daniel's reply was the same, "I moved about thirty wheelbarrow loads," or, "No, just dirt."

Having to say it aloud was a constant reminder of his deceitfulness. With each passing day the weight of his lie and his subsequent angst grew. One day McMaster would build up enough gumption to 'come have a look' as he frequently threatened. He would soon want to see the progress for himself. In truth, that inevitability was closer with each passing day and McMaster was not the kind of man to forewarn anyone of his intentions.

When first discovered, the corpse's eyes invoked fear. Now, they bore the eerie admonition, 'Be careful, Daniel. The secret to your freedom is down here, but you'll have to be careful. Soon your chance for escape will come.' Daniel didn't know if the words came from Grundpark's ghost, or if they originated from his own mind, a reflection of his grim determination. Either way, he would have to hide the remains.

Moving the man had been one thing, but Daniel knew he could not rebury the body without finding out for himself what it could tell him about its previous life. With trepidation, Daniel examined each of the man's pockets, feeling like a grave robber as he tucked each item he found into his own pockets. There was not enough light or time to examine them. Taking inventory would have to wait until later. He pulled dirt from the wall above the body. When he was done, the mound looked like a natural part of the cavern. He hoped it would suffice. Removing any more material from the wall would reveal an abnormal indentation in the side of the passage.

With the body safely hidden, he returned to work in the tunnel. Although he would have liked to have been able to forget about Grundpark, at least he didn't have to worry as much anymore.

Daniel returned to his task in earnest, torn by the desire to work slowly versus the need to please McMaster. At some point his job would be finished, revealing all of the work that Grundpark had accomplished. And when the mine was open, McMaster might no longer need him.

Although the thought of escape usually consumed him, the artifacts knocking around in his pockets provided a welcomed distraction. His mind wandered away from his predicament as his fingers meandered to the effects he'd gathered. He toyed with the damp leather pouch he'd taken from an inside coat pocket; surely strange and wonderful objects lay hidden inside. He would have loved to spend the afternoon sitting in the sun, exploring its contents and daydreaming.

Click. Reality came crashing home and he was back inside the cave pushing the empty barrow toward the flood-lamps. Sadly, he wasn't a kid—not really, anyway. And he couldn't remember a time when he had ever sat in the sun and played with anything. As enjoyable as daydreaming was, it was impossible to maintain alluring delusions when faced with the worry of what might happen in the next week, month, or even year.

He needn't have worried. Overcome by exhaustion and the need for a meal, he passed under McMaster's gaze, routinely answering his questions. His head fell into his lap on the ride to the barn and he only woke with a jerk when McMaster killed the engine.

The nightly routine of cleaning up and eating revived him. Even the short nap on the way back from the mine had helped. For the first time, he was happy when McMaster closed and locked the barn doors, leaving him alone in the loft. He pulled the items from his pockets and placed them in an organized array across the bed.

First was a leather wallet as ancient as Grundpark, but still not much different from the billfold McMaster carried, its basic function unchanged over time. After years underground, it was soggy and bloated. Daniel eased the thick halves apart. Grundpark had jammed them full of papers that were too important to keep anywhere but with him. Daniel rippled with excitement.

The contents might be too delicate to move a second time, so he shifted them from his bed to the floor. He pulled the mass of paper out as a single wad then carefully separated each sheet. For some, water had broken the fibrous bonds reducing those pages to unsalvageable pulp. The others he laid out flat and positioned them deep under the bed to dry.

Some items were still recognizable. There were faded receipts, a driver's license issued in April, 1937 to a man named Jacob Grundpark, born on March 23, 1888, and several odd bills, like nothing he'd ever seen before. The elements had abolished the itemized list on one slip, but the business name, *The Hudson Bay Company,* was still evident. The wallet had a coin pouch. Daniel pulled on the snap and was saddened when it came right out of the leather. He sighed and opened the flap. Inside were several coins of varying denominations. One of the coins had a picture of an Indian on it. In the same pouch was a small key with a round barrel and intricately detailed teeth. Daniel set the cash, coin, and key aside. Although the key was intriguing, he couldn't imagine what it might have been for or whether a corresponding lock even existed.

He forced himself to move on, filled with bittersweet sentiment, to the small satchel. Opening it represented the last mystery; he had always liked to save the best for last. Back on his bed, Daniel examined his prize. It was made of leather but, unlike the wallet, the leather on this satchel was thin. He could only imagine it had once been extremely fine, perhaps even as delicate as cloth. Looped around the top was a sturdy cord securing whatever items were inside. Time, moisture, and filth had hardened both leather and cord. Limbering and releasing the string was easy enough, but he'd have to work carefully with the tough material if he hoped to save the bag. There was something fascinating about the old pouch. It would be wonderful if he could restore it and use it again.

He managed to pry the mouth open and poured the contents onto the bed. Two gnarled yellow stones which he assumed, or rather hoped, were enormous gold nuggets and a small black dowel, tumbled out. The wooden pin was immediately recognizable. If his dream had been accurate, it was some sort of key.

Daniel would have liked to explore the treasures further, but time had run short. McMaster could notice the light at any moment and come to see what was so vital that could keep a dog-tired boy awake. He flicked the lights off and crawled into bed. The best for last, he reminded himself. The dowel would have to wait.

Daniel lay awake in the dark. If the nuggets were any indication of what was to come, McMaster was certainly going to be a wealthy man. Would Daniel have a place among those riches? He drifted asleep to images of treasures and justice. He was the king of his imaginary castle lavishing the rewards of his labor, while McMaster struggled, penniless and alone.

CHAPTER 16

As he worked, bathed in sweat, Daniel's thoughts turned to the papers drying beneath his bed. What secrets did his treasures hold? Could they lead to a means for his escape? Later, at the dining room table, he tried to hide his eager anticipation of returning to his room. When dinner was over and he sat on the edge of his bed, proud of his charade, he was sure McMaster hadn't suspected a thing.

He dropped to his knees and gathered his new belongings from under the bed. The papers were dry and brittle as was the pouch. He rolled the wooden dowel between his fingers and something inside rattled. Odd. In his dream Grundpark had definitely used it as a key, but it appeared to be nothing more than a container of some kind. He shook it with puzzled skepticism. Could there be a connection between the implement and the strange door from his dream? It was more likely a mere figment of his vivid imagination and Grundpark a strange coincidence. Torn, he sat on the bed rolling the object in his fingers. Bonk, clink, rattle, bonk ... what could it be? Figuring out how to open it would end the surprise, yet it was so enticing. Daniel savored the mystery and slid it beneath his pillow. Tomorrow. Maybe tomorrow he'd get it right. Maybe.

He turned his attention to the wallet. Although it had held no surprises, it deserved further scrutiny. Time had washed the ink away on most of the items, but some kind of membership card—Cattlemen's Assoc.—whatever that was, and the driver's license were still legible. Must be one of the very first driver's licenses ever, he thought.

Daniel folded each artifact carefully, returned them to the wallet, which was dry and now much thinner with only the surviving articles inside, and placed it under his pillow. He climbed into bed and stared at the ceiling, turning the canister in his hands, pondering the sound of whatever rolled inside. When he was too tired to stay awake any longer, he stowed the canister under his pillow and fell asleep.

***

McMaster sat troubled at the dinner table. There was definitely something different about the boy, but what? Justin wasn't making any attempts to escape. He never offered a word unless it was required of him. He came in silently, ate his meal, excused himself and left the table just as he always did. Still, there was something different. Something was up, but there was no way to tell what.

In front of the television, he sat replaying the events of the evening, wondering what was so bothersome about Justin's behavior. No, it wasn't purely the boy's behavior; it was his demeanor. For a boy who had spent the last three years broken and resigned to his fate, the change was glaring. What had happened? What had caused this transformation?

McMaster flipped through the channels, distracted. Has he been lying about something? Is he planning something? Did he find something and isn't saying anything about it? *That's it.* That's *exactly* what the sneaky little bugger did. I'll bet my life on it.

In frustration and anger, he jumped up and stormed out to the barn, stopping long enough to grab an axe handle from the shed. He climbed the ladder and stood towering over the sleeping boy.

For a long time, McMaster stood over the boy. His calculating nature came to bear. Without the boy he would lose his investment, his worker and his chance to find out if the boy had any secrets to share. He lowered the haft and returned to the house.

McMaster lay awake for a long time, tossing and turning, unable to find a comfortable position. When he drifted into tormented sleep, images of the boy with an evil grin taunted him throughout the night.

CHAPTER 17

The morning sun rose in a cloudless blue sky, producing surprising warmth considering the early hour. The fine weather did nothing to quell McMaster's suspicions, leaving him no perceivable choice but to inspect the mine himself. He prepared for the day's challenge in Yoga-like fashion, taking deep cleansing breaths, approximating hyperventilation.

He studied the boy during breakfast. Whatever was different the night before was still evident. He fought his urge to reach across the table and hammer the kid. He finished his meal as frustrated as ever.

He reminded himself that the boy was no more than a glorified dog. A dog's duty was to be loyal and obedient, ready to do its master's bidding. A good dog was grateful for any kindness it was given. A good dog was worth its weight in gold. Until now, he had always considered Justin to be a good dog. Feisty at first and for some time, yes, but that showed spirit. Once broken in, he'd been a good dog. What causes a good dog to turn bad? Today he was determined to find out.

McMaster stood on the platform suspended over the shaft and shuddered as he descended, along with Justin, into the dark pit. He mouthed his mantra, *Sonofabitch, sonofabitch sonofabitch*. He knew his feelings were irrational. Looking up, he held his gaze on the tiny patch of sky as it grew smaller the farther he descended. His mind screamed its warning, telling him that soon the light would be gone, trapping him underground.

The platform came to a startling halt. His knees buckled and he grabbed at the bracing for support while craning upward, until some deep part of his brain seemed satisfied the light would remain and it would be waiting for him on his return. He faltered as he stepped to the ground but faced the darkness.

Justin stepped into the passage and waited for him. McMaster couldn't help but sense the boy's feelings of disgust, or … amusement? He dismissed the thought. Dogs don't feel such complex emotions. It was too dark to read the whelp's expression anyway.

He followed Justin into the black, but progress was slow. He leaned against the stone wall, pretending to scrutinize the boy's work. Every step forward was painful. He didn't know if Justin recognized the halts for what they were, ploys to regain his composure. He didn't care. He couldn't breathe and the sweat was running down his forehead and into his blurred and stinging eyes. It was all he could do not to bolt to the light, which would have been unacceptable in every way. Let the boy think what he wanted, no discomfort was so great that could cause him to break down and run.

***

McMaster moved slowly through the tunnel getting ever nearer to the large boulder and the grave. McMaster appeared to notice everything. Although he had covered Grundpark with loose dirt, Daniel never planned on the burial site withstanding deliberate scrutiny.

McMaster halted. The corpse lay no more than a foot from his boot. He eyed the small opening to the right of the blockage. Above, a second smaller boulder balanced, cramping the opening even more and leaving just enough room to pass hunched over with the wheelbarrow.

Daniel recognized the opportunity. The man was distracted and Daniel felt sure that he'd never stay behind alone. Daniel stepped through the narrow opening, leaving McMaster to cringe on the other side.

As he had hoped, McMaster hastened to catch up as though the opening might collapse at any moment. The shaft widened again as soon as they were beyond the rock. He couldn't see McMaster's face, but he heard the rush of air escape his lungs as he came through.

Daniel too, let out a sigh of relief. McMaster had walked by Grundpark's resting place without a glance.

The passage turned slightly to the right and progressed another fifty feet where it came to an abrupt end. The halogen work light waited unwaveringly on its stand. Daniel flipped the switch, flooding the passage in near daylight and stood back awaiting instructions.

***

With flashlight in hand, McMaster examined the work thus far. The support beams were well placed, the floor was smooth and flat. Justin's work was that of an artisan. It continued to be a worthwhile endeavor and was a noteworthy accomplishment. Maybe the change he'd sensed in Justin was because he too could sense that they were close. Was it so unreasonable that Justin would be excited to see what might lie on the other side?

Nothing seemed amiss and progress was good. He stepped past Justin and took long quick strides toward the exit.

At the bottom of the well, McMaster turned, "You've come a long way and you may be almost through the cave-in. Let me know the moment you break through." He didn't wait for Justin to acknowledge the directive, but turned his head skyward as they rode the lift toward daylight.

***

Above ground, Daniel gathered his tools and returned to his dark sanctuary. Less to fear down here than up there, he thought as he parked the barrow in front of his worksite.

The thought that Grundpark's belongings might lead to some great secret faded as the hours of manual labor dragged on. Hours eventually added to make days until his enthusiasm became a shadow of a memory. It was possible that Grundpark's possessions were no more than the mundane personal effects of someone from a time long passed. He was comforted to know the gold nuggets had real value. He had slaved for McMaster for ... how long now? He counted back the winters. Winters were hardest and easiest to remember. He had slaved for four years and deserved some compensation. Grundpark had become his secret benefactor. Each time he passed by the grave, he silently thanked the man.

He climbed into bed at the end of the day. Tonight was the night. He removed the container from under his pillow and went back to rotating it, inspecting it carefully following a thin line around one end. At first, he thought it was an interesting quirk of the wood grain, but it dawned on him as he stared at it that this was in fact a seam separating two individual pieces of wood. He grasped the ends and simultaneously pulled and twisted as hard as he dared. The two halves gave and, for a moment, he thought he had broken it. But they slid apart exactly as Grundpark had intended. He inverted the canister and a tiny silver locket tumbled out, a flowery design adorning the front. Daniel turned it over. "To Francis with love," the engraving professed. He pried it open, revealing two black and white photos, yellowed by time: one of a woman, the other, of a man and each no larger than a fingernail. The faces were stiff and emotionless. To Daniel, they seemed like older versions of the McMasters.

Other than the pendant, the tube was empty. He gathered the items from the bag and prepared to drop them into the container when he noticed a distinct discoloration inside. *Was it painted*? He explored the interior with his finger and produced a scrap of paper. He worked it free. Afraid it would tear, he carefully unraveled it to discover it was mostly blank except for a series of letters and numbers.

10CCW-3CW-2CCW-4CW-1CCW

Daniel studied the odd markings trying to connect them with anything from his previous experiences, but nothing came to mind. He released the paper and it sprang back to its original shape. He dropped the pendant into the vessel, pulled the metal nuggets from under his pillow and placed them inside the cylinder as well. Now, what should I do with this strange treasure, he wondered as he looked around the building for a hiding place.

The barn was a remarkable structure, really, almost a work of art. As far as Daniel could tell, they had made the entire building without nails. For whatever reason, some holes, which may have once held dowels, were empty. He had already used several to store what few toiletries he owned. In one of these was a toothbrush and in another a comb. Higher up on the same post was another unused hole. He stood on his bed and slid the canister inside. It slid into the hole to the bottom leaving only an inch or so sticking out. It was easy to retrieve and appeared as though it belonged there. Perfect. He returned to his bed and turned out the light. He fell asleep dreaming about the meaning of the paper. What made it so valuable that Grundpark had taken such care to preserve it for so long?

CHAPTER 18

The following day began like every other, but when Daniel pushed the wheelbarrow passed Grundpark's shallow grave, his stomach lurched. Fresh soil had fallen from above, littering the floor. He raised his flashlight. There was a black gap in the wall near the ceiling. The only explanation was that the passage forked. Dread replaced Daniel's feelings of surprise when he realized what a terrible piece of bad luck had befallen him. Dirt had sloughed off adding a further layer over the corpse. *How can I tell McMaster about the new passage without proving I've known about Grundpark all along?* Moving Grundpark's frail remains seemed too risky to attempt. McMaster would find out about Grundpark sooner or later, but Daniel wanted it to be on his terms and not because of some twist of fate.

The problem weighed heavier with each load of dirt he hauled. By the end of the day, the problem had grown graver than anything Daniel had ever had to endure. That evening he rode the lift into the dimming light, crushed by the weight of his dilemma.

***

From McMaster's perspective, the dining area was refreshingly silent. Matilda brought the dishes and laid them on the table saying nothing. As far as the boy was concerned, it was difficult to surmise. Only the top of his head was visible, his face dipped almost to the table.

After Matilda had finished laying out the meal and had seated herself, McMaster waited a while longer, knowing that no one would begin eating until he had given his say-so. When he felt the wait had been sufficient, he picked up the bowl of potatoes and scooped a mound onto his plate then held the bowl to his left. He waited another moment as one might do when training a dog to stay, and then he cleared his throat. Daniel raised his head and took the dish. In the McMaster household, those who do real work eat first. Matilda could wait. The meal had officially begun.

The only sounds at the table were of chewing and swallowing. These were subdued to such a degree they seemed almost apologetic. Matilda hadn't acknowledged him upon his arrival in the house, but that was likely due to the spat they'd had from the previous evening. McMaster appreciated her most when she was silent. If not for her cooking skills, there was little benefit of having her around.

The boy ate without looking up. McMaster watched him with interest and noted that his appetite was healthy enough, while at the same time he appeared satisfactorily disheartened. For now, the boy had returned to his normal self. It disturbed McMaster to see him change in character with no apparent provocation. There was a positive aspect to the boy's demeanor, though. In his current state there was little chance of rebellion and that was all that really mattered.

CHAPTER 19

Daniel found no pleasure in the bright early morning sun on the way back to the mine. He rode the lift down and pushed his barrow into the dark. He arrived at the cave-in and, to his surprise, the ceiling had collapsed further. Now, there was no doubt that a second shaft existed, a fact that would be impossible to hide from McMaster. The new passage was obvious in the aftermath of the most recent cave-in. Daniel would have to tell McMaster immediately.

McMaster was furious with Daniel's unexpected return. It was easy to see by the way the big man stomped toward the entrance.

He opened his mouth, but before he could berate Daniel, he said, "Mister McMaster! You need to come down here right away!"

"What for?" he bellowed.

"There's been a cave in."

The color in McMaster's face rose. What would he be furious about the most? Daniel's return, the potential delay, or would it be some other impossible to predict cause?

Daniel raced on, hoping to douse McMaster's mounting anger. "It's opened up a new passage."

McMaster's hands shook.

"What do you want me to do?" Daniel said.

"Can you wait one damn minute?" McMaster yanked his briefcase from the front seat and took it to the tailgate, where he removed some papers and busied himself studying them. Daniel recognized the blueprints of the elevator which hadn't been useful in years. After flipping through them in one direction and then back again, he stood and said, "I guess we'll have to check it out."

It seemed that although it had only been a couple of days since McMaster's initiation to the mine, he remained as fearful as ever. McMaster took hold of the framework with one hand and slid the other into his pocket, but Daniel could still see his shaking hand through the denim. Daniel toggled the switch and the elevator began its descent. He watched intrigued and noticed that McMaster did not exhale until they settled at the bottom and he had stepped onto solid ground. Even then, his breaths were stunted and sharp.

If the man had been kinder, maybe Daniel would have helped him along. He might have given him a word of encouragement. Instead, he relished the moment, grinning broadly from behind each time McMaster leaned his heavy mass against the supporting framework, crippled.

The blockage was not far. At first glance, all of Daniel's previous progress seemed obliterated. There was an audible tremble in McMaster's voice. "You brought me down here to see that my efforts have been for nothing?"

"No Sir. It's not a complete cave in. I can dig it out. There's something else you should see."

"Just tell me what the hell you've found." Sweat poured from his brow and his cheeks flushed.

Daniel pointed his light in the direction of the mound of debris so McMaster could see. "When the tunnel caved in, it opened a new passageway. You wanted me to tell you when I found something. There's another shaft right through there."

Daniel waited in agony while McMaster deliberated. It startled Daniel when he spun saying, "Follow me!" He did not wait to see if Daniel would follow. He strode in the direction of the lift without looking back.

McMaster went directly to the truck and sat on the tailgate taking deep recovering breaths. "How long do you think it will take you to move the debris and shore up the ceiling there?"

Daniel took a moment to think about it. "Maybe a week or two. I could probably finish moving the dirt in a week and it would take at least another four days to do the brace work." Daniel didn't care if McMaster accepted his estimate or not. In things relating to the mine, his opinion was all that mattered. It felt good to be in control for once. The man would have to accept whatever he told him.

"I'll give you a week. If you get done before that, I want to know. Get to work," he said, closing the compound gate between them and locking it. He slid behind the wheel and drove away.

He couldn't move the dirt any faster than he had been and McMaster couldn't make him work faster than he was capable. Daniel stood alone in the enclosure. The two generators lay idle, resting until Daniel called them to work. *Lucky bastards.*

Daniel stood in front of the slide. The dirt was loose and soft. *One week.* Ironically, it was probably the amount of time it would take to finish the task. Too bad McMaster hadn't gone for the two. Still, he might be able to trim that back and end up with some free time yet. Maybe a week was all he would need to orchestrate his escape. He had no idea how to get around McMaster's fortifications and, if his escape attempt failed, he still needed to show that he had completed enough work to account for the time spent. There was a lot to think about and more to do.

At Daniel's feet, Grundpark rested beneath eight feet of fresh rock and dirt. There was no point relocating the body now. It occurred to Daniel that the circumstances were perfect. When he dug down to Grundpark, he'd inform McMaster. Let him decide what to do next. At least then, Grundpark would cease to be one of his worries.

By the end of the second day, Daniel had moved most of the loose rock and soil. The cavern was exposed and it was only with the greatest effort that Daniel resisted exploring it. He knew McMaster would be looking for any signs that Daniel had jumped ahead without his permission. He worked with precision and care, knowing that Grundpark's body lay within a few scant inches. He eased the shovel into the loosely packed dirt until his shovel struck. Using his hands, he scraped away enough dirt to expose part of Grundpark's trousers. Satisfied with the scene, he stopped work. McMaster would have his very own discovery.

Daniel returned to the surface. The truck was nowhere in sight and Brute lay guarding outside the gate. He was two days ahead of schedule and the circumstances for escape would not improve. Brute was now his most significant obstacle. The fence was keeping Daniel in, but it was also keeping Brute out. He might have to kill the dog if it came to that. If only he could get Brute to jump up on the electrified fence … that would take care of the dog and the fence at the same time. Maybe.

"Here boy. Here, Brute. Come on, boy," he coaxed. The dog shifted its gaze, unsettling a fly that had been feasting on the yellow sleep gathering in the crook of his eye. The fly hovered for a moment and then landed again.

This is stupid. The dog would have to do a whole lot more than look in Daniel's direction. What could he do to get the dog to make a leap like that? He tried everything. He yelled. He whistled. He waved his shirt. He even tried to coax it over with part of his lunch; Brute just lay there in the dust like an ugly canine statue. "You're just a stupid ol' lazy dog, aren't you?" he said, mocking affection.

Daniel searched his brain. The hours slipped by and the sun began its descent. McMaster was due to return soon and he still had no good idea about how he might circumvent the electric fence or the dog. And there he sat in frustrated impotence, chewing the cud of empty possibilities when the roar of the truck drew him from his stupor. Daniel hopped up and raced to the shaft. He pushed the button and the elevator called the generator to action. The engine coughed and roared to life; the lift began to drop. *Faster, faster*, Daniel willed it, knowing that it would do no good. Helpless, Daniel envisioned the truck growing nearer. In his mind's eye he could see McMaster removing the keys from the ignition and clambering from the truck. He would hear the generator roaring while Daniel rode the elevator down and then he'd know that Daniel had not been working. What excuse would he have? Not Grundpark. It was too soon. He'd lose his chance to escape.

Daniel knew the generator would not quiet above until the lift had reached the bottom. Hurry, hurry, he pleaded.

As the truck approached, the power plant screamed its warning. Rocks and pebbles skipped ahead of the vehicle heralding the inevitable. The truck engine stopped and McMaster stepped out amidst a cloud of dust wafting around him. Two generators idling were the only sounds in the otherwise silent compound.

He called in the direction of the well, "Time to call it a day, Justin."

Daniel waited a few moments, guessing at the time it would take him to walk from Grundpark's burial place and then pushed the button to return to the surface. The generator revved and the lift began its assent. Daniel felt relieved, thankful and mentally exhausted at the same time.

Disappointed, but unable to show it, he rode to the farmhouse having made no significant progress with regard to his escape. With luck, he'd have another chance soon.

CHAPTER 20

Daniel gathered his belongings. Everything of value he owned, he'd stolen from his dead companion. On the upside, everything he owned would fit into his pockets. So the time it took him to dress was all the time necessary to be ready to leave. *Today is the day.*

McMaster dropped him off in the compound, locked the gate, and started the generator. He released Brute to roam freely and then sidled his bulky frame into the truck before driving away, for what Daniel hoped would be the entire day.

He didn't even wait for me to go into the mine, Daniel thought as he stood watching the truck disappear down the rough track, kicking up miniature dust devils as it went. He turned his attention to the fence, thinking back to school and his lessons in basic electricity. McMaster's design was obvious. If Daniel climbed the fence and touched any of the top wires, he would complete the circuit and create a dead short—literally. Whether or not the current was strong enough to kill him was an issue he would prefer not to test.

If I get out today, I'll be far away before he realizes I've escaped. He might come back at noon, but if he doesn't return until the evening, I'll be safe. He won't be able to begin a search till morning.

The generator idled on the opposite side of the fence, a patient, humming accompanist to Daniel's whirlwind of thoughts. His shovel lay next to the wheelbarrow giving Daniel an idea. That might do it, he thought. Guarding his eyes against the potential shower of sparks, he reached up and jammed the spade between the top wire and the fence. Instead of the sparks he expected, the engine sputtered and died, unable to pick up speed fast enough to compensate for the sudden draw of electricity. Daniel's heart leapt at his triumph.

The dog remained resting in front of the gate, lethargic and unaffected by anything going on inside the compound. *Maybe Brute is nothing more than a ploy. It could be the dog is not vicious at all.*

"Hey Brute, come 'ere boy," Daniel invited.

The dog lifted its snout in vague acknowledgement, but then dropped it to the ground once more.

"Come here you lazy brute," Daniel coaxed.

The dog remained still, an apathetic gargoyle.

Daniel scaled the fence, hoisted himself over the top and began to climb down the other side. The dog remained motionless. Daniel dropped another tenuous foot toward the ground. He was within the dog's reach now, but it only lifted its snout, uninterested in Daniel's progress.

Only a couple of feet from the ground now, Daniel prepared to hop down. Suddenly Brute bounced up and raced around the enclosure in his direction. Daniel scrambled toward safety. His bulky boots peeled out on the fence as he clawed his way to the top. Daniel glanced over his shoulder. Brute was coming hard and dust flew from his paws as he skidded around the final corner, shoulders pounding up and down like pistons. A moment later the dog was upon him and leapt in one fluid motion, much higher than Daniel would have thought possible. Daniel wrapped his arms around the top pipe and tensed his muscles, calling on all the strength and endurance his upper body had accrued. His feet swung upward, but as quick as he was, Brute was almost fast enough to nab him. Jaws closed too soon and ivory teeth slammed against Daniel's steel toe. Then Daniel was up and out of the dog's reach.

Daniel hung, draped across the barbed wire while the dog repeatedly jumped at him attempting to snag a bootlace, the cuff of his pants or anything else that might dangle close enough to reach.

Staying atop the fence was easy enough, but moving off the barbs proved to be more difficult. As a result of his rapid retreat, the wire had snagged his clothes in a half a dozen places. He could not risk moving toward Brute in his efforts to dislodge them; the dog had not given up and was still leaping maniacally. Daniel labored to free his jacket until he was able to maneuver into a sitting position. Only his pants kept him from returning to the safety of the compound.

Daniel sat up when he heard the sound of the truck. The cloud of dust was fast approaching. If the truck was in plain view to Daniel then Daniel must be in plain view of McMaster. He released one final barb and leapt toward the ground. His coat sleeve caught and he dangled momentarily before the fabric ripped. Daniel leaned toward the ground and ran to the well. He leapt onto the lift and dove for the controls. Lying as low as he could, he waited while the elevator sank.

The truck thundered to a stop. Daniel released the switch. The generator dropped to an idle. The truck engine died. Daniel looked down. The bottom of the well was still twenty feet away. He rose to his feet and flipped the switch to change directions. He could not continue to the bottom. McMaster would know that something was amiss. He had to go up. Daniel came into view just as McMaster walked up to the well.

"What the hell are you doing? You don't come out of there unless you're pushing a load."

Daniel searched his mind, but no excuse would come. The fraction of a second that he stood mute seemed an eternity, when … suddenly the right words came. "I—I w-was c-coming up to, ah … to find you. I found s-some—something else you should know about. There's a body down there." He forced his eyes wide, in hopes that he was approximating the appropriate look of surprise. McMaster didn't seem to notice one way or the other. He had already fixated on Daniel's final words.

"A body? Are you sure?"

Daniel nodded, and thought with a silent sigh, He hasn't noticed the fence generator is not running—damn lucky I came up with something compelling enough to distract him.

McMaster edged closer.

"Do you want to see it?"

McMaster backed away. "Of course. But it'll require preparation. I'll check it out first thing in the morning. Come on. We're calling it a day."

CHAPTER 21

In the moments before sleep, and with a clear head, Daniel considered what his future might hold. Am I in danger at the hands of McMaster? No. There's more threat of a fit of rage. Besides, the man's scared shitless every time he goes into the mine. The home of the dead and buried would likely remain Daniel's domain. He closed his eyes and felt himself begin to drift off, relieved to be rid of his secret at last.

The following morning, McMaster did not behave as Daniel had become accustomed. During the ride to the mine he said nothing derogatory or mean. Although his fear was evident, McMaster climbed aboard the lift without hesitation. The same rigidness showed in his movements, but he lacked the hesitation of his previous visits. Daniel led McMaster to the corpse. While McMaster cowered in the darkness, Daniel went to the light stand and flipped a switch filling the cavern with radiance. He moved the floodlights into place but apparently he was too slow for McMaster's approval. No sooner had he positioned the light and illuminated the body than McMaster shoved past him and began to examine the rotting fabric Daniel had exposed. He slid his fingers through slices in the cloth where Daniel's spade first pierced. He sat there for a long time and then his attention shifted to the new tunnel beyond the corpse. He examined the strata. "Have you been down here yet," he asked, nodding in the direction of the shadows.

"No," Daniel said and offered McMaster his flashlight.

McMaster took the light, shone it around the dark space beyond and then passed it to Daniel. "You go first."

Daniel moved forward a short distance. McMaster clung to the rocks behind, evidently undisturbed by the corpse, but incapable of exploring the new cave. Daniel stopped a short way inside. "There's another branch," he said, pointing to the left. It goes down and it's blocked with rocks."

"Maybe it's another cave-in," said McMaster.

Above ground, the small hillock next to the well had been mistaken for an old root cellar. There was not enough material there to account for the network of caves that was unfolding. Daniel supposed that, after Grundpark had finished mining one shaft, he deposited the debris from another part of the mine to avoid unnecessary hauling of waste material to the surface. This was no random act of nature. But this supposition, Daniel kept to himself. How many more closed off mine shafts will I find, he wondered.

Daniel moved into the main tunnel and his light revealed that Grundpark had cut through solid stone as he followed a vein. Again, it was the only logical explanation that Daniel could think might explain the winding tunnel. The passage veered left into the darkness. Daniel proceeded through the long sweeping corner. In the tunnel behind him, McMaster's light faded.

"Stop!" cried McMaster as Daniel disappeared from view. "Where do you think you're going?"

Daniel could see the end of the passage just ahead. A few steps farther and he'd be able to see up close the work that Grundpark had been doing in his final days. The tunnel terminated in a rounded cup. It looked as though a giant wood grub had eaten its way through soil and rock instead of a man. "I'm coming," he called and started his way back to McMaster.

McMaster's pallid face was a crescent moon above his beard. He stood with his arms folded across his chest intending to portray the pillar of strength and power he supposed himself to be. His glare was an ineffectual mask and with arms folded too high on his chest he resembled a child imitating an adult. Rather than appearing serious as he must have intended, McMaster looked like a man close to a breakdown. Go ahead, stand there and cry, you stupid obese slob. You're pathetic.

"What did you find down there?"

Daniel enjoyed giving his cryptic, casual reply, "The tunnel ends just around the corner."

"Take the wheelbarrow and bring back a few samples of ore."

McMaster's quick recovery was astonishing. Daniel wondered what had precipitated it. How deep did the man's fear go? Was it just of close spaces, or was it more than that? Daniel would try to figure the man out if he could, but in the mean time there was the task at hand to attend to. He gathered a few tools, tossed them into the barrow and trundled passed McMaster into the black, oblivious to whatever unseen danger that seemed to threaten McMaster.

Daniel collected the samples and returned. As he walked, his light bounced across the rocks, illuminating McMaster like a strobe light. Strobe. McMaster sat bent against the cold stone, eyes closed. Deep creases furrowed his brow. Strobe. McMaster now sitting upright, eyes as large as saucers. Strobe. He stood rigid, his face framing his familiar scowl. Strobe.

As much as McMaster would deny it, the headlamp had illuminated the weaknesses he was too small a man to admit. *Pathetic.*

McMaster picked up a rock from the wheelbarrow and examined it. He rolled it over in his hand investigating every facet as though he possessed the special knowledge necessary to make an educated determination of its value. It seemed impossible that this man in this environment could manage to think clearly about much of anything.

McMaster tossed the stone back into to the handcart and turned to leave. He stopped mid stride to kneel beside the body. "Bring the wheelbarrow. I'm not coming back down here again today."

McMaster pulled at the corpse, tearing at its clothing like an animal. He threw each bone to the side, and flung the remnants into the handcart in a heap, more interested in the man's possessions than in the man himself. Once he had desecrated Grundpark and had tossed anything of value in the wheelbarrow, he left the shaft with arms pumping in time with long quick strides. He wheeled his findings to the pickup and left Daniel behind to continue his work.

Later that night McMaster was silent at the dinner table. Daniel expected no less, considering McMaster had an old set of clothes and a handful of rocks to inspect. Daniel took advantage of this rare opportunity. Without the added worry that McMaster might suddenly barge into the barn, he would have time to do his own research.

He retrieved Grundpark's belongings from their respective hiding places and arranged them on the bed. He opened the wallet and took inventory. Besides the driver's license, there was the paper money colored in greens, reds and blues, exceptionally vibrant considering all those years in the damp earth. There were the few remaining receipts and there was the key. He put the key aside along with the coins and cash, all ancient treasures.

The only mystery left was the small piece of paper from Grundpark's jacket pocket, kept safe inside the wooden container. It must have been important.

10CCW-3CW-2CCW-4CW-1CCW

He wracked his mind. Had he seen anything like it before? He rolled the cylinder in his hands. The wood was hard and beautiful. It was a deep dark, rich brown and heavy. It was nothing like anything he'd seen before. The wood grain at the bottom ran in the opposite direction from the grain on the sides, suggesting the artist might have carved it from a single piece of wood.

Daniel stared at it for a long time, but having exhausted his imagination he put it to rest in the post above his bed and lay down, interlocking fingers of both hands beneath his head. He fell asleep to thoughts of the key, the locket, and the strange dowel.

Even after waking, thoughts of the paper lingered. *What could it all mean?* He took the canister down and studied it again. He ran his fingers along the polished wood. It was faint, but was there a second seam? Daniel held the tube and twisted, pulling hard at the same time. It gave. The bottom portion separated from the main tube. Daniel's eyes widened at the sight of a star. Memories of his dream rushed back and he knew the canister was the key he had seen in his dream.

CHAPTER 22

McMaster's excitement had grown; that much was obvious. Though he shared nothing of his findings, he sent Daniel to continue laboring in the main shaft where Daniel dedicated himself to his work with newfound enthusiasm, spurred on by his discovery of the key. It seemed that the more time he spent meditating on the clues, the more those bizarre thoughts and images resurfaced, so vivid and convincing that they had to be more than mere dreams. They had to have been memories. He could see himself struggling on horseback through the rain. He felt his aching muscles digging trenches defending the entrance from advancing floodwater. He was overwhelmed by horror as wet earth poured down, smothering him. He *remembered* dying.

Where did these 'memories' come from? Were they some sort of message from Grundpark? Could he be Grundpark reincarnated? He didn't know much about reincarnation, but he understood the concept. The once foremost and all-consuming thought of escape diminished — slipping away into the recesses of his mind. He could not leave this place until he had unlocked its mysteries and his connection with Grundpark. He had to keep digging.

Daniel dropped the wheelbarrow in front of the work area and began filling it. His shovel struck a large rock, like so many others he had come across. He dug away the dirt around it until it was loose enough to pick up and heave into the barrow, but when he reached down to pick it up, rather than roll down the slope toward him, the boulder rolled away into the darkness beyond.

The great door must be nearby. Everything inside him told him so. He began digging into the mound with renewed vigor and soon created a hole large enough to crawl through. On his belly, he inched inside. The tunnel continued for a short distance and then widened before splitting into two. There had been no fork in his dream. Would he forever be second-guessing himself, he wondered.

He shone his light into the dark to where Grundpark's rough passage came to an abrupt end. The new tunnel's cross-section formed a semicircle and his light reflected from the polished stone.

He took a step forward. His toe caught a pebble. It rolled ahead of him into the dust, leaving its telltale trail behind. He would not be able to hide the traces he'd leave. Daniel eased backwards and returned to the surface where he found McMaster and described what he found.

"A natural cavern?" McMaster looked quizzical.

"No. The walls are smooth. It's wider and higher than anything I've worked before."

McMaster returned to the pickup. He opened the glove box and retrieved a vinyl case. He unzipped it revealing a digital camera and handed to Daniel. "Take some pictures."

Daniel accepted the camera and turned to go.

"Take enough so I can tell what's down there."

"Sure." Of course, you idiot.

The photos proved Daniel's analysis was correct. There were none of the signs of mining that had been evident everywhere else. It must have taken a specialized crew of workmen years to complete just the work within view. Was it possible that Grundpark had dug his way into a preexisting labyrinth?

McMaster scrolled through the pictures. "I'm not going down there, but I can be there," he said. Daniel waited for further clarification, but none came.

Over the years, the vicinity of the well had begun to take on the appearance of a small community. Besides the power plants that supplied Daniel with light and McMaster with his security fence, there was the elevator, a trailer that was McMaster's office, lumber supplies and a small front-end loader. McMaster used the last to move the rubble to a large pile some distance away. Daniel regarded the awesome heap with the bittersweet knowledge that he had shoveled every ounce of the material in the mountain.

McMaster led Daniel to a small stack of unopened boxes in one corner of the trailer and pointed to one of the larger ones. "Open that one first. It's the monitor. Set it up on the counter over there."

Daniel had worked with computers in school, and sometimes Leonard and Hilda had allowed him to play games on theirs, but that was years ago. The hardware he unpacked now looked space-aged. When he finished unpacking and placing the last item on the countertop, it seemed like it could be the bridge of a spacecraft. McMaster fluttered from element to element, running cables as he went. He stood back and, with everything in order, proceeded to fire up the computer.

"This is a recording system," he said, pointing to the monitor. "What the camera sees, I'll see here. I can choose to record the images as video and even take still shots." He moved to the speaker system. "There's a built-in mike. When you speak, I'll hear that as well. I'll instruct you moment by moment. You'll be my hands, my eyes and my ears."

Though McMaster didn't come right out and say so, it was clear that if there was risk involved, it would be Daniel's to take. He was fine with that. Even more fine with the fact that McMaster wouldn't be working next to him. Except now he would literally be McMaster's puppet and that meant the man would be watching every move he made.

McMaster took Daniel's headlamp and mounted a small digital camera to it. *Very cool.* Even Daniel had to admit that. Next to it, McMaster mounted the battery pack and lastly, he handed Daniel a two-way radio. "Keep this on," he said. "I can hear you through the camera, but I might need to talk to you, so don't turn it off."

Daniel nodded, and descended into the mine while McMaster barked directions over the radio. Daniel walked through the tunnel turning from side to side describing what he saw until he arrived at his dig. He panned the area. McMaster must have realized the hole to the other side was still too small to crawl through. His voice crackled over the radio "Finish clearing the tunnel until it's completely open and shored up."

Daniel hung the walkie-talkie from his belt and started to dig. But when he leaned forward, the weight on the headlamp shifted on his head and the band slipped over his eyes. He pushed it back and dumped the shovelful of dirt in the wheelbarrow, but it wasn't long before it slipped down again. He tightened the strap, but now the darn thing was giving him a headache. The shovel caught the radio and knocked it to the ground. "Damn." He picked it up and put it out of the way.

"Justin, what are you doing?"

"Nothing. The radio fell." He returned to his work.

McMaster met him as he rolled the wheelbarrow off the platform to dump it. "I've been trying to talk to you. Where's the radio?" he scolded.

"Sorry," Daniel said, disdain clear in his voice. "I forgot it." He dumped the load and then he made his way down into the mine again.

He was halfway finished with filling the handcart when the radio crackled. "You'll have your lunch up here today."

Daniel ran over to the walkie-talkie to say, "Yes Sir," and went back to work.

A short while later McMaster interrupted again. "You're not working fast enough!"

"How the hell am I supposed to get anything done with all these stupid extra things you've got me carrying around and you interrupting me every ten seconds?" he said under his breath as he walked to the radio for the umpteenth time. But when he depressed the talk button, he said, "Yes Sir."

He ate his lunch in angry silence. What was so important that he had to come up for? The light was too bright and the company was too dim, way too dim. Daniel chuckled inwardly, the edges of his mouth rising in a tiny private grin. And just as fast, Daniel returned to his sulk.

"What's your problem?" McMaster demanded.

Daniel paused and then spewed, "This stupid thing keeps falling. It's uncomfortable and it's slowing me down. I bet pretty soon you're going to start hitting me because you think I'm not working fast enough." By the time Daniel finished, he was yelling. Letting his anger escape seemed to help relieve his frustration. Somehow he managed to leave out how badly he wanted to stomp the radio into the dirt. He dropped his head and braced himself for the inevitable backhand.

He would never know what stayed McMaster's hand, but Daniel was beyond caring. Hit me if you want, he thought. You've hit me for less. One day you'll get yours.

"Well, yes. I suppose it would be frustrating. Why don't you leave the camera with me?" He paused. "I'll try not to interrupt you 'every ten seconds' for the next little while."

Daniel flushed. That's right; he can see me down there. He knew what was going on. He let me suffer with that thing for hours. Now I'll make better time and that's what he wants anyway. He's not doing me any favors.

The cool dank air calmed him as he strode along the passage. Claustrophobia my ass. You don't have a clue what that is. Try working down here. He jammed his shovel into the dirt, imagining he was ramming it into McMaster's mouth, smashing teeth out —something he did frequently for enjoyment.

Unlike the rough primitive shafts hewn by Grundpark, the artisans had carved this section of the labyrinth from solid stone. The walls were as smooth as troweled concrete. The ceiling was a high curved arch, a perfect semicircle from one side to the other.

"This is definitely not a natural cave," he said out loud.

"..atural cave, ave, ave," the chamber called back.

"Helloooo," he called.

"Helloooo, ellooo," it echoed.

Daniel ventured forward, moving with haste. He walked to the junction between Grundpark's work and the newfound section. He turned to the right. After a short distance, the passage opened into a bona fide cavern with a higher ceiling, arced in the same manner as the tunnel, only larger. It seemed like he was standing inside a half submerged sphere. It was immediately obvious that Grundpark's permanent quarters had been set up here. Furniture was everywhere.

The crackle of the radio and McMaster's impatient voice snapped Daniel to attention. He raced back, grabbed the radio, and said as calmly as he could, "Yes, sir?"

"What the hell is going on down there? What's taking you so long?"

"I'm just finishing up. Cleaning up the last of it. I'll bring this last load out and I'll be done."

"Hurry your ass up."

Daniel filled the barrow and wheeled it out. He dumped it while McMaster towered over him.

"Well ...." he prompted when Daniel offered nothing.

"It's big. I don't think whoever mined down there made it. It's amazing." Daniel didn't want to sound interested, but he did. He couldn't help himself. He couldn't imagine anyone excavating it, especially not an old miner like Grundpark. Aliens?

McMaster wasted no time. He brought out a hardhat with some modifications. He had mounted a real mining lamp to the front. There was a flat spot on the side designed for ear protection. Here he had securely fastened the camera. A belt with a nylon pouch for the batteries formed the second part of the apparatus.

Once Daniel had donned the helmet and buckled the belt, McMaster ran a thin wire from the camera to the power supply. He toggled a switch and an image popped on the monitor.

"Get back down there and show me what you've been working on," he said.

Daniel rode the elevator down feeling like he was on a scientific quest. At the worksite, he stopped and panned from one side of the passage to the other, showing McMaster his accomplishment.

"Fine," the voice on the radio said. "Move slowly down the passage."

There was a whir from the camera. Daniel knew McMaster was either zooming in or widening the lens. He reached the intersection and pivoted to show McMaster both directions.

"Move slower. You're making me sick."

Daniel slowed his movements, trying to be conscientious of what the image above might look like. Now he really felt like an astronaut doing a moonwalk. "I'm Darth Vader," he said aloud, taking deep rasping breaths and imagining he was walking along inside a space station.

"What are you saying, boy?"

"Sorry about that. Nothing, Mister McMaster."

"Pay attention to what you're doing. Keep to the left."

Daniel inched forward. There was little to see. The corridor rounded a corner then ended in a precipitous halt. A small cache of kitchen items was stacked to one side.

McMaster cursed. "Damn, another cave-in!"

"It doesn't look like a cave in to me, sir." Daniel noticed the floor had begun to ascend. There was no evidence the rock was unstable. It appeared to Daniel as if it had been backfilled. Someone had blocked the tunnel off from the other side. He wondered if he was looking at the original entrance; who would have buried it and why?

"Shut your mouth and stick to what you know best—digging. There's nothing down here. Go back to where you started."

Daniel followed the hallway until it opened into the large chamber.

"Stop," McMaster said. "Turn around slowly so I can see the entire area."

Daniel rotated.

"Good."

His headlamp tracked with the movement of his head and illuminated the room wherever he looked. The shapes of a vintage dresser, a timeworn wood stove, and a brass bed came into view. Dust-coated relics of an age gone by were scattered throughout the long abandoned dwelling.

"I want a record of everything that's down there. Move around the room to your right. Stop at each object so I can get a good look."

Daniel proceeded in deliberate, slow motion, turning to the large armoire.

"Hold it there. Look in each drawer starting from the top."

After examining the armoire, Daniel continued from one object to the next. Then he stopped, transfixed. He stood in silent awe. It was the door from his dream. Its beauty far exceeded his memories. Even through the layers of dust his lamplight glistened on the stone-studded door. Just as he'd seen in his visions, the stones were brilliant.

The brainless blimp blared, "All right, it's wonderful. Can we move along?"

Having completed his introduction to the chamber, McMaster said, "Justin, bring the lamps and get some more light in there."

Daniel retrieved the light stands and moved them into place, but there was not enough cord to supply power, so a trip to the surface was necessary for more extension cords. Once connected, the lights illuminated a roomy chamber. The door was located directly across on the far side. Grundpark's sleeping quarters had been set up on the right and he prepared food in the area to the left. The furniture was ornate. Grundpark had not been a poor man by any means.

"You about done down there," came the dolt's dithering over the radio.

"Yes, sir. Just now."

"Get up here then."

A stack of tripods waited for Daniel upon his arrival.

"Take these light stands and place them every twenty feet or so. When you're done, I have a string of lights. Set them up starting from the entrance of the chamber. String them along the hallway as far as they'll go."

The lights lit the great hall to near daylight and the bulbs provided enough radiant heat that Daniel could feel the warmth rise. I've spent years working in the cold dark, when I could have had this. You cheap asshole.

Daniel helped load tools, including a hand truck, into the pickup. "It's moving day," said McMaster.

McMaster had scrutinized his work, Daniel was well aware, through the entire job. And although Daniel was able to view each of the objects he packed, either in newspaper, in boxes, or just in plastic bags, he also knew not one of the items was his to share in. McMaster would save them all for his private enjoyment. But none of that mattered. Daniel knew that Grundpark's real treasures were already in his possession.

Two full days later he had finished moving all of Grundpark's belongings into McMaster's home.

CHAPTER 23

"You'll be working here until you're finished," McMaster said, tossing a pitchfork and shovel on the ground in front of him. Daniel wondered why the man could never offer any form of respect. He retrieved the implement and went to work cleaning stalls in the horse barn. Tines instead of a spade, that's all. Other than that, there wasn't much difference between the two. The handle hefted about the same except when he tried to lift a large lopsided forkful. It was almost as bad as an off balance wheelbarrow. Not exactly a challenge though.

Days of nothingness ensued. Daniel missed the quiet and dark of the mine.

Since he'd filmed the Grundpark's chamber, McMaster had never mentioned the door. Except for the first pass with the camera, he hadn't asked Daniel to examine it. Why was that, Daniel wondered. Wasn't there a potential for great wealth behind it?

With each passing day, Daniel's curiosity grew. He had the key. As certain as anyone could be, he knew that funky wooden dowel would open the ancient mystical door. In time, the door and its secrets would be his. *If I can help it, Old McPig will never see the other side of it.*

The door was not the only curiosity. Why had McMaster not asked him to go back down in the cavern? And what was he spending his time doing in the house for all these days? What about the shaft that looked like someone dug it out with a giant ice cream scoop? Weren't there a hundred other things more important than horse manure?

Two weeks slipped by before McMaster called on him to go back to the mine.

"Look in every corner," he said.

It's a round room, you idiot.

"Double-check every passage."

I lived in every passage.

"Bring back anything you can find—anything at all."

Daniel ambled through his assignment being dutiful. He covered every inch of every floor, just as McMaster instructed him. He was the astronaut again. Back and forth he walked, filming every square inch of the cavern from every angle, giving McMaster a thorough photographic diary of everything … nothing. Whatever McMaster was looking for, he did not find. There had been nothing left behind.

When Daniel was finished with the general inspection of the cavern, McMaster sent him back to where he'd found Grundpark's body. He was to collect all the bones and dirt in the immediate vicinity and bring them to the surface. He was to dig into the floor and create a hollow around the body.

Daniel obeyed, feeling McMaster watching him work from the office monitors.

Daniel loaded Grundpark's remains in the cart, brought them to the surface and dumped them on a bright blue tarp McMaster had put there for that purpose. One load of dirt followed another. When he had finished, the floor of the cavern under Grundpark was a foot lower for twenty feet in front of and behind the boulder. He shaved the walls back beyond their original boundaries. If there had been something valuable in the area, it was in the debris. Not that it mattered, he thought with a smug smile; McMaster has me digging in the wrong place.

McMaster brought out a big wooden box with a screen on the bottom. "Sift all of this. Bring me anything you find." A camera poised on a tripod nearby made Daniel feel as though he was working in a fishbowl. Now and again McMaster would rush over yelling, "Hold on!" or, "Wait a second!" Then he'd push Daniel aside and take a closer look at the rock he'd just tossed away. One shovel full at a time, he sifted and sorted until not a teaspoon of dirt remained on the sheet of plastic.

It took Daniel a week to sort through the same mountain it had taken only a few days to create. When he had sifted the last shovel full of dirt and there was nothing fruitful to report, McMaster became furious. He stomped and screamed at Daniel, "You are a carelessly lazy, good-for-nothin' shit. It was there, but you lost it. You shoveled it into the pile with everything else."

Daniel stood still, waiting for the McMaster storm to pass. The man had stood over him, watched him, and hounded him for the entire week, and he knew Daniel was not guilty of his accusations. Daniel remained motionless, uncaring. *Howl at the moon you stupid old dog.*

CHAPTER 24

Daniel would endure any amount of McMaster's abuse, but he prayed that some good luck would come his way before it was too late. Until then, he followed McMaster's directives. Armed with pry bars, he descended into the mine. He stood before the beautiful stone door, prepared to do whatever McMaster ordered him to, while the key lay impotent inside his pocket. He positioned himself in front of the door, bar poised. There was the bronze seal, the metal exquisitely etched and in the center of it, a round indentation about an inch in diameter. Inside the depression was a star shaped protrusion, the exact inverse match to the star in the end of the wooden cylinder.

Daniel's hand drifted to his pocket, the key in his hidden grasp while McMaster sat above in the trailer watching everything. He couldn't use the pry bar on the door. If he were successful, McMaster will have won it all. He couldn't allow that to happen.

"What's going on? Get the bar on that door!" McMaster yelled through the radio.

Daniel placed the bar in the crack at the edge of the door and in a moment of brilliance—or stupidity?—he feigned leaning into the bar, allowed it to slip and slammed the camera and his head into the wall. He pictured McMaster in the trailer, the image on the screen flickering and going out.

"What's going on down there, Justin?" McMaster yelled.

Daniel fumbled with the radio. "I slipped, Mister McMaster, but I think I can get it working again."

"Well, get on it!"

The lens was cracked. Daniel unplugged it from the battery pack and slammed it into the wall once more for good measure, hoping there was enough damage that neither McMaster nor anyone else could fix it. He reached into his pocket, took out the wooden cylinder, and slid it into the hole in the middle of the bronze plate. It fit perfectly. Daniel's excitement grew. He pulled at the bottom and the two halves separated, revealing a carving of the star hidden in the end. He positioned the wooden key, pushed it into the hole and attempted to rotate it, but it wouldn't move. He twisted harder and alternated the key's direction. Nothing worked.

Maybe the lock has rusted solid. Maybe I didn't insert it deep enough. Why didn't I pay closer attention to the dream?

He pushed with increased force and twisted simultaneously. The key slid farther into the keyhole. Something released inside. The key turned more. Repeated audible clicking sounds followed as he rotated it.

The radio came on and Daniel leapt back, startled. "What the hell are you doing down there?"

Daniel could hear the thoughts going through McMaster's head, "You lazy-good-for-nothing-son-of-a-bitch." He said the phrase with such rapid-fire that it sounded like a single word. Daniel knew what 'lazy-good-for-nothing' meant, but he never really understood what a son-of-a-bitch was. McMaster used it every time he felt compelled to blame Daniel for something that had gone wrong.

Daniel fumbled the key out of the lock, dropped it on the ground, retrieved it, slammed the end back in place, and tucked it in his pocket.

"Boy! If I have to come down there to find out what the hell is going on, I'm going to kick the livin' shit outta you." There was a pause. "Answer me!"

Daniel raced to the radio, groped with it and then answered, "I'm right here."

"What's going on down there?"

Think fast. "I can't seem to get the radio to work. It's all staticky. I think it might be broken, too." He winced at how lame he must sound.

"It better not be or I'll be takin' it outta your hide! I hope you're reading *that* loud and static-free down there. Get that camera on. I wanna see what's goin' on."

Daniel hastened to hook up the camera.

McMaster again, "Get up here."

Daniel stood helplessly while McMaster fiddled with the camera equipment. When it wouldn't work, he assessed the radio. "It seems to be working fine. Maybe it's just the batteries." He slipped the battery cover from the radio, slapped it in the palm of his hands knocking a half a dozen batteries out and replaced them with a fresh set. Daniel was happy to see that the camera was a wash. He had cracked the casing and busted the lens.

Shaking the camera at Daniel, McMaster rebuked him. "This is a load of shit. Do you know how much this cost? I can't just go out and get another one. They don't even have anything like this around here." Daniel expected the tirade to go on longer, but McMaster fired the camera to the floor where it exploded in pieces, leaving no chance for repair.

***

That night Daniel dreamed. He stood facing the great door. He held the key in his hand. He stabbed it into the lock and it seated with ease. He pushed it in farther and then rotated it. It turned making smooth, even clicks. He twisted the key in one direction and then the in the other. He repeated the process several times and then stopped. Gears turned somewhere deep inside the door. Clanging sounds and metal scraping against metal ran up and down the full length of the door and then ... the noises stopped. The door twisted partially in its frame, one side forward and the other side back.

It was heavy, but once he got it moving, it slid easily enough. Not unexpectedly, there was dark beyond. He pulled the door open until the floodlights illuminated the space inside.

Am I me or am I Grundpark? Is this a memory? How will I know?

He walked forward in the new passage. He wondered absently why McMaster was nowhere around. He walked cautiously through the opening onto a suspended wooden floor. He ambled on and the light dimmed behind him.

He looked down, transfixed by the strange floor, unable to explain its existence, and walked ... for hours it seemed. Then, as if coming out of a trance, he raised his head and looked back the way he'd come. The great door was no more than a speck of light in the distance. Suddenly, he had the urge to go back, but he was torn. That was the way back to McMaster. That was the way back to captivity. He fought his fears and forced himself forward in the dark unknown passage.

Partial memories invaded his dreams, but beneath him always were the hard boards under his feet. How far had he come? The light speck marking the entry was gone. He stood alone in a glow that followed him and thought of Grundpark heading for home with a lantern held high, him at the center of his own halo.

His frame of reference had disappeared. Black was everywhere. He spun one way and then the other. There was nothing to indicate which direction he should go. He ran blindly. Part of him hoped to find the door he'd left behind, the assurance of a meal, and the knowledge of a place to sleep. Part of him wanted to run toward the night...away.

The sound of his thumping boots echoed from the wooden floor and the light around him dimmed until there was no light at all. He reached out with both hands and he could touch the cold stone walls with his fingertips. His fingers bounced along the stone like cards slapping spokes, the rock wearing them raw, and he raced, blind in the dark. The only sounds were of his feet on wood and his fingers on stone.

He slammed to a halt in the darkness and fell backwards. By all accounts, his face should have been a bloody mess. He ran his fingers over his nose. No pain. He stood and reached out in front of him like a sightless man. The passage had ended. There was another door. He could feel its edges. There were its hinges. His fingers found the handle. It had a thumb lever. He pressed it and the door opened.

He stood on a ledge on the side of a mountain. A valley stretched before him, dotted with wooded groves and fields. A wide river wound its way along the bottom. The sky was blue except for the occasional white wispy cloud. The sun was warm and welcoming. He was free. *Please let this be real.*

He stood on the precipice, overlooking utopia, but there was no way down. The sheer drop meant certain death if he fell, so he sat and watched the lazy clouds drift across the sky.

***

He woke in his bed, half expecting to see the splendid valley still extending out before him. Instead, he was in the darkness facing the all too familiar barn ceiling. He lay there blinking in the night, tracing his dream backward, afraid that if he didn't keep it in his mind, in a moment it would be gone forever. What were the important parts? Not the running. He remembered the long hallway. He remembered the excitement of opening the giant stone door. He let his mind slip back to the beginning of the dream knowing, somehow, there was a moment too valuable to lose. He reached back in time. He saw himself slide the key into the lock.

He bolted up. That's it!

He had turned it one way and then the other and back again. It was a combination! Grundpark had kept the secret to opening the door stored safely inside the key. Daniel flicked the light on, retrieved the cylinder and fished out the small piece of paper. He studied the strange code with new eyes.

10CCW-3CW-2CCW-4CW-1CCW.

The numbers might fall into place if only he could figure out what CCW and CW meant.

***

In the house, McMaster rose from his bed. His visits to the bathroom were still like clockwork and for that he was grateful, though sometimes he found it hard to fall back to sleep. It helped if he never allowed his eyes to adjust to light, so he stood positioned over the toilet with his eyes closed facing the glazed window. Was that light coming from outside? He head jerked up. False alarm. If there had been a light on in the barn, it was off. Maybe it had only been his imagination. He pulled up his drawers and stumbled back to bed.

***

Daniel snapped out the light and lay down. It *was* a combination! He wanted to slap himself for not seeing it sooner. How was he going to fall asleep now?

He woke in the morning at the scheduled time and emptied the canister … except for the slip of paper. He donned his clothes and was ready when McMaster opened the door. Later, he sat in the passenger seat willing McMaster to drive faster. Why was it that today he seemed to crawl, when every other day he careened along the bumpy track? Daniel swayed as the truck popped from rut to rut.

McMaster pulled into the compound and stopped. He handed him the walkie-talkie and an old digital camera. "I want pictures of everything. Do you hear? As soon as you have something to report, I want you back up here."

Daniel ran along the passage. When he arrived at the door, the key was already in his hand. He referred briefly to the slip of paper, which he now read as – 10 turns counter clockwise – 3 turns clockwise – 2 turns counter clockwise – 4 turns clockwise – 1 turn counter clockwise.

The key slipped in with ease. He pushed it farther, felt the spring inside give, and then turned it. He followed the directions as he understood them, but when he made the final counter clockwise turn, nothing happened. He pulled the key out of the hole and shone the light into the lock. What was he doing wrong? There was the star in the middle, but from each of the points, engraved into the bronze plate, were rays. Five points on the star and five grooves on the plate.

The canister was another matter. There was a narrow groove that ran the full length of one side. Until now, he had considered the marker as a scratch that might have happened sometime during its long life. Maybe it was more than that. He slid the key into the lock with the channel facing the top, and then pushed it into the second position and began to turn it.

Had he somehow foreseen the future? He didn't think so. If that was true, why could he not see other things? Besides, except for the first bit, his dream was a hodgepodge of images.

He completed the cycle once more, but nothing happened. What could he have done wrong? He tried again. Still nothing. Had he assumed too much? If the numbers didn't mean turns, then what did they mean? The radio crackled.

"I want an update!" McMaster roared from the speaker.

"I'm trying to get enough rock chipped away to get the pry bar in," Daniel lied.

"What's taking so long?"

"The rock is very hard, sir. I'm working on it."

"Well hurry it up."

Daniel dropped the radio and went back to the key. Click, click, click came from the mechanism as he turned it. Then it dawned on him. He returned to the lock.

Left ten clicks … click, click, click, click, click, click, click, click, click, click, Daniel counted carefully.

Right three clicks … click, click, click.

Left two clicks … click, click.

Right four clicks … click, click, click, click.

Left one click … click.

Somewhere inside wheels and cogs slid into place and parts moved within the stone door. The bronze seal slid out of the door becoming a handle of sorts. Daniel stowed the key, grasped the handle and twisted it. Unlike a conventional door, it pivoted on some central focal just as his dream portrayed. Instantly, light poured from the opening filling Grundpark's cave.

Shielding his eyes, Daniel stepped inside and found himself in an oval room surrounded by crystals uniformly covering every wall in the cavity. Squinting, Daniel's eyes roamed from the brilliance of the light to other aspects of the chamber. A walkway made of roughly hewn timbers and lumber disappeared in the bright light inside. Daniel proceeded.

A short distance in, he turned to look back the way he had come. The door and the wooden path were the only objects in the chamber that did not emit blinding white light. He continued through the forest of crystals feeling like he was living the negative version of his dream. Water streamed from his eyes. He focused on the wooden floor. Looking anywhere else was unbearable. It occurred to him that somehow he had gone from the real world, to an opposite world of un-reality. Before he finished his thought, he found himself standing before a second door.

Had he inadvertently turned himself around and walked back the way he'd come? No. This door was different. For one, it was closed … and locked.

"Boy! You down here?" McMaster's gruff voice, ripped through the light from behind him.

Daniel's first thought was, Definitely a different door, overlapped with, *oh my shit!*

Glaring light obliterated everything in McMaster's direction. Daniel stood dumbfounded and trapped while seconds slipped by. He was a fly in a bottle and came to the only conclusion he could. "Yes sir," he called.

More agonizing time passed. Reluctantly, he started toward the opened door like a child bringing a switch to his own beating when McMaster's booming voice reverberated through the chamber, "You're one dead kid, b—"

The door slammed closed, cutting off the final word.

CHAPTER 25

Once the door thumped shut, the light in Grundpark's old digs quartered. McMaster's eyes turned into saucers as the gravity of his situation dawned. The path up to this point was a simple single avenue with only one side passage to avoid, but that knowledge was no match for his fear of enclosed spaces. The darkness astronomically increased the effects of his claustrophobia. His body immediately reacted. His breaths came in quick sharp bursts. Where was the air? He sat with his back to the cold stone door and pulled his knees to his chest. His internal voice screamed. Pull yourself together. Control the situation. What are you if you can't control the situation?

Salt water seeped from the corner of his eyes and his chest constricted. He could taste his fear and resisted his urge to pee. The reasoning part of his brain knew he was on the losing side of a battle with terror. Some deeper, primitive part was running things now. His diaphragm dropped, pulling hard to draw air into his chest, but the cavern seemed devoid of oxygen. He sucked harder, faster. The lights around him dimmed and stars circled on the backside of his eyes. Stay conscious, he ordered himself. No. No. No. Stay conscious.

And then … there was nothing.

***

When he woke, his first awareness was that the chamber was black and a chill had seeped into his body. Memories flooded back and his fear returned strong, acrid and instantly consuming. He fought it. He willed himself to stay calm. He forced himself to control the circumstances. "Think. Think. Think," he chanted. Can't stay here. Got to keep moving.

There were no side tunnels to the left. Stay to the left. Stay to the left. He dropped to his hands and knees and crawled on all fours. The left leads straight to the well. Straight to the well. Gotta get out. He crawled for a seeming eternity while his stomach grew increasingly sick with fear. *Oh my God.* His gut lurched and he spewed his stomach's contents. Please be done. Gotta get moving. He heaved again and then again. I'm breathing. That's good. Deep breath. Good.

He started crawling again … straight through. Stay to the left. The left is out. Can't get lost. Can't get lost. Chanting helped. It kept him focused, kept him in control. Left hand, touch the wall. Right hand, move ahead. Legs, follow. Left hand, touch the wall, he ordered. A thousand choruses, no verses, he chanted until his hand touched the elevator. He stood, caked with filth and puke, and screamed to the stars in animal triumph. God had tested him and he had passed. His tears flowed freely.

Pallid, in the night he stood exhausted yet relieved. The small square of open beckoned above him. He found the power cable for the elevator and followed it to the controller. He fumbled at the buttons. *'Down' is close to the cable. 'Up' is at the other end.* His fingers found it and he pushed. Nothing. Pushed again. Nothing. Push. Push. Push. Nothing.

"Why?" he screamed to the sky.

The primitive was back and whispered in his ear, *You're gonna die. Just like the boy. You're gonna die. Naaa NaNa, NaNa Naaa. You're going to die.*

"*Shut up.* Shut up!" He strode in small circles on the platform, hands over his ears as if it was going to help quell the voice. He looked up. Sky, he thought, as tears rolled down his cheeks.

Angled braces and beams stretched to the top, not even a challenge for a twelve year old. McMaster reached up as far as he could. The first step was the equivalent of two rungs on a ladder; too far for an overweight man who could barely tie his shoes. He pulled himself up. The tip of his toe found something, just a sliver, really. His gut pushed against his diaphragm making it impossible to breathe. He slithered his foot forward and pushed with all his might. His giant mass rose.

For the longest time he clung there, panting. When he had rested, he reached up again and, somehow, found the strength to continue. The sun was rising when he fell onto the solid ground above. Sweat poured from him. In the clean night air, he could smell his own old-man-stench—sweat and vomit—and puked again, a dry heave that produced acidic spittle and traces of blood.

Eventually he picked himself up. He slid into the driver seat and puttered home, avoiding bumps and ruts. *Waltzing Matilda, Waltzing Matilda, you'll come a waltzing Matilda with me.* He was feeling better already. Thoughts turned to his wife. She'd need an explanation. She had grown uncomfortably close to the boy. He had warned her about that and it should never have happened.

By the time he reached the house, he decided to break the news to her in stride. There was no point feigning concern or regret when he'd never had those feelings in the past. He didn't have to look at the clock to know it was early morning. His appetite was back. He pulled out a loaf of bread, butter, peanut butter, and a jug of milk. The jug and the loaf were all but gone when he strode into the bathroom to have a shower. When he crawled into bed there was enough light that he didn't feel the urge to turn one on. Matilda lay on her side of the bed, barely using any covers. She wouldn't even notice he'd been gone. He closed his eyes and hated her until he slept.

When he woke it was late afternoon. He went nonchalantly through the house and found his wife where he expected, working in the kitchen. He sat at the table, a practice he'd established when they were first married. This routine dictated she serve a cup of coffee. He liked it with a little whole cream and a tablespoon of sugar. The perfect amount of cream resulted in a rich caramel color with which, even he had to admit, the woman had become an expert. He waited until the steaming beverage arrived. "There's been an accident," he said.

If Matilda had been concerned about his late arrival, she showed no interest. Maybe she would react to this news.

McMaster's fingers rotated the warm cup on the table allowing the information to steep. Then he carried on. "The passage Justin was working in collapsed. He didn't make it out." McMaster took a sip from his mug.

Matilda gave a short nod then returned to tending her roast.

McMaster watched her turn away. That went better than I expected. Not even a word about the loss or an attempt at a guilt trip. He finished his coffee in silence and went to the barn. He'd have to clear away all the evidence that Daniel had been there. It wouldn't be difficult. Except for his clothing, the boy owned nothing. McMaster stripped the bed and tossed the blankets in a heap for the dog. After dropping the sheets and clothes into the burn barrel, he poured a small amount of gasoline on the top, struck a match, and was already walking away when the clothes ignited in a woof of flame. He lifted the mattress to toss it to the barn floor when he discovered the items Daniel had stashed beneath it. He paused long enough to give them a cursory inspection and pocketed the lot. Sure as hell, you're getting exactly what you deserve!

CHAPTER 26

Daniel ran toward the way out, but the door closed. He listened, but the thick stone prevented any sound from penetrating. Nothing resembling a receptacle for the key was apparent. Besides, even if he could find a way to open the door, McMaster might still be out there, waiting.

There was the other door. Maybe it held the secret. He raced across the bridge. Close scrutiny revealed nothing more than its construction was the same as the first. A set of twin doors leading into the same boulder filled with crystals, from opposite directions. He sat wondering what to do.

At least he was safe. McMaster had no way of getting in and was scared shitless to be in the mine. He didn't know that a key existed, so maybe he'd think he could figure out the door for himself. A vacuous thought had Daniel half-wondering if the old shit would use explosives. He didn't think so. McMaster wouldn't want to risk a cave-in or the possibility of damaging his treasure.

Daniel had a serious problem to solve. In all likelihood he'd have the time. He'd probably have until McMaster had the courage to come back, or until he died—whichever came first.

Daniel paced from one end of the corridor to the other. He grew hungry, thirsty, and still he paced. He grew tired. His pacing slowed. Eventually weariness overcame him and he succumbed to sleep.

Daniel awoke in pitch black with cold stone chilling his body, his back welded by the stiffness that had crept inside. Slow and deliberate movements limbered his rigid joints.

Whatever magical energy the crystals emitted had expired. The remarkable crystals had absorbed light from when he first opened the door, stored it, and reflected it until it had spent its charge; that much was clear. What would happen if this stone had access to the sun's rays? It was a question for another day. He pointed his flashlight upward and flipped the switch on and off. The effect was immediate and blinding. He winced and shut his eyes, opening them only to slits until they adjusted.

Daniel turned to the problem of the door. With such ingenuity, surely whoever built it would have made it possible to get out if someone accidentally locked himself inside. He scanned its surface, but could see nothing. There were no shadows. Light had found every crevice. He placed his fingers on the door looking for imperfections. And they were there. He felt opposite to where the door handle would have been if he were on the other side and there was something. *A seam?*

He pushed a little and a section in the middle of the door moved inward. Is that all there is to it? He pushed the door, but nothing gave. Still locked, or just latched? He wondered.

Surely, Grundpark had not built this place, as McMaster had believed. Daniel speculated how many times had it been lost and found through the eons. How many millions of years ago had it formed?

He thought back to all the times he wished for death rather than wake to another day of working for McMaster: innumerable. And just as countless were the times he willed the cavern to fall in on him as it had on Grundpark. He heaved a mighty sigh. McMaster had put an impenetrable wall between them, and there was a strange comfort in that.

That there was more to the secret door was obvious. As he pondered his predicament, his thoughts returned to the crystals. Was light the only thing they could capture and amplify? What drew people to this place? What drew Grundpark to live in the mine? What drew McMaster? Who built it and why had they abandoned and forgotten it?

Grundpark was long dead, so there was no explaining his behavior, but what of McMaster's? Nothing about the man seemed levelheaded. The bastard lived in a world of extremes.

The thought teetered on the edge of his mind and then … he knew he had the answer. There *was* a relationship between the two men, a relationship that only the crystals could explain. Both of these men lived in a world of poles, incapable of monitoring their responses to the world around them. McMaster was certainly insane and Grundpark must have been. Why else would he choose to live in a cave?

Understanding and fear collided. If exposure to the crystals caused such strange behavior in Grundpark and McMaster, what might it do to him? What *had* it done to him? He had worked in close proximity to the chamber for years.

It seemed unlikely that the crystals could communicate. If they could, there was that second door and he had no idea what was behind it. Nor had his dream been entirely accurate. Without the influence of the crystals, would he have been able to make the connection between the wooden dowel and the door lock? Would he have thought to check for the faint lines on the door? And even if he did, would he have supposed they had a purpose?

Somehow, the stones seemed to have the capability of improving his ability to apply himself to the problem at hand. Was it possible they were able to store and impart mental images? It would have explained his dream of Grundpark's final moments. Maybe later he would dream about McMaster and his fight with claustrophobia.

Assumptions aside, he slipped his hand into the cavity inside the door. The portion of the door was a cleverly disguised handle. He grasped it and turned. Loud clicking sounds came from within. Unseen latches moved and the door twisted on its center post. Daniel pulled the edge of the door toward him, revealing a second passageway extending as far as he could see. The height and width of the corridor were just large enough to accommodate the door's swing, giving it a personal, almost secret feel. At head height, two strips of the strange gemstone decorated the corridor resembling long florescent tubes. They were made of innumerable crystals, each perfectly placed end-to-end, creating what Daniel thought might be the world's first incandescent light bulb, an impressive thousand feet long. The polished granite surface gleamed in the near daylight.

The path dipped downhill and opened into a large domed temple, larger still than Grundpark's antechamber. The path continued around the circumference of the sunken room as a narrow raised platform, creating both a bench and walkway around a central altar. The crystal décor wound around the room in a continuous loop that started and stopped at the sunroom—as Daniel had come to think of it. Dead center was an altar, the shape of an upside down, miniature pyramid, stuffed halfway into the ground point first.

Encircling the perimeter, below the ribbon of light, was a series of ancient markings similar in form and design to those on the door. As indecipherable as they were, he knew instinctively that they told a story, possibly the history of the temple. He'd like to return one day with the knowledge necessary to answer all his questions.

As interesting as the temple might be, he had allowed himself to become preoccupied. There was a new idea blossoming in his consciousness, more urgent and alien from all his previous experiences. As the idea took shape in his mind saliva filled his mouth. The idea was 'freedom'. As confounding as the labyrinth might be and as wonderful as his new discovery might seem, all would forever be sallow wax in comparison to the knowledge that he was no longer captive. He was free.

On the heels of that thought followed the thought of McMaster.

He had slept, but for how long? Would McMaster be out there, waiting for him? Probably not. McMaster wouldn't have been able to stay down here for five minutes by himself. If he were waiting anywhere, it would be above ground and then, only if he thought Daniel could get out. McMaster would have made sure that he couldn't escape.

Daniel ran his fingers over the door and found the telltale grooves outlining the hidden mechanism. He pressed and the stone block slid into the door. It opened and McMaster was nowhere in sight. The floodlights were out. Only the crystals illuminated the cavern. He paused to consider how deathly scared the old fart must have been if he'd counted on the crystal's glow to light his way out and then got hit with the harsh reality of dealing with not only his claustrophobia, but also groping his way in pitch blackness. Daniel smiled at that possibility.

A single gem could make both a brilliant and long lasting light, but he'd have to break one off. A stone would make a suitable hammer. He knelt at the edge of the suspended deck; the gems were close and much smaller. He picked out one he'd be able to conceal in his hand and brought the rock down hard. Instead of knocking just one loose, the stone cleared away an unexpected swath the length of his arm. Broken crystals exploded into tiny powder-sized fragments.

He discarded the stone and grasped a crystal at its base, adding incremental pressure until it broke free. As he predicted, it preserved its properties of storing light. Maybe it retained whatever other properties it might possess as well, a scary and, at the same time, exciting thought. He placed it on the floor and pointed the flashlight at it, then toggled the switch to recharge it. The transformation was instant. The light from the crystal became overwhelming. He closed his eyes against the frigid luminosity, changing his eyelids into translucent red lenses.

After securing the door behind him, he marched toward the entrance, grateful for the refreshing darkness in the passage. He held the crystal palm down. The glow turned his flesh a bright pink. Veins crisscrossed in a darker red and his bones appeared as dark lines, the only material dense enough to block the light.

Daniel stopped short of the entry. If the flashlight could charge the crystal with unbearably bright light, what would the sun do? It would be better if he didn't find out. He knelt and buried the crystal in the dirt before tentatively approaching the opening.

Early morning light poured in. The elevator rested at the bottom of the shaft. Daniel froze, terrified. There was only one immediate explanation and that was that McMaster was in the tunnel somewhere. Daniel spun, listening. There was no sound, only pervasive silence.

Daniel looked up into the shaft, still craning to hear noise of any kind. He began his ascent. The timbers were like old friends and in moments he crouched at the edge of the well overlooking the familiar worksite in the warm morning sun. The opened gate listed sideways, as if bowing in apology for its years of regrettable service.

Daniel crossed the compound. Deep easy breaths filled his lungs with air. These were his first breaths of freedom. His face was to the morning sky when he heard the rush of paws pounding earth. He knew that sound and ran without looking back. Brute was close behind.

Daniel scrambled up the hill of dirt. His hand found a fist sized stone. He clawed it free and pulled it with him. Brute's breath was strong. Daniel spun and launched the stone. Brute was only an arm's length away. The rock had barely left his hand before crashing into the dog's skull. Daniel rolled to the side and toppled down the mountain of dirt, each tumble giving him a new view of the vicious hound. Brute stood and shook his head, gathered his bearings and then bolted down the hill.

The poplar tree next to the well was tall and strong. He'd be safe if he could get to it. Daniel sprinted and jumped. His hand found a limb, dead and dry as the lower branches of poplars are, just a suggestion of a branch. It bore his weight then Brute had him. The dog's jaw clamped down on the sole of his boot and pulled hard. The twig broke and the two tumbled to the ground, Daniel kicking with his free leg. His foot connected with the dog's head and Brute released his grip. Daniel scuttled away, kick, scoot, kick, until his hand slipped into the well behind him—throwing him off balance. He had begun to fall head first into the well when Brute bit deep into his calf and pulled. Pain ripped into Daniel's leg, but it was a small price to pay. He was even thankful for a moment. Daniel twisted away, kicking and screaming, "Let go of me." His boot made solid contact again, knocking the mongrel away. Brute paused only long enough to find a new target. He lunged at Daniel's face.

Daniel caught the massive neck in two hands. Brute's hind feet dug into the ground. Daniel held the dog in a vicious stalemate. Daniel's powerful arms rippled. The dog moved back an inch. Daniel relaxed. The dog raced forward. Daniel threw his head to one side and heaved. The dog's momentum carried him forward. A tooth grazed Daniel's face as the dog traveled through the air. There was a short yelp from far below and then quiet. Daniel rolled over to be sure. Brute lay at the bottom of the shaft. He could have been sleeping … except for the blood oozing from between his open jaws.

It was still early morning when he walked up to the house. There was no sign of McMaster. There were items in the barn that could be useful. The yard was quiet when he stole across it. There was no movement from the house. The way seemed clear. Once inside he raced up the ladder to find the empty loft. McMaster had come and now nothing remained. The wallet and the locket were gone, as were the money and the stones. There was no time to look back and no ties for which he felt the urge to reminisce. There was nothing here. There never had been.

He was halfway between the ladder and the barn door when it swung open and Mrs. McMaster appeared. She ran toward him. Fear slammed into his chest. There was no time to react. It took her all of three strides before she was upon him. And then her arms were around him.

"Thank God you're all right."

Daniel wasn't listening. McMaster would be right behind her. He shoved her away.

"No. No. He's not coming. He's asleep."

He didn't know whether to cry or scream. "What do you want from me?" he said, in a harsh whisper, still trying to push her aside.

"Shhhh. It's over. You're okay." She was still holding on to his shoulders. "Here," she said, handing him a wad of creased and wrinkled bills. She stuffed the money into his hand. "Mad money," she added, as if it was supposed to mean something. "I know it's not much, but it should get you away from here." Her eyes were bright with tears.

"Thank you so much," he said, neither grateful nor angry. He ran.

CHAPTER 27

And he ran.

Mrs. McMaster had said there was a little town close by called Vanderhoof, but as he sprinted along the driveway toward his freedom he realized there were other things he must do. The bus depot could not be his immediate destination. He came to a halt and with trepidation turned back. Little time remained. He must be gone before McMaster awakened.

The strength gained from three years of hard labor came to his aid. He ran tirelessly and soon he was standing at the door of the trailer next to the mine. On the floor inside was his backpack. It was made of thick canvas the color of sand. He used it to tote equipment to and from his work site. It still contained many items, some useful and others not so much. He tossed out the battery pack and walkie-talkie, but kept the flashlight and the remains of a two day old lunch consisting of half a sandwich and an apple. The peanut butter and jelly had kept well. The bread was crusty and stale, but it would suffice. At least it would take the edge off his hunger.

Having taken what he could, there was the matter of the crystals. He climbed into the well. Once inside the chamber he brought out his steel lunchbox and filled it with as many crystals as he could. Light shone from it like a miniature sun. He closed the lid and shut the light inside.

Daniel crawled out of the hole. It was already midmorning. He ran west to the fence line. He could skirt the farmhouse, follow the property line and emerge on the main road. In just a few hours, he'd be far away.

Mrs. McMaster had said there was a bus station in town and from there he could go anywhere he wanted. Maybe he didn't know exactly where yet, but by the time he arrived, perhaps he'd have some idea. Daniel ran from the sleeping tyrant. The roar of an approaching vehicle sent him scurrying into the brush. *Not McMaster ... yes? ... no!* He was back on the road running again.

There was an off chance that McMaster would make a trip to town. That was enough of a threat to keep him diving toward the ditch at every approaching sound coming from behind.

CHAPTER 28

An hour later, a pale eighteen-year-old boy, with scraggily long hair and the beginnings of a full beard, wearing shredded clothes that showed more skin than they covered, walked into the small farming and logging town. He wandered through the streets, too afraid to ask for directions.

As fearful as he was, he did eventually stop at a busy intersection. A tall red brick building, maybe the oldest in town, stood on his left. He didn't need to read posted signs; watching people come and go with stacks of mail was all that was required to know it was the post office. In the front was a two-legged bulletin board filled with overlapping pages of upcoming events and miscellaneous items for sale. No one seemed interested. Daniel wondered if anyone ever stopped to try to make sense of the clutter.

Around the side next to the bar and hotel a group of younger people, not much older than he, stood near an old pickup. It looked as though it might have once been red, but it may have merely lost its battle with rust. Daniel felt out of place.

"Hey," one of them called in his direction.

The guy must be talking to someone behind him. Daniel turned to look, but there was no one there. Daniel smiled and nodded.

"I'm Steve. Which crew are you working with?"

Daniel shrugged. "I'm not sure what you're talking about."

"You're kidding, right?" but he could see that the kid wasn't. "We're planting trees around here for the summer. I thought you might be working with one of the crews."

There was a long empty silence. When Daniel said nothing the stranger carried on. "People drop out all of the time. You should think about joining us."

Daniel shrugged. "Thanks for the offer. Maybe."

"A bunch of us are headed into the bar. Why don't you join us?"

Friends? The prospect was suddenly frightening; scarier than McMaster even. "Thanks, but I've got a few things I need to take care of right now."

"Maybe later, then." Steve headed into the bar.

"Hey, do you know where the bus depot is?"

"Yeah sure. It's a no-brainer. Just follow this street straight down through the lights. You'll see it as soon as you see the mall."

"Thanks, man." Like Steve had suggested, it was a 'no-brainer', except for one thing. What Steve had described as a mall was an unimaginative rectangular building covered in metal siding. There was an awning over a sidewalk that ran the full length of the structure which sported equally ordinary signs for each of the establishments. Daniel stood before Greyhound Bus Depot and the locked door. It wouldn't be open again until after eight p.m. His gaze roamed to the mirror surface of the darkened window and his reflection. A young man stood before him with a shaggy, brownish blonde beard. His clothes were baggy on him and he'd tied his pants with a short length of cord instead of a belt. The ends hung down, each ending in a large knot with frayed tips. His shirt was threadbare and tattered. The coat he wore was a heavy throw away with a broken zipper. There were dark oil stains on the sleeves and tufts of the lining poked out through every hole. As well as all of that, he was filthy. I'm one scary son-of-a-bitch, he thought, and it was McMaster's voice he heard, not his own.

Daniel spent the day walking around town. It didn't take long to become familiar with the village. The core consisted of about sixteen square blocks, but the main part of business area was made up of the central four. That midtown corner was marked by one of the five sets of traffic lights, a theatre, a bank, a gas station and a pizzeria.

The sun slipped through the sky then dipped away. Daniel had expected to see McMaster at one point or another, but either he had not come into town, or Daniel had missed seeing him. Even with fear hanging over his head, it had been a terrific day.

Suddenly, Daniel heard the howl of the Greyhound. He raced to the depot. The office was dark and vacant. He watched the bus as it rolled out of town. *He'd missed it and there was nowhere for him to go.*

The theatre had long since begun to bear the signs of age. Over the years the stucco on and adjacent to each of the corners had been knocked off exposing the chicken wire beneath. There was a small parking area behind the structure with a space between the theatre and the neighboring building. An exit door opened into the alcove where two large homemade wooden waste bins bulged with black garbage bags. They emanated of popcorn and candy. Daniel's stomach gnawed at him.

He wasn't the first to have taken refuge in the small alley. There were numerous empty wine bottles, big green ones that said 'Royal Red' on the side. Maybe it was a good place to hunker down. Others had done it.

A movie was playing inside. The speakers were close, just a few boards away. Although the dialogue was subdued, it came through clearly. He remembered the last, and only, time he'd gone to a movie. His foster parents had taken him. He didn't remember the story, but he recalled how much he enjoyed it and how special it felt to be able to go out. He sat, exhausted. There was no picture, but he was entertained anyway. Soon he was engrossed in the story and forgot both his hunger and fatigue.

The good guy, Andy, was in prison for a murder he didn't commit. And there was also a man named Red. Together they were the whole story. They were two men dedicated to friendship. Daniel cried when Andy gave Red a harmonica, but the real kicker began with Andy's escape. It was long and wonderful and Daniel couldn't pick one part to like more. When the two men stood reunited on the beach somewhere in Mexico and much older now, Daniel sat in the alley and cried tears he could not understand. It was just a story after all. It had nothing to do with him, did it?

Rustling from inside sent him scurrying into the shadows. A door opened, maybe on the street side of the building, followed by a flurry of activity. Animated conversations and the sound of starting vehicles painted a vivid picture of a movie theater exodus. Daniel hid next to the bin, his eyes squeezed closed and his legs pulled to his chest, willing the door to remain closed, praying the tens or hundreds of people would leave through any other door but this one.

The mad rush dwindled and Daniel was thankful no one had used the exit.

The din died away until only a few voices remained. Daniel's tension eased until the door swung open unexpectedly. A boy, a few years younger than he, hoisted full garbage bags onto the growing heap in the bin then disappeared inside, closing the door behind him. A vehicle engine started shortly afterward and headlights shone into the alley, briefly lighting the area. It backed away and disappeared, leaving Daniel alone and in the dark. No more sounds came from within. The whole town had grown quiet. There must be nothing left to do in the village but sleep, was his vacuous thought.

Sleep may have come. His thoughts rambled the way they do in dreams, but the cold was always there, making it feel like he might be daydreaming in the dark. Asleep or not, he was alert in a flash when a staggering group of people wandered into the alcove. Someone spoke. Faces were dark and mysterious, not that it mattered. "Who th' hell're you?" the voice asked. Daniel couldn't tell if it was a slur or an accent, maybe a little of both.

"Daniel."

"I don' care who the hell you are. Shaddup."

Daniel did. There were McMasters everywhere.

"Listen, I didn't mean anything by that. Maybe you could spare a few bucks so we could get some coffee?" His arm made a broad lazy sweep across the group.

If a few dollars would buy his privacy, he could afford that. He reached into his pocket and drew out his crumpled wad of bills. A hand darted out. Before he could close his fingers, it had scooped everything from his palm.

"Thanks, man."

"Wait! That's everything I have. I need that," Daniel said.

"We won' f'getcha. We're good for it," he returned in that slurred accent.

Daniel counted the silhouettes. There were five ... too many. He watched them go, taking his life away with them. He cursed himself for being weak. Was he no more than what McMaster had always accused him of being? Had he become what he loathed? He hated McMaster. He hated the thieves. But more than that, he hated himself for being frightened.

He had saved all his money for the bus fare because he couldn't know what it would cost and hadn't been willing to risk coming up short. The stale peanut butter sandwich and apple were long gone; hours upon hours gone. Since then he had fasted. After he'd bought the bus ticket, breakfast was going to be so good. That thought had been enough to give him the strength to hold out until morning.

He didn't want to, but he wept angry, bitter tears. He was supposed to be on the bus already, riding in a plush comfortable seat on his way to anywhere-but-here. He wished he'd held back the apple at least. Now he had nothing. *I don't deserve freedom*, he scolded himself.

The smell of fresh popcorn wafted from the garbage container and his stomach launched another attack. As distasteful as digging into bags full of garbage seemed, his empty stomach was not in agreement.

The bags were bursting, not with stale old rotting food, but with leftover popcorn. These were fresh leftovers, he reasoned. Daniel pulled the one closest into his lap. The knot came loose easily and some of the contents spilled out. Most of the garbage was empty popcorn containers, paper cups and candy wrappers, but the aroma was strong and pleasing, too strong for there to be nothing. He pulled out the bags and cups tossing them in a pile beside him. The trash grew around him. The image of burying himself in garbage was more than he could stand, even if he was damn hungry. He began to stack the cups and fold the empty bags. Always the responsible one, he thought.

His hand came across an upright full bag, pinched closed at the top. Someone must have bought the bag and never even touched it. He could see the workers flitting among the chairs picking up after the moviegoers. People are slobs and there would have been popcorn strewn on the floor. But there would be the odd bag, such as this one, which they would have picked up carefully from the seat and placed in the garbage to avoid adding to the already formidable mess. Well, maybe not, but it was a vision that made the popcorn not only edible, but enjoyable as well. He pushed handful after handful into his gaping mouth and didn't stop until the bag was empty.

Daniel systematically rummaged through the rest of the trash, adding leftovers until he had filled two bags with good clean popcorn. He ate one of the bags and folded the top down on the other, putting it into his pack for later. It occurred to him, as he slid the zipper tab, making his next meal safe, that he had no idea how much had been taken from him. Why hadn't he taken the time to straighten the bills and count them? Why hadn't he just said no, I don't have any change?

Full, and both emotionally and physically exhausted, Daniel closed his eyes. He was too tired to care that the night chill had set in. He curled up in a ball and wrapped himself in his tattered coat. Eventually he slept.

Daniel awoke to the sound of a voice. "Hey! You! Skeennay Steeck!"

Daniel heard, 'skinny stick'.

"Get outta my place. Yuh go fine summerelse ta sleep."

The man made a sweeping motion with his foot but lost his balance and fell against the wall. He steadied himself and then let his feet slide out from under him. He landed awkwardly on his butt with a bottle of Jack Daniels firmly in his hand.

"Oh hell weet it. I'm too damn drunk. Doe'n steal anythin', okay? Yeah … you're a good guy aren't yuh. Yuh look like ya need a drink." He held the bottle out at arm's length to Daniel. "Yuh wanna sit an' drink with me?"

Daniel said nothing.

"What! You too good for me? You're juss another stuck-up whitey. You, you son-of-a-bitch." The man took a pull on his bottle and let his arm flail to the ground as if holding it up had been the most difficult task he had ever attempted. He threw his head sideways and it flopped in Daniel's direction like a sack of potatoes. He regarded Daniel briefly as if sizing him up, then gathered his strength and swung the bottle up and let it drop onto Daniel's chest, never losing his grip on it.

"Here. Go head. Have a drink."

Daniel looked down on it. The smell was nasty. The man and the bottle reeked of the same stuff.

"What? Are you too good tuh drink with your ole fren Raphael? Come on. Take a drink."

The man had leaned in close. The combination of alcohol on his breath and the strong smell of rotten teeth made Daniel's stomach lurch. He wasn't going to get rid of the guy until he shared a drink with him. He took a swig, passed the bottle back to Raphael and immediately wondered where he had misplaced his spine. His throat burned and he started to cough. Whatever Raphael was drinking tasted like poison.

"You're alright, buddy. Wass your name anyway?" Raphael chuckled.

"Daniel."

"Daniel! My good buddy Daniel, You can drink with me any time ya want to."

The man fell asleep, still gripping the open bottle.

Daniel woke before his guest and spent the day wandering the town. He avoided making eye contact and kept a lookout for either the old pickup or the red Ford sedan the McMasters drove. Few vehicles in a town this size could be mistaken for those. Besides, McMaster would have a hard time grabbing him in public. Daniel could scream and run. He'd be safe enough.

A tap from behind him sent Daniel spinning, ready to bolt.

"Can you spare a quarter for a coffee?" a small native man with a bulbous red nose asked.

Daniel managed, "No. I don't have anything myself," but he thought, holy shit, this guy has one foot in the grave.

The small man walked away muttering something like 'cheap white bastard' and Daniel wondered in bemusement about racism. It seemed like everyone hated the color of his skin. He had noticed there were two groups of people living in Vanderhoof, the 'Indians' and the 'white' people. Apparently, they didn't like each other much. So far he'd only met people who wanted his money.

He puzzled over the concept of money, realizing he'd never had enough tangible experience with it to know its value and the relative gain or loss of having it or not. He was learning. Still hurt, having lost his possible bus fare escape money. He stood in front of the theatre looking at posters of coming attractions and practiced a skill it had been long since he used: reading. He read everything. *Speed,* with Keanu Reeves was coming soon. He pronounced it Keenoo. It looked exciting. *Forest Gump* was on another poster, some story about a retarded kid. He couldn't imagine anyone wanting to go to that. Then there was *The Mask* with some guy name Jim Carrey. Now that looked like a movie worth watching. The Shawshank Redemption starring Morgan Freeman and Tim Robbins was showing at seven-thirty. It was due to run until Friday. Since there was nothing else to do he'd return at seven-thirty and hear the story again. This time he would listen to the whole thing.

The theatre billboard included the current time and temperature. It was five forty-five and the current temperature was sixty-eight degrees.

He moved along.

Chicken wings and fried rice were on special at the New Pagoda Inn. The building looked like it was a hundred years old and wasn't doing so well either.

He moved on.

There were posters in every window of every building. He read them all. One of his teachers had told him that he'd find reading fun one day. At the time he thought she was crazy, but she hadn't been wrong. Reading was like candy and he couldn't get enough of it.

He was sitting next to the dumpster when the movie started up. There were short films advertising the movies he'd read about. They'd all sounded like they'd be great to watch and not just listen to.

The movie ended, the doors opened and the patrons dispersed. The same rustling from inside the theatre followed. This time an elderly man about five foot ten and of a medium build delivered the bags of rubbish to the container outside. Someone had come to collect the garbage since the previous night. Except for the new bags the man now tossed in, the waste containers were empty.

The man did not return to the door immediately. He looked up and down the short alley and his eyes fell upon Daniel. "Hey there," he said, and paused as if waiting for a response.

Daniel nodded.

"What arc you doing back here?"

It sounded more like an accusation than a question. Daniel hesitated, his mouth open as if he was about to speak.

The man squinted up his eyes as if trying to keep the sun out of them. "Have you been drinking?"

Daniel shook his head.

The old man pressed. "What are you doing back here?"

"I was listening to the movie," he said, and he realized he was probably talking to the owner. He didn't know how he would feel if someone was trespassing on his property, but he knew what McMaster would think. "I'm really sorry. I didn't mean to cause any problems. Do you think it would be all right if I stayed here for just one more night and then I'll find somewhere else to go?"

"How long have you been staying back here?"

"Oh no. Not long at all. Just last night," Daniel said quickly, trying to minimize the infraction.

"Where are you from?"

Daniel hesitated. The truth seemed impossible to tell, so he lied. "West of here. I wanted to see the country, but I ran out of money."

"You didn't get very far did you?" The man didn't wait for Daniel to reply "Where are you from?"

Daniel knew the answer to that one. "Alberta."

There was a thoughtful pause. "Travelin' from the west, eh? How long you been on the road?" The man paused in thought, stroking his chin. Daniel could tell he was trying to add the one plus one he'd lied about so far to see if it added up right. The creases forming on the man's face told Daniel he wasn't buying his story so far.

Sweat was beginning to bead on Daniel's forehead. *How long, how long?* He blurted out the first thing that came to mind. "Six months."

"That's a long time. That's a heck of a long time to be out on the road."

If the man didn't believe him, he gave no sign of it.

The man continued. "You can't sleep out here. Come on and you can join us this evening. My wife can throw something together once we get home.

Daniel was speechless and for a long time he just stood there.

"Well, are you coming or not?" he said, now standing as a silhouette in the doorframe of the theater.

Daniel followed the man inside.

Although the theatre appeared as if it was about ready to fall down on the outside, the inside looked as though it had been recently gutted and completely renovated. Gleaming hardwood floors stretched to every corner. Rows of brand new seats covered in dark blue upholstery arced from one side of the room to the other. Daniel followed the man uphill toward the front of the building. In the foyer, magnificent bright hardwood was everywhere. On his left was the concession area, on his right the entrance. He looked through the glass doors and recognized the street beyond, where earlier he had stood reading posters. If the seating area was beautiful, this was ten times that. An older woman stood behind the counter, cleaning up.

"Honey, we've got a guest," the man said to her. And then he turned to Daniel. "This is my wife, Phoebe, and I'm William."

She looked up from her work and reached across the counter and offered Daniel her hand. "Pleased to meet you," she said, smiling.

Her hands were warm and gentle. Daniel was surprised when she didn't let go right away. He looked down, embarrassed. His hands were grimy and the contrast was startling.

Phoebe turned toward her husband with a questioning look.

"This boy was planning on sleeping in the alley next to the garbage cans. I told him we'd be glad to have him over for the night."

"What's his name?" she said, still smiling.

"You know? I didn't even ask him." He turned to Daniel, his expression requiring an answer.

There was a long empty moment and then suddenly Daniel blurted out, "Justin." It caught in his throat immediately. It had been the only name McMaster had called him for the last five years. "I-I mean, Daniel."

"So, is it Daniel or Justin?"

Daniel's mind scrambled, groping for words of explanation with any sense. "It's a little of both. My real name is Daniel, but my friends call me Justin. It was my dad's name and they thought I looked so much like him that, when he died, everyone just started calling me Justin." He paused for a moment. Looking down, shuffling his feet with a timid sigh, he said, "My real name is Daniel. Daniel Sterling."

Daniel followed them to the truck and crawled into the back seat. Even though there was an old sheet covering the nearly brand new seats, it did nothing to hide the fact that they were luxurious and comfortable.

They stopped briefly at the lights before turning right and Daniel was immediately aware that they were traveling in the direction of McMaster's farm. No problem, he chanted under his breath. After all, there were lots of homes in that direction and McMaster's was only one of them. They crossed the bridge and turned right, still traveling toward McMaster's farm. The truck sped up the steep hill and rounded a sweeping corner. They were still heading in the direction of McMaster's farm. It was all too soon and too familiar. Daniel's heartbeat began to quicken. His agitation grew as they approached Sturgeon Point Road. Grundpark Road teed off it. Daniel thought in prayer, Please God, don't let him turn right. Please don't let him turn right, but the sound of the blinker and the slowing truck told him that God wasn't listening today. Grundpark Road was still a long way away and the Bernard driveway could be anywhere along the road.

A driveway approached. *Turn here. Please turn here.* But the Bernards drove by without slowing.

They were coming to another driveway and Daniel prayed silently, "Let it be this one, please let it be this one." But the driveway was behind them without a sideways glance. Daniel's heart rate continued to rise.

The miles went by in distressing rapid succession. The sick feeling in Daniel's stomach doubled and then tripled. Soon the pressure inside his head would burst out through his eardrums, he was sure of it.

Grundpark Road loomed ahead and Daniel's prayers became a frantic breathy repetition, too quiet for the older people to hear in the front seat. Now he could see the light glint off the reflective paint of the road sign. "Mister and Missus Bernard, I just want to thank you so much for your warm invitation. I've been thinking about it and I really don't want to trouble you. If you just let me off here I'll find my own way back to town."

"Nonsense. You aren't putting us out at all. We would enjoy the company," said Mrs. Bernard.

It was not too late. Mr. Bernard might drive right on by. He might live beyond Grundpark Road. "Please drive by. Oh, Please drive by," he repeated to himself. To his dismay the truck began to slow. Mr. Bernard reached over and flipped on the blinker. Daniel's heart raced. This can't be happening. They seemed like such nice people. They seemed so trustworthy.

The truck was nearly halfway through the turn on to Grundpark when he reached for the door handle, but it wasn't where he thought it should be. He felt around and finally his fingers wrapped themselves around it, but … when he pulled, nothing happened. *Had they locked him in?* There was no indication that they had. Why wouldn't the door open? There was no more time to think about it. His opportunity to escape was gone.

The truck had sped up again. The mailbox with McMaster's name on the side of it was just ahead on the left. Daniel was a rabbit trapped in a snare. Breathing was hard as if he had a wire wrapped around his neck constricting his airway. He was beginning to feel faint. Let me die, he prayed, but … God wasn't listening today.

The truck slowed. Daniel heard the blinker clicking on and off and knew that they were returning him to McMaster. There was no other explanation for what was happening. How did they know? Was his attempt at producing a rational explanation for who he was and where he came from that bad? That transparent? Daniel stared out the window, his body already leaning in the direction of the turn into McMaster's drive. Suddenly his head bonked the window as the truck veered away and the mailbox slipped by. *The truck was moving away from it.* They had made a right turn instead of a left. They were not going to McMaster's house at all.

Daniel's heart never slowed a beat in his transition from fear to relief. Neighbors. That's all they were, just neighbors. The Bernards were nice people after all. They probably don't even know the McMasters. Nice people don't have much to do with not nice people, or was it the other way around? No matter, the truck was slowing as it entered a carport.

Although it was dark, it was easy enough to see that the house was massive. The vehicle had pulled into a covered area large enough to hold at least six vehicles. Above, a railed deck the size of a basketball court sprawled out as the roof over the massive space.

The Bernards had both left the vehicle and almost to the door before they realized that he had not followed. Daniel rapped at the window. Mr. Bernard returned to the door. "Sorry about that," he said, "child locks." He let Daniel out of the truck.

Mr. Bernard led the way into the house. He didn't hesitate at the door. Apparently, there was no need for a key. The door was unlocked. Who were these people? Were they crazy freaks of nature?

The basement was unfinished. The walls had a white stucco texture. It reminded Daniel of the outside of the theatre, but he had no reason to think that there was a connection between the two. An ancient pool table was set up in the far corner with two lights suspended from chains hanging over the center.

To the right was a heater or furnace of some kind. By the looks of it, there was more than one. The Bernards slipped off their shoes, Daniel followed suit and they proceeded to the stairs.

Daniel followed them to the kitchen and dining room, unsure he'd be able to find his way back. From what he'd already seen, it was a very large house. There was carpet in the living room and a glance was all that was required to see the furniture was made of leather. This they strode past and were in the kitchen. The flooring was linoleum.

Daniel realized he had barely looked up. The house was made of perfectly round logs, machined in some giant lathe. The logs were finished in a way that gave them a perpetual look of wood that has never seen the damaging rays of sun. They were not white, but there was not a better word that Daniel could come up with to describe the color.

"Are you ready for the grand tour," Mrs. Bernard asked with a hint of pride.

Daniel nodded.

They started with the kitchen and bathroom on the main floor and then proceeded to the family room. From there they showed him to the guest bedroom, but not the one he would be staying in, they informed him, and the den. In the family room, a set of stairs led to a floor above.

Phoebe led the way up the stairs and passed many rooms.

"We wanted a house big enough so that each of our children could have a room. We got what we wanted, but they're all grown up and gone now. We'd hoped they'd visit more often, but we see a lot of them at the theater and that's nice," she explained.

At the end of the hallway was the bathroom, where the tour ended. She showed Daniel the towels, gave him brief instructions about the shower and indicated the laundry chute.

"You don't have to wash my clothes," he blurted.

Phoebe smiled. "Yes. I do. But don't you worry about it, not even a little bit."

He felt terrible, but his clothes needed it so badly. She left him alone and he started the shower, dropped his filthy clothes down the chute, and stepped into the water's warm caress. It did more than warm his body and was by far the best shower he had ever had. Probably, he thought, because it was his first shower as a free man.

When he turned the shower off and emerged, he felt fresh and alive. He glanced at the old clock on the wall. Twenty minutes had gone by? Felt like no more than five at most. With a towel wrapped around his waist, he slipped into the bedroom that Phoebe had prepared. He found a pair of pajamas waiting for him. He sat on the edge of the bed and toyed with the fabric. It was soft; softer than a tee shirt and a bit fuzzy. They'd be warm. He slid into them and immediately knew what cozy was. He had never experienced it before but he knew he liked it.

He stepped into the hallway. When he got to the kitchen, the Bernards were waiting at the table. "Thanks so much for the loan," he said, indicating his borrowed pajamas.

"You're welcome. You ready to eat?" Mr. Bernard said.

Daniel sat. Although the meal came from plastic bowls that had been in the refrigerator, it was better fare than he could remember. All of the leftovers were gone by the time Daniel was finished.

"Can I get you something more?" said Mrs. Bernard.

"Oh, no. I couldn't eat anything else. Thanks so much."

Daniel was exhausted. His stomach was full and all he could think about was the warm bed waiting for him as he excused himself from the table, thanked them again, and climbed the stairs.

He slid into bed and pulled the covers to his chin. It was at least twice the size of the one he normally slept in. It lacked both the musty smell and the steel springs that he had learned to arch his body around so they didn't poke him while he slept. The sheets had a fresh smell … a flowery, but foreign scent. He had heard, somewhere in the far past, about additives you could put in your wash to make them soft and smell good. He wondered if Mrs. McMaster had *ever* changed the sheets in the barn. He didn't think she had.

***

The morning came and went. It was as if his body clock had decided to take a holiday. McMaster ensured he was up every day at six. Sleeping in had been unheard of. Each day for Daniel had been the same dull routine, marked only by the changing seasons.

It was almost noon when he opened his eyes. He supposed it was the smell of cooking that did it. So many new experiences in a single day were difficult to take in. He could not remember waking up to anything other than the smell of hay. Did people really live like this? Was this a real home and real people or was it the Bernards who were abnormal and not the McMasters? Whatever the truth, Daniel felt as though he were in heaven. He knew eventually he must leave but, for now, he wouldn't think too much about it.

He arrived in the kitchen and Phoebe was laying out the last of the grilled cheese sandwiches. Soup was steaming on a potholder. There were three places set at the table. It was clear which one belonged to Mr. Bernard. His was the captain's chair at the head of the table. The other two place settings were on either side of it. Daniel couldn't decide which one to sit at and so he waited.

"Would you like a cup of coffee," asked Phoebe.

"Yes, please."

She brought the cup to the table and placed it in front of the setting to the left of the captain's chair. With his question answered, he sat in front of it.

"Would you like some cream or sugar?"

Daniel thought for a moment. He had never had coffee before. He had seen McMaster drink it, but it had always been a light brown color, not like the nearly black stuff sitting in front of him now. It did smell good. "Thanks. I'll just try it like this."

He took a sip and nearly spit it back into the mug. The stuff tasted like acid in his mouth. He winced. "Do you think I could try it with a little cream?" he said, hoping he wasn't being offensive.

Phoebe brought the cream and sugar to the table. Daniel poured it until the liquid in the cup was close to the brim. It looked a little paler than what he could remember McMaster drinking. Hopefully it would taste a lot better. The cream took the edge off, but the underlying bitter flavor came strongly through. Was it possible that coffee was the foulest tasting stuff he had ever tried?

He added sugar. That helped quite a bit, but he noticed Phoebe watching him as he put the fourth heaping spoonful into it and was embarrassed. With the excessive cream, the beverage was lukewarm, but at least it was sweet. He couldn't bring himself to waste the drink so he nursed it. He noticed a grin of amusement on Phoebe's face, but she said nothing. He was glad about that as he continued to struggle with this new experience. *She knows, but she's not belittling me. Nice lady.*

By the time William came in a few minutes later, Daniel's cup was half empty. They all sat together, a prayer by William followed, and they commenced eating. To Daniel it was the most wonderful food he had ever tasted. Maybe it wasn't so much the food, but the generosity with which they served it.

Daniel could feel their curious eyes upon him. There were questions burning there, but for whatever reason neither William nor Phoebe asked. Eventually they'd want to know that Daniel had a good reason for being penniless and without a roof over his head. They'd want to know where his parents lived and why they hadn't supported him. This was no stretch in logic. These were questions he'd have wanted answers to as well. But he had no good response. The truth would surely sound like an outlandish lie, while a lie might seem closer to the truth.

Daniel kept closed lipped while those inquisitive eyes smoldered into him. He hoped that his silence came across as shyness. He smiled bashfully and hoped it would suffice until he was gone away. Away to where? Away to anywhere.

CHAPTER 29

"Why don't you change and give me a hand with some chores?" William said after lunch was over and Phoebe had cleared the dishes. Daniel didn't miss the sideways wink William flashed in her direction.

"You bet."

Daniel followed William to the shop and a parked tractor within. William climbed into the seat. "Hop up on the step. There's a solid hold right there. You should be fine."

Daniel crawled up.

"I need to feed a couple of bales to the cows and we'll be done. I thought you might like the ride."

The tractor rocked from one side to the other as it crawled through mud holes and across ruts. William dropped a grader blade and pulled dirt behind, leveling the road as he went. Cows ambled on the other side of a barbed wire fence. Although there was ample room to roam, they mulled around near large steel feeders. These were empty now and it was self-evident that when their chores were finished, they would have remedied this.

William lined up the tractor along the fence and drove toward a short row of large round bales at the other end. There was only one small stack remaining from what must have been an immense reserve. The tractor treads left a map showing the length of each row and their numbers. Of those, there were twenty or so remaining.

As one who has done a thing countless times, William moved toward the stack while he ran the hydraulics. Twin forks moved into place and skewered the top most bale. It reminded Daniel of a giant brown marshmallow, carefully turned and fresh from the fire. When they reached the pasture, Daniel leaped to the ground and opened the gate. William drove through and waited until he had climbed aboard again. William dropped the bale into the feeder and they were busily cutting the fifty or more feet of string off it when William spoke. "You seem pretty lost, Daniel."

He thought about that for a moment, measuring his response, trying to decide what he should give away or keep. He settled with, "Yeah. I guess I am."

"You know, not a lot of what you said last night made sense."

There was another long pause. "I'm really sorry about that."

"Is your name even Daniel?"

Daniel nodded, but he could tell that William was beginning to find his lack of reasonable responses frustrating. William's face reddened a bit, and an angry tone edged its way into his voice. "Listen boy, I don't owe you anything. You had better start making some sense real soon."

William was suddenly sounding very much like McMaster. Of course he would. He and everyone else are all the same. They all want a little part of you. Why would he have thought the Bernards were any different?

Daniel retaliated, his voice a shriek. "I don't know where *here* is! I came from Alberta and now I'm here. That's all I know."

William rubbed his temples and slid his palms over his face in one long exasperated motion. He ended this thoughtful maneuver with his fingers clasped prayerfully in front of his mouth. Time seemed to slow. The cows were like statutes. Their tails counted seconds. Ravens circled ominously overhead. The tractor droned. The entire world waited.

"I feel torn."

Each word was a measure. Each one weighed greater than its predecessor did, and as a group, they had mass. Daniel could choose to leave now, because now was the pivotal moment. He could, he realized. It was as simple as that. This man, this family, was of no value to him. They would lose nothing without his presence and gain … what? — if he stayed. He had almost convinced himself it would be better if he left. He would have, too, had his thoughts not moved forward and he posed the one question that almost no one asks themselves in the heat of emotion. What then?

The cows' tails twitched. Ravens circled. The tractor idled. The world waited.

"I can tell you that I have nowhere to go. I don't have family and I don't have any money. I am lost." He stressed the word 'am'. "But I don't know what to say to make it better for you."

It was William's turn to respond and it was a shorter time in coming. "Open the gate. We've got one more bale to feed."

The cows slipped their heads into the feeder. The ravens settled. The tractor roared toward the gate with Daniel clinging to the side. Time resumed.

The conversation wasn't over. How could it be? He had answered none of William's questions and the man let him be. Not forever, he was sure. Maybe not even until supper.

Daniel felt guilty, and it was an unnerving emotion — one he'd never before dealt with. Guilt is a difficult feeling to live with, he mused. It aged him, somehow, and he pondered thoughts that made him feel old — like adults with decades of hiding and living with guilt must feel — the regret and remorse peeling away layers of the soul the way he'd experienced rough sand paper can peel away layers of skin. He owed the Bernards something more. He couldn't take their hospitality without giving something back. The Bernards had reached out to him at his lowest and asked for only one thing, his story, and he had been too weak to tell it. They wanted to know that their generosity wasn't for nothing. They wanted to know that his needs were genuine. And they were. He needed a little respite—or a lot—he didn't know which, but he knew he needed a rest. His wellbeing was as fragile as his light-starved pale skin. By the time he stepped out of the shower, guilt had worn it raw.

The house was quiet when he walked down the steps to the main floor. Voices seemed to be coming from the kitchen. He followed the sounds, but they were not coming from the kitchen as he first surmised. They were coming from the master bedroom. Daniel raised his hand to knock, but stopped at the sound of his name.

"Do you think 'Daniel' is even his real name?" Phoebe said.

"I wish I could guess. He seemed sincere enough. I don't wonder if he's got amnesia or something. I don't think I've ever heard such silly lies. What do you think's going on?"

Daniel could almost hear Mrs. Bernard's mind working during the long pause that followed.

"Did you notice how scared he seemed when we brought him home?"

"I did. It's just the craziest thing. Do you think he might have a mental disorder of some kind? Have you ever come across anything like it before?"

Outside of the room Daniel's eyes grew wide. Phoebe seemed to take the question in stride, almost as if it was reasonable to ask. "I've read about cases like his, but he seems more 'with it' than I would have expected. He doesn't seem to know where he is, and I can't explain that. Someone with those kinds of problems wouldn't be able to survive without some kind of support and, unfortunately, we don't have facilities to help him here."

Daniel knocked.

"Come in,' William called through the door.

Daniel eased the door open and peered inside. Nightstand lamps cast long shadows everywhere except on the two figures sitting in bed. They looked like twins, each with a book resting on their laps and spectacles perched on the ends of their noses.

"You've wanted to know about me and I think I should tell you." He rushed on to release them of any obligation they might feel. "I don't want you to feel sorry for me. It's okay if you don't want me around. I will be fine," he lied. He did want them to feel sorry for him and he didn't want to go.

"We would appreciate that," said William.

The room fell silent and then he began, "I came from Red Deer, but I don't know how I got here." Daniel took a deep breath, blew it out loud and long, flapping his lips, then proceeded to tell the true story of his enslavement.

The Bernards listened as if they believed. They interrupted him from time to time with simple questions, such as, what was the kitchen like, or, can you describe the woodshed, just little things that allowed them to test for the truth.

When Daniel concluded, Phoebe was incredulous—both hands clasping her cheeks, her jaw dropped open. "We had them over for Christmas last year," she said, as she looked first at Daniel and then at her husband.

"You believe me, then?" Daniel said with relief.

"I believe you've spent a lot of time across the road, but this is something the police need to deal with," William said as he reached for the phone. "They can get to the bottom of it and then it won't matter whether you're telling me the truth or not."

"You can't," Daniel pleaded, his words coming in machinegun fire succession, "He thinks I'm dead. Everyone thinks I'm dead. I don't exist anymore. He'll come and find me."

William's finger paused and then he returned the phone to its cradle. "You don't want to see him punished for what he's done?"

"I do. I would." Daniel's head drooped, and then, in a voice no more than a whisper he said, "I don't want to be scared anymore."

CHAPTER 30

The Bernards didn't call the police that day or any other day after that. Each morning began with an invitation to accompany William on the next job and Daniel gladly obliged.

It seemed that William was always busy with one project or another. One day they worked on the tractor. The next they mended a fence. The following day they hauled a load of firewood. All the while, the grass grew higher. It would be a good crop — a bumper crop — and William had begun to hint that he'd appreciate a little help with it.

The summer slipped by in much the same manner as every other summer had during his stay with McMaster. Daniel worked from dawn until dusk. The Bernards paid for his efforts with the clothes on his back, the food in his stomach and a bed to sleep in, but the similarities between this life and his previous one ended there. The conversations were infinitely more interesting. The food was incalculably tastier and there wasn't a single spring poking out of the mattress or a single hole in any of the blankets. Daniel felt like a peer, working no more and no less than William did.

The Bernards certainly needed his help, he figured, but what he got back from them was nearly priceless.

"Daniel, have you ever had a haircut," Phoebe asked one day.

"Sure. A few times, I guess." Some trimming in the past had knocked down the front and sides, leaving him with a raggedy cut reminiscent of the late '70s.

"I think it's something we need to take care of."

A few days after that, Daniel stepped into Wendy's salon chair. She was a daughter-in-law to the Bernards but, more importantly, she was a renowned stylist. Phoebe had gone to great lengths to ensure that he understood that he was in for a real treat. "He was a new man in the making," she'd said.

Wendy chuckled, showing her good-nature as she ran her fingers through his hair. "You've got to let me get rid of this funky mullet you've got goin' on. Do you want to keep your beard or do you want it cut off?"

He watched her in the mirror toy with his hair and half-wondered if he had already fallen in love. "Whatever you think will make me look good is what I want." It occurred to him much later that he sounded embarrassingly flirtatious the way his voice had gone up and down with too much enthusiasm. She probably thought he was just a stupid kid.

"I like short cuts on guys. You've got nice thick hair and I think a Caesar might look great on you. What do you think?"

"I don't know what a Caesar is, but sure. It sounds great."

She pulled out clippers that looked big enough to shear sheep and turned them on. They must have worked well because Daniel barely felt them tug as she made fast sweeping strokes from the nape of his neck to the top of his head. Hair dropped to the ground in heaping handfuls.

A few minutes later, she traded clippers for shears and began to make the final adjustments. It was a chore that took Mrs. McMaster half an hour to accomplish poorly. Wendy had done it in less than ten minutes. She spun him toward her so he couldn't see himself in the mirror and began again with the clippers, but this time on his face. She switched tools and trimmed his mustache and brows.

She brushed the hair off his neck and clothes. "How about a quick rinse to get all the loose hair out? My niece loves it. She doesn't like cuts. She comes for the washes." If Wendy had pampered him with the cut, she sent him to heaven with the water. It felt like a warm wet massage and he wished it didn't have to end. It was sad when she brought a towel down over his face giving him a friendly ruffle.

"Would you like some gel?" she said.

He gave her a questioning look.

"You'll like it. It'll only take a second."

Daniel was elated and then disappointed at the same time.

Wendy dropped a dab of goo onto her hands and rubbed them together. "This is going to give you a trendy look that will drive the girls wild."

"Will it drive you wild?"

Wendy just smiled and spun him around, ignoring the question. "What do you think?"

Daniel hardly recognized himself. His features were unfamiliar. Not surprising, as there had been no mirror in the barn at the McMaster farm. All these years, hidden beneath thick locks, my face has been changing from a boy's to a man's. Daniel sat there for a long time, contemplating the stranger staring back at him.

He was clean-cut, that was for sure. He'd never admit it out loud. It would be pretentious, but yeah, he thought, that *is* a handsome guy looking back at me.

They stopped in town and picked up a shirt, a pair of jeans, and a new pair of shoes. Daniel knew that not even McMaster would have recognized him if he saw him. At the house, his raggedy clothes were tossed. He felt badly about everything that the Bernards had done for him, but William had said not to think twice about it. It was a cheap price to pay for Daniel's help.

Haying continued. In the evenings, after the dew had settled and they could bale no more, Daniel and William returned home, exhausted but satisfied. Sundays were special for the Bernards. William and Phoebe never missed going to church. Afterward they would return to the house and from then on it was a day of rest.

"What you can't finish in six days isn't worth finishing in seven," William always said.

A day of rest, hmm. This alone was a big change for Daniel.

The summer trickled by.

CHAPTER 31

Daniel often went to the theater with the Bernards to help out, but tonight he decided not to go. They expected the turnout to be small and they probably wouldn't need his help anyway. For a while, he sat in front of the TV, but it was a brief enjoyment. His old canvas bag that he had tucked into his closet beckoned to him. It had been weeks since he arrived and he had not brought it out. It still reeked of the too familiar smell of his old life. It was a smell that made him want to vomit. He sat for a moment with his head between his legs knowing well it was only in his head. It was the same feeling he experienced every time he rode past the McMaster driveway or saw a vehicle he thought he recognized. That part of his life was over, and still McMaster had control over him.

Other people knew that Daniel existed now and even if he ever came face to face with the man, he was no longer McMaster's secret pet and no one could ever make him go back.

Daniel's stomach churned. To be safe, he walked to the bathroom and fortunately only burped. The acidic taste filled his mouth, but his stomach felt better. This is stupid, he thought. I am not sick. I do not have to feel this way. He willed his stomach to settle. He knew the trigger. He just needed to train his body to forget.

He returned to the satchel, this time breathing through his mouth. He liked the old bag and it was not the cause of his feelings. He turned it upside down and the lunch box fell out onto the bed. The bag represented triumph. He did not want to part with it just because of the dirt on it. He dropped it down the laundry shoot.

He sat with the lunchbox on his lap. The crystals lay inside. He wondered if they were dormant. In the quiet of the house, he could almost feel them pulse. He envisioned them a pale blue that he would never be able to verify since any amount of light that fell upon them turned them into cold fire.

These crystals had other properties; Daniel was convinced of this. There was power here that he could harness. If he had enough knowledge and creativity, he could unlock their secrets.

Daniel went into the basement where the bag lay with its poisonous aura. Picking it up with two fingers, he dropped it into the washing machine along with twice the recommended soap. Later he dried it with an extra dryer sheet and took it back upstairs. With the crystals safely stowed inside, he slid it under his bed.

When the Bernards came home, he was sitting in front of the TV watching an old movie on the western channel.

CHAPTER 32

Below his bed, only a few inches away, the crystals pulsed like a living organism. His room had become a radiation chamber and at night, Daniel slept and bathed in it.

While he slept, his body functions increased their efficiencies. His blood supply increased and his body reacted to it. Worn discs from years of backbreaking labor began to repair themselves. His immune system strengthened. New neural pathways formed, first as small tendrils, and later as entirely new networks. Daniel slept unaware of these changes taking place.

During the day, he felt tireless and he accredited it to the long years of his work in the mine. Problems seemed easy to solve, but he accredited that to the years he had longed to learn and never had the chance.

William had a lathe and welder that he allowed Daniel to try. "I can't believe how quickly you have caught on," he said to Daniel. He said the same thing almost every time Daniel dropped the welding visor. Daniel thrived.

When Daniel wasn't working or sleeping, he read. He read every book on the shelf and the ones he liked, he read several times. He hadn't realized how much he would grow to enjoy reading and began to finish two and sometimes three books a night, depending on whether it was a Saturday. Saturday nights he always read more. He didn't have to work on Sunday. He searched for more books. He remembered everything, not almost everything. Reading had become more than a pleasure. It had become an obsession.

"Daniel, have you ever thought about going to a university?" Phoebe said at the dinner table one night. His pause was all the evidence she needed to know that he hadn't. "You should, you know."

What would he need to do to go to school? He finished his meal in thoughtful silence.

CHAPTER 33

Daniel came to realize he needn't have worried about whether or not he would overstay his welcome. William had a never-ending list of things he needed done and he was getting too old to do much of it on his own. Once the hay was stacked in the yard, there was still the winter supply of wood they needed to bring in before it got too cold or before the wet season of early fall made it too difficult.

Daniel spent the winter there. The family weathered hard times caused by the Mad Cow plague that ravaged the whole country, but especially brutal in the northwest. There wasn't a country in the world that wanted to accept Canadian beef. Any farmer that depended on beef was bound to be devastated.

It was a good thing the Bernards had what William called a 'hobby farm'. For a short time, he considered getting out of the cattle business all together. It just didn't seem to be worth the effort any more, he had said. Farming was a losing proposition and he was getting tired of the constant repairs and hard work. The money was going out, but never coming in.

The tractor needed an oil change and William was vocal about his thankfulness he had a heated shop to work in. He lay on his back, squinting against the dirt that flaked from everywhere he touched and half the places he didn't. "Did you read that article about the McMasters," he asked Daniel, who stood nearby. Without waiting, he added, "Can you pass me a half-inch socket?"

Daniel rustled through the toolbox until he found what William needed. "No. I guess I haven't got to that one yet." His stomach did a triple flip with a double rotation, but he handed William the half-inch socket as if nothing was wrong.

"They randomly checked the larger cattle farms for mad cow disease. McMaster was one of the farmers they checked. Can you cut the side out of that jug? I need something to drain this oil into."

Daniel found the razor knife and began to slice through the thin plastic of the empty two-gallon oil container. "Oh, is that right? What happened?"

"Well, the only way to test an animal is to remove the brain."

"Yeah, I read about that part." Daniel's stomach lurched. Why did he have to talk about McMaster?

William had crawled out while a shiny black stream of oil ran into the jug. "They sampled a third of his herd, originally. I was surprised they would kill so many," he said, wiping his hands on a grease rag that was once probably an old tee-shirt.

"I guess he's getting what he deserves." Daniel's voice was flat.

"I suppose," William said. "What goes around comes around. So far there hasn't been any compensation and that's not even the whole story. Do you remember all the commotion over there last week?"

Daniel nodded.

"Apparently, his herd was contaminated. They came back and killed every animal he had and then they hauled the carcasses away and burned them. I didn't think it would hit so close to home. I guess in that regard, I'm lucky," he said.

Daniel let the conversation drop.

CHAPTER 34

Between books, Daniel let his mind wander in an effort to touch bases with those memories of people that he could consider family. He traced backward from Hilda and Leonard Harbinger or Coffinger ... Salinger. That's what it was, Salinger. He remembered he turned thirteen when he was living with them. They were the nicest of all the foster families he could remember. He had only been there just over a year when he woke up one night, and ... instead of being in his warm bed he was in a wooden box in McMaster's barn. He had come to believe they had betrayed him and wondered why. It was a fruitless train of thought, so he stepped passed them as he had done with Grundpark so many times and reached farther into his past. The Salinger's were corpses to him.

He followed his wisps of memories back in time. They were difficult to recall, partially because they were more like individual pictures — disconnected and without continuity. He dedicated some time to it, starting a journal to try to document his experiences. First, he began to document his memories by describing what he saw in them, but later he began to piece the pictures together and they slowly became flashes of memory, but no more than an adjacent frame or two. The flashes became glimpses and eventually those glimpses became bona fide memories. As disjointed and sad as his childhood had been, he began to see its story.

He remembered when he was about ten years old. He was the oldest of four other foster children. He could not recall the children's names or the parents'. He remembered changing diapers. Smells were a good reminder and although those ones had been strong, they had not been unpleasant. He remembered that going to school had been enjoyable. It was the one time he could escape into the world of regular people. Daniel had liked school that year, especially the teacher. She was nice and often complimented him. She had said he was a cute boy and she really liked him. He chose to believe her.

That seemed far back, but he knew there were earlier memories. He had bounced around from one foster home to another, never growing attached. For him it was easier to leave. He was, what he liked to call, cerebral. He was not often emotional when it came to others. It was one of his strengths.

Christmas this year was a new experience. Thirty people came, filling the house with happy noisy bodies. He felt like more than a guest. He felt like they had come to *his* home. He got teary and hoped no one noticed.

The children unwrapped gifts while their proud parents sat around the room watching. William busily made memories on the video camera.

Daniel opened a package. It was a pair of socks, the same kind that each of the brothers opened as well. When had Mrs. Bernard had time to buy and wrap the gifts? His feelings suddenly split in two. He knew he should feel special. They had accepted him as one of the family. But he wasn't special, was he. He was just a charity case, not really part of the family at all. Who was he anyway?

There wasn't much contact with the other family members after Christmas. It was good not to worry about fitting in or not fitting in. Daniel saw them occasionally at the theatre and that was about all.

Spring approached like a tease. Warm weather in February cleared the roads. Then one snow after the other added two feet to the two that were already lying on the ground. March came with another warm bout and then kicked everyone with a lunge of freezing temperatures. The Bernards hunted Easter eggs inside because there was still not a patch of green on the lawn. The neatly stacked hay marched away with the cold. But the days were growing longer and that was something. The groundhog had not seen its shadow and that was something else.

Cabin fever had set in and Daniel had begun to hint to William and Phoebe that it was time for him to move on. They asked him about his plans. He would have liked to tell them, but he had no idea what they were. In a sense he wasn't lying when he told them that it was just time for him to stop taking advantage of their charity.

It was one evening in mid April as they sat in front of the TV watching the Portland Trailblazers take on the Seattle Sonics when Phoebe asked, "Daniel, when's your birthday."

The question caught him off guard. It occurred to him that he might not be able to remember it. He had never celebrated it in the past few years. He grabbed the first date that popped into his head that he thought might be correct. "June thirteenth." It was a good date. He thought he would be gone by then for sure … he hoped.

Unfortunately, the month of June came and went and Daniel found himself helping William through another haying season. Logistics and guilt played important roles. Logistically, he had not graduated and could attend no university without a high school transcript. Because he was familiar with both the equipment and their quirks, he felt obligated to stay. He did celebrate his birthday on June the thirteenth and, as it turned out, that date had been correct. It was a good day because it was his day and he didn't have to share it with anyone, unlike Christmas.

Being nineteen had its advantages. Trying to find out about his past life earlier would have been impossible. A minor requires written permission from his guardian and he was glad that he was beyond all that.

His goal had become to attend university. He was sure of that much. Of course, there were two issues he needed to deal with. One was the fact that he had no money. The other more serious issue was that he had no education beyond grade seven. He had no report cards, no birth certificate, and none of the documents required to prove who he was.

He needed a birth certificate. He couldn't get a high school diploma with out one. Hell, he'd need that for everything … a Social Insurance Number, driver's license, bank accounts… everything. If he could come up with that, he might learn a lot about himself. There was a problem. How could he get a birth certificate if he couldn't prove his identity? How could he prove that without a birth certificate? And that was as far as he could get without help.

Under these sorts of circumstances, the Internet had proven extremely useful. He had found countless answers to unlimited questions and he started there more often than not. A quick search provided a toll free number that promised he could call to talk to someone in person about his problem. He dialed the numbers. His hands shook. He pressed a four instead of a seven and had to restart. The next time he hit the eight twice in a row. He cursed and dialed a third time.

The woman on the other end answered in a disinterested monotone. Daniel explained his situation. That would be no problem once he supplied his Social Insurance Number.

"I don't have one."

'Do you have any other ID?"

He didn't.

"Sir, your predicament is unheard of. It's against this office's policy to release records without the proper identification. You'll need to give me something more than a story before I can release any information to you. For all I know you could be asking for information belonging to someone else."

There was a long pause while Daniel seesawed about what to say next. Finally, he had an idea. "I've been in foster care, but there were no documents for me when I left. I have no idea where my family might be or even what their names are." Most of this was true.

The woman's attitude shifted as if she had flipped a switch. The bitch disappeared. "If you go to child services, they should have some record of you somewhere. They are not as sticky about such things since they would like nothing more than to see families reunited. Why don't you try that?"

"Thank you so much!" Daniel hung up. He thought about what the woman had said with the phone still resting in the curve of his palm. The words she had chosen had given him pause to think. 'They should have some record of you' she had said. He might find answers about his past, which suggested there might be more to discover than the identity of his egg and sperm donors. He jerked when the phone screamed at him with a series of high-pitched tones. Then a voice came on, not unlike the dry, matter-of-fact voice of the woman he'd spoken to at the beginning of his call. "Please, hang up, and try your call again."

CHAPTER 35

There was one vehicle in the front of the squat, one story building that sprawled across the lot. Painted with a bland shade of cream, it was the kind of structure that left no lasting impression. Daniel entered, frightened that he might have opened the door to another dead end. His heart raced.

They would want a story, an explanation of some kind, and he did not know what he would say. He could not account for the last six years. And he felt sure they would ask. At least he could explain one of them—the last one with the Bernards. Maybe he could stretch that out a bit.

"Excuse me? Ma'am?" he said from the counter to a woman seated across the room.

She looked up with little interest. "Yes?"

"My name is Daniel Sterling. I'm trying to locate some records. I was told that I might be able to find them here."

The phone rang. "Just one moment please," she said to Daniel in that same disinterested tone. The woman didn't wait for Daniel to respond before picking up the receiver.

He didn't want to seem rude so he turned away to give the woman some privacy. By the sudden change in her tone, she seemed to be speaking to a family member, a child by the sounds of it, who seemed to be trying to negotiate a ride home.

The woman grew agitated. "Honey, catch the bus. I've got to go." The voice on the other end must have responded affirmatively because the lady said, "Good-bye," and hung up the phone. She turned to Daniel. "Yes. Can I help you?"

Daniel started again and the lady listened attentively to his entire story.

When he was finished she said, "What was your name again?"

Oh my God, Daniel thought. He felt like asking, *Are* you going to have me start all over again? But instead he said, "Daniel Sterling."

She jotted it down. "Please just have a seat over there." Taking the slip of paper with her, she disappeared through a door. Daniel imagined her winding down flights of steps into the annals, though the reality was probably less interesting.

The waiting area was as uninteresting as the rest of the building. Outdated magazines littered the end tables that seemed, themselves, littered about the room. Daniel perused through one of them looking for something that might be of interest. They were all geared toward women. He picked up one, which featured a scantily dressed model and turned though the pages enjoying the pictures. They were beauties; there was no doubt about that.

He was about ready to move onto another magazine when a side door opened and a young woman, not ten years older than he, walked through. "Daniel Sterling?" she said.

"Yes?"

"You're Daniel Sterling?

"Yes."

"Will you please follow me?"

Bewildered, Daniel rose to his feet and tagged along. They continued down a corridor with a series of offices on either side. Some of the doors bore names, but most of them were empty with just a number to identify them. The same mind-numbing cream color seemed to have been an epidemic that had infected the entire building, outside as well as in. They continued past doors until they reached one with a label that read, 'Mrs. Talbot.' She pushed the door opened and motioned for Daniel to enter.

"Won't you please have a seat," she invited.

The woman sat at what Daniel believed was her own desk and began tapping her pencil on the blotting pad. The silence was unnerving but Daniel remained stoic. She finally looked up.

"Daniel, I'm Missus Talbot." Daniel waited for her to tell him something he didn't already know. "Did you know that you've been missing and presumed dead for over five years?"

CHAPTER 36

From that point forward, things became simple. Mrs. Talbot brought the records up on her computer. She showed him one of the last photos they had on file. It was a school photo from his first months at the highschool in Alberta. There was no doubt that he was Daniel. His last known address had been with the Salinger family from which he had reportedly run away. Mrs. Talbot turned a computer screen toward Daniel to reveal a complete profile up to that date. She scrolled through copies of his birth certificate and school records. Documents included written reports from child services and newspaper articles as well.

"What happened to you, Daniel? Where have you been all of these years?"

Daniel's mouth dropped open. His plan was unraveling as the saliva dried in his mouth. The story he had conjured would sound ridiculous. He grasped for something to say, but his vocal chords were on strike.

Anyone else might have jumped at the opportunity to break the silence. He had information that would ruin the lives of both the Salingers and the McMasters. His reluctance did not come from the knowledge that he would feel responsible for their downfall, but that it would be a further waste of his time. None of the tragedies was worth one more moment of his life.

"Here and there," he answered with, what he hoped was, enough disdain to appear to be that disgruntled youth they believed ran away so many years earlier.

"There were people who were worried," she scolded, but stopped before finishing. "Where are you staying now?"

Daniel gave her William and Phoebe's home address and phone number.

"I'll make copies for you and send them out as soon as I can." She paused before continuing, "Wow, what an exciting day," she finally said, standing. "The authorities may contact you to make a statement and explain where you've been all this time. This is all new to me, so I'm not sure."

She shook Daniel's hand and escorted him to the door.

CHAPTER 37

The documents arrived weeks later. He expected the package to be thicker, more substantial than it was. He hefted it and although some part of him felt elated, there were other prominent emotions too. There was fear. What would he learn about his mother, his father or the events that led him to all those foster homes? There was disappointment. How could a whole life be contained within a single thin package? It seemed pathetic.

He turned the official looking envelope over in his hands and there, typed neatly across the front, was his name. The ministry's logo and address were stamped prominently in the upper left corner. Daniel pushed his finger between the envelope and its flap. He took a breath and then tore into his past. The envelope contained another packet with no identifying information. There were no stamps or tags. Instead of glue, two metal tangs secured the packet. For a second time Daniel confronted the task of facing his unknown. He drew the tabs together.

At first, he flipped through the pages, reading none. They had reduced his childhood to a short diary written from a sadly clinical perspective. They were required reports made by disinterested doctors and social workers, each profession having its own specialized gibberish. He flipped back to the beginning of the chronologically arranged documents hoping to find an explanation for his beginnings.

Following a cover sheet stating whose file the pages pertained to, was an intake form. He contemplated the title. That his life had always been pretty much the same, even in recent years, struck him. McMaster had called him livestock and referred to him as an acquisition. But, even though McMaster had succeeded in making him feel small, he had never felt as worthless as he did looking at those cold white pages. He had not been 'taken in.' He had been 'intake'… inventory. Unwanted by his family, authorities placed him in society's flea market and they called that flea market 'foster care'.

His eyes moved down and there was his mother's name, long forgotten. And he realized that he had never missed her. He had only longed for belonging, but not for his mother. How could he miss someone he'd never known? He read on about the appalling circumstances of his intake. Child neglect was the cause of the intervention. Social workers arrived in Allie Sterling's home to discover a naked toddler playing alone in the living room. They found the room littered with beer bottles. No adults were present.

Daniel closed his eyes and ran his hands over his face, pushing his palm into his forehead then read on. She had made several attempts to win back custody of her only child, but had failed with each. The sixth intervention was the last. After that, he had become a permanent ward of the province. The remaining pages served as nothing more than filling, describing the various places he'd been. His mother had been incapable of taking care of him; he came into foster care and eventually ended up with the Salingers. The in-between stuff didn't matter much.

It was by his will alone that he'd placed himself in the world as an equal. No one had ever invited him into the company of real people, until now. Filled with uncertainty, he glanced around his borrowed room. The Bernards' selflessness stared back from every corner. Whatever it was that his mother and father may have owed him, they had been unable to give it. He had come to believe that neither the world nor fairytales have much to do with fairness. If he wanted anything from the world, he'd have to earn it.

Daniel shuffled to the bottom of the stack to the final custody order he knew would be there. At the top of the page were familiar names, Leonard and Hilda Salinger. He was not surprised to see little other than his transfer there. It had been the hallmark of his placements and he often thought back to his time there as he slaved for McMaster. He flipped past it to the last page. It was a police report. Of course there would be a report. The Salingers would have looked for him. When he didn't come home from school they would have called the police and there would have been a search, just like on TV.

As he read, cold realization replaced the warmth inside him. It was not a document describing a police investigation at all. It was a missing person report filled out and filed by the Salingers. A tsunami of emotion swelled and slammed into him with full force. On the bottom of the page was Leonard's explanation. "We went into Daniel's room yesterday morning to wake him up and he wasn't there. He had been having troubles. He didn't come home from school and we haven't seen him since. He must have run away."

He had imagined there was some form of betrayal, but why would the Salinger's say he had run away? He hadn't been having troubles there and he was doing well at school, too. He had been taken forcibly from the home; that much he knew for sure. There should have been some evidence of a struggle. McMaster was telling the truth. He had bought him, just like he said and the Salinger's sold him. Leonard's signature at the bottom of the statement had ended the investigation and at the same time it had ended his life.

Fury clouded his coherence. *"Why,"* he asked the empty room. "I thought you loved me!" His voice trailed off, "I thought ... you loved me."

He sat on his bed cradling the envelope, allowing numbness to seep inside him. How could such a small package contain so much sorrow?

But it did contain more than that, didn't it. It held pages and pages of facts pertaining to the life of a kid he barely remembered … a kid named Daniel Sterling. Even with all of that, none of the memories of his youth had been there, like the time he learned to ride his bike by coasting down the hill behind the old apartment building where he had lived, or the time he made a slingshot and knocked cans off fenceposts in the back lot. No, the envelope did not contain memories; it held opportunity. The lady at child services told him there would be a birth certificate inside, but he hadn't seen it. He turned the envelope upside-down and a third, smaller envelope dropped out. He knew the documents he had been waiting for would be inside.

The first was his birth certificate. The second was a small plastic card with a series of nine numbers and the words 'Social Insurance Number' printed across the top. He may have lived his life happily without all of the other papers, but these two documents were the keys to everything. He could finally talk to William about learning to drive and he'd be able to get on with high school too.

According to the birth certificate, he'd been born in Calgary. His mother's name was Allie Sterling and his father was Marcus Habernash. He was born on June thirteenth, a date he had almost forgotten. It was probably a Friday, he decided.

CHAPTER 38

That night at the dinner table, Daniel brought the envelope with him.

Phoebe looked first at the envelope, then at him. "Is that what you've been looking for at the post office everyday for so long?"

"I was planning on showing it to you after dinner ... if, ahm ... if you wanted to see it that is," he said, eyes down. He had told the Bernards his story before, but it somehow seemed more real now that he had tangible evidence to prove that their trust had not been misplaced.

As usual, they were kind and nodded in all the right places. Some part of Daniel still believed that their responses were not honest. In his experience real people were not kind and loving. Real people didn't express their thoughts and feelings. A person couldn't just tell people what he felt because feelings are fragile things. But the Bernards did it all the time, tossing about what was on their minds and in their hearts like it was confetti. As uncomfortable as it was, Daniel had begun to understand that each smile and kind word was a small gift.

Daniel wasted no time in beginning his studies. What took others years to accomplish, he finished in one. By the end of June he was ready to take his final exams. As he sat amongst late blooming scholars, the stress and worry imprinted on their faces was all that was necessary to see that the GED was serious business. The teacher gave his preliminary speech and began his timer. Daniel zipped through the pages, slowed only by the speed of his hand. He was thankful that most of the questions were multiple-choice, not because reading was a problem, but because writing was.

When it came to the English portion, his progress slowed to a crawl and for a bit, as he looked around at the other students, he thought that his face might carry the same signs of worry as theirs. A chill flittered over his skin and goosebumps rose in its wake as he laid the pages onto the desk at the front of the room. "Thanks so much," he said.

"I hope it went well," said the teacher.

"Yeah, me too."

As the door swung closed behind him, Daniel wondered whether he had raced through the test too quickly. Had he got any of the questions right at all? It would be weeks before the results would be in. He would have plenty of time to second-guess himself.

It is not possible to say that the weeks slipped by or even drifted by. They didn't crawl or inch. Torturous self-doubt filled the first day and those that followed worsened. When the manila envelope finally arrived he held it fearfully. It was a decree. Would it proclaim, 'Daniel, you shall have success from henceforth and always,' or would it herald the opposite? Part of him wanted to tear it open, but another part of him wanted to put it away, too afraid to find out that he'd failed, so ... he stood staring at it and did neither.

The second hand on the clock made one jerky revolution after another. He turned the envelope over in his hands, found a gap in the fold, and inserted the edge of his thumb. Even as he tore the top of the packet, his body fought against it. He peeked a little and then a lot. His eyes widened. It was a good day. It was a very good day.

As Daniel lay in bed, he thought back to another night so many years earlier. He had woken, one eye was swollen shut and he had wondered if it might be blind. He remembered his prayer. Had God answered? Maybe He had because some things seemed to have 'unhappened'.

BOOK II

CHAPTER 39

The mineshaft seemed darker than Daniel remembered. His shoulder brushed against the old familiar boulder and dampness from it found its way to his skin. Tremors rolled up his spine. The girl fell into him from behind. He steadied her with a hand and they carried on up the passage.

They came to the main dome. Daniel's light shone about the room. Suddenly Camille screamed. Daniel turned and followed her gaze with the beam. Light fell up upon a human form slouched forward, its back against the door.

Daniel drew Camille close, letting his light rest on the humped remains. Who could it be? There had been no ladder leading down and there were no lights. All the equipment had been removed. It could not be McMaster. McMaster would never have the balls to climb down the beams and wade through the dark. Daniel inched toward the slumped figure.

"We should leave," Camille said.

"I've lived half my life down here. Everything's fine. Whoever this is can't hurt anyone anymore," Daniel said.

CHAPTER 40

(Four months earlier)

Daniel sat next to the aisle near the centre of the auditorium. At the front of the class, Professor Ingstrom droned about the importance of learning the dead languages. So far, his lecture offered nothing that Daniel hadn't picked up from the assigned readings, but professors were usually leaders in their fields and some of them were even worth getting to know. So he had done this. But, in order to meet the right people, there were protocols. He could just knock on a door and say, "Hi, I'm Daniel Sterling," but that would get him an introduction and nothing more. He had to prove he was worth remembering. It had become easy enough to do. He looked around the room at thirty other students writing vigorously, barely looking up from their notebooks. It wasn't that he was pompous. He didn't look down on them. It was just that his competition wasn't particularly steep. In fact, he appreciated every one of them. It is easier to rise to the top in a world of mediocrity.

Daniel listened while his pencil moved randomly on his paper now and again, adding doodles to a mostly blank page. He rarely took notes. He just listened. Lectures were enjoyable, but only on the rare occasion did they offer a fresh perspective. Even when there was no new point of view, they helped him to focus on the issues. Instead of relying on information from class, he used the class to guide his reading. Real value came from books. Every minute spent reading was equal to ten wasted in the auditorium.

Daniel found learning intoxicating. McMaster had starved him and now he feasted. Unfortunately this lecture was not one of the good ones. The professor rambled on in the background, regurgitating material he'd assigned, making Daniel's presence a sad waste of time. Daniel tuned in for a moment and then he tuned out again. Maybe something interesting would come out of the discussion, but a glance at his watch told him that there wouldn't be one today.

Daniel took pride in the status he'd attained. The students in the class knew him as an articulate expert. He understood that there is precious little difference between an articulate expert and an annoying know-it-all. Gaining respect from peers had been a tricky skill to develop. If he appeared overtly keen, he invited their resentment. If he was silent, he would be invisible. Most students wanted their fair share of the glory, so he left it to them, gathering only the leftovers by offering his opinion on questions that left all the others stumped. He thought of it as holding out for the nuggets.

Things had changed since he entered university as a first year student, a degree and a half ago, bright eyed and innocent. He could see that now. That first year, he had known nothing. But it hadn't taken long to learn that most people attend class for no good purpose. Most students know little about their fields and desire to get through with only a rudimentary understanding of the material. It was frustrating. Everyone seemed to want something for nothing.

He had joined a study group once, but in short order had found their strategies a waste of time. They seemed to focus on rote memorization of basic facts that they believed would appear on the test. It was sad. If they could only see that if they possessed true understanding, vocabulary would fall into place. The kids were nice enough and they were driven, but they had a strange habit of expending energy where it was least useful.

"Mister Sterling."

Daniel looked up from the cartoon frog he had mindlessly drawn. The voice belonged to Professor Ingstrom, whose curved finger beckoned Daniel to the podium. Students were already flooding out of the class, so Daniel waited rather than wade against the current of students.

"I'm sorry you were bored today," Professor Ingstrom said when Daniel arrived at his desk.

Daniel flushed.

"Not many students come to class having read the assignment, but it is imperative that all students be exposed to this particular material, hence the redundancy."

"I'm sorry I seemed uninterested. I didn't know you were watching me."

"It's difficult not to notice a student who seems to come by understanding so effortlessly. While other students are dropping out from the pressure, you carry on coolly. I'm impressed."

"Thank you, Professor Ingstrom." There was little else to say. Though his words were few, Daniel's response was neither flippant nor shallow. Professor Ingstrom was a man who deserved his respect and Daniel gave it openly and honestly. Even though he had calculated the importance of this acquaintance, Professor Ingstrom was a good man and Daniel liked him.

When Professor Ingstrom said nothing more, Daniel smiled with a slight nod, and followed the other students out of the auditorium.

CHAPTER 41

Camille noticed the boy long before she decided to talk to him. She had watched him in class for a month, contriving to sit behind him now and again. She found it disgusting that what he put down on paper were no more than scribbles, yet he spoke as though he knew everything and she couldn't remember a time when he had ever asked a question.

Why was she sitting here now, behind a boy of average good looks? She was pretty enough and there was rarely a day when a stranger didn't comment on that fact or stutter a weak invitation for a date. Camille had received a lot of attention over the years and had learned how to filter the good and the bad. To her endless frustration, her beauty was more often a disadvantage and she found it difficult to gain respect when it mattered most.

Then there was Daniel. He was the only boy in class who hadn't shown an interest in her. There wasn't another guy who was as intriguing and at the same time as frustrating as Daniel Sterling was. Not only did he take no notice whatsoever, he was popular and didn't even seem to know it.

Every time he spoke, the entire class would turn in melodramatic unison and hang on to every word. First there was the Prof. and then there was Daniel. How could someone his age know so much? She found it impossible not to notice him and yet he was oblivious to her, simply oblivious.

Camille was distracted. It was hard to concentrate in class and impossible to study out of it. She went to the library under the pretense of research only to find his table and then sit close by. She'd open a book and then never read a word.

"You're infatuated with this guy," said Cally, her best friend.

"No I'm not," Camille said. "I'm not some fifteen-year-old with stars in her eyes."

Cally gave Camille her 'yeah, right' nod.

"He's unique and genuinely interesting." He was interesting enough to make her want to cancel meetings with friends in order to hang out by herself in the library to spy on him, even though he didn't know she existed. "Fine. Maybe I'm a little bit infatuated," she finally admitted.

Camille was walking across campus when she caught sight of Daniel coming out of his anthropology class. It was the only class they didn't share. Predictably, he didn't pause to visit with anyone from class or head in the direction of the student union building for coffee. She knew where he was going because he always went to the same place: the library. He was off to the silence and the solitude of the innumerable shelves of books, better known as the stacks.

Today that was going to change. She was going to see to that! She paced herself perfectly and merged onto the path so that the two of them walked shoulder to shoulder. She smiled at him with her best come-and-get-me look and he smiled back ... awkward, though. Did she have something in her teeth? She persevered. "Hi. I'm Camille. I'm in your geology class."

"Yeah, I know."

If she was a bug, he'd probably slap her dead. She couldn't believe it. Just 'Yeah, I know'? Nothing more? Now what? A line like that for any other boy would have had him drooling. This was not at all going as she planned. "Where are you going," she asked, hoping he hadn't picked up on the cheerleader tone that came out cracking like a thirteen-year-old boy whose voice is changing.

"To the library. You?"

She hadn't expected a question. She wasn't going anywhere because she didn't have anything to do. She was going where he was going. It came out cumbersome with just enough of a pause to sound flaky. "I'm ... going to the library."

"Good stuff."

'Good stuff? Good grief! It was like talking to a wall. She had heard him have dozens of conversations with other people that included more than two words. She continued to walk beside him, but felt contrived. If she ducked out of going to the library now she'd look like an idiot, though she wanted nothing more than to spin in her tracks. Once inside, he could go wherever he wanted and she could ditch him then.

They were almost in the building when he spoke. "What are you studying?"

"I've got a research project that I'm a bit behind on for our geology class. I haven't even decided what I'm going to do yet."

This wasn't a lie and maybe that's why it sounded as natural as it did.

"That's the same project I'm working on. It's fascinating. It's really been taking up a lot of my time."

And just like that she was bound to go with him. They walked together to the third floor where the geology stacks were and found a quiet table. Camille dropped her pack with a thud, eliciting raised eyebrows from other students, then produced a notebook. Daniel disappeared among the dark trenches lined with infinite volumes.

Camille sat alone. What, on earth, was she thinking? It was true that she had the same project to work on, but she had no interest in it at all and certainly hadn't planned on working on it today. What kind of guy was she interested in anyway? If he was Superman in class, he was a consummate Clark Kent everywhere else.

Daniel returned with a tall heap of books, precariously balanced in his arms. He leaned forward to put them onto the table, but they fell— sliding across the surface splaying a variety of titles. Camille glanced at them curiously. They were not at all the kinds of books she was expecting. One was named 'Mystic Stones'. Another was entitled 'Properties that Matter'. Though each was clearly about rocks and minerals, none of them was what Camille would have expected. "What's all this?"

"My research project." Pride colored the tone of his voice.

"Are you sure that this is what Millenburg wanted when he gave us our assignment?"

"Maybe not, but I think it's got merit. Don't you?"

"Not really. He wants us to tell him about the real and tangible characteristics of minerals. He doesn't want myths and legends."

"He'll get both."

Maybe this boy is a bit off balanced. Then again, maybe he's just eccentric. She picked up one of the texts from the table and began to leaf through it while Daniel continued.

"Did you know that there is a remarkable consistency in the ancient classifications of crystals? Even experts in the field of geology give these a passing acknowledgment. They refer to them using words like historical, magical, and mystical. But there's no denying that crystals have played an important part in human lives since cavemen first dug them out of the earth. Besides their great value, mystery has always surrounded them. Did you know they grow crystals in outer space because out there they grow with fewer defects? This will be one of the most interesting essays that this professor is ever going to read." There was no trace of doubt in his voice.

When Daniel first began to speak she wondered if he was some kind of cultist, but she soon realized he was looking at crystals in a way she hadn't considered before. What if crystals really had innate qualities as part of their make up that science had failed to measure and categorize? This was an interesting concept; improvable, but interesting nonetheless. "What if I were to work with you?"

Daniel gave her a skeptical look. "Why would you want to do that?"

"I don't have a geology project yet. I started a bit late and when I went looking, there wasn't a whole lot left to choose from. I wanted to come up with something unique, but I'm having the hardest time."

"So, if you didn't have any idea about what you were going to do, why did you bother to come to the library?"

"I guess I was planning on window shopping, you know, looking for inspiration. And maybe I found what I was looking for." She gave him a coquettish smile, but it was lost on him. He had already returned to his reading.

If only he would put his book down and talk for a minute, maybe she could make some headway, either with her personal project or with her geology assignment. Either one would be good.

She turned through her pages, barely aware of the print on them while he mechanically worked through his. He was going much too fast to be reading and much too slow to be browsing. Exasperated, she interrupted, "Are you going to read anything? Isn't it just a waste of time to spend hours in the library and do nothing at all?"

"It would be easier if you weren't bothering me."

"You're not even reading."

His silence told her that he disagreed and that he was uninterested in idle prattle. "No one can read that fast."

"I suppose that would be me then … Mister No One," he said without looking up.

Camille reached out and snatched his book. "Prove it," she said.

She thumbed through the initial pages; the ones he claimed to have read.

"What page are you looking at?" he said.

"Three."

Daniel began his recital. Camille followed on the page. "How is that possible?"

"It's not. No one can read that fast." He snatched the book away and found his page.

"That's amazing. You're probably the only one in the world who can read like that. You could be doing so many other things with a talent like this!"

He looked up as if the thought had never occurred to him. "Then I wouldn't have time to do the things I like. I like reading." He went back to his book.

She placed one finger on the top of the spine and tugged it forward. "You didn't just read that. You memorized it too!"

"I'd like to finish at least one of these before it's time for supper." His impatience was all too clear.

"I can't believe you," she said in disgust. "I've got to go. I'll talk to you later."

"Sure." If he noticed her anger, he didn't show any sign of it.

She walked to the cafeteria with her head down watching the seams in the concrete path go by. Who is this boy? How is it possible that he can do the things he does? No wonder he doesn't take any notes.

In the days that followed, Camille became a study partner of sorts. She knew he didn't need her around, but her curiosity would not leave her alone. Everyday after class he went to the library. She thought he might find her presence annoying, but he seemed to like her questions, as long as it was about a subject he was interested in.

The fact that he never asked about her or her interests was annoying, but what could she do about that? In time, she began to feel like she didn't matter to him at all. She decided to test it.

For several days she sat as far away from him as she could, periodically looking up to see if he missed her. Nothing. It only served to strengthen her resolve. For the rest of the week she avoided him but as far as she could tell, he continued through his daily routine without as much as a hiccup. If he missed the trysts, he gave no indication. By Friday, she stopped looking and even managed to take a few notes of her own.

The weekend had arrived and it was time to kick her heels back. A few friends were standing outside the student union building. She walked over. Someone suggested grabbing a bite and heading over to Romeo and Juliet's, two downtown clubs situated next to each other. It was a popular place loaded with hard bodies. She gave herself up to the moment and, for a short time, Daniel was mercifully off her mind.

The music blared and the floor writhed. Camille ignored all but a few invitations to dance, choosing instead to sit at the back of the booth nursing one Rye-and-Coke after another. When the evening ended, she accepted Joni's invitation and crashed at her place. She fell asleep on the couch with *Sleepless in Seattle* playing in the background.

It was mid afternoon the following day by the time she arrived at home, feeling queasy and dopy. Half the weekend gone with nothing to show for it, she thought, and cursed herself. She hated it when she made bonehead decisions like that.

There were messages on the phone and she pushed the button to listen:

"Hey Cam. It's Cally. Thought you might like to shoot some hoops. Call me."

She pressed the seven key without waiting for the prompt.

"Your message has been deleted," the voice responded in mechanical monotone.

There were several other messages and Camille ploughed through them. She was pretty good about keeping in touch with her friends and they knew that if she was out on a Friday night she wouldn't be likely to return calls until Sunday for obvious reasons. The disgust she felt earlier at the thought of wasting half the weekend returned.

She flopped into the couch and snapped on the TV. An Oprah commercial was playing … something about a big car give-away. The TV acted as a sedative and before the commercial was over her breaths were lengthening.

The telephone rang and snatched her out of her dream. Before she was fully awake it rang again. She picked it up in time to hear the sound of her own voice, "Hi, this is Camille. I'm probably home; I'm just avoiding someone. Leave me a message, and if I don't call back, it was you." She had thought it was hysterical when she first recorded it, but something like that was only funny once. She'd have to change it.

"Hi. Camille? It's Daniel. I was just calling to see if you were all right. My num…"

She punched at the buttons trying to find the right one, and managed to shift the call to the speaker. Daniel finished his message and hung up. Frustrated, she punched the play button. She felt giddy. In an instant all the anger and frustration she'd experienced during the week vanished.

Her fingers roamed the pad pecking out his number. It rang twice before he picked up.

"Hello?"

"Hi Daniel. It's me, Camille. I just got your message."

"Hey. I'm glad you called back. I thought you were avoiding me."

He must be talking about last week. "What? I wouldn't do something like that."

"You're answering machine said you were avoiding someone. I was afraid it was me."

"Oh, no. Daniel, that's just a joke. I'm not trying to avoid anyone. I was, ahm …." she paused as her mind raced. I don't want to say I was out late drinking up a storm and was completely toasted. On the other hand, I don't want to sound lazy either. Am I crazy? Why do I care?

"I was just outside and couldn't get to the phone in time."

"What are you doing?"

Great, now he wants small talk. She snatched another thought from her creative depths, "Taking in a little sun on the deck." She could have been. It was only a white lie. The sun was out and she often did that.

"I was just wondering how your essay's going?"

"It's fine. Is that all you called about?"

"No. I mean, yes, but … you mentioned that we might work on this project together, and I thought I'd like to take you up on that offer. I was wondering if you keyboard well."

"You want me to be your secretary?"

"N-no. Not, not just … not just that. Not at all."

She enjoyed hearing him stammer. Cute, she thought as he went on.

"I thought that if I shared with you what I've got, you could help me out too, and we'd end up helping each other."

She had thought he hadn't noticed her, figured he didn't even care. Did he really need her help at all? With the way he reads? She didn't think so. Then again, maybe the one skill he *doesn't* have is keying, so ….

"I could, if what you've got is worthwhile," she warned, but the humor was lost on him.

"Oh that would be great. I'm sure you'll be interested. It's a deal then?"

"Sure."

"Okay, great … well, see you soon then. Bye."

"Yup. Bye, now."

The TV was still talking to the walls. She clicked it off, buried her face in her pillow, and kicked her feet in joy.

CHAPTER 42

It felt strange to Daniel—having never asked a girl out before. Not that this was really a date. It was better than that. She was coming over. He looked around the room. *What a mess.*

His apartment was a meager bachelor pad. On one side of the single room was the kitchen. An island counter separated the two parts of the living area. The counter was wide. The kitchen sink dominated one side. The other side was a bar which acted as the only table in the apartment. He used stools as chairs that he stored under the ledge on the living room side, if one could call it that. His futon, converting into a bed, was one of his few pieces of furniture. In truth, it had been months since it had transformed into anything. He had no need for a couch.

He owned two sets of sheets and a pillowcase match for each. Both had been gifts from Mrs. Bernard, but now they were threadbare and dolefully similar to those from that unspeakable time in his life he preferred not to dwell on. Camille would be his first visitor.

He stripped the bed and put on clean sheets. He folded the futon into a shape that was almost foreign and tossed his pillow down as a cushion. He whipped across the room to the kitchen. He had neglected washing dishes until now. Almost every one lay filthy in the sink. The Kraft Dinner he'd eaten on Monday was yellow concrete in the bottom of his only pot. His bedside table doubled as a desk and dresser. He swept the papers together and slid them under the bed, leaving a family picture of *the Bernard Clan*, as Phoebe liked to call them. He dusted the room and dragged a broom across the floor. Then there was the lunch box. He couldn't have it lying around. He slid it under the futon, out of sight.

Now that the mad rush was over, he allowed himself a moment to sit down. His apartment was the cleanest it had been since he moved in. He was satisfied about that. He leaned back with arms behind his head and then it suddenly dawned on him: the toilet! He didn't have to ask himself. He knew that he hadn't cleaned it since he had moved in. He looked at the clock. In ten minutes she'd be here.

He finished and dropped the toilet lid just as the phone rang. As he expected it was a call from the lobby. "Hello?"

"Hi, Daniel. I'm here."

He buzzed her in. Moments were hours. As he waited, he thrust his hands deep in his jean pockets.

CHAPTER 43

Camille stood at the entrance to the apartment block. She was early and, if she rang up now, she might seem too eager. She waited, smiling apologetically at each visitor or tenant who came through the door. She primped using her fuzzy reflection from the matrix of stainless steel mailboxes. *What am I all worked up about? After all, Daniel hasn't really asked me out on a date.*

She pushed the square black plastic button. His voice came over the intercom and he buzzed her up.

She knocked when she reached his door and Daniel answered it.

"Hey, come on in."

If he noticed that she had made an effort with her appearance he didn't show it, but she nodded and smiled anyway.

"Well, here it is," he said, and his arm swept across the room. Then he added, "Except the bathroom. It's through there. Can I get you something to drink?"

The apartment was tiny. There were no other doors except the small one Daniel indicated was the bathroom. She wondered where he slept, but didn't ask.

"Yes, please. How about a glass of water?"

"I've got lots of other things to drink ya know."

She sipped her water while Daniel sat still, observing her like a staring deaf-mute. The silence grew from uncomfortable to eventually unbearable. "Is this all there is? Where's your bedroom," she asked, embarrassed the moment the words escaped her lips.

"You're standing in it. The futon folds out into a bed." Her surprised reaction was noticeable enough for him to hurry and add, "But don't worry, I just changed the sheets. It's clean."

Okay, she thought, unsure whether what he seemed to have suggested was what he meant. *How could it be?* She sat on the futon, but she felt strange knowing it was his bed.

They sat and talked, but all the while Camille couldn't shake the uneasy feeling she'd been having.

"Camille?"

"Oh, sorry. What were you saying?"

"Nothing important. You just seem a little preoccupied."

CHAPTER 44

The crystals pulsed without intelligence. What cannot be explained with science seems magical and so, in a way, the crystals worked their magic. Had this meeting been a singular event, nothing may have come of it. The two may not have become anything more than passing acquaintances, ending their story. But as Daniel and Camille sat talking, inklings of desire stirred and in the weeks that followed, affection bloomed.

"You know that project I've been working on? I've got something I've wanted to show you," Daniel said one day. He slid a rough tray from under the bed. There must have been at least a hundred different crystals adorning it.

Camille's eyes shot open. Some of the stones, she recognized. Some, she thought might be precious. Others may have been mere rocks, for she had no way of knowing their purpose in the collection. "These are beautiful," she said. "May I touch them?"

Daniel nodded and smiled at the one she chose. "That's an uncut diamond."

It was a half inch in diameter. "No way," she said, but there was no teasing in the look he returned. "How did you get this?"

"It was a gift from one of my Profs. I think she got it from a mine up north, some of which she donated to the university and this was the smallest. She gave it to me in a small box with a note that said, 'Never give up. Your dreams can be more than dreams.'"

"You think she was hitting on you?"

Daniel laughed and then said thoughtfully, "Maybe."

Camille raised her eyebrows.

"She was sixty-five. She knew I was collecting crystals, and that there would be some I'd never be able to have. If she loved me, then she loved me like a grandmother."

Camille was skeptical. "This really is an amazing collection. Do you have them all?"

"Not at all. I'm missing lots. That's the only one with real value. The rest are just rocks. That one's an agate and that's amethyst," he said, pointing to one and then another.

"What are you going to do with all these?"

"I'm going to prove that crystals have unique and measurable qualities, just like those suggested in new age books. Crystals seem magical because they are ... kind of."

"Daniel, it's not that I don't agree with you or believe you, but what makes you think that you can prove this? What if you can't prove it?"

"Oh, I already know I can prove it, but that's not the problem. I want to prove it with known substances. Even if I can't prove it, I'll write the paper anyway. I think the Prof will understand. Even if he doesn't it's only one assignment. I'll make up the grade somewhere else if I have to. I'm planning on this being a test run for my master's thesis."

"You can prove it? How is that possible? You haven't shown me anything I couldn't learn from a rock shop jeweler. And how come you never told me you had a degree already?" Daniel didn't say anything for a long time. She wondered if she had hurt his feelings.

"I didn't tell you about the degree because it didn't occur to me."

She drew back a bit, regarding him. "That seems awfully odd to me."

"I guess, but I've been busy with other things on my mind. I just didn't think about it."

Fine, but what about your *unknown* substance?"

He stroked his chin, then cradled it in his thumb and forefinger. His eyes locked on hers. "Do you trust me?"

"I was just wondering about that."

He nodded, popped his lips. "Yeah, I figured."

That's it? Daniel could be so flat. That alone was by far the most difficult aspect of Daniel's personality to take. What he was suggesting didn't seem possible. Why should she sacrifice her security for his crazy ideas? Trust was a lot to ask.

"By the way, Camille, I do apologize for not saying anything before. It's a little late I know, but I do have one degree so far and I'd like to get more. There is one other thing you should know. I've never lied to you, and I'll never lie to you."

"Since you haven't lost my trust, that means I trust you, I guess. As for whether or not you'll never lie? That remains to be seen."

Daniel stared at the floor.

"What's the matter?"

"Nothing. You'd be the first, that's all … and maybe the last."

She leaned back, scowling. "It can't be that serious."

"It is," he said, and the look on his face told her it was.

Daniel poked around in one of the kitchen drawers and returned with a small flashlight. He pulled the canvas bag from under the futon.

"Come with me," he said.

Camille folded her arms. "Come with you where?" She flipped a hand out. "There's nowhere to go."

"The bathroom." He nodded that way.

"Come on, Daniel. No one is going to see anything in here. What on earth is there for the two of us to do in the bathroom?"

"I have to show you in the bathroom, or I can't show you at all. You said you trusted me."

She sighed, shook her head, and rose to follow him.

The bathroom was the size of a small closet. The door swung inward and cleared the toilet by no more than a quarter of an inch, forcing one to stand between the toilet and the tub in order to close the door before sitting down on the privy. Daniel walked in and Camille followed. Together they filled the small space. Camille looked into Daniel's serious eyes, tipped up on her toes, and kissed him on his unprepared lips. "Thank you for trusting me," she said.

She would have loved to see his reaction. She hoped she hadn't embarrassed him. She hoped that she hadn't embarrassed herself. The moments ticked by. Whatever Daniel was fiddling with was taking too long.

Daniel fiddled for some time. Camille grew impatient. "Would it help if I gave you some light? I feel the light switch right he—"

"No! Don't touch that. Whatever you do, *do not* turn the light on."

Camille slipped her hand into her pocket. "Sorry."

Daniel separated one crystal from the others, laid it in the bathtub then closed and resealed the lunch kit. "Are you ready?"

"*Yes*. Whatever you're going to do, *just do it*."

Daniel turned on the flashlight. The crystal flashed into brilliance, filling every nook and blinding the bathroom's two occupants.

Camille screamed. "Daniel! What's happening? I have to get out of here!"

"No, Camille." She was already scrambling for the knob, but the sound of his voice stopped her. "It's only light." Daniel wrapped the crystal in the black cloth.

"What is it?"

"It's a crystal. It grew naturally—as far as I know."

"How is that possible? What happened just then?"

"Let me get it back in the box and I'll tell you all about it."

"Can I turn the light on now?"

"No, not yet. I'll let you know when it's safe." Daniel slipped the crystal into the tin box and snapped the clasps closed. "Done," he said.

Camille flicked the light switch.

The image of the bright crystal still burned on Daniel's retinas and his eyes could not adjust. They moved to the sofa, Camille waited while Daniel struggled to find the right words to say. Camille finally broke the silence, "I don't understand."

He shrugged. "It was a crystal."

"A crystal can't do that." Again her arms folded.

"That one can. Later, after the light is dimmer, I can show you. It'll stay bright like that for a long time … hours."

She stared at him, arms remaining locked together. "How do you know this? Where did the crystal come from?"

"That's a long story and I'm trying to forget it."

"*I can't believe this,*" Camille nearly screamed, with both hands flailing. "You talk about trust like it's something that only goes one way. You ask me into a bathroom and turn the light out and give me nothing. I followed you blindly and then you say that I am out of place for asking for your trust in return?"

"Camille, I'm so sorry. I didn't mean to offend you. I've only told the story once and I feel like I shouldn't have. You wouldn't believe me if I told you."

"An impossible to believe story? Then what difference does it make? Why won't you trust me with it?"

"It isn't about you."

"I'll talk to you later," she said as she walked to the door.

Daniel pleaded. Camille ignored his incoherent excuses. Her hand was at the door when she heard the words that stopped her. "It's a secret I don't want you to bear. I've carried if for years and it still crushes me."

Her hand hovered over the doorknob. "I know what skeletons are, Daniel. If you trust me to know about the crystal, how can you not tell me everything?"

Daniel's shoulders dropped. "Would you like a cup of tea? I have some chamomile. It made me think of you, so I bought it."

Her hand released its grip. "That sounds fine," she said, and took a stool across the counter from him as he heated water in the microwave.

Camille imagined that in the dark of the box the crystals were glowing, turning the cloth nearly transparent. She heard barking down the street. Maybe the crystals emitted a sound only dogs could hear. Daniel brought the tea and sat beside her.

"I think the power in these crystals is greater than anything known in the world today. The potential for the crystals could be limitless." Daniel went on for a long time, explaining all he knew and all of what he conjectured.

Camille listened patiently. When he was finished she said, "I thought you were going to tell me *your* story. That's what I stayed for."

"I will ... before you leave. I promise. It'll still take a few more hours before the light is dim enough."

They sat together on the couch, waiting, a marathon of patience. Camille slumped to one side, lying against him. She awoke with his arm draped across her, unsure whether he stole it over her during the night or whether she pulled it across her for warmth. Either way, she would not have objected. She liked the way his arm felt in the crook of her side.

Daniel's eyes opened.

"You were asleep."

He rubbed his eyes. "I don't think the light will last much longer. If you want to see the crystal, it has to be now."

They crossed to the bathroom and Camille closed the door behind her. She took her place on the toilet seat and turned out the light when Daniel was ready. She heard a familiar clicking sound as Daniel unlocked and opened the box. The crystals bathed the room in an eerie glow, the light from one having transferred to them all. Daniel unwrapped one and offered it to her.

She held out her hands to receive it, all the while her face bathed in firelight glow. It weighed almost nothing.

"It's very delicate. Be careful," said Daniel.

She smiled her understanding.

The crystal was smooth and surprisingly cool to touch. She held on to it as if it was a living thing, afraid to crush the life and light out of it. She stood and stepped into the tub. She beckoned Daniel to follow. They sat as if around a campfire, basking in the crystal's phosphorescence, two magi holding a séance while the sun rose outside.

By the eerie light, Daniel related his story in a low whisper like a small boy telling a scary tale to friends with the woods and the creatures of the night surrounding him. Camille sat transfixed and listened.

Maybe there was no other way that Daniel could have told his story in order to make it sound believable. Was it the power of the crystal or was it just him? She wasn't sure. Whatever the case, Camille sat riveted while cramps seeped into her legs and back. As his story came to an end, so did the light.

They sat in the dark as if the telling and absorbing the new information required absolute silence and concentration. Daniel broke the ambiance by returning the crystal to its metal container. When he leaned forward to stand, Camille reached out and found his cheek. She tilted his chin down and kissed him. His lips were both soft and gentle.

The sun was high when they exited. It was almost two forty-five in the afternoon. "Would you like me to make some lunch," Daniel asked.

"I'm tempted to, but I need to get going. I've still got some studying to do and I feel like a wreck."

***

It was an awkward good-bye. Camille was faintly aware of her fading feelings of ecstasy as she left the building. By the time she got into her car, the cramps subsided, and she felt almost normal. Daniel's story was unbelievable just as he'd said. In his apartment, it had seemed so plausible, but as she drove away a feeling of unreality washed over her.

The kiss though, that had been something she had been thinking about for a long time. It was everything she had hoped for, fresh, innocent, and passionate. It was the most honest, natural kiss she had ever received. It was a first kiss all over again. She felt almost sure it was one that would remain with her a lifetime.

At home, she stepped into the shower. She let the warm water cascade over her. She slept without stirring until the alarm clock slapped her awake. She left the house without checking her phone messages. It seemed petty somehow. There probably wasn't anything worth listening to.

She met Daniel in class, as she always did. Instead of sitting behind him, as she was accustomed to, she sat next to him. He smiled when she arrived and, although he was as driven as he had always been, he seemed softer—softer toward her anyway.

After class, they stole away to the library and Camille was happy to go ... a fellow conspirator now.

The weeks before the reading break were a blur. As a duo, they were voracious. Camille had become a sponge. She credited her newfound skills to her growing interest.

Daniel's studies didn't end with geology. His second major was ancient history and Camille found that equally fascinating. She read with him as often as she could, but she had other classes to focus on as well. Sometimes she went to her own apartment to study for them, but it was so much easier to get her work done when she was with Daniel.

CHAPTER 45

Camille gave Daniel a warm smile and tender kiss before she disappeared through the airport security. He had turned down her invitation to come home with her to meet her family. He had planned to stay in the city. It was just as well. There was enough to discuss with her parents once she arrived.

She cleared security, found an empty row of seats near the window, and sat with vague hopes that no one would disturb her. The spring reading break was one of her favorite times. It was the getaway before the final push and, although there was often some work to complete, she used it more often than not to recharge. She stared through the glass barely aware of the busy workers and the passing planes on the tarmac. In a few hours, things were going to get serious.

By the time the plane landed, Camille's feelings of self-doubt had all but subsided. I'm an adult, after all. I can make my own decisions. This is what she kept telling herself. She knew it was a lie.

"Honey!"

Camille recognized the voice immediately and wondered how many others looked up expectantly at the vague salutation. "Hey, Mom. Thanks for coming to pick me up."

Jackie gave her a wink that said, 'Of course I came to pick you up. What kind of mother would I be if I didn't?'

"Where's Dad?"

"He wanted to stay home and paint that silly trailer he's been working on. He says he wants to haul the quads on it. He and your Uncle Robert want to take it hunting this year. You know him, always thinking a year ahead. I guess that's a good thing. I don't know why he couldn't leave it alone for a few hours. Anyway, he'll be waiting for us when we get there."

It was always the same with her mother. Ask one simple question and get an entire story. Camille turned to the window and let her thoughts turn inward. Trees, fields, and buildings flashed by like cards shuffled in slow motion. She had hoped to use the ride home to break the news, but telling her mother first would just complicate matters. She'd respond with something like, 'Oh, that's very nice, honey. Why don't we just wait until we get home and see what your dad thinks.' She'd never come right out and give her support or not. Her opinion would come later and only then to parrot her father's. If Camille had any regret, it was that her relationship with her mother had no depth. If only her mother could say what was in her heart.

Camille walked through the front door into familiar surroundings. Jackie preferred what she called 'timeless' décor. That's not what it was, though. The hutch was an heirloom handed down from her grandmother. 'When I'm gone, I'll pass it on to you,' her mother would often say morbidly. Camille didn't know how she felt about that. The memories she associated with it were words of warning and scolding. It didn't have value to her other than what it might bring at auction. The table was an anniversary gift to her mother from a time before she was born. Unlike the hutch, it had survived herself and her three younger brothers. Her dad had eventually refinished it, but that had been six years ago or more. Her mother still acted as though only yesterday it returned to the house looking like new. Since then she had become the queen of the coasters, ensuring that every glass had a protective disc between it and the table.

"Mom, Dad," she started, feeling her way, a bit tentative as they sat around the table. "There's something I need to talk to you about."

They looked up in anticipation. When Camille said nothing more, her father prompted, "What is it, hon?"

"I've decided to change my major." There she had said it. She didn't ask. She didn't waver. She just said it like it was. The ball was in their court now.

"This seems so sudden," her mother said, a near verbatim rendition of what Camille had predicted.

"It's not, Mom. I've been thinking about it for a long time."

Dad picked up his fork, looked at her. "What direction were you thinking about going in?"

There he goes making it sound like it's still up for discussion when it's not. "I'm going to be a geologist," she said, and wondered if she could have been more decisive.

He frowned, set his fork down. "You've never been interested in geology before, Camille."

"I never knew that I would be. I find it so fascinating. I'm particularly interested in man's use of minerals throughout history. I might even go into archeology."

"So you're really not sure?"

"I'm sure that I don't want to teach. I know it's what you did, but it's not what I want."

Her father nodded.

"Honey, what about all those years you put into school already? Will you just throw them away?"

"They won't be a waste, Mom. They haven't been."

The discussion went back and forth for hours. At times, she felt she was gaining ground, and at others she felt like the debate would carry on for hours more. While her long account was a plea for support, their interrogation served to measure her resolve.

Camille was just happy that the grilling was finally over.

The following day it was unclear whether her parents had come to terms with her decision or whether they would prolong her agony by waiting a little to broach the subject again in a new attempt to sway her decision, but … by the end of the second day she began to relax a little. By the third, it felt like every other visit home, her mother making her favorite meals.

Camille eased into a parking spot outside the mall in the old Mercury Sable she had learned to drive in. The green 'N' she had no longer required since she passed her final driving test lay dusty in the rear window. Her mom said she'd make that broccoli casserole she loved if she'd pick up the ingredients. The automatic door opened so slowly that it forced Camille to slow her stride. Jennifer Dickinson met her on the other side. "Camille! How are you?"

"Hey, Jennifer. It's good to be home."

"How long you back in town for?"

"Just until Sunday."

"I've got to go right now, but we should get together before you leave. It's great to see you."

Camille smiled as she watched her old friend cross the parking lot. There were a half a dozen of the same kind of encounters before she got back to her own car. They were one of the reasons she was happy to run the errand—the allure of the small town. It was bittersweet, too. The same phenomenon occurred every summer. After a week, the hubbub concluded and she was just another local. Once the novelty was over, she felt like she had never left.

The week passed too quickly and Camille mounted the steps of the Boeing 737 breathing new life. She was no longer following the footsteps of her father. She was on a new path, one of her own design.

She stepped off the plane in Victoria as a woman who had sloughed the bindings of childhood, having lost nothing in the process. She now understood that all adult decisions were hers to make and that knowledge had changed her. Until now, her parents had mapped out her life, taking over each of her dreams and orchestrating them to fruition before she even knew that she had them. With clear goals of her own, she crossed to the bus.

CHAPTER 46

Dr. Ronald Millenburg sat marking papers in his office. Once a stack of a hundred, it made for an impressive twenty-four inch high pile. It was the one part of his job he detested. First and second year students tended to produce regurgitated drivel sometimes quoted directly out of the texts. He was so familiar with the contents of the library that he could quote the book based on the work before him. Bibliographies were merely a required formality.

It was getting late. Marjorie had hoped he would be home early. Unfortunately, it was that time of the year. If he brought the work home, there would be a hundred different things that would keep him from it and it only made it worse to drag it out. Twenty years of marriage had been enough to work out the kinks. And there had been kinks.

Students believed that spring break was for their benefit. They were mistaken. It required teachers to work extended hours and they needed the entire week to catch up on the deluge of work that term papers created. This mad rush happened six times between September and May. It was a dreadful period, but he always managed to get through it. Thank God for work-study employees and student helpers, otherwise the load would be unbearable.

He slapped a C+ on the paper in front of him after scrawling of few words of encouragement and criticism on the last page. Not likely to do too much for a mediocre student with no real ambition, but there would be no one to come biting his ass later for not doing his job. It had been ten years since he had made any significant changes to his assignments. Familiarity had its benefits.

He was no more than three quarters of the way through the pile. Maybe he could get through five more before he called it a night. He pulled one from the stack in front of him. 'Daniel Sterling', it said in the top right corner. *Ah, yes.* He remembered the boy. *Amazing kid.* "Let's see what you've got to show me, Daniel," he said aloud.

Interesting. The kid demonstrates an understanding of the concept. Good. What's this? An outlandish twist.

He read on like a child hooked on a good book. Only a few minutes later he had completed the essay and wanted to know more. How refreshing. A smile crossed his face as he wrote a comment he had not been able to put on a second year paper for longer than he could remember. "Excellent work, Daniel. I was thoroughly impressed with your understanding of the subject matter and I was pleasantly surprised with your unique perspective. It's true that it is likely there are minerals and compounds that man has not discovered. Though we have our theories about the deep core of the planet, who's to say what lies there? Very nice work. A+"

Maybe he could get through six. That one didn't take too long at all. He pulled another one from the pile, but the energy went out of him before he got through the introductory paragraph. "Please, someone, teach these kids to write!" he vocalized.

The next few that followed were as bad as the last making it hard to give them even a mediocre grade. *Last one for the night.* He sighed as he read the name. Camille Robertson.

What are the odds of that? Millenburg flipped through the last essays and selected Daniel's work. He laid the two side by side and began to scrutinize them one page at a time. He reached the end and then compared the bibliographies. *Interesting.* Probably study partners. There was certainly no law against that. Very similar ideas from both, but at the same time still unique. Remarkable, he thought.

He placed the two papers aside, pushed himself away from the desk, snatched his jacket from the hook and headed to the car. It had been a long time since any student had surprised him. It was almost enough to rekindle his love of the subject.

Ron Millenburg arrived at home. His wife was in bed reading. It was nice to find that she wasn't asleep, and he told her so; then he went to the bathroom to get ready for bed. When he returned she was just sliding her bookmark into the novel. "Ready for lights out, sweetie?"

He gave her the standard nod and slipped into bed to the sound of the light switch. She had already rolled over as she always did and he sidled up behind her, wrapping his arm around her and kissing the back of her neck.

"I thought you'd be exhausted," she said.

"Oh, I am. But the thought of you waiting up for me even after all these years does it for me. Thanks *so much,* darling."

She rolled toward him and gave him a tender, feathery kiss. They made love the way they used to and she remembered that she loved him.

Dr. Ron Millenburg didn't have Daniel's class the next day, or Camille's. But he would see both students on the following Wednesday. At noon he went to the faculty lounge as was his custom. The same fogies showed up, and they visited over lunch followed by a cup of coffee. Most of the men in the geography department were hard-core environmentalists. The body and the world we live in are shrines, was their communal belief which meant that none of them had any vices to speak of. They were all men on the straight and narrow.

As it turned out, Millenburg discovered during his chats with the other professors, Camille and Daniel stood out in other classes as well. Apparently the two students had been shining in all of the classes they attended together. What were the chances of having two prodigies in the same year? This was definitely something worth checking into.

Class began and ended on Wednesday in the same fashion as it always did. Ron recognized Daniel when he saw him and, as he suspected, Camille sat next to him. When the hour was up, he dismissed the class and began to walk toward the two students.

Daniel was quick to stand and made way for Camille. A moment later there were thirty people in the aisle between them. Rather than call out at the cost of his dignity, Millenburg watched them go.

CHAPTER 47

Camille began the semester focused and determined. She and Daniel sat in his small apartment sharing the reading and regurgitating the crux of it.

"Have you checked this out," Daniel asked, holding up a copy of National Geographic. "There's an article about a mythical gem discovered in South America."

Camille flipped a page of her current selection. "I read that this morning. Maybe you'll get a chance to find out if the stories are true once you become rich and famous." She smiled without looking up and tossed another page. "When are you scheduled to meet with Doctor Millenburg?"

"Yeah, in about twenty minutes. I better get going." Daniel dropped his book onto the floor and reached for his coat.

"Let me know how it goes. I hope he's not going to tell you that our project missed the point, otherwise I'm sure I'll be meeting with him next."

"I doubt he has a problem with it," a confident Daniel said. "I'll be back in a bit." He went out, seeing Camille returning to her book out of the corner of his eye as he closed the door.

Living close to the university had its advantages. Within a few minutes Daniel was walking down the hall toward Millenburg's office.

He stopped at the door and gave two quick raps.

Daniel listened for either the professor's footsteps or his voice. If Dr. Millenburg called from his desk, it might mean that he was too busy to get up or that Daniel's visit was trivial, but if the man made the short trip across the office, that would suggest something more. Daniel hoped for the latter.

"Take a seat for a moment, Daniel. I'll be right out," Millenburg's voice came through the old wooden door.

Four empty upholstered chairs lined the wall. Daniel sat in one and pondered the reasons for the meeting while listening to muffled murmurings from inside. Shortly afterward the door opened and Dr. Millenburg ushered his previous appointment out of the room. "Come on in, Daniel."

Daniel followed him into the office and sat in the seat the professor indicated.

"I'll get right to the point. Your essay was interesting. What's more is that you write with such conviction … as if you know something no one else does."

Daniel nodded, unsure yet how to respond.

"Under normal circumstances, I would have probably dismissed this paper. You'd be surprised at how often I must read works from students who believe they're writing their thesis and that they've got something to teach me."

"I'm sorry, Doctor Millenburg. I didn't mean to seem presumptuous."

"That's not why I asked you in. If that were the case, I would have written a note at the bottom of the page saying as much and left it at that. I brought you in for something else all together."

Daniel nodded.

"Here's the crazy thing. As I read your paper, I found myself wanting to believe it. You piqued my interest when you described the device you have in mind for measuring the qualities crystals might have. Maybe what you've touched on here is the appeal that draws many of us to geology. I think it's the same fascination treasure hunting has for archeologists. These romantic dreams are not a reality of the work we do, but you've made me think they could be."

"I apprecia—"

Millenburg shot an open palm in the air. "I couldn't help noticing that Miss Robertson had some very similar ideas."

Daniel backpedaled. "Yes, she does. We do. We work closely together, but we try hard not to copy each other's work."

Millenburg held the submissions up. "Would you mind if I hold on to these?"

CHAPTER 48

Daniel regretted having convinced Camille to take time off to let their relationship settle over summer break. His logic had been that they'd both be too busy anyway. Reluctant at first, she had finally agreed.

He had envisioned that his post at the local museum would consume him. It hadn't. His job was to conserve artifacts. He had hoped there would be specialized training that would encompass a wide variety of materials. He'd assumed there would be special procedures for everything. There weren't.

He arrived at the museum office ahead of time. It was a squat, white single story building; an artifact itself. The museum society was slowly erecting a miniature historic village. There was the old Royal Bank, the Okay Café and an old log cabin, once occupied by the Royal Canadian Mounted Police. In the latter, even though the holding cell no longer existed, after its conversion to a residence, steel bars remained set into the logs making its original purpose obvious. The buildings spoke of a rustic time when settlers plugged drafts with moss and a hearty blaze kept the chills away. Wooden sidewalks connected each of the buildings as they would have during the period.

Daniel thought of Grundpark and the ruins there. He'd never seen McMaster since his escape, but thinking of the place sent shivers racing to the base of his skull. He enjoyed his visits with the Bernards, but each time they returned to Grundpark Road his guts lurched. It was only with strength of will that he didn't vomit. But in those weak moments, he *found* strength, too. To hell with you, was the thought that was the best medicine for a queasy stomach.

Since Vanderhoof was originally a farming community, what they called artifacts included such gems as wagon wheels, plough sheers, ancient steam tractor parts, and the like. He'd at least expected the assignment of assistant to the curator to be stimulating work, but it turned out to be nothing more than a strange sort of painting job. The brush was a normal household paintbrush, but the paint was a watery chemical that, when dry, produced no visible change in the steel. The elements were gradually reclaiming the metal, but the point was not to refurbish the scrap steel; it was to keep it in its present condition indefinitely. Every steel artifact required the treatment. That was what the curator had hired him to do. Through long hot days in the yard, or inside on rainy ones, the task was always the same: paint rusty steel with tannic acid.

It had been two months since Daniel started, but this day he was hardly aware of the tedium. At the beginning of the summer, Camille had agreed to come for a visit and her bus would arrive this afternoon. He knew she wanted to see him, but he had also promised to show her the cavern. She said it didn't matter if he did or didn't, but it was back to the trust issue. If he were satisfied to call an end to their relationship, he could refuse. He wasn't willing to give her up, so not showing her where he found the crystals was not an option. She'd said she would understand if he didn't think he could do it. He never thought of himself as macho, but letting her think that he couldn't handle it seemed too wimpy to admit.

She was riding in on the Greyhound bus. Mixed feelings welled up again. He had ridden those buses enough to know how unpleasant and tiring it could be. He could envision it now. Camille would sit in a seat by herself, next to the window. Just when she thought she could relax and get some rest, some lowlife drug addict would ask if the seat next to her was taken. She wouldn't be able to lie, so he'd sit next to her and stink up her seat with his nasty reeking stench for a hundred miles, hoping that each time he got off the bus for a smoke it would be his stop and he wouldn't get back on. Daniel empathized with her predicament, but he was too glad she was coming to care very much that her ride was going to be hell.

He could see the bus depot from the local Bakery so he sat sipping coffee and nibbling on a donut. The bus arrived on schedule, dwarfing every other vehicle around. Daniel took a final sip and raced across the street. He was waiting as the door swung open and a herd of nicotine addicts barreled out, pulling at rumpled packages even before their feet touched concrete.

Then she was there, framed in the door, her hair a mottled wreath around her head. Her eyes were bloodshot from too many hours of sleep, but she never looked so good. She fell into his arms, kissing him between words.

"I. Missed. You. So. Much."

Daniel gathered her bags and escorted her to a vehicle the Bernards had been kind enough to lend him for the summer. Camille would want to know about where she was going, so along the way he pointed out landmarks that had only become familiar in recent years. Too soon, Grundpark Road loomed ahead. Since his escape he had coped with this stretch of road by speeding along it, but now it required a tour guide's commentary. He slowed, turned left, then pulled off to the side. The air inside the vehicle suddenly seemed cold. Daniel reached for the heater lever and pushed it fully into the red.

When the Bernards had moved into the area thirty years earlier, the ancient cabin stood alone in its clearing void of even the smallest tree. Back then it stood in its entirety, a rustic structure complete with hand hewn shingles and moss chinked logs. But time had not been kind. The roof lay in rotten shambles inside the few rounds of timbers that remained, camouflaged among a dense growth of young trees. Daniel pointed. "That's where Grundpark used to live. He threw his garbage just down the hill over there."

"Is that all you know of him?"

"I know what I've been told and I know what I dreamed. He lived in a cave and then he died there." Daniel dropped the car into gear. "Everything important is about a half a mile up ahead."

The road was fenced on the left and lined with trees on the right. Daniel dropped down the hill and rolled along the flat at the bottom. On the other side he climbed a knoll and stopped the car at the top adjacent to a barbed wire gate in the fence. Daniel's voice quivered. "The mine is just through there … on the other side of those trees." The equipment and the trailer were gone now. Not even the piles of dirt remained.

Camille pointed toward a field to her right. "What's over there?"

"Those are the Bernard's hayfields. Let me show you." Daniel pulled the car off the road and crossed through a small ravine. He stopped the car under a Douglas fir tree with alfalfa growing all around and they kissed. "We'd better get up to the house now."

William and Phoebe had taken the night off. They had been expecting Camille. Daniel knew that Phoebe would be making a special meal. With Camille's hand in his, he grasped the knocker and rapped on the door.

CHAPTER 49

Although Daniel knew Camille was anxious to see the evidence he spoke of, he would not insult the Bernards by disappearing immediately after supper. Daniel already knew that their first night there, in terms of any excursion, would be a loss.

After dinner they played card games and talked until the early hours. It wasn't until the following evening when it was William's and Phoebe's turn to play the movie when they had an opportunity to slip away. Daniel watched William back out of the driveway and then led Camille across the road and through the field. They stood overlooking the well and, although he hadn't expected things to remain the same during the previous few years, he was surprised at his discovery. The site had been stripped. All the equipment was gone. The tall fence that once held him prisoner had been removed. Even the piles of dirt and rock that he had heaped high with his own hands were nowhere to be seen. Grass grew on the flattened area erasing all evidence of the years he had spent there.

A worn realtor's sign looked like it must have been posted less than a year after his escape. The secret of the well would be safe as long as there were no buyers.

Daniel stood near the edge and looked in. The lift he had expected to see was gone. There was no evidence of it except for the trellis of beams that crisscrossed into the dark. He could see his shadowy reflection in a standing pool of water at the bottom. No one who passed by would guess it was anything more than a well. If McMaster's intention was to disguise the site, he was successful. But Daniel would have to find another way to the bottom.

They made the short trek back to William's shop and found an extension ladder hanging on the wall. Camille took one end making an easy job easier. It was a trait he cherished. She was always willing to jump right in and lend a hand.

Maneuvering across the barbwire fence required little effort, and within a few minutes they were standing back at the abandoned well. Daniel stretched the ladder to its full length and guided it into the abyss. There was a splash when it hit the bottom and he didn't have to climb down to know the water was only a few inches deep. Daniel looked up. Summer days were long and there were still hours before the light would be gone from the sky. He pulled the camera from his pocket and snapped a few pictures before stepping onto the ladder. It felt flimsy and made a racket with each step, but it was a descent he was accustomed to.

Camille stood watching as Daniel went down. He cast a glance up at her, smiling in knowing amusement at her expression of excitement and fear. When Daniel stepped off the ladder he was no more than a shadow in the darkness. He called up. "The water's not deep. Come on down."

"Are you sure it's safe?"

"I'll hold on to the ladder. Just take your time."

Camille stepped out and felt the aluminum flex. "It doesn't seem sturdy."

"It's built to carry someone a lot heavier than you. You can do it."

It took some coaxing and numerous promises that she'd be safe, but eventually Camille began her descent.

She stepped into the cold water. "Oh," she cried. "The cold hurts." She pumped her heels up and down, alternately bringing each ankle clear of the water.

Daniel took her by the hand. "Come on. It rises a bit just ahead and there won't be any water there." He had only come prepared for the conditions he was familiar with years ago and the unanticipated water brought something else to mind. There might have been another cave-in since he was last here. If that were the case, their adventure would come to an abrupt end.

Daniel led the way with the flashlight's beam bouncing off the walls. The mineshaft seemed darker than Daniel remembered. His shoulder brushed against the old familiar boulder and dampness from it found its way to his skin. Tremors rolled up his spine. Camille fell into him from behind. He steadied her with a hand and they carried on up the passage.

"Sorry, about that. I was still thinking about my feet."

Daniel smiled. "This is where I reburied Grundpark after I found him the first time. His bones are still scattered around here. McMaster took everything else."

Camille scooted to the opposite wall and inched behind Daniel. To his left the beginning of a passage loomed. Daniel waved the beam into the shaft. "It was a mine before it was anything else. There's no telling how much ore might be left. I don't think Grundpark did very much digging after he found something a little more interesting."

"Do we have to go down there?"

"No. We want to go around the other side of this rock."

Camille sighed.

Daniel led the way, the supporting beams like strands of humanity winding into the dark. In contrast to the dark stone and earth, they seemed to have been installed only days earlier rather than years in the past.

"I can't believe you did all of this yourself," Camille said from the darkness behind him.

"I can't believe it myself." A shiver ran across the nape of his neck and he realized he'd whispered it.

The scenery remained unchanging until the passage terminated at an intersection where the stonework was remarkably more refined than anything they'd passed through thus far.

"Did you dig this out too?" Camille said.

"No. But it's a mystery I'd love to be able to solve. I would give anything to understand these passages … who built them and where those people came from. It's not far now … just down this way." Daniel waved her toward the right artery. "This is where Grundpark spent his final years. I don't know how long he stayed down here, but this was where he lived for a long time," he said as he walked into the open chamber that was once Grundpark's home.

Daniel's light shone about the room, slow, silent, this way and that … it was a timeless feeling, until ….

Camille screamed. Daniel jumped, whipped around and followed her gaze with the beam. Light fell up upon a human form slouched forward, its back against the wall.

Daniel drew Camille close, letting his light rest on the humped remains. Who could it be? There had been no ladder leading down and there were no lights. All the equipment had been removed. It could not be McMaster. McMaster would never have the balls to climb down the beams and wade through the dark. Daniel inched toward the slumped figure.

"We should leave," Camille said.

"I've lived half my life down here. Everything's fine. Whoever this is can't hurt anyone anymore."

A whimper escaped from Camille, but Daniel strode forward, unafraid and barely aware of the woman behind him or the terror that captivated her. The dark had always been his friend. He pushed the form to the side and the body splayed out on the ground. Although bloated and rotting, it was unmistakably McMaster. The cool air acted as a natural refrigerator making it impossible to tell how long he had been dead. Daniel grabbed McMaster's coat at the shoulders and dragged the body away from the door. As he pulled, one of McMaster's legs twisted oddly to the side immediately telling a story about his climb into the well. Impotent hatred raged inside Daniel. He was glad Camille could not see the grimace contorting his features as he fought to contain himself.

What had driven a man who feared closed spaces and the dark to come down in this hole to die? Then it occurred to him. McMaster had lost everything. His farm had been repossessed before he could exploit his find. With any luck, Mrs. McMaster had fled before he had a chance to hurt her. Even in her coldness, she had been more human than

McMaster ever was. Unfortunately, her story was bound to remain a mystery.

The truth dawned on Daniel. McMaster had died believing that Daniel was on the other side of the door. He would have believed it was Daniel's fault he'd lost everything. That thought must have been infuriating. Daniel wondered how far had he climbed down the lattice before he fell. With his leg broken, how long had he lain in the water before embarking on his excruciating journey? And once at his destination, how long had it taken before he took his last breath? Daniel hoped it had been a ghastly and long, drawn-out time. He mused it would have been better, more gratifying, to find him alive … suffering in that state of utter despair.

Daniel pulled McMaster's jacket open and began to rifle through his pockets.

"Oh my gosh … Daniel, what are you doing?"

Daniel didn't look up. "He has some things that belong to me."

"But you're stealing from a dead man!"

"I'm not stealing anything. This bastard took more from me than I could ever hope to take from him."

Grundpark had decided to live next to the object of his worship. McMaster had decided to die beside it. Would that make the items that the two men carried to their deaths markedly different? Daniel shuffled items into his pockets as he found them. He could always throw out what he deemed useless later. When he had run his hands through McMaster's coat, breast and trouser pockets, and was sure there was nothing left behind, he sat back against the door, which, although still standing glorious, was overshadowed by the cold death surrounding it. Daniel dropped his face into his hands. "Why?" he yelled, but his muffled pleas bounced from wall to ceiling and were eventually absorbed by the dank earth and pitiless stone.

Camille moved to his side and wrapped her arms around his shaking shoulders. "It's over now. He can't hurt you anymore."

"He should have suffered more. I owed him that." Daniel took a calming breath. "I'm fine. You're right. It's over." He stood up, fumbled through his pack for his camera and, taking care that McMaster was not in any of the frames, he began to snap pictures of the door. What a moment ago had been an exciting adventure had now turned into a dreary escapade.

"Are you ready?"

Camille nodded.

Daniel aligned key and lock.

"We don't have to do this, Daniel. I believe you. You know that, don't you?"

Camille had misinterpreted everything. She had no idea how he felt and her presumptions only made matters worse. "I'm fine, really. And we do have to do this. I need some pictures because I don't know when I'll be able to come back."

"What's in there?"

"You'll see."

Daniel turned the key. The mechanism glided in smooth precision, just as it had the last time he was here. The numbers came to his mind as if the paper was in his hand. With a final click the door swung inward awakening memories that seemed like dreams now. The glint from the flashlight got inside and the room jumped to life. The place was ancient beyond human existence. Daniel wondered what it must have been like when a torch and not a flashlight caused the crystals to respond. Camille flinched as though she had never seen the like before. Daniel knew that in a way she hadn't. If the light from a single crystal had seemed unbearable, the light from a million would be like standing inside the sun.

Daniel took several pictures. Sadly the result was what he had expected. The photos came out white. The brilliance of the scene before them could not be translated. Individual crystals were obliterated by their own light and Daniel knew the only way to capture them on film was to wait it out and take pictures them when their charge began to fade.

He led Camille across the wooden bridge. The stone he used to break a swath of crystals still lay on the planks. He bent down to show her the broken shards, but the crystals had regenerated. He expected to see the residue, but there was none.

They meandered along the walkway, shielding their eyes from the brightness. Daniel halted when he reached the opposite door. "Come up here," he coaxed Camille. "I want you to see something." He took Camille's hand and placed it on the surface of the door allowing her to feel ridges that must surely be microscopic. He let his memory guide him, with her hand beneath his. "There," he said. "Just push right there."

Camille gasped as her hand disappeared into the door.

"You should find a kind of doorknob. Can you feel it?"

Camille responded with a nod and turned the handle. As the door swiveled, light poured into the passage beyond. "The walls," she said, touching them, "they are unbelievably sleek. This is impossible. Daniel, it's as if we've crossed a threshold into an ancient, and … until now, undiscovered world."

Daniel nodded, said nothing and, following his previous footprints in the ageless dust, led the way. They were as clear and defined as the first day he'd shuffled through, reminding him of pictures of man's first steps on the moon. There had been nothing to disturb these or erode them away. He wondered how long they would remain. Would they still be here a thousand years from now?

The passage wound downward and ended abruptly as it opened in a domed chamber dwarfing Grundpark's living quarters. Daniel stopped, allowing Camille to step ahead of him. She entered the sacred hall, her body trembling. A small noise escaped her; neither a moan nor a sigh. It bounced from wall to wall, sounding amplified at first, before finally fading away into the dark recesses of the hall. The walls were as glassy as the stone in the previous passage and the dome could be nothing less than a perfect hemisphere. Camille stood in awe.

Daniel pulled the pack from his shoulders and laid it on the ground. With camera in hand he began his examination. Individual images, each framed in stone wound around the room like an ancient art gallery. Each casing began at the knee and ended somewhere above his head. Daniel circled the room snapping one picture after another, marveling at the workmanship of each. Every panel was an intricate mosaic made of small, flat stones, brilliant in color and polished to a shine. Each was cut in such a way that the small joints were the lines that delineated individual leaves, imperfections in the bark of the trees and even the delicate facial features of every elaborate figure. Some of the images depicted peaceful times, while others portrayed scenes of war. On those, even the scowls on the faces of the victorious had been forever captured in a medium infinitely more permanent than ink or dye, far exceeding the capability of the Egyptians or the Mayans.

Camille, standing close behind Daniel, tapped his shoulder. "Do you think we could go soon?"

"I won't be long. Just hang on, okay?" Another flash lit up the room.

"It's creepy down here. And I can't get that awful corpse out by the entrance out of my mind. How much longer do you think it will take?"

"It'll take as long as it takes. I thought you would be excited to see this." Daniel could feel familiar anger rise.

"I was. I've seen it and now I want to go."

The girl was behaving ridiculously. After having spent years below the surface there was one thing Daniel knew better than anyone; there was less to be afraid of down here than anywhere. The terror in Camille's voice was obvious. "I don't know what your problem is, but you can leave whenever you want. I'm not going until I'm finished."

"What's wrong with you? Why are you treating me this way?"

"Nothing's wrong with me!" Daniel's face turned red. "Why are *you* being so irrational?"

"Irrational? There's a man dead outside and we're the only ones who know he's there. You don't think that's a tad worrisome? And I can't believe you're not bothered by it."

"Trust me. No one will care. And for your information, I wish we hadn't found him dead." A long silence was a loud punctuation to his next statement. "I wish I could have killed him myself."

The look on Camille's face was enough to see that she was appalled, but he was beyond caring. He turned his back, said, "Do whatever you want," and continued snapping pictures.

"I will," she said, and stormed up the passage.

Having finished photographing the sculptured art, Daniel explored the rest of the space, taking in every detail. The floor was a seamless flat stone. In the center, the altar was an inverted pyramid. It seemed to be the only element in the room besides the art. Daniel moved to the table, snapping pictures from all directions. Below the edifice he found the only other variation in the room, a wooden grate set into the floor. He shone his light downward through the slats, but could see nothing but darkness below. Maybe it was an ancient storm drain. There was no way to tell and no time to surmise. Daniel consulted his watch. The Bernards would stay at the theatre for a little time after the movie, but there was no guessing how long. Preferring to err on the side of caution, he gathered his pack, tucked the camera inside it and began his trek out with barely a thought of where Camille had disappeared to.

The light pouring from the crystal chamber was still blinding as he entered. It wasn't until he almost tripped on her that he found Camille hunkered on the path, her body trembling and her eyes staring blankly into the light.

"I thought you decided to leave?"

Camille did not respond.

"Hey, I'm over it. Let's go." He prodded her gently on the shoulder, but Camille's body merely rocked a bit and then returned to center, reminding Daniel of a weighted punching bag he'd played with as a kid.

Daniel bent. Camille's eyes were wide and unseeing. Was she crying? It didn't appear so. Although tears trickled down her cheeks in a steady stream, her jaw was slack and her face emotionless. "Camille," he said with more concern, but still there was no reaction. A growing worry replaced his fading anger. Her state seemed comatose and he could think of no explanation for it.

He donned his pack and hoisted Camille's slight frame onto his shoulder. He eased through the open door and pushed it closed, shutting the light in … and leaving them in absolute dark. He slapped at his pockets until he found his flashlight and with the beacon in hand he began the walk to safety with his burden. He breathed easier as the distance from the chamber grew and his anger further subsided. Is that what she's become … a burden? he thought as he stood at the base of the

ladder. At the moment it occurred to him, he knew it wasn't true. Camille was so much more than that.

He stepped onto the first rung and pulled himself up, but the extra weight on his shoulders pulled him backward. He stumbled and with only the greatest effort avoided slamming Camille into the wall behind him as he struggled to balance himself. Adjusting her on his shoulder, he leaned forward hugging the ladder to center his weight over the balls of his feet and started up again. He pulled hard with his arms. Thankfully, Camille did not weigh more, as each inch he gained sapped his energy. At the top he managed to roll her onto the ground before hauling himself up the last few steps.

Daniel heaved the ladder up and tossed it to the ground. He'd have to make a separate trip to retrieve it. He stooped and looked into Camille's eyes. Nobody home. Of the considerable rage he had felt earlier, none remained. And for all he knew he was the cause of her state. His back groaned as he hefted her from the ground, this time choosing to carry her in his arms rather than over his shoulder. He trudged across the open field and shortly afterward staggered down the empty driveway. He had returned before the Bernards.

He stood inside the entry with knees of jelly. The two flights of stairs looming ahead of him seemed insurmountable. It would require only one step at a time. He counted thirteen. Panting, Daniel dropped Camille onto her bed and she sat there, eyes vacant, with her hands limp in her lap. After removing her shoes, he forced her into a supine position. Obediently, Camille allowed herself to fall then pulled her knees to her chest and stared at the wall. The sound of an approaching vehicle drew Daniel away.

When William and Phoebe walked into the house, Daniel was lounging in front of the television watching an old black and white film. They said their pleasant hellos and he was relieved they didn't ask the title of the movie because he wouldn't have been able to tell them.

"Where's Camille," Phoebe asked.

"The bus ride must have finished her. She said she was beat and turned in early."

"It is getting late. I think we're off to bed too. We'll see you in the morning." William left the room with Phoebe in tow, leaving Daniel to fret in solitude. He pulled a cushion under his head and his thoughts turned inward.

How many friends had he had in his life—one, or two … *maybe*? And those were short-lived. But Camille had been different. She had been his only real companion and she wanted nothing more than to share his dreams. Now she lay in peril and all because of his senselessness. Had he not sent her away in anger, she would not be in this state.

The house was dark and quiet when Daniel stood to go upstairs. He passed Camille's bedroom and a weak call from her stopped him. Relief flooded in and his chest ached because of it. "Camille?" he said, making quick steps to her side.

"Where am I?"

"Shhhh … you're in your room … at the Bernards'."

There was silence for a long time before Camille said more. "Did you get all the pictures you wanted?"

"Yes … I did. You need to rest."

Camille nodded. "You were angry."

"Yes. I was. I'm sorry."

"You're never mad."

"I am, can be … but hardly ever like that." Even now the emotions he felt within the temple seemed surreal. His behavior had been reprehensible. *Will Camille ever be able to forgive me for my coldness?*

"Yes."

What? He looked close at her. "Yes?"

"Yes. You were an ass, but I forgive you."

"But … but, I … I didn't say anything."

"Daniel, stop it. Be nice."

Daniel gave her an awkward apologetic smile. "What do you remember from the temple?"

There was a long pause before Camille answered. "I remember being scared … really scared. And you were angry, but I didn't know why."

Daniel raised a self-incriminating eyebrow.

"And you were mean and you wouldn't listen. Then I walked away. That's the last thing I remember … until now."

"Are you tired?"

"No. I feel fine. I'm glad we're out of there though. Daniel, you were right. It *was* amazing."

Have I imagined it? I'm sure I said nothing. Maybe a little rest will help me to figure things out, he thought, hoping for a response. He waited on the off chance she'd heard him, but if she did, she said nothing. "I think I'd …," he started, but when he turned around, Camille was asleep. "Apparently you weren't as fine as you thought," he said as he pulled a blanket over her before retiring.

CHAPTER 50

Daniel slept. Images swam behind his fluttering lids. His dreaming eyes snapped open. He knew he was seeing the world through McMaster's eyes.

He stood in an open field and wrapped his arms around his chest to keep the warmth in. So cold, he thought, looking up at the night sky. A full moon reflected off a fresh skiff of snow, bathing the field in strange daylight. The well loomed before him. The heaps of earth were gone, the trailer was gone and so was the high fence. With trepidation McMaster moved forward. He stood before the gaping hole and wiped the sweat from his eyes. Fear coursed through him. Acidic vomit rose in his throat and he choked it back then spit to clear his mouth.

Standing at the brink of the abyss, he looked down. The lift no longer filled the hole. He knelt in the snow and it melted through his pants. The cold wet seeped into his knees. Out of breath he lay on his stomach and inched his legs into the well. He slithered out until he suddenly bent at the waist and the weight of his legs pulled him down. He clawed at the frozen ground and caught himself before he fell. His feet dangled in the dark and when he was calm enough, he felt around with outstretched toes until he touched wood. Hoarfrost on the beams sparkled in the moonlight, a dazzling warning of the danger of ice. None of that mattered. Terror was a shadow to his need to return to the door.

He crept along angled beams, clutching at them as a frightened child clings to his parent. *His foot slipped.* He pedaled for purchase until it finally caught in the crux of two beams. He rested there … longer than his body needed, but not long enough to regain his confidence. That was already lost forever. Slowly he bent at his knees and eased into a squatting position, crouching for the impossibly long step to the next junction. Like an inchworm he worked his way into the well. The moon was no longer directly above, but he could see the gray ice below. Almost to the bottom now, he thought.

He slid his hand along the beam when unexpectedly it jammed into something sharp, barely enough to break his skin, but he jerked from the pain. Instinctively, he released the beam. His lone hand, unable to support his bulk, tore free. As he fell backward, his foot lodged in a junction of beams. It carried the weight of his body until with a yank his boot came free. He landed in a heap at the bottom of the well. Though his foot ached, he was thankful that he hadn't hurt himself too seriously.

McMaster readied to stand, attributing the throb in his calf to the stress it had undergone. He rose to discover an unbearable pain shooting up his leg and into his back. He dropped to the ground, gasping while the cold numbed his knees and palms. It wasn't until the pain in his leg had begun to subside that his predicament registered. "I'm going to die down here," he said. It had been his unspoken intent until now. The well was the noose around his neck. Once he got down, he knew there was no going back. What little chance he may have had of changing his mind was now gone. Hunger and thirst could no longer overcome his fear and drive him from his chosen resting place.

McMaster screamed as he rolled onto his back and he screamed again with every inch as he dragged himself down the long passage. He stopped to catch his breath and though the feeling had long since left his hands, his arms shook and sweat poured from his brow. No hurry. No worries. I've got the rest of my life, he thought, and pulled himself another few inches toward his goal.

He followed the wall and stopped only when he found the cold metal of the door. He propped himself against it and rested.

***

Daniel awoke. If the pain and fear that he had experienced in the dream had in any way been a measure of what McMaster had felt every day, maybe the man had come close to paying for his sins. Whatever McMaster had taken from him, he had paid karma a hundred fold. Daniel's pity stopped there. He was glad the man was dead, but nothing could change the fact that in dying, McMaster had robbed him of satisfaction.

CHAPTER 51

Daniel rose with the morning rays to discover Camille was not in her bed. It was freshly made. Had she gotten up early and gone back to the well without telling him? It was a fleeting thought, expelled by the sound of rustling paper somewhere below. He found Camille in the kitchen sipping coffee and reading a magazine with a stack of others beside her. "How long have you been up?"

"A while. I've read these," she said, pointing to the pile. "I couldn't sleep."

"Maybe we should talk." He was growing concerned, and his tone bore witness to it. "Something strange is going on. I don't understand it at all and you seem oblivious to everything that's happening."

"It's crazy. I know I should be mad at you, but I feel ...," she searched her mind for the word, "... euphoric."

"Camille it *is* crazy. That's not how you should be feeling at all. As soon as we got to the well you were afraid. We hardly got inside and you could barely stand it. We found McMaster and that just about killed you. And from there on it only got worse.

"As for me, in the beginning I wasn't angry. But then I saw McMaster and I couldn't control myself. At first I was mad because of him and then I got increasingly enraged. I don't know when, but it changed, and then I was furious with you. I knew that I was being mean, but ... I couldn't help it. After that you left and when I found you, you were in some kind of trance. I had to carry you out of there."

"I remember all of that too ... all except the part where you carried me out. Of course you were angry. Who wouldn't be after all you've been through. As for me? I don't know why I was so scared. It seems so silly now that I think back on it. We should go back."

"I've got everything I need. We don't need to go back." *Everything except the ladder.*

"You have to go back."

"Why?" He turned a hand up.

"You left the ladder behind," she said with an impish glint.

"I do have to go back, but you don't have to come with me."

"We'll see."

Daniel traipsed across the open field. The fact that Camille was close behind was the only testament necessary to show who lost the argument. The ladder lay in the grass where he had left it, the silver of the aluminum easy enough to discern in the green clover. Daniel bent to retrieve it.

"Just one more time, Daniel. Please?" Camille pleaded.

Daniel raised a palm and wrinkled his forehead. "Why would you want to risk it? It didn't go so well for you the last time."

She shook her head, scratched her forehead. "I think it was me. I think it didn't go so well because of us."

"What makes you think it'll be different?"

"There won't be any surprises … just like it was for you all that time."

"Surprises?"

She nodded. "I think you're right. There is a reaction and I think you saved my life. But we can control this. I know it."

He sighed. "What are we doing, then?"

Camille looked into the well. "We're just going to have a look around. Check out all the tunnels. I want to see everything."

"What if something happens?"

"You'll be fine. I already know that. You can keep an eye on me." She looked up and found his eyes. "We can learn something from this."

Daniel lowered the ladder and started down. Camille was climbing down before he had reached the bottom and was with him only moments later. "What did you do with Camille?"

"Nothing. Nothing at all. She's back."

And she was.

Daniel led her to the stone and was about to pass through the narrow opening when Camille stopped him. Oh my gosh, we're not even there yet. Is she struggling already?

"Don't worry. I'm not afraid. We haven't been down there, yet," she said, pointing to the side passage.

What kind of sign had he given to allow her to read him so accurately? "How did you know that was what I was thinking?"

"Daniel, I didn't need to read your mind or hear your thoughts. I just know you."

Daniel's lips raised in a minute smile as he brushed passed and led her into the secondary passage.

There wasn't much to show, or see for that matter, so the detour was brief. He showed her the second side tee and the end. Within fifteen minutes of entering the mine, Daniel and Camille stood before the bejeweled door once more. Looks like McMaster hasn't moved, Daniel thought, a smug smirk on his lips.

CHAPTER 52

Camille stood outside the great stone door mesmerized by its beauty yet struggling with the fear it invoked. To her left McMaster sprawled and, although he was dead, the stories that Daniel told somehow gave him life. The feeling she was living a ghost story would not go away.

She looked down at her shaking hand, willing it to quiet … needing it to be still. Had the confidence she felt upon entering been a figment of her imagination? It couldn't have been.

Daniel put a hand on her shoulder. "Are you all right?"

"I'm fine. Just give me a minute."

"We can go whenever you want." He patted her.

"I know. Just give me a minute," she hissed.

Daniel waited.

"Okay. I think we can go in now. I just want to get inside the stone." She looked to Daniel.

His eyes narrowed as he peered at her. *You* think *we can go in?*

Camille caught her breath. Daniel lips hadn't stirred. It was no illusion. His lips had not moved and yet she heard him in her mind. It was as if the mechanics of her hearing had been bypassed and the message had gone straight to her brain. Fear became excitement. She wondered if there was a psychosis that would describe her alternating feelings of terror and exhilaration.

Daniel inserted the key and sent it through its series of turns. Soon the door was open.

Camille pushed by.

Could you get any ruder?

Camille knew instinctively that he hadn't said it. She ignored the meaning of what Daniel thought and instead chose to listen. *Thoughts are so much faster than words.* Daniel's ideas poured into her mind. First, information from the surface of his brain flooded through and then his memories and even his knowledge. It would have taken a lifetime to assimilate all the information one mind could store with the slowness of words. It was as if she were living his entire life in mere moments. Complete images, feelings and sounds poured in. Daniel was an open container and she could have it all. But it was more than a deluge. There was pressure. Information forced its way in with no valve to slow it. Camille struggled to keep up. Daniel's mind was running full out and hers was too. For a moment she understood that the stones were merely acting as a catalyst but, unlike light, she could not close her eyes against the onslaught. Two minds were filling a space meant for one.

Camille told her legs to run. She collided into something, but blindly pushed it aside. She could only hope her legs were responding. She ran. With her mind feeling like white noise, her data-overload daze was brought to a shocking halt as she crashed into something and fell to the ground.

CHAPTER 53

Could you get any ruder? Daniel thought as Camille brushed passed him. She went just a few steps inside before she turned toward him. He watched as her eyes grew wide. A grin spread across her face as if there was a joke that only she understood. But the grin dropped and she grew serious. Her eyes were focused on nothing and Daniel knew that wherever she had gone the day before she was going there again.

He stepped forward to take her by the hand and lead her out, but she began to shamble toward him simultaneously. She bumped into him, managed to correct herself and then fell to the ground outside the chamber. Daniel tried to help her to her feet, but her mind was elsewhere … and that same haunting look filled her eyes. Daniel picked her up once more and raced out of the cavern. He stopped at the stone half blocking the passage, set her on the cool earth … and waited.

Camille's eyes fluttered open. The vacant look disappeared. "Hey, do I have a lump on my head?"

"No. Why would you?"

"I figured I would have a knot from the wall I ran into."

"You didn't run into a wall. You staggered out of there and then fell down. I carried you here."

"Really?" She was quiet for a while and then continued. "Daniel, I know this is going to sound a bit crazy, but I want to go back … without you."

Are you crazy? Daniel thought, with a vigorous shake of the head. "Camille, that's not happening. We're done here and I'm not risking this any further."

Camille widened her stance, planted both hands on her hips. "It's not your risk."

"It is. Ignoring the fact that I don't know what I'd do without you, what would I tell everyone if this symptom, this never-seen-before characteristic, was permanent? How would I explain it?" *I love you,* he thought.

"I love you too."

He jerked. "I *never* said that out loud."

"I know you didn't."

It was Daniel's turn to be astonished. "You said being able to remember everything that I read was amazing. What you have going on, walks all over that."

"It's nothing. It's almost gone already. It feels like shadows in my head … dreams that were never mine."

He sighed, looked down, then straight at her. "Camille, I ... I don't understand."

"I don't understand much either, but there was a moment of clarity, like what's happening right now. You've got to listen while I still remember some of it.

"It was like everything about you tried to get inside my mind all at once. At first it was nothing, just kind of fun. That didn't last very long, though. It was too much, like too much electricity in a circuit. Or maybe it was like a computer with not enough memory. One thing is for sure. It was definitely an overload of some kind."

"Why would you want to go back in there?"

"Because it wasn't the crystals that I was overloaded with, Daniel." She got direct eye contact. "It was you."

"Now that's a comforting thought. I didn't think you could get too much of me." Daniel winked.

She gave him a playful punch on the arm. "You know that's not what I meant. I don't know what the limitations of the crystals are, but whatever they are, they're a lot greater than ours. And that's the problem. I think that's why there hasn't been anyone here for eons. People just aren't that strong."

"If you believe that's true, then why in this godforsaken world do you want to go back?"

"Because I know that *you* are the reason. I don't think I'd experience anything if you weren't close."

He hunched his shoulders. "Why doesn't it happen to me too, then?"

Camille shrugged. "It happens to me. That's all I know."

Daniel paced. The risk was too great. How much could one person's mind withstand? His curiosity and need for understanding were great as well. If only a little common sense could prevail. Camille seemed to think it would be all right, and he did want to know. "Five minutes. That's all you'll get. After five minutes I'm coming to get you."

Camille snatched the light and was off, a firefly bouncing through the dark.

Daniel glanced at his watch and began to count down the seconds. It would take one of those minutes for her to get there. In four he'd go after her whether she was on her way back or not. Agonizing seconds wore on. The excruciating silence was worse than any pain he'd been subjected to. Why had he agreed to let her go?

Just then the passage brightened. She was returning.

"Well?"

"Nothing," she said.

"Nothing? What do you mean?"

"Just a second. Let me concentrate." Camille's fingertips migrated to her temples. She stood that way for a long time. "Nothing. Everything's fine."

"How would you know?"

"Trust me. I'd know. I think I understand something about these crystals."

"And what do you think that is?" That sounded harsh. It wasn't what I intended. Camille could have knowledge of the crystals, but shouldn't it be my knowledge first? Having spent so long in the proximity of the crystals wasn't it reasonable that I have the greater understanding?

"I'm different from you."

"What do you mean?"

"I'm different from you and that's why we respond differently. There's something in my makeup that's different from yours."

"That's it?"

"It's everything. The other thing is that people are too weak. I think of it like feedback. I start to get a little scared and then I get near the crystal. Then I get a little more scared and the crystal makes that fear stronger. Pretty soon I'm too terrified to function. If I control myself, it seems like I can control the crystal."

Daniel's head was in a slow wag. "I don't think you control the crystal at all. I think you just control yourself."

The truth of Daniel's statement seemed obvious to her the moment he said it. "You're right. That's exactly what happens!"

Camille helped pull the ladder up and together they returned it to the hooks in William's shop. The rest of the weekend shot by and before long Daniel found he was kissing Camille good-bye once more. It was an unpleasant and long ride home and he prayed that she would be all right. He watched the bus as it crept up the hill that led out of town. It may have been crawling, but it was still too fast and too soon for Daniel's liking.

The remainder of the summer passed, filled with loneliness, but otherwise without incident.

CHAPTER 54

Millenburg sat hunched with the two essays side by side on the desk between bent elbows. His clasped hands created the apex of a triangle which supported his chin. Last year, he'd asked the students if he could hang on to them. They stood apart. The 'A+' scrawled across the top of each made its statement. The paper on the left belonged to Daniel Sterling. The one on the right belonged to Camille Robertson.

With a nod to himself he took up a notepad. *These are the two. They'll be perfect.* He'd need to talk to them, but anything he didn't write down he soon forgot. He scribbled a few words that were barely legible. Doctors and professors must have this in common, he thought, and slapped a yellow Post-it onto each essay.

***

Camille and Daniel sat where they always did. After class Millenburg wandered toward Camille and Daniel, speaking generally to the class about his expectations for the year. He paused momentarily to lay a note on Daniel and Camille's desks.

"I'd like to meet with the two of you. Can you see me for a moment after class today to arrange an appointment?"

Daniel nodded and Millenburg sallied back to the front of the room, lecturing as he went. Daniel read his note.

"What does it say," Camille asked.

"Same thing that he just said."

"Mine too." She gave him an 'oh my god, what's up?' look, and he responded with a shrug. They'd have to wait and see.

Dr. Millenburg arranged papers and gathered his materials as he waited until the lecture hall was nearly empty and then turned to the two lingering students. "I'm astounded by the work you've done."

'Astounded' did not really indicate good or bad, but then again, Dr. Millenburg wasn't frowning. That was a good thing.

"I'd like to talk to you about some of your ideas and see if we can't get you into doing some work that will do a better job of capitalizing on your talents. Can you come to my office this afternoon?"

Daniel answered for both of them. "That shouldn't be a problem."

"Will one o'clock work for you?"

"We can do that." Neither of them had classes then. In fact there were no classes scheduled for Friday afternoons and Daniel knew that Millenburg was just as aware of that fact as he and Camille were.

"Thanks so much, Doctor Millenburg," said Camille. She gave Daniel's sleeve a tug as she headed up the aisle toward the door. She waited until they were outside before she said anything further. "Daniel … this could be that opportunity you've been hoping for. You know that? He said he wanted to put our talents to good use."

"I hope so, but you can't dismiss the possibility that he's looking for a classroom aid. He didn't exactly say which of our talents he wanted to put to use."

"No, he didn't. But I have to tell you that I'm pretty sure that's not what he meant."

"What are you talking about?"

"Well, I've been working at my skills. I'm not sure about it, but I'm trying to trust my feelings on these things. I don't think he's looking for an aide. I think he's going to ask us to be involved in something exciting."

"That's your gut instinct?"

"Yeah, I guess so. That's my feeling. I've read that's the way it always has been, thinkers and feelers, but you're not the *only* one who can *think*, you know."

Daniel chuckled. "Did your feelers get hurt?"

Camille punched him as he pushed the door open and they entered the student lounge. By the time they'd finished eating it was time for their meeting.

CHAPTER 55

The hallways were narrow in the faculty building. Daniel remembered the strange difference. Spaces provided for students were generally wide and welcoming. Apparently the same consideration had not been given to the professors. Here the offices were crammed together and it seemed as if the powers-that-be allotted no more than the space necessary for a couple of filing cabinets, a desk and a small space for seating. He recognized Dr. Millenburg's rectangular name plaque and knocked on the door.

Millenburg called from inside, inviting them in. He picked up a pen and tapped it on his desk. "I'm going to get straight to the point. I wanted to tell you that, even considering your age and experience, your research represents some of the best I've ever read. One of our many philanthropists has provided an endowment with this project specifically in mind. I thought that you two might like to help me with a unique opportunity."

"What kind of opportunity are you talking about?" Daniel said.

"People have wanted to believe for centuries that the properties of crystals extend beyond their obvious physical attributes. I've been given the task of heading a project to determine whether or not any known crystals have any characteristics beyond what we already know."

Daniel said, "Of course we want to be involved." Camille nodded her agreement.

"Good then. I've made the arrangements and the facility is ready." Millenburg said, producing keys and two white plastic cards from his desk drawer. "Come with me."

Daniel and Camille followed.

Dr. Millenburg led them into the basement, stopped at the first door, inserted a key and opened it. Inside he swept his palm across a bank of switches. Fluorescent lights flickered to life. They were inside a sterile white room with a low ceiling. There was a workbench along one wall and a rolling worktable in the center.

"This is where we'll be setting up the lab. I know there's not much here, but that will change come Monday, when the real work will start. Here. After-hours you'll need this passkey to get into the building and here's a key for the lab. I need to get back to the office, but stay as long as you like. We'll start after the weekend. Get plenty of rest. This might be the kind of big adventure everyone dreams of." Millenburg left the room.

Daniel and Camille wandered through the empty room for a bit. There wasn't much to see, but it was exciting just the same. "We should get going," Daniel said after a few minutes. They locked the door behind them and Daniel glanced at his watch. "Let's get to the library before it closes."

***

In the weeks that followed, the empty storage room filled. Equipment arrived, followed soon after by specialists to install it. While technicians furnished the lab, Daniel and Camille familiarized themselves with the apparatus. 'There won't be a university in the country with a geology lab that will compare,' Millenburg often said, and Daniel began to believe it as well as he stood over a crate labeled MS7.

"What's that?" Camille said from behind him.

"According to this," he said, pointing to the label, "it's a seventh generation multi-sensor. I think it's exactly what we've been dreaming about."

CHAPTER 56

Camille worked across the room from Daniel, polishing and preparing samples. Her cotton gloves ensured she would leave no fingerprints on the quartz crystal as she placed it with care on a stainless steel tray.

"Camille, put the crystal into the crucible whenever you're ready," Daniel said.

Camille swiveled toward the keyboard, selected the appropriate program, typed her password and tapped the enter key. She punched in a series of instructions and a robotic arm swung on its base beginning its predetermined journey. Hydraulic clamps closed on the quartz shard, maneuvered it into the testing compartment, placed it on the receptacle, and then retracted. The glass door of the MS7 slid closed. Daniel glanced at the pressure gauge and watched the needle drop. He waited until the vacuum was complete and then flipped a switch. The apparatus hummed. A look at another meter confirmed that two thousand volts bombarded the crystal. A timer counted down the seconds. When the LCD displayed zero, the humming ceased and the machine went silent. Daniel stood mute while he scanned a second set of readouts. "Damn!"

Camille shot him a look. "What is it?"

"This is the last of the crystals to go through the residual current test. According to all of the instruments … there's nothing to measure." Daniel flopped into his chair with a thud. His shoulders slumped forward and he pounded his forehead with his fist. "Hell, you'd think one of these crystals would respond!" he yelled at no one in particular.

At first Camille allowed him his frustration, but when his pouting continued, she tried to quash it. "Any ideas?" It was the only thing she could think of to say. She knew it wasn't helpful, but anything seemed better than the growing silence spawned by Daniel's unprovoked aggravation. Still, she was surprised at his reply.

"No! I don't have any ideas!" he said, slamming his hands onto the desk. "Do you?"

His glare burned into her and she wondered at moments like these whether he liked her at all. His angry outbursts had all but become commonplace. And although they usually subsided as quickly as they began, it didn't change the fact that they were hurtful.

"Listen, Camille, I'm really sorry. I shouldn't take my frustrations out on you."

Give yourself a slap girl, Camille thought. He does this to you all the time. "I'm outta here, Daniel. Sort it out on your own." She stormed up the stairs and managed to get through the door before he had a chance to say what she knew would be coming. Even as she crashed through the doors and onto the campus grounds, something unintelligible wafted from the depths of the basement, but she ignored it. He'd need to do something more than offer a lame-ass apology from a hundred feet away. She ran out to the parking lot.

CHAPTER 57

Daniel watched Camille run out. Why couldn't anything go the way he planned? "Son of a bitch," he said to the empty room and flung a pen into the waste bin. The phrase flowed out in easy rhythm as if he'd been saying it his whole life. 'Son-of-a-bitch.' How had he come to own those words after all these years? When he thought he had finally put the past behind him, it seemed to sneak back when he least expected it. *McMaster, when will you leave me alone?* Even Daniel's angry outbursts were reminiscent of the man he had hated all these years. What inherent weakness is it that causes me to behave in ways I detest?

Daniel stared at the display. The zeros mocked him. He felt fury rise and he grimaced against it. How many times had he lashed out in the past month? Four? Five? How many times had he managed to keep it in check? Twenty? Was he on the losing end of a battle with his temper?

Hopelessness filled him as he perused the empty lab. How desolate it seemed. He was more than alone. In ways it was worse than being a slave. He had been abandoned. He shrugged away those feelings as well and began the nightly routine of powering down the lab. Maybe tomorrow would bring new answers. He let out a sarcastic chuckle. He'd been telling himself that for weeks and still disappointment flavored every day. He turned out the lights. He was becoming an emotional misfit and learning to control it was beyond him.

The night air was crisp and cold. He breathed deep and the wisps of cobwebs that clouded his thinking eased their hold. He walked, staring at a patch of ground between his toes and forced himself to look up when he realized he wasn't paying attention to where he was going. No insects hovered in the halos of the streetlamps. Much too cold for them, he thought. But the stars seemed more tenacious. Even against the city lights, the brightest shone through. Daniel stuffed his hands up to his wrists in his pockets and ambled home.

CHAPTER 58

Camille's early arrival at the lab the following morning was no accident. She managed to avoid Daniel the previous day. Let him be the one to walk into the uncomfortable situation he created, she thought. The weekend had been long and silent. He hadn't called and she had no intention of being the one to mend the fences he had torn down.

The lab was dark and cold. She flicked on light switches and turned the thermostat up. It said the temperature was seventy degrees, but it felt more like fifty. With light to work by and extra heat to replace the cold feeling in her heart, she went to the journals and turned to some of the original entries. She found what she was looking for and began to read.

Purpose: To determine whether any known crystals possess latent properties or whether these same crystals retain any residual effects from the bombardment of a variety of wavelengths and energies. See appendix for the breakdown of proposed tests which include, but are not limited to: infrared, ultraviolet, x-ray and electrical energy.

Camille flipped forward and found the results of the long-wave infrared testing. They had been conclusive. There was no significant difference between any of the samples, other than to say there was the expected direct correlation between density and the amount of energy radiated during the cooling period. There was nothing in their findings to suggest that any crystal possessed the ability to produce more or less energy than it had absorbed.

Camille picked up the pad they'd used to record the raw data from the electrical tests. The findings were equally dismal. Electrical energy had been converted to heat energy and so the results mimicked the previous tests. If any crystal was able to retain an electrical charge, the results did not show it.

Camille was scouring their notes when Daniel arrived.

"Hey, Camille. You're here already."

She ignored him. Is every guy the same? Leave a mess for a few days and hope it will clean itself. If that was the way the world worked, doing nothing would be the best solution for every problem. She turned another page.

Daniel stood before the MS7. "This isn't right. There's got to be a better way."

"You're damn right this isn't working. I'm sick of it."

"Maybe we can make some modifications."

"Modifications? Is that what you think is going to solve our problem?"

"I don't know. I've tried everything I can think of and this thing is just not working."

"What the hell are you talking about?"

"The MS7—maybe we can modify it. What did you think I was talking about?" *Please don't start talking about the other night. I don't have anything I can say.*

Camille shook her head in resignation. "I'm not talking about anything that's coming out of your mouth and if you've really got nothing to say, then there is no point talking at all."

Daniel stood dumbfounded.

"I'm giving my notice to Doctor Millenburg today. I'll stay until the end of the week. Either you'll realize you don't need me or Millenburg will find someone to replace me. Either way, I'm gone. I need a coffee." With that she left the room leaving Daniel standing in a stupor. *How can we hope to get along if Daniel is unable to talk about his problems?*

Camille kept her word. When Millenburg came to the lab, only moments after she'd returned with her coffee, she told him she was resigning. He did as she expected. He took her aside and asked her to reconsider, but she declined. When he asked her why, she burst into tears and ran out.

CHAPTER 59

Daniel sorted through the pages of his journal. In the two weeks that had passed since Camille's emotional exodus he'd made unprecedented strides. Already the journal was full of carefully documented notes. Only the last few pages remained blank. These he'd saved for the summary of his findings. He had been wise to find a bigger notebook. There would be only one volume to guard; one master diary of his discoveries. The others lined a small shelf over the desk, all but forgotten. Each page contained painful reminders of his failures—failures with Camille and failures in the lab. He'd get back to them when Millenburg demanded it. Until then he could claim that progress was slow and that there were no discoveries warranting report.

Daniel sat at the desk; the equipment in the lab lay quiet and cold. The task of making meaning of the experiments did not require more technology. The thousand authors he'd read lay silent in the stacks. He'd exhausted every source and not one could explain the origins or predict the meaning of anything. That was his task now. He'd have to be the one to make sense of it.

He sat with only the desk lamp glaring at the pages while he jotted down his findings. As he worked, the act of writing down his thoughts brought clarity. The subdued lighting and the silence acted as catalysts. On impulse Daniel sat back in his chair allowing understanding to wash over him. Elation filled him until he could no longer contain himself. He whooped in triumph. His chair rocked back and his yell echoed in the empty room, but it was not enough. He stood and turned on all the lights. He threw his arms in the air and bellowed a primal howl. Still, it was not enough. He raced around the room starting every machine until the room buzzed with electricity. He ran laps around the lab, skipping and yelling. And still ... it was not enough. Exhausted, he sat down and the grin would not leave his face.

And then it did.

None of the work mattered. The crystals didn't matter. Whether or not quartz was anything more than a pretty stone didn't matter. Grundpark and McMaster could not have comprehended. Perhaps the priests that once roamed the ancient halls of the buried temple had understood. Perhaps not. Regardless, everyone was long dead and neither they nor the stones could offer him what he needed. Grundpark and McMaster had sacrificed family for a dream. Daniel would not do the same.

Camille.

Daniel stormed from the lab and up the steps. The campus was quiet … dark again. Time had been lost to him, but now it was all that mattered. He raced along the sidewalk toward Camille's apartment. He ran down McKenzie Avenue and didn't pause at the corner grocery store or the gas station, but turned and ran along Shelbourne toward Cedar Hill Cross Roads. He slowed when he reached the lights of Maude Hunter's Pub and *only* then. He knew Camille's apartment was just a few blocks further up the road. His lungs would burst if he didn't catch his breath.

Daniel strode to the door gulping air. He pressed the buttons and waited. Silence dragged. He buzzed her again and then pulled his sleeve up to check his watch. Just after two in the morning. Oh shit. What the hell am I doing? But before he could go, her groggy voice came over the crackling intercom. "H-hullo? Who iz this?"

Embarrassed, he answered, "It's Daniel, Camille."

Her voice became instantly clear. "Daniel, go home. I don't have anything to say to you."

"Camille. I'm sorry. I didn't realize how late it was. I just ran down here from the school. Can I please talk to you?"

"Why should I listen now?" The crackles added a hissing feel to her demanding query.

"I was wrong." He winced, bit his lower lip. "I know I was wrong and I know I can be me again."

"I'm not sure I ever knew you." A crepitating pause. "Why don't you just go home, Daniel?"

"Please, Camille." His voice had grown quiet. "If I can explain and you still want me to go, I'll leave you alone. I promise. I'll never bother you again."

Daniel waited, searching his mind for something more to say … anything that would change her mind, but there was nothing. Maybe it was better this way. Loving Camille only complicated matters. Perhaps it was time to say good-bye. He reached for the intercom button when the sound of a buzz filled the foyer. Daniel pulled the door open and raced to the elevator. The door had hardly closed before he regretted not taking the stairs. Camille was waiting in the hall when the doors finally opened.

"Camille, thank you so much." Her outstretched palm stopped him before he could say anything more making it clear that any conversation was going to take place in the hall.

"What do you want?" She folded her arms under her breasts.

"To tell you that you were right, that I'm sorry and … to tell you that I figured it out."

No movement. "How is any of this supposed to make me happy?"

Daniel thought about that. She was right, after all. He'd run to tell her all he'd learned, because he wanted to feel better. He wanted her in his life. He'd never considered how she would feel having been woken in the middle of the night. He hadn't considered how she'd feel to find out he'd discovered everything and she hadn't been part of it. Maybe it *was* too late. "You're right. I came to make me happy. I should get going." He sighed, droop shouldered. "Camille, I just wanted you to know that I'm really sorry."

She lingered. Did she want him to sweat? He was. "Oh, come inside."

Daniel stepped in and she closed the door. "So what is so important that can't wait?" She went into the kitchen and filled a mug with water. "I'm having some tea. Do you want anything?"

"Coffee?"

"You'll have to make it yourself. It'll keep me up all night. But I'll make you a tea if that's what you're having."

"I was thinking of instant coffee … sorry."

"Stop saying you're sorry. I'm sick of it already."

Daniel started to apologize again, but caught himself. "Okay."

The microwave beeped and Camille brought out two steaming cups. "So what did you run all the way down here to tell me at two in the morning? You've already apologized and I don't care about that."

"Two things, I guess. I realized what the link is between Grundpark and McMaster."

Camille's eyebrows took a slow journey upward. She said nothing, lifted her cup and blew the steam off the top.

"Please, Camille, just hear me out. Grundpark and McMaster became obsessed with the crystals. They even sacrificed everything just to be near them in the end. They sacrificed their families. You may not be able to believe me just yet, but that won't happen to me. I won't sacrifice you, so please don't give up on me—not yet anyway."

"We'll see. I'm not making any promises I won't keep." The force of her tone wasn't entirely convincing. Her expression softened some. "What's the second thing you wanted to talk about?"

"I understand the crystals now." His voice became animated. "They amplify waves. That's all there is to it."

"That doesn't explain *anything*."

"It explains *everything*. The way the crystal reacts to different wavelengths does vary. For example, the crystals absorb and amplify light. We've seen this clearly with the white light produced by a flashlight, but the same is true of any band of visible light. Bombarded with red light, the crystals intensify it and produce red light. It has a memory, so will continue to produce whatever the last source it received."

"That's not a stretch. You haven't told me anything I couldn't have guessed."

Daniel spun around, came to a halt facing her, leaning forward with both palms in the air, imploring her to *listen*. "This morning I sat in front of my notes and I had an idea. It was a brainwave." He tapped his temple with two fingers. "We have brainwaves!"

"So you're saying that our brainwaves are absorbed by the crystals?"

"*Absolutely.* Once the crystals intensify the waves, they broadcast them back. These waves haven't changed their signature; they've just changed their intensity. Our minds can't tell the difference between the waves that we produce and the ones coming from the crystals. Because of this increased stimulation some of our reasoning capacity has been increased as well. Memory and processing speed are the most obvious changes, but there are others that are not so benign."

Camille's left hand came from under her right breast and folded open toward Daniel. "How do you explain what happened to me?"

"I struggled with that too. My proximity was a requirement for your reaction. With the help of the crystals, your mind was able to assimilate waves that originated from me. Rather than having a positive loop originating from yourself, you ended up on the receiving end of a whole second mind, one that was also in a state of constant excitement. Not unlike a computer, you just crashed. I think your ability to hear what I was thinking was simply a residual effect that occurred as you recovered from the overload."

"There's more, isn't there?"

"Yes." Daniel thrust a forefinger in the air. "Emotion is a real problem. Our emotion is one of our strengths, but in this case it can be detrimental. Since they do not stem from rational thought, once amplified, they become impossible to control. You simply can't reason them away. Those base feelings can consume a person. That's what happened to Grundpark and McMaster. Who knows? Maybe that's what's happened to everyone who came in contact with the crystals. It would explain why the original entrance had been buried."

"You want me to believe that the reason you've been such an asshole is that the rocks made you do it? Daniel, you need counseling." Her arms went back into their folded position.

"That's actually a good idea."

"What?"

"You're absolutely right, Camille. I can't blame my problems on anyone but me; and you shouldn't suffer because of them. Every time I've been angry with you, it has been my failure. I am truly sorry I put you through so much, Camille."

"I think you've had one too many epiphanies for any one man. Maybe it's time you went home."

"Yeah, you're probably right." He paused, pulled on his cheek. "There is one other thing I wanted to ask you though."

"Can it be the last thing?"

"Absolutely. I was hoping you'd reconsider and come back to the lab. I don't want to work with anyone else, and besides, it's not my work anyway. It's our work and it's not the same without you."

"Let me get through tonight, would you?"

"Oh yeah … for sure. Thanks for listening, Camille. You're the only one I can talk to."

His walk home was long and cold. Although he could hear traffic from other parts of the city, only an ambulance passed him, sirens blaring. Daniel crawled into bed, optimistic about the day to come.

CHAPTER 60

Camille swiped her card and pushed through the door. She hesitated at the top of the stairs before starting down, wondering again why she had chosen to come. Daniel had been correct when he said it was her project too. As much as he had been her original inspiration, the project was more a part of her than anything ever had been. So what if Daniel had more intimate knowledge of the temple; it didn't make any of this exclusively his.

She opened the door to the lab and stepped inside. "I want to make something perfectly clear. I didn't come back for you or for anyone else. I'm here for me."

"I'm just glad your back."

"And Daniel … there's just one more thing."

"Anything, Camille. Whatever you want."

"The next time you take your anger out on me, you'll be the one who's leaving." Daniel's silence was enough of an answer. "What do I need to know to get up to speed with things?"

Daniel pushed his journal in her direction.

"Oh, and Daniel, one last thing. Don't expect me to carry on as a glorified assistant. I didn't come back for that either."

Daniel nodded. "Whatever you want," he said as he popped the lid off of a can of black spray paint.

"What are you doing with that?" Daniel had disassembled a sizable portion of the MS7 and arranged the pieces across the length of one of the workbenches. The glass vacuum cabinet from the MS7 lay on splayed newspapers in front of him.

"Just making some minor modifications." Black paint misted from the can covering the once transparent compartment.

"Have you okayed this with Doctor Millenburg?"

Daniel turned the cube and resumed spraying. "No, but when he sees the results, I'm sure he'll be fine with it."

"How is the paint supposed to help?"

"I want to use one of my crystals as an amplifier, but I need to isolate the chamber from outside stimuli in order for it to work."

"An amplifier?"

"Just because our instruments don't measure changes in our sample crystals doesn't mean they don't possess other measurable properties. My crystals are hypersensitive and will increase the intensity of the waves we expose them to. If we run a specific test on an amethyst, let's say, and then expose that to one of my crystals, there might be a reaction. With the help of my crystals, we'd be able to record the event."

"What about putting together some baseline data first?"

He stopped what he was doing, looked at her. "What did you have in mind?"

Camille snatched a tablet and pencil from a nearby desk and began to sketch a chart. "If we use one of your crystals as the norm, we could use those figures to calculate actual levels emitted from our sample substances. If the output for a particular wave is two hundred times the input, we can use that known result to work backwards to discover the input from any crystal we're testing. Then we'd have useful data even if the base measures were so small that the original instruments couldn't detect them."

Daniel put the paint aside to give his undivided attention to Camille's ideas. "I have to finish my improvements on this compartment and then partition it in two sections so that I can stimulate the samples on one side and take readings from the other."

Camille turned the page and began another plan. "We'll need to fabricate a second crucible as well and then it'll be necessary to split the feeds. I can get to work on that while you finish up with — whatever it is you're doing. Maybe by the time you're done, I'll have the cup ready for the other tests."

***

They had worked into the early hours of the morning refusing to leave the lab until most of the work was complete. Daniel entered his apartment too wired to sleep and too tired to do anything else. He knelt at the kitchen sink and reached into the corner until his fingers found his thermos. It would make a perfect container to transport a crystal.

In the darkness of the bathroom, he removed one of the crystals from the lunchbox. Using the serrated edge of a butter knife, he cut through it. The texture was similar to chalk and it was no harder than a macadamia nut. A few chucks broke off of one end. He wrapped them in a cloth and dropped them into the thermos, then returned the rest of the crystals to their place in the lunchbox. The thermos he put on the counter so he wouldn't forget it the following morning.

Daniel slept restlessly and rose before the sun. He met Camille and they stole into the lab knowing that Millenburg had classes to attend and it would be hours before he came in ... if he came in at all. In the darkened room, Daniel moved the crystal from the thermos to its new home. With the chamber closed and sealed, Daniel called to Camille to turn the lights on. Daniel flipped switches and the MS7 hummed as if alive. "Any thoughts on how we should proceed," he asked as Camille joined him.

"Small. I think you want to start very small."

Spurred on by adrenaline, Daniel and Camille worked through the day and night with no unwanted Millenburg appearances to disrupt them. By mid afternoon the following day they had several sheets of organized data which included data on the rate of absorption as well as radiation.

"The output values are out of this world," Camille said. "Why are we bothering to continue the work with any of the other crystals? Shouldn't we focus on this one? There must be limitless experiments we could do."

"I wish we could, but I have no intention of telling Millenburg about my crystals and that's the only way we'd be able to change the focus using this equipment. We've got to keep up the pretense of doing the work we were hired to do. Besides, I know how we can do both."

"Won't it slow us down?"

"Some, but I don't see a way around it."

"What are you thinking?"

"We'll have to run each sample through every experiment that we design. There's one crystal that's already set up for that. We run our tests in the empty machine first, establish our data and then run the other tests as planned. We'll design our experiments for my crystal and we may even learn some interesting things about the others in the mean time."

CHAPTER 61

Millenburg appeared at the door followed by a stranger. "Daniel, Camille. I'd like to introduce you to Mister Davenport."

Tom Davenport was a giant of a man wearing a black, tailored, pinstriped suit. His size might have been attributed to fat except that his ribbed neck and chiseled features suggested any extra weight he might be carrying was more likely muscle. He was clean-shaven and his serious mask discouraged any pleasantries.

Davenport nodded after the introduction, but his hands remained clasped behind his back. He didn't look like the sort that would be interested in experiments. He looked more like a guy who broke legs for a living.

"Mister Davenport is representing Vance Feldman and Mister Feldman is our backer. We owe him our cooperation. Could you two please show Mister Davenport around and answer any questions he might have," said Millenburg, before he left the room.

The young scientists followed the man through the lab as he wandered from one apparatus to another, who was silent until he came to the MS7 and then said, "Tell me about this."

"It measures various outputs from the crystals," Daniel told him.

"What is this for?" he said pointing to the receptacle inside the vacuum chamber.

"It's for the samples. It has a number of sensors built into it and it isolates the samples from other external factors such as light and heat."

"Interesting. Why is it encased in glass?"

"All of our experiments are conducted in a vacuum." Mr. Davenport's vacant look revealed much about his understanding. "That's so that we can control the environment more effectively," Daniel said.

"Interesting," Davenport repeated. "Well I think that's all I need. Thanks for your time. I'm sure Mister Feldman will be pleased with your work." There was no warmth in his sentiment and without waiting for a response he left the room, brushing past a returning Millenburg on his way out.

"How did it go?"

"It went fine, Doctor Millenburg, but what was it all about?" Camille said.

"I'm not entirely sure. Vance Feldman is the money behind this project. He is also responsible for almost all of the oil exploration in the province and off the coast as well. We are lucky to have such a man backing us."

"That's not all that's going on though, is it?"

"Well, our agreement with Vance Feldman has not come without a few strings, but that isn't anything you need to concern yourselves with. Suffice it to say that there will be more visits. I've had to agree to keep him informed. So please be polite to the occasional visitor and I'm sure everything will work out."

Camille wasn't satisfied, shifting her weight from one leg to the other, crossing her arms. "Is there anything else we should know?"

"Just keep me informed and don't embarrass me."

Work continued without enthusiasm after Millenburg's departure, until it was time for supper. "Let's get out of here," said Daniel.

Camille slapped the light out and punched the keypad on the recently installed coded entrance. Millenburg had added the security measure after they demonstrated that amethyst emitted a faint residual radio signal.

***

Camille tossed in her bed that night. Sleep came only with difficulty and when she finally did fall asleep troubling images filled her dreams. She had barely closed her eyes when Davenport's eyes gleamed from the dark. She shot up into sitting position, but the room was dark and quiet. She lay back, staring at the ceiling until she dozed off once again and dreamt.

The beach reached out in front of her. She walked in the water, the sand squishing up between her toes with every step. Camille looked up from her utopia to see that the beach had come to an end. Before her, cliffs plunged into the water. Weather-beaten concrete stairs wound from the rocks above onto the sandy alcove. Above, the shingled peaks of some wealthy estate overlooked the water. She stopped there and her mouth dropped open. Davenport stood above her, wagging a warning finger in her direction. She knew that she should go back the way she had come, but she couldn't help herself. She took another step toward him and he began to descend. The man was massive. She studied him as he approached. His chest beneath his jacket bulged, strangely rectangular for a mass of solid muscle. Then the wind came up and blew his jacket open. She could see it clearly now … cold steel in a leather holster.

Camille bolted upright. The sun was not up, but had begun to lighten the sky. She looked at her bedside clock. Oh great, six in the morning. I'll never get back to sleep now.

CHAPTER 62

An old man sat at his workbench in the basement of British Columbia's provincial museum. With gnarled fingers he turned yellowed pages of a journal that had been kept by a long dead farmer who once lived nearby. It was a testament to a life and proof that there had been simpler times.

He paused a moment to consider his surroundings. Why was it that all museum curators seemed to relegate this kind of work to the basement? Light and moisture were the reasons, the two enemies of all that is old. And so maybe it was fitting then that the old man sat at his desk, a relic among his beloved artifacts.

With furrowed brow, Faber Smith leaned forward and immersed himself in his work. So long had the ancient past consumed him that he had all but rejected his need for anything from the present. His work was the reason the world would remember him when he was gone. It was a sad sentiment really, for he doubted his loved ones, few as *they* were, would remember or miss him all that much. Or would they? He wasn't sure.

He lifted his head at the sound of a squeaking hinge echoing among the shelves, bouncing off ancient stones and other objects, reminiscent of an apologetic entrance of a child who is afraid of the dark. It was the kind of sound only a stranger to the catacomb could make, for that was what he called the artifact room, 'The Catacomb'.

My God! How slow can a door open? Faber thought. Soft footfalls drew closer. A double echo indicated there were dual intruders. Whoever they were, they hadn't called out to introduce themselves nor had they managed to find their way to his desk. They were probably just a couple of new employees on their rounds to become familiar with the building. It happened two or three times a year.

He swiveled in his chair to discover it was worse than he thought. A boy and a girl drifted into view, lucky enough not to have knocked something over in the dim light. "If it's something you're selling, I don't want any and I will never want any. If it's something you need, there are a thousand other people who can help you and I'm not one of them," he groused, then elevated his voice for emphatic finality, "*Go away and leave me alone.*"

The boy wearing jeans and a tee shirt, looking to his ancient eyes barely old enough to grow facial hair, spoke first. "Mister Smith. I'm Daniel Sterling."

A waste of time, that's what this is. "I thought I told you I wasn't interested. Get out of here so I can get to work."

"I promise we'll go, but we need your help."

Damn kids. "I'll give you two minutes if you promise to leave afterward."

"We were told that you were the most knowledgeable man in your field. The curator said he was lucky to have you on staff. He also said you'd never see us."

"He was right—on all counts. Was there something else on your mind? Your two minutes is nearly gone."

Daniel unrolled a large photograph and spread it out in front of the old man.

Smith snorted. "What do you have there? A map to a buried treasure? The original plans for Noah's ark?" He rolled his eyes.

"No, Mister Smith, nothing like that. If you could take a look at this, I only want to know if you've seen anything like it before or if you know where I might go next to do more research."

The boy's sincerity was apparent and, from a glance, the picture did look interesting. "What is it?"

"It's a photograph of some hieroglyphs I found. I've done as much research as I can and I still don't know anything about it. I can't find any source that will help me identify the culture responsible."

"This has to be a prank," he said more to himself than his unwelcome guests. Although there were familiar aspects, there was nothing in the photograph to associate it with any of the common cultures. "Where did you get this? Is this some kind of a hoax? Don't you have anything better to do?"

"I know it sounds crazy, but this photo is authentic. I guarantee it. I took it myself."

"Sorry if I'm not jumping up and down here. I guess I haven't made myself perfectly clear. Your guarantee means *jack shit* to me." Faber returned to the photo and pulled his magnifier down over his eyes. "What do you think you have here?"

"Maybe it has something to do with a culture we've never seen before. I don't know. I haven't been able to find anything that resembles it. I just wanted to know if it's something you've ever seen. After that I'd be more than happy to leave and never come back."

Faber studied the picture in silence. He liked nothing better than a good puzzle. "Where'd you come by this?"

Daniel stammered.

Becoming impatient, Smith continued. "Listen, this picture has a story. You don't tell me your story then I don't tell you mine." He held the photo out toward Daniel.

Daniel refused to take it. "Mister Smith, I know that the images you're seeing appear authentic enough to you, and that it seems impossible. Maybe you think every ancient culture on the planet has been discovered, and that might be true, but I don't think you want to miss out on this."

The girl spoke up. "Neither of us wants to share what we know yet. If your curiosity is strong enough, you'll help if you can."

"Damn spunky little gal, aren't you?" he said as more of a statement than a question, returning his attention to the picture. "Fine, tell me where and when the picture was taken and then I'll give you my opinion."

Daniel and Camille gave each other a nod and Daniel spoke. "It was taken in a cave up north. I took it about a month ago."

"I was with him," Camille added.

"That's not good enough. If you want my help, you're going to have to give me something I can use."

More stalling. "The site is sixty miles or so west of Prince George. It's located on private property outside a farming community," said Daniel.

"And you're not the owner?"

"No."

"Then why are you here and not him?"

"Well, he's dead and the property is up for sale."

Faber cocked his head. His look must have given his thoughts away.

"No. No, sir. We didn't kill him, but I knew him."

"If there's even the slightest credibility to this photo, I'm going to have a lot more questions." Faber adjusted the light and bent to look at the print.

"I knew you would be curious," the girl said.

Smith snapped back, "Shut your mouth, Missy. I'm workin'."

Camille did.

Daniel and Camille waited a long time in the muted light of the museum's basement while Smith studied, working his way carefully from one edge to the other and then slowly inching his way to the bottom. He hovered over the lower right hand corner for a long time and then removed the magnifier from his forehead. The bench was nearly chest high and Smith sat on a stool, placing him at a comfortable height. When he stood up he shrunk by an apparent four inches. The man couldn't have been more than five feet tall. He rolled the picture up and handed it back to Daniel.

"Interesting. I'm almost positive that it's a hoax, but I'll tell you what it looks like to me. There's some combination of Native American and Inuit, but the medium is nothing they would have used. It's too advanced for either of those cultures."

Daniel waited for him to continue, but he didn't. "Is there anything else?"

"Nothing. That's it. That's all. There is nothing more." Faber paused as if considering what to do next. "I've done what you asked at the risk of looking the fool over a prank. It's a very nice job. Now, good-bye." His last words were crisp and clean. The interview was over.

CHAPTER 63

Faber sat at his bench long after the students were gone. Although he declined to accept the photo, they had left it behind. Pinned by a fossil on one corner and his empty coffee cup on another, Faber studied it. As he sat fascinated, his eyes brightened and the years seemed to roll away from his face. He remembered the passion he'd once had. His dreams of making his mark in his field and on the world had been gone long ago. The dungeon he now abided in was not so much a disappointment as it was a necessary compromise. Only two years from retirement and what had he accomplished? Yes, it was a fine museum, but its mandate covered nothing more than the provincial history and the odd exhibit such as the recent Titanic rediscovery. That exhibit was an antic to increase the visitor count and nothing more. In fact, there was little at the museum that could challenge him and set him apart as the leader in anthropological research that he'd been hired as.

He reflected back to the private Catholic school he attended as a child. His mother felt anthropology was the best thing for him at the time, probably because he was a loner and the other kids often picked on him at the public school. Of course he had been kind of strange, especially when he'd run around the house dressed like a cat. He smiled at the memory. Back then he had been Faber the saber-toothed tiger. Every year he'd kept the same costume, making only minor modifications, but those days ended abruptly when he entered high school. Contending with being beaten up and stuffed in lockers was different from the constant teasing in elementary school. At least he had been able to ignore that, but in high school the bruises were real. Although no one would ever associate him with being 'normal', he had made his choice to try and fit in. It was a turning point in his life. That decision was etched into his memory like a scratch on glass.

The days he had spent with his best friend Timothy were long in the past. Back then they could be found excavating in the gully behind the soccer field. He used to spend every moment possible digging in the moist dirt under the Aspen trees behind the fence. By the time he finished grade seven he had developed a sizable collection of bottles and trinkets. The nunnery was adjacent to the soccer field and years earlier the gulley had been a dump. The most interesting items were the tiny collectable souvenirs that came from Red Rose tea. It didn't occur to Timothy or Faber that it was simply an indication that the nuns who came primarily from Ireland and England were devoted tea drinkers. He wouldn't make these kinds of connections until he was studying archaeology at a university in his early twenties.

That love of treasure hunting and unearthing buried ruins had taken Faber into his adult years and had eventually led him to this seat at the counter staring longingly at this strange snapshot. As if the photo were actually as old as the artwork it depicted, Faber studied with a keener eye. Was it a hoax or did this art really exist somewhere? It was a digital photograph after all, and would have been very easy to alter. He studied it for signs that it might have been tampered with.

Faber Smith sat in the near dark as the outside light waned. He packed up his belongings, walked out to the parking lot and fired up the old clunker that still got him back and forth, and from here to there. Although he was not yet ready to admit it to himself, there was no evidence to indicate the photograph was anything less than authentic. The meaning of such a thing was mind-boggling. If it was indeed genuine, this single photograph could turn the world upside down about its beliefs and understanding of ancient history. Faber's excitement grew.

At home Faber went through his evening regimen without much thought and then crawled into bed. With the bedside lamp's dull burn and the photograph spread out in front of him there was scant difference between his life at work and the one at home. Faber fell asleep with the picture in his lap and the lamp still shining.

CHAPTER 64

A little after seven in the morning the phone rang. Daniel stumbled out of bed toward the kitchen counter. He picked it up on the fourth ring. "Hello?"

"Mister Sterling?"

"Who is this? Do you know how early it is?"

"I'm terribly sorry about that. This is Faber Smith."

A maladroit silence followed.

"Mister Sterling? I've been looking closely at the photograph you left me and I have to admit that I'm more than a little intrigued. I was wondering if you have any more photos that I could take a look at."

"Yes, I do, but I really wanted to research them myself."

"I don't blame you, Mister Sterling. I understand completely and that's the other reason I'm calling. You probably could do the work yourself, but attaining the skills and certification to authenticate this find will take you a dozen years or more. If this is indeed authentic, the significance of this find is inestimable. If you want results in less than fifteen years, you need my help."

"Thanks, Mister Smith. I'll give it some thought and get back to you but, like I said, I was really hoping you could point me to research materials that could help."

"That's what I'm trying to tell you, Mister Sterling. There are no textbooks. There are no primary sources of information. To my knowledge, nothing like this exists in the world today. If you want to find out what all of this means, I can help you."

"Thanks so much for your offer, Mister Smith. I have to get ready for school. I'll let you know, though."

Mr. Smith reiterated his offer while Daniel nodded to the phone, afraid he'd have to hang up on the pathetic old man. Thank goodness Smith ended the conversation himself. Daniel laid the phone in its cradle. The clock on the oven told him he had little time for his morning routine.

As Daniel hiked toward the university his thoughts deepened and his step slowed. He had to remind himself to keep a swift pace, periodically putting on a burst of speed. The old man was probably right. He may very well need help from an outsider, but he would get the help on his terms. On the other hand, choosing a recluse like Smith over someone like Dr. Millenburg offered the benefit of less risk. Who else but a recluse to trust with such a secret?

Although he was late for class, he found Camille waiting on the park bench outside the building. She stood as he approached. "What's up? You look like you've just heard some bad news."

"Faber Smith called."

"The old man from the museum?"

"Yes."

"Well?"

She shrugged.

"What did he want?"

"He wants to look at some more of the photos we took. Now he thinks they might be real, but he says it'll be years before we can authenticate the site and since there's never been anything like it before, there's no point trying to research it. He says we won't find anything."

"Do you think we should listen to him?"

"I don't know. We better get to class."

CHAPTER 65

The sky was a bright blue and the air was winter crisp. The city bus roared along the streets. Camille pulled the cord above her seat. Daniel Sterling and Camille Robertson stood up from their seats as the bus veered to the right and came to a stop across from the museum. The doors opened and they stepped onto the sidewalk.

"What can I do for you," the receptionist asked.

"We're here to see Mister Smith."

She pointed to a door that stated 'Employees Only'. "He's right through there. Just follow the stairs down."

They found Mister Smith where they'd left him, a wrinkled imp on a stool. He may very well have made the call from there. Camille called out to him. She was not surprised to hear his familiar grunt of acknowledgement. When he glanced up from his work, his demeanor changed with his recognition. *"You've come back.* Come in. Come in. What did you decide?"

The grin appeared odd on him. It seemed as though it could have been copied and pasted from an image belonging to someone else. For a moment he barely looked like the same gnarled old curmudgeon. The smile had taken ten years off his age and there was a craving in his eyes. He reminded Camille of one of the many garden gnomes her grandmother collected: small, squat and jovial.

"This morning you said we needed your help. We've decided to give you the chance to prove it," Camille said.

Faber glowed. "You need to understand that if this is authentic, from an historical perspective, it's probably the most significant find in this millennium. Even though you can study every culture and ancient writing individually, there is nothing like this anywhere. You'll be ready to begin the process of translation with some rudimentary skills years from now. Even then, the process of translation will take you many more years to complete. It is likely that you'll be old and grey before you understand the final significance of your find. With my help you could cut years off that."

Mr. Smith's certainty gave Camille the feeling of a small child about to embark on an impossibly long journey. Already she was restless with the waiting. Camille and Daniel glanced at each other and then back to Faber Smith. "Do you think you can translate this one?" Daniel asked as he placed the next photograph in front of the old man.

Faber studied it silently for a long time before the words "Fascinating. Simply fascinating," slipped from his mouth.

Minutes became hours as the two sat patiently watching and waiting. In truth they had expected Faber to study it briefly and tell them immediately the meaning of it all. Instead he looked at each symbol carefully and even began to take notes. Camille looked at the list he wrote. It was a bibliography. She recognized some of the titles. Without a doubt, Daniel recognized many more. She looked across to see if he'd come to the same conclusion. His face turned toward her and the look in his eyes told her that he had.

Since their falling out, Daniel had kept to his word to keep his temper in check. He had controlled himself and had spoken no word to her in anger since then. She dropped her hand and let it slip into his. He did not brush it away.

They had been watching the old man work for nearly two hours when he finally put his pen down and turned to his visitors. They waited expectantly. The moments ticked by and still he said nothing. He just sat there with a silly grin that seemed better suited to a child's face.

It was Camille who finally broke the silence. "What can you tell us about the photos, Mister Smith?"

Faber was almost giddy. "My curiosity is most definitely piqued. If there is a real place on this planet where these images exist, it's very exciting. This second photo has helped me greatly. I can tell that these mosaics were probably side-by-side. You gave me the first in a series and I believe that this is the second."

Daniel nodded, indicating Mr. Smith was correct.

Faber continued. "These panels seem to tell a story. It's impossible to say how many there will be or even what the true nature of the story is. I hope I live long enough to see where it is you came upon these fascinating samples."

"There are more," said Daniel

"How many?"

"About two hundred."

"What do you plan to do with them? The world must know about this find sooner or later."

"We're not ready for that and if you're going to be a risk to us, we're done right now. We're not ready for some government agency or some renowned expert to take this over. We're the experts." Daniel face had grown flush. Camille could sense the heat growing inside him. He took a breath and looked to Camille. Her nod seemed to be all he needed. "Faber, will you swear to us that the information you gather will remain only between us and that you will not share it with anyone?"

Faber did not hesitate. "Absolutely. You have my word. You can know that I won't be saying anything, especially if there is a chance that it means losing any of the professional respect I've worked so hard for."

He paused to remove his spectacles, lean toward them with one elbow on his desk, his glasses dangling by one stem from his hand. His eyes narrowed, and his words seemed chosen and spoken for measured impact. "I'm an old mean shit of a man, so this better not turn out to be some sort of a scam."

CHAPTER 66

Following a hectic midterm schedule, the break seemed to race forward at a harrowing speed. Camille returned to her family's home. As disappointing as it was, Camille could not follow Daniel. His plans were set. He had to return to Vanderhoof where, with any luck at all, the cavern remained undiscovered.

Daniel shared a taxi to the airport with Camille. They had scheduled themselves on the same flight from Victoria to Vancouver, but that was as much of their journey they could share. Camille would board a plane east while Daniel traveled north.

They stood in a corridor halfway between their gates in the silent reluctance of a new couple. A muffled announcement blared over the PA, "Daniel Sterling, this is your final call to board flight thirty-seven to Prince George. Daniel Sterling, please make your way immediately to gate one."

"Camille. I gotta go," he said and started past her.

Camille leaned forward and pulled him toward her. "You know I love you, don't you?"

The best sort of pain shot into his chest. "I was kinda hoping."

"Call me when you get home."

Daniel raced toward the gate and paused briefly in front of the waiting attendant. Her hand was outstretched, palm up, before he arrived. He passed her his driver's license and boarding pass. The woman in blue polyester swiped his pass and handed the paperwork back to him. "Have a good flight," she said with one of those plastered-on professional-duty smiles. He slung his pack over his shoulder and ran down the ramp to the cockpit.

Daniel had no sooner strapped himself into his seat than the stewardess began miming the standard auto-spiel. The plane soared north and he immersed himself into a book ignoring the humdrum drone of the engines and the intermittent lurches caused by air pockets. Air pocket, he thought, an oxymoron if he'd ever heard one. Since planes fly through the air, how can a pocket of air cause them to suddenly fall? That makes about as much sense as a boat suddenly sinking when it passes through a pocket of water.

The plane landed in Prince George on a runway with a skiff of freshly fallen snow. Fence posts wore small white hats. The Bernards met him as he strode into arrivals. After a greeting and a short wait for his luggage, the unconventional family drove home. Their turn onto Sturgeon Point Road revealed that the country roads were spared the deluge of salt and sand and their white frock made a perfect winter homecoming.

Though Daniel had been looking forward to the break, his worry grew as they neared the farm. The car slowed and made the turn onto Grundpark. He scanned the McMaster driveway. The 'For Sale' sign was looking the worse for the winter wear and had an unattended look which was a good sign; he smiled inwardly at his pun. The driveway was unplowed and there was no trail to indicate that anyone had made the trek to view the house. He turned to William. "I see the old McMaster place is still up for sale."

"Yeah, I imagine it'll probably stay that way. Ever since the US closed the border to beef exports, ranchers have been going out of business left and right. I used to think raising cows would be a nice way to retire. Now, it's just a losing proposition all the way around. I'm thinking about getting out of the cattle business myself. It just isn't worth it anymore."

Daniel held back a sigh. Maybe there would be a little more time after all and that was all he needed.

He woke early that first morning for a stroll outside. He stopped to look over the fence toward the poplar trees that towered near the well. The fresh blanket of snow stretched out like delicate flooring. Any footprint would draw attention to the very thing he was there to protect. Though his curiosity was nearly unbearable, Daniel could not risk creating a path to the well. Even if the property sold, as long as there was snow on the ground, the well would be safe.

The Bernards saw him off at the airport. As much as the welcome was always warm, the good-byes were always tearful. This departure was particularly stressful. Daniel couldn't ignore his sense of foreboding. He watched from his window seat as the plane taxied down the runway and prayed for a little luck and a lot of patience.

CHAPTER 67

In Vancouver the passengers deplaned. Camille's arrival had not coincided with his and although they had made plans to meet in the food court, that rendezvous was still two hours away. He headed to the baggage carrousel, allowing the other hurried passengers to overtake him.

Before long the other passengers were far ahead, leaving him alone in the long corridor. When he arrived at the baggage claim area the last of the passengers were departing. Apparently there were no other arrivals—which provided a lull in activity. The luggage carrousel churned, carrying his lone satchel on its endless ride.

Daniel retrieved his bag and wandered toward the exit. A tall man in the black suit held a sign with his name on it. Daniel recognized him as the same man who had come for a visit at the lab. He walked to him. "I'm Daniel," he said.

The man smiled humorlessly. "I've been ordered to pick you up."

"Where are we going?"

"Back to the lab. Professor Millenburg has asked that I bring you right over."

"What about Camille? I told her that I'd meet her here when her plane got in."

"There'll be someone here to pick her up as well. Can you come with me please? I've been asked to hurry."

It was almost comical how little expression was in his voice. Not a man with many social skills, Daniel thought.

He followed the man to the front of the terminal where a limousine waited in the temporary parking zone reserved for taxis. The bruiser opened the rear passenger door and after Daniel climbed in he closed the door behind him. The mystery was disconcerting, but the man behind the wheel appeared to be a bona fide limousine driver. The mafia guy, so Daniel had come to think of him, got into the front passenger seat before the car pulled away from the curb. Neither of the men offered any clarification. Daniel rode in silence, watching the scenery and wondering what the emergency might be.

His imagination drifted randomly and some time passed before he suddenly realized they were not taking a route that would lead them to the university. "I thought we were going to the lab."

Tom turned in his seat. "We are going to the lab. Doctor Millenburg is waiting there and it is an emergency. I never said we were going to the university. Please relax. You have as much information as I am at liberty to share."

Daniel's heart began to race. There was no doubt that this strange meeting had to do with the work he had been doing at the university, but that was as far as his deductive reasoning would allow him to surmise. He patiently waited while the unfamiliar scenery sped by.

The cityscape gave way to hills and trees as they entered a part of the city inhabited only by the very rich. The limo slowed … Daniel could hear the faint clicking of the blinker. They stopped in front of an ornate steel gate. The driver reached through the window and punched a series of buttons on a touchpad supported at window height by a metal stand. His rapid finger motions made it obvious he had done this before.

They passed by numerous homes, none of which could be described as anything other than a mansion. The limo again slowed and stopped in front of a second gate. Here, there were no code pad entries and the driver waited. A moment later, as if obeying instructions by some command station in the sky, dual gates swung open and the driver proceeded into the largest estate Daniel had ever seen. Trees dotted the flawlessly kept lawn for as far as he could see in every direction. They crested a small hill and, on a crag overlooking the ocean, stood an old castle out of place and time. It wasn't the dilapidated sort you would expect to see in Scotland or Britain. It had a newness and modern look about it. Daniel sat mesmerized by its extravagance.

The car stopped in front of a set of stairs as wide as the length of two stretched limos. The stone steps led to the main entrance fifteen feet above them to heavy wooden doors set between marble pillars. Mafia man led Daniel to the doors which opened before they reached them. A butler ushered Daniel inside and took his jacket before leading him down a wide hall. The place looked more like a museum than a home and the feeling that something was just not right grew within him. Though he had made plans to remember where he'd been, after passing innumerable doors and corridors it wasn't long before he was completely lost. Somewhere near the centre of the labyrinth they came to a great hall. Stairs wound around the perimeter leading to upper floors and at the center another flight of stairs descended. The butler led them down the steps and to an elevator at the bottom. A guard sat on a chair outside the stainless steel door.

Mafia man pushed the down arrow and the doors slid open. Clean sleek stainless steel also covered the interior. Instead of a series of floor buttons there was only one. The symbol beside it indicated it was for both up and down. There would be only one stop. When they were inside the man pushed the button and they began their descent. The trip lasted longer than Daniel would have guessed. The elevator was traveling either extremely slow or terribly far.

The doors finally opened, revealing a large room laid out much the same as the lab at the university. A closer look revealed that the equipment in the room was his. He had known something was wrong about the trip all along and yet … he had still fallen for the charade. Daniel bolted to the elevator, but the doors had already closed and the behemoth barred the way. Now his jacket was splayed open revealing a handgun nesting in a holster strapped beneath his arm. Daniel was trapped, a prisoner once more.

His hands grew clammy. The color left his face. He felt like vomiting. How could it be happening again? What did he do to deserve this fate that seemed so unavoidable? He braced his stance, jutted his chin. "What do you want with me?"

The man took a more permanent position, legs apart and arms folded across his chest like a strange version of a palace guard. He reminded Daniel of a sentry in front of Buckingham Palace without the red jacket or the fuzzy black hat. The man lifted one eyebrow. It was doubtful the over-sized oaf knew why he was doing his job. More than likely he was simply following orders.

If mafia man wasn't going to do any more than prevent him from leaving, he might as well explore his new prison. The lab was more spacious than the one at the university had been. There were extra tables and chairs. Whoever had planned this abduction intended that he be comfortable. Daniel sat.

His thoughts turned to Camille. Tom had said they were picking her up as well. Had he said that to make his story convincing, or had they scheduled her for the same fate. He thought about Faber and hoped they had made no connection between them. Daniel sat, consumed in gloom, trying to reason through a chain of events that seemed impossible to fathom. Why would they need me?

Daniel shifted in his chair, unable to find a comfortable position. He stood and walked around the room. He glanced at the clock on the wall with obsessive regularity logging each minute that ticked by. Two torturous hours had passed before he heard the whine of an electric motor somewhere high above them. Someone had called the elevator to the top. More long moments passed before the elevator stopped at the bottom and the doors slid open.

Camille stepped out, ushered in by an older, distinguished looking man that Daniel had never seen before, but his heart nearly broke as he watched her expression change as she realized what was actually happening. Her eyes bulged as she took in the lab with which she had become so familiar. Like him, Camille turned to flee, but the Brobdingnagian caught her in his cold grip, then held her out like a rag doll. She jerked herself free and ran to Daniel. Her back to their captors, she mouthed to Daniel, "Let's get out of here."

She turned and raced toward the elevator only to find her way blocked once more by the hulking thug. This time he forced her into the room and threw her unceremoniously into a couch that was part of the living area. Daniel stood, paralyzed and helpless, as he watched Camille. Defiant, she stood and began screaming. "You can't keep us here! You don't have the right to do this! You let us go this minute!"

If her rampage had any impact on their captors, they showed no sign of it. The man who had escorted her into the lab spoke with irritating mildness, "Miss Robertson, please make yourself comfortable. I'm sure that you've noticed that you are several stories below ground. There is just this single entrance. If you glance around the room you will also notice numerous cameras surrounding you. Rather than captives, I would prefer you to think of yourselves as guests. The rest of this," he said gesturing to the room, "is merely my way of protecting my investment, which I can assure you has been substantial. Please rest up. I know that you've had a long journey. I'll be seeing you in the morning after you've become a little more accustomed to your surroundings."

He reentered the elevator with the guard following. With the brute gone Camille spun around to Daniel. "Why didn't you do something? We could have gotten out of here if you had helped! We could have at least tried!"

Daniel hung his head. "Can't you see that there's no way out?"

"Oh, there's a way out. And I can tell you right now that I'm going to find it."

Daniel voice was low and resigned. "The man said it himself. We're a long way underground and the only way out is in the elevator."

Camille turned on him, her disgust thick in her voice. "I don't care how far below the surface we are. I'm not giving up."

There was no response that could have helped Camille face the obvious so Daniel drifted to one corner hoping to avoid her accusing stare. In his head he knew hope was a necessity, but at the same time it was a commodity he lacked. Camille would need to hold out hope for both of them.

The suite was divided into three main parts: the lab, a small bachelor pad and a separate portion that could only be the bathroom. There was a Japanese folding divider with a bed on either side; the rest of the space was delineated by furniture. Other than the furnishings, there were the electronics. As the man had pointed out, cameras were everywhere. There didn't appear to be a place in the room that either Camille or Daniel could stand in without being under scrutiny. Camille crossed the room toward Daniel. He heard the rustle of her jeans and turned his gaze to the floor. She could berate him as much as she needed to, but he would not return her anger. They could not afford to turn on each other.

Camille stepped up to him. He waited for her onslaught. Instead he felt gentle fingers through his hair and then on the side of his face. She pulled him to her and he allowed it. She held his head next to her chest for a long time. The sound of her heartbeat mesmerized him. After long moments she stepped back and leaned forward in one easy movement. She tilted his head back and he let her. She kissed him.

Daniel kissed her back. Somehow, while he wallowed in his greatest moment of shame, she had set herself aside and allowed him to save face. He loved her for it.

A small buzzing sound came from one of the cameras as it swiveled on its base and the focus ring turned automatically. Daniel glanced up. The tenderness he had felt disappeared as his eyes narrowed and his upper lip curled into a scowl.

CHAPTER 68

Feldman sat in his wine colored leather chair that matched his mahogany desk, an elegantly crafted expanse of wood and leather. An expansive computer monitor was the dominating element, split into half a dozen sections; one of them focused and zoomed in on Daniel's face. Feldman hit a key and the image grew until it filled the screen. Was this the face of a broken boy or was it that of a dog who was about to bite?

The young man stood and began to move out of view. With his miniature joystick Feldman maneuvered the camera and followed. Even with the knowledge that he was anonymous behind his desk and there was the technology between them, the lad's intensity burned into Feldman.

This time, when Daniel moved out of view, Feldman punched another key which returned the monitor to its normal configuration. In the lab, the camera moved to its neutral position and widened its field of view.

The girl spoke. "I think he's trying to make a point," Camille whispered, not taking her eyes from the camera.

"Very good, Miss Robertson. I'm impressed. Again, please enjoy your stay." There was a small click from the speaker indicating the end of the transmission.

***

Camille leaned over and whispered into Daniel's ear. His eyes opened wide. Camille stood and took his hand. Reluctantly he followed. They walked to the elevator. Camille pushed the single triangular button that pointed up. The familiar sound of the descending elevator followed, growing louder as it neared, then came to an abrupt stop with a thump. The doors slid open. A rush of air suddenly escaped Daniel's mouth and for the first time, he realized he had been holding his breath. No goon waited to make sure they remained below. Camille stepped inside and again Daniel followed.

Holding his hand, Camille pushed the button. The doors closed and the elevator ascended. Would Feldman simply allow them to walk out? It seemed so until the doors open and they faced Tom who, as always, showed no surprise.

He gave them his customary humorless smile as he reached in and pushed the down arrow without uttering a word. When the doors opened again the young scientists stepped into their prison once more.

There was nothing else Daniel could do. He walked over to the equipment and examined it. Was the crystal still where it belonged? The two lead globes were just as he recalled having left them. He turned to Camille, "What do you think?"

Camille glared, not letting the cameras see.

Daniel understood and closed his mouth. He took Camille by the hand. "We ought to take a closer look at this place, don't you think?" he said, smiling at her.

The mystery man would certainly expect them to carefully inspect the area. Why not complete the examination as obviously as possible? They began at the elevator and then circled the room looking for anything that might be a light switch but there was none. Darkness was clearly not an option unless their captors decided there should be.

Camille gazed at Daniel. He studied her face. She seemed she was coming to realize the futility of their plight. She wrapped her fingers behind his elbows, pulled him closer, and ran her cold hands up the back of his arms beneath his shirt.

Daniel shivered. His first thought was how freezing Camille's hands were and the fact that she was frightened, but something else leapt to mind—taking priority over the needed concern for her for now. He went to where the crystal was contained. He opened the metal sphere to place samples and touched the sensors inside.

Camille went to the console and the readouts. If the crystal was still in place and functioning then the temperature should read out Daniel's body heat. It did.

His thoughts jumped to the crystals in the apartment. If the one in the crucible was undiscovered, then it was likely that the others were still safe. And if the crystals weren't what brought them here, then what was the reason behind their kidnapping?

The clock continued its steady movement with the minute hand making one tortoise-like revolution after another. At nine fifty-five their captor's voice boomed over the intercom. "In five minutes the lights will automatically turn out. A timer controls them and they will not be on again until six in the morning. Don't be alarmed. There will be just enough light to ensure that the cameras can continue to function."

Camille screamed shrilly at the faceless voice, "Why are we here?"

A maddening click indicated the end of the transmission.

Just as the man had stated, at ten o'clock the lights went out. They readied themselves for bed in the reduced visibility and lay down to rest. For now there was nothing else they could do. Small red lights flashed intermittently from each of the cameras mounted around the room. Even as they reclined in bed, the cameras blinked incessantly at them.

CHAPTER 69

If the sounds had been coming from an apartment they would have been easy to ignore. In their prison the sound of the fan behind the constant whir of the cameras gave the place an alien quality. Sleep was slow in coming. Between the tossing of one and the turning of the other, Daniel and Camille slept little. After what seemed like an hour or more had passed, Daniel glanced at the clock, only to note that a mere fifteen minutes had gone by. This insufferable situation went on into the night, sleep eventually stealing its way into them.

At six in the morning Daniel's eyes were yanked open by the rude awakening of lights turning on, as per their captor's non-negotiable contract, right on schedule.

At six-thirty the elevator dinged. Davenport stepped out carrying a platter of covered dishes. It could only be breakfast. "Mister Feldman will arrive at nine o'clock for your briefing. Please be prepared." All that was missing was an English accent and he could have been a butler. He turned, reentered the elevator and disappeared behind the shining steel doors, leaving the captives alone once more.

At nine o'clock the elevator ushered in the distinguished looking man as promised. They stood, with fearful anticipation.

"No, no. Do sit down. There's so much we need to discuss," he said, his tone approximating pleasantness. If you haven't already surmised, my name is Mister Feldman."

What followed was not so much a discussion, but more a series of unimaginably long monologues that lasted much longer than either Daniel or Camille would have guessed: twice as long as their buttocks would have allowed—had there been another option.

"Please think of yourselves as my honored guests. The work that you are doing is simply astounding and the results will change the way we see the world. I'm absolutely convinced of this. Unfortunately, I'm not ready for the world to discover what I'm up to."

The deadpan stares from Daniel and Camille did nothing to slow his speech.

"Everything you need will be provided. I will have meals delivered three times daily as well as a variety of other things to snack on. If it's not an emergency, just state your needs out loud. I personally review the tapes every day. I'm sure I've thought of everything, though."

Feldman turned to go, but stopped midway, "Have you heard about Doctor Millenburg? Unfortunately, he was not particularly cooperative. He thought I was trying to steal his fame. I was sad to hear of his involvement in that fatal collision over the holidays. One should never drink and drive. Please continue your work. And, do let me know if you need anything?" Finished, he clicked his Italian-leathered heels, spun round and began his pompous exit.

Feldman walked into the elevator and turned to face the prisoners once more. "Oh, and by the way, I should tell you that you've officially dropped out of school and you've run off together. Camille, the note you left for your mother was very moving." He reached to push the button.

"Mister Feldman!" Daniel said.

Feldman's hand stayed.

"There are some things that I left behind at the apartment. I need to get them."

"What is it that you need?" an impatient Feldman responded.

"Just some personal items," Daniel returned.

"I was planning on sending someone for them," Feldman quipped.

"No, sir. I want to get them for myself."

Feldman's composure and the sweetness in his voice vanished. "You'll do no. Such. Thing."

Daniel was frightened, but he remained calm. "I need to pick up *these* things myself." He continued, ostensibly assuring, but with sly calculation, "If I forget anything important, an investigation might lead authorities to the idea that I did not leave voluntarily … especially if there was something left behind I would never have gone away without." Daniel watched Feldman's reaction with intense scrutiny, hoping he'd made an impression.

Feldman pushed the elevator button without acknowledging Daniel. The doors closed.

Normally it was impossible to know where Feldman was, but at the moment he was riding in the elevator, so he could not be watching. Daniel leaned over and spoke quickly into Camille's ear, "He's going to have to take us there. We need to find a way to talk."

There were really only three items in the apartment that Daniel wanted. If Feldman allowed him to go, as he hoped, Feldman's men would search him for any belongings that he brought out and they would probably do a thorough job of it, too.

CHAPTER 70

Three weeks of constant surveillance had passed. Feldman sat in his plush leather chair examining the lab from his office. The kid was smart. He had tried to play Feldman's own game and had managed to pull off a pretty impressive attempt. The kid just didn't seem to realize that unfortunately he wasn't holding any of the aces. He'd also brought up something that Feldman hadn't given much thought to. The professor had died and his protégés had disappeared. There very well could be an investigation, and an investigation could lead back to him. After all, it was his money that linked him to Millenburg and the kids. Like it or not, he still needed them.

The intercom buzzed. Feldman punched the button, irritated. "I asked not to be disturbed. Thank you."

The secretary pressed on. "Mister Feldman? I'm sorry, but John Foreman is on line two and has asked me to make *sure* you knew that it was him."

"Thank you."

He reached for the phone, brought the receiver to his ear and paused with his finger over the flashing red light that indicated a waiting call. As if he had speed dialed a new identity, his demeanor changed. His eyes brightened and he answered the phone. "Hello, John," he said with all the cheerfulness and confidence he could muster.

"Vance. How are you?"

"Fine thanks," he said, but a bead of sweat snuck down his cheek.

Foreman's tone was intense. "Do you have that situation under control yet?"

"Oh yes. Things are coming along just fine. I've got it under control." How stupid, repeating the man's words. Too late now, just carry on, he scolded himself.

"I'm glad to hear that," he said, and added in a too-civil manner to be believable, "You take care, Vance, and be sure to keep me apprised of any new developments."

"I will. Thank you."

Somewhere in the middle of that sentence there was a click from the other end and the phone line went silent.

Thank you? How dumb can you make yourself sound, Feldman thought. "Gotta love the game," he said sarcastically to himself as he tossed the phone onto the desk.

With his elbow propped on the desk he rubbed his forehead with the palm of his hand. Everything's under control, right? Really, everything is under control, he tried to convince himself.

He pondered the problem for only a moment before forcing his mind back to the most important issue at hand—those too-damn-smart kids. He had to have a viable plan. There could be no mistakes. There would be no investigation.

The solution came to him all at once. It was simple, really. His original plan had been that Daniel and Camille would merely disappear. Unfortunately, this was impossible. They needed to be available to correspond with their families. If they weren't missing, there would be no reason to investigate. Millenburg's death would continue to be a tragic accident and there would be no connection between his death and the missing university students who worked under him.

CHAPTER 71

Two days had passed since Feldman visited the lab and Daniel had not been able to force Feldman's hand. It was frustrating to think that he had been wrong. He knew Feldman could not risk an investigation. He couldn't afford to have any connection with Millenburg's death. Feldman would have to ensure there was no evidence that might lead to suspicion falling on him.

Daniel went into the bathroom. It was the only place in the lab where he felt he had any privacy. He sat on the toilet and racked his mind for a solution. It seemed that even expressing his thoughts with Camille had become impossible. He reached his hand out idly and began to twirl the roll on its spindle. The paper was rough, almost the texture of newspaper. All at once he had an idea. From the time he began his college career, he had developed the habit of carrying a pen or pencil behind his ear and, even now, there was one there at his disposal. On a strip of paper he began to scribble his thoughts as fast as they came.

Camille,

I was thinking that you could use this note for its intended purpose after you've finished reading it. I plan on using the bathroom at least three or four times a day, maybe more. We should be able to communicate freely.

Love you babe,
Daniel

CHAPTER 72

Tom Davenport had never been a happy man. Normally he looked like a crocodile having a bad decade. Today he was much worse than that. Feldman had sent him to clean out an apartment. When he had asked why, Feldman had blared, "Because it's what I pay you to do, that's why."

That prick.

He turned the key in the lock and entered the small pad. He tossed the moving boxes he had brought in the middle of the floor along with all of the plastic bags, except one. He collected the blankets and began to stuff them in. When that bag filled he stuffed it into an open box. He threw the kid's stupid rock samples into it. Another plastic bag held almost all the clothes that hung in the closet. He worked as efficiently as he could. He'd be damned if he was going to spend any more time on this errand than necessary. It was bullshit. There was nothing more he could say about it. This whole errand was a petty load of crap.

With the truck loaded to the hilt, he drove back to the Feldman estate and parked at the rear entrance reserved for serving staff and those with less status. There was a sign posted outside the double doors. "For Loading and Unloading ONLY." His part of the job was done. It was up to the house staff to figure out what to do with the garbage from here on out.

The following day, when Tom returned to move the truck, he was happy to see it was empty. He slammed the rear doors closed and took the truck back to the garage.

CHAPTER 73

Several days had passed in the lab and so far work had been easy to avoid. Feldman had given no specific instructions and he hadn't been back since Daniel had threatened him. There was a TV, but there were only two channels. One was a weather channel and the other was the Discovery channel. Neither provided news from the outside world.

They sat watching a rerun of the Crocodile Hunter. A large snake had just bitten the host who was in the process of explaining how it wasn't the snake's fault, when the elevator door opened and a man dressed like a technician entered. He walked over to the desk and began the work of installing a phone. Maybe they weren't going to be using the intercom as the main source of communication after all. The man finished his work and tested the phone. Satisfied that it worked properly, he gathered his tools and left without saying anything. Daniel wondered what lie Feldman told the man before he had been allowed to get into the elevator.

Once the doors were closed Camille crossed to the desk and put the receiver to her ear. "Daniel, there's a dial tone." She began to dial the number to her parents' house. She mouthed to Daniel, *It's ringing.* Her enthusiasm disappeared and her heart sank when the ringing stopped and an automated female voice spoke clearly into her ear, "Please hang up and try your call again." Camille continued to listen. There was a pause and then the voice repeated the automated response. A moment later the phone returned to the steady dial tone signal. She tried a long distance call to her sister, but again the same message greeted her.

She turned to Daniel, "I don't know. It doesn't work. Why would he have a phone installed that doesn't work?"

"My guess is that he wouldn't," Daniel said.

A voice came from the speakers, "*Very good*, Daniel. You posed an interesting and problematic question. It compelled me to deal with the issue in a way I hadn't planned on. I can't say that I'm completely satisfied with the solution, but I think it will suffice for now.

"The phone in front of you looks like and is a regular phone in every way. There are some special features that I had installed. One, it will not allow outgoing calls of any kind. Well, that's not entirely true. There is a special dial function that I control from up here. Why don't you hit zero now?"

Camille followed his directions. There was a ringing on the other end and this time a familiar voice answered, "*Very good.* Can you please push the speaker phone button?"

Camille did and Feldman's next words came clearly from the phone. "That's my direct number and it will only be available to you when I wish it to be. Any other time you will hear a recording that will allow you to record a voice message. Please do not abuse this feature or I will have it removed. It's really that simple. I debated whether it would be useful at all, but I thought that you might have a need to instigate a call now and again. It'll also be easier than using the intercom or watching the monitor for comments or concerns you might have.

"The main feature for this phone is for incoming calls." He laughed. "I can see your wheels turning, Daniel. Whatever it is that you're already scheming, you can forget about it. All calls this phone receives have been redirected from your old home number. I will screen all calls and only those I feel necessary for you to respond to will be forwarded to you. The rest? They can leave a voice message if they choose to.

"For now, you have given up your lease and dropped out of school. That only leaves your parents who might want to contact you. And from the looks of your phone bills, they don't call very often. Every phone call that I forward to you will be monitored. If it appears that you are trying to get some kind of message out, I will terminate the call. Please don't make it more costly to keep you around than you're worth."

There was a click from the other end and the phone went dead. Daniel excused himself to go to the bathroom.

CHAPTER 74

A young man wearing a white smock wheeled a trolley out of the elevator. A rich breakfast aroma rolled out from under the covered dishes. Along with the delicious smell rose a faint white vapor that denoted the hot food that lay beneath. He rolled the trolley into the hall, stepped back into the elevator and pushed a button. He stood statuesque until the doors closed.

Daniel and Camille took their dishes and sat in front of the TV. They had been eating silently for a time when Camille stopped chewing mid-bite and began to stare at her steaming cup of coffee.

"Camille, stop zonin'," Daniel said.

She stood absently, brushing his hand away. She walked over to the trolley and lifted the lid on the teapot. Steam wafted up. Her behavior made no sense.

"What are you doing," Daniel asked.

Camille ignored him.

Daniel crossed to the breakfast trolley to see what she was staring at. She jerked around and walked to the bathroom. She snatched a blanket from her bed and draped it around her shoulders like a superman cape. She ran to the sofa, jumped on that and ran from one end to the other. She raced back to the trolley and stopped just long enough to kiss Daniel and then sat down to stuff a huge bite of egg into her mouth. She was up again in a flash skipping around the room once more. When enough of her energy was spent, she sat down a little calmer.

Daniel stared at her. "I repeat. What are you doing?

"I just love bacon and eggs," she said, beaming.

Something was either up or she had blown a fuse somewhere. He'd just have to wait until after breakfast to find out what it was.

After the meal Camille called out, "First dibs on the bathroom," and raced to the door.

Daniel sat on the couch and began to read a magazine while he waited. He had finished rereading an old article when the bathroom door opened and Camille emerged. "Finally. I though you were never coming out of there."

He sat on the toilet. The roll of toilet paper had been unwound and then rewrapped. There were dark ink marks that had bled through in the places where she scribbled her note. Daniel unwound the roll and began to read.

This is so cool, Daniel. It occurred to me that this place has to have access for heat, electrical and air circulation. While the vent out there is closely monitored, the one in here is not. We could remove the bathroom fan! I think the hole would be big enough that we could get out through it. It would just take a screwdriver to take a closer look. One of us could do that during lunch today. By tonight when we're having our showers we could be well on our way to getting out of here. I love you babe!

It was a good idea. Feldman thought he had taken everything into account, but maybe this is one thing he hadn't. The fan cover was fairly large. If the hole behind it was big enough, he might be able to fit through. The cover was about sixteen inches square. He tossed out Camille's message and scrawled a quick one of his own.

Camille made her bathroom visit and emerged in good spirits. It was all the evidence Daniel needed in order to know she had made progress. He would have to wait to find out how much. This was no longer about communicating, this was their best chance for escape and it was unlikely they would get another. If this failed, Feldman would make repairs and prevent something similar from happening again.

By the time the day came to a close, they were able to remove the guts of the fan and a hole, too dark to see into, was exposed. The fan sat on the rafters somewhere above the ceiling and the wires hung limply beside it.

Daniel rose early the next morning and stole into the bathroom. The hole where the exhaust fan had been was in the center of the room, a little off the edge of the toilet bowl. Daniel climbed onto the toilet and balanced on the tank. He leaned forward to get his torso into the hole but, even so, he wasn't tall enough to crawl up without some kind of a boost from below.

He waited there for a few minutes while his eyes became accustomed to the near absolute blackness. Slowly a kind of definition began to appear as he oriented himself to the faint images around him. There were a series of steel trusses supporting the ceiling. The ceiling was merely a cap to a pit. There were tendrils of cables and wires attached to the trusses stretching out somewhere behind him. Daniel turned carefully inside the hole to see where they led.

Every cable and all of the ductwork came to a junction next to the area that Daniel had always considered just an elevator shaft. In reality it was simply a structure in the corner of the great empty space that supported and guided the stainless steel metal box between the floors. The elevator was currently poised at the top waiting for someone to make the next trip down.

In the black it was impossible to tell where the ductwork terminated. The darkness and the unknown space was much like the mineshaft back on McMaster's farm. There was little he could do at the moment. He was nearly out of time and he still needed to take a quick shower. He stepped off the tank and dangled from the hole. Using only his upper body strength he lowered himself down onto the toilet lid. He flipped the shower on and scribbled a brief note to Camille before jumping in. No more than two minutes later he was drying off and stepping through the door. Breakfast would arrive soon and Camille would want to take an opportunity to discover for herself what lay above them.

When he emerged Camille appeared to be asleep in her bed. He crossed the room and sat beside her. She rolled over as if she was just waking up, but Daniel could tell there was no sign of sleep or drowsiness in her eyes. She rose and carried on her charade all the way through the bathroom door. She closed and locked the door behind her. It was Daniel's turn to wonder what was going on in there.

***

Camille pulled out the portion of paper that Daniel had scribbled on. She had expected to see more, but he had written only one word, "Cool." He must have thought that she could solve the problem of getting up into the hole in the ceiling on her own. She stood on the toilet seat as she had done in the past to work on removing the fan, but that only got her closer. She was much shorter than Daniel and not nearly as strong. She crawled up on top of the tank and reached over to the hole in the ceiling. Her body swayed. She pushed off from the tank. It slammed into the wall. For a moment, she wondered how far the sound would carry. She was able to hold her head into the open space before dropping down once more onto the toilet. In disgust she jumped to the floor only to discover that she had stepped into a growing puddle of water.

She turned to see that the water was coming from the now broken toilet tank. She spun around trying to figure out what to do to stop the water, but nothing sprang to mind. She bent down. Under the toilet, just ahead of the flexible water supply line was a valve. She reached behind the tank, felt around until her hand came to rest on the metal knob and turned it until the sound of running water stopped. Water still poured from the tank, so she flushed the toilet. She threw a few towels on the floor to sop up the mess and then took a shower of her own.

Sick and disappointed, she robotically cleaned herself. There was no way they could recover from this. How long could they go without a toilet? What on earth could they do now?

As had already become habit, she scribbled a brief apology and expressed her anger that Daniel hadn't left a more detailed message. Then she left the bathroom. She was angry and frustrated with herself, so when Daniel asked her what happened she replied, quite naturally, "I slipped and slammed my shin into the toilet bowl." She paused. "Everything's fine," she said with pursed lips.

They went back to work as Feldman requested but the task was tedious and uninteresting. Side by side they puttered at the workbench making no headway and not caring. The problem with their tactic was that it made waiting more difficult. They had agreed to run old experiments. Double checking the results was always a good idea and it made them look busy, but it bored them. And as long as escape was all consuming, nothing else mattered.

They worked through the morning hardly speaking. All of the important conversations took place on the toilet paper roll. Camille walked over to the toolbox and began rummaging through it. She burrowed her way to the bottom and produced a partial roll of duct tape. How could she get Daniel to take it with him the next time he went? She placed it where he could plainly see it, careful to be casual about it, not drawing undue attention, and continued the menial task she had been working on. Occasionally she'd glance over to see if he noticed what she had done. He hadn't.

For God's sake, Daniel, *duct tape? You don't think that's a little odd?* She waited patiently for thirty minutes, all the while her frustration growing. She even walked past him, moving the roll of tape closer to him on the way — again, not being conspicuous, but surely he'd get the ... *oh no,* he scooted it away from him, like anything else not needed for his task at the moment. Why? He doesn't seem occupied with anything of significance.

***

Images from the space above them cluttered Daniel's mind as he worked through his plans. Beside him, Camille worked alone and that was fine. He glanced up at the clock, disappointed by its slow progress.

Camille interrupted him by placing some object beside him for the third time. He hadn't been paying attention to her or whatever the object was, but the slightly more emphatic gesture this time gave him pause to look and see what was so important. Duct tape. *Duct tape?*

Duct tape.

There it was, as plain as the message now was obvious. He raised his eyebrows in understanding. She rolled her eyes as if to say, *it's about time.* He needed to have the tape with him during his next potty break. It was unimportant to understand why at this point. Something had happened in the bathroom earlier in the morning and he would need the duct tape; that much was clear.

***

The floor was still damp when he arrived inside. He hadn't expected to have to repair the toilet before using it, and was in need of defecating … *soon*. When Camille slammed the toilet against the wall it had created a large triangular crack in the back of the tank. The bottom of the 'V' was lower than the highest point the water filled to. It was obvious that the water would run continuously and would never be able to fill the reservoir if he did not repair the crack. To add to the trouble, one part of the crack extended almost to the bottom of the tank.

He hastened to sop out the remaining water and dry it out as well as he could. If only the tape would stick to the inside of the tank. It did. Holding his near-bursting bowels at bay, he started near the bottom and worked his way up the crack to the top, making what he hoped would be a watertight seal. Once finished, he hurried—his bowels now about to explode—to replace the lid, turn on the water supply, lower the seat, sit, and … finally get relief.

The regular cleaning staff came down once a week to do a thorough cleaning of the lab. That included the bathroom. They were due again in just two days. Daniel glanced at the hole in the ceiling and then down at the floor. The combination of dust and water made mud, which now covered a large amount of the linoleum. They had destroyed the fan, but it sat above the ceiling out of the way. Daniel was grateful he didn't have to try to dispose of it.

There was just time enough to scrawl a quick note and clear the area. Stay calm, slow down and let's make it work so we can get the hell out of here, he thought. In his note, Daniel suggested that he take on the task of repairing the hole in the ceiling, while Camille could work at cleaning up the bathroom. He pictured her smiling ironically to herself at his proposed division of labor. Once again, leave it to the woman to do the cleaning. But she'd understand the logic. She didn't have the height necessary to work on the ceiling, so the suggestion that she do the cleaning made more sense.

Twenty-four hours passed since Daniel repaired the toilet. When he reentered, the duct tape looked to be holding. Now that the tank lid was in place it was impossible to see the crack that snaked across the back. Camille had done a great job of cleaning the bathroom. She had gone through almost a full roll of toilet paper, but the room looked nearly as clean as it did when the staff finished their job.

In order to fix the hole in the ceiling, Daniel had started with two metal clothes hangers. He shaped the wire and attached it to the backside of the plastic grate. He shaped the hangers to form tabs that could hang onto the joists above. They crossed the cover like a 'plus' sign. He put the screen forty-five degrees out of position, aligning the tangs with the corners of the hole. He pushed the cover up into the opening and when he turned it in place it covered the hole nicely. The wires did a good job of holding the grating in place, but it did not fit as tight against the ceiling as Daniel had hoped. After several fittings, he had made it work as well as he could. Standing from the floor and glancing up, only a discerning eye would notice that something was out of place.

Time was running short, and he needed to rig some kind of a way for Camille to get easy access to the hatch so that she too could get up through the ceiling.

***

Camille sat with her breakfast plate pushed aside. Bright patches of light had begun to swirl behind her eyes. She closed them, hoping the sensation would go away, but the brightness sharpened. Her hands found their way to her temples as she tried to focus.

"Camille, are you all right?"

"Yea, I'm fine. Just give me sec."

"You don't look so good."

"Shhh. Just hold on a minute." His worried look didn't soften, but at least he stopped talking. The images began to clear somewhat. She could see delicate hands that must belong to a woman. The hands were on the handle of some kind of a trolley. The contents of the cart bounced up and down with every step. Beyond the cart was a hallway that Camille did not recognize. The trolley was made of stainless steel. There was a variety of plastic bottles on the top tray.

"Daniel, the maid's coming."

"She's not supposed to come until tomorrow."

"Well she's coming early." The images were growing clearer. Proximity was important. The elevator door came into view. "I'll be right back. I've got to go to the toilet."

Camille busied herself double checking the toilet. She stripped a few sheets of paper off where the scribbles of the last message could still be seen. She tossed them into the toilet and flushed it. Daniel could rewrite the message if he needed to. The floor was dry, so she knew the duct tape was holding. She glanced up at the fan cover. It looked properly in place.

She ignored the sound of the descending elevator. It confirmed what she had known for some time. If Daniel didn't understand what she meant or the significance of it, he'd know in a few moments.

The maid appeared in the elevator door. She wheeled a trolley equipped with a large garbage can and all of the supplies needed for a thorough cleaning. Now that she had arrived, Camille scrutinized her hands and imagined the view she'd have from the woman's perspective. It was the verification she had hoped for. The things she saw in her mind were not approximations as she had feared. Everything she was now looking at, she saw moments earlier as the woman made her way down the corridor.

Camille glanced at Daniel. She had no desire to address his look of bewilderment. He was a smart man. He'd figure it out, if he hadn't already. The persistent exposure to the crystal, even in this small amount, had begun to affect her. Flashes had begun to happen a while ago, but they had never been like this. They were never as clear before and there had been no way to know that what she saw was even real. Now she knew for certain that what she saw in her mind was really happening.

The custodian began her work in the restroom. Had Camille been thorough enough? She could only hope. She walked by the bathroom trying to appear nonchalant and, on each pass, the woman looked as though she was carrying out her job in the way she always had. Camille tried to see inside the janitor's mind, but all that was clear was the woman's hatred for her work. No need for clairvoyance, Camille could see that much from the woman's demeanor. Several hours passed and she left without acknowledging either of them.

CHAPTER 75

Camille was developing an interesting skill set; this much Daniel was sure of. Rather than risk another catastrophe trying to help Camille up into the ceiling, Daniel would prepare for the escape.

The work was easier than Daniel could have hoped, interrupted briefly by a single visit from Feldman that Camille had been able to predict. He had come to make sure they were making progress to his satisfaction. Since he had no real understanding of what they were doing, it was a simple enough to tell him everything was going well and they would report anything as soon as they could.

As they talked, Feldman wandered around the room. He paused in the sleeping area and then wandered into the bathroom. Camille shuddered as she watched him make his way around the cell. She knew the purpose of his visit had not been to get an update on progress. She wondered what they might have let slip. Feldman's fingertip found the light switch in the bathroom and he flipped it on. Camille prayed he would not flip the second switch as well—the one for the exhaust fan. She held her breath as he reached for it … then breathed easy when there was no second click.

His head moved around the room giving some indication of where he was looking. He glanced at the sink, toilet and bathtub. He stopped for a short look into the wastebasket. Camille had written the last note, and it lay hidden rerolled under a couple of layers of paper waiting for Daniel to read it. Would he notice anything different about the toilet paper roll? After what felt like a day beyond eternity … he left the restroom, without glancing toward the ceiling.

His inspection was apparently complete. "In reviewing the tapes, I couldn't help but notice your frequent use of the restroom. It occurred to me that something might be going on. I cannot imagine what you could be doing that takes you so long in there, but if you do not wish to have the walls around the toilet removed altogether, I suggest you spend a little less time in there."

Without saying more, he and his small entourage disappeared into the elevator. The crushing angst was mitigated at last, seeing them go and knowing their secret was still intact. But time was now of the essence … it had all but run out.

Daniel waited until late that night. He found that once he got into the space above the cell it was easy enough to scale the girders supporting the elevator and climb to the floor above. A vent cover was all that was between him and the outside. From his vantage point he could see a guard sitting beside the elevator door. There was no way of telling what might be going on in the surveillance room, but with a guard outside and the prisoners asleep, he hoped the cameras were running with no one to man them. Since they had never attempted an escape before, Daniel thought it was a reasonable bet that even if there were a guard on duty, he wouldn't be watching the monitors the entire time. They would have do this soon—the following night was decided upon.

Daniel waited until 1:30 in the morning, then nudged Camille as the signal to get moving. He could see her blinking in the near darkness. He would go first. It would have been nice if they could have taken some belongings, but the risk was too high. It had been hard enough to leave a few clothes in a backpack in the bathtub the previous day. He had worn a double set of clothes for the better part of the morning before he had an opportunity to go the bathroom and ditch them there. He placed his pillow strategically for the camera so that a casual glance might give the impression he was still in bed. He slid his feet into his runners and staggered to the bathroom where he changed his clothes, turned out the light and waited for Camille.

About a half an hour had passed, the door opened. Camille flipped the light switch on. She slipped into her clothes while Daniel opened the hatch above. Daniel boosted Camille up and when she had her hands firmly anchored on a rafter above, he lifted her the rest of the way. Seconds later she vanished into the darkness.

Daniel looked around the room to make sure they were leaving nothing behind. Camille's nightgown still lay in the tub. He picked it up, stuffed it into the pack and pushed it up into the opening. Camille's hand appeared, snaked down and took it from him. Daniel tore off a few sheets of toilet paper just to make sure he left no evidence behind, flushed the toilet and turned out the light before climbing up into the hole.

Holding onto the wire tangs, he lowered the cover through the hole and then pulled it back up into place. He turned it a quarter of a turn to square it with the ceiling. They made their way across the beams to the elevator and began their ascent. Kneeling before the vent cover they could see the guard sitting in his chair reading a magazine. At least he wasn't sleeping, Daniel had the ironic thought, for a second imagining himself the guard's employer. Eventually, he put the magazine down, locked the elevator, and left his post.

Clips in each corner held the metal cover in place. Daniel pushed until the top clips gave way, but the panel tipped forward out of his control. The grate was on its way toward the floor. Daniel reached out toward it, but he missed. There was no time for a second try. He was at the end of his lunge.

Camille's hand darted past him. She reached low where it was still attached to the frame. She was able to hold it there, but she was off balance and reaching around Daniel at the same time. She wheezed at him to help her.

It was the time Daniel needed. He was able to get hold of the grate as well. He moved it out of the way and crawled through the opening. Camille followed and replaced the vent cover. They stole up the staircase and toward the front door.

CHAPTER 76

It was the breakfast boy who was unfortunate enough to discover that the captives were missing. Ignoring the steaming trolley, he raced to the centre of the room and called out frantically to the cameras and sensors, "They're gone!" He then turned and rushed to the elevator and waited impatiently for it to reach the top.

***

Tom Davenport had been working for Feldman for years. He had begun his work as Feldman's personal limousine driver. Back then he was single and unattached. He had a background in self-defense. His black belt in Karate was enough to satisfy Feldman that his training was sufficient for the post. While Tom was intelligent enough and could have held a job doing anything he wanted, his real love was hand-to-hand combat and he had been looking for an occupation that might give him an opportunity to use his extensive training.

The first few years had been disappointing. Although Feldman was wealthy, he was not as threatened as he may have thought he was. Tom had considered giving up the job on more than one occasion and he did not hesitate to let Feldman know about it. He was merely a foreman with occasional fill in work to do. Today he had taken the morning shift outside the lab elevator. The regular guy had called in sick and Tom had been available.

The elevator door opened and the kitchen boy scrambled out in a panic. It took Davenport a moment to make sense of his jabbering, but when he did, he pulled his cell phone from his pocket and hit the speed dial for his second–in–command. "Send backup down to the lab immediately." Though his voice was cold and emotionless, the urgency in it was clear. Several men appeared within moments and he rattled off a series of orders, pointing at the men in turn with his directives. "You, stay here and keep an eye on the elevator. You three, lock down the house and make sure no one leaves the building. You two organize the dogs. We may need them." With his final words he was already stepping into the elevator.

He reached the lab and began to scour the apartment. There were no hiding places in the room. The only area left without surveillance was the bathroom. He ripped the door open and slid his hand upward against the switches. The light came on and he scanned the room. Nothing out of order, but he began his investigation anyway, starting with the garbage can. There were just a few tissues inside. He dumped the contents on the floor. Nothing of interest there. He moved to the sink and ran his hands along the bottom edge. Nothing out of place. Davenport opened the medicine cabinet and pulled everything from the shelves. He removed the lid from the toilet's water closet and immediately noticed the copious amount of duct tape. How might the broken toilet fit into what was appearing to be an amazing escape?

The only other place he could think that they might have tried to escape from was the air vent. It was in the lab and had a camera dedicated to it. How could they have escaped through it eluding the cameras? This exit had been bolted shut during construction. He pulled at the screen noticing that it was still mounted firmly to the wall. No way could they have refastened it after escaping.

The elevator dinged. The doors opened and a furious Feldman stalked into the room. "Have you found anything?"

"Nothing that I can report so far, Mister Feldman. I'm hoping the tapes will reveal something." He paused. "There *was* something out of place in the bathroom, but I can't figure out what it might mean."

"What is it? Spit it out!"

Davenport hated it when Feldman treated him like a child. "The toilet tank is busted and they repaired it with duct tape."

"Really?" It was a rhetorical question. Feldman didn't wait for an answer. He went to the bathroom, flipped the light switch on and went straight to the toilet to examine it. He leaned the cover against the wall and sat down on the toilet seat. He sat there, glancing around the room, looking for clues when his eyes came to rest on the exhaust fan in the ceiling.

Davenport began to feel uneasy. He should be doing something, but he couldn't figure out what. Feldman had looked up at the fan. It occurred to them suddenly as if the two men were thinking as one. Feldman was already climbing up on the toilet seat examining the fan's screen. He noticed right away there were no screws holding it on. He took hold of the edges and yarded the useless piece of plastic out of the ceiling. Where there should have been a fan, there was only a gaping hole. He looked around for something to stand on and the toilet came to mind immediately. It was instantly apparent how the toilet tank had broken. Feldman climbed up on it. Not being a particularly tall man, he could not see beyond the top of the rafter above.

"Where can they get to from here?" he demanded.

"It's just an open hole, sir. The only exit from this room is by the elevator."

"If that's true, then they are still in there. Bring in a crew and search the area. In the meantime, send the dogs out. If they've already gotten out of the building I want them stopped."

Feldman climbed down leaving Davenport to solve the problems he'd given him. Davenport pulled out his cell and punched more numbers. "I need three more men. Send them down right away." As an afterthought he threw in, "Have them bring a step ladder and a flash light when they come."

It took less than five minutes for the three men to arrive with the ladder and light. Davenport took the ladder and slid it into place below the hole in the ceiling. He climbed up and called for the flashlight. He switched it on and peered around. There were no surprises. It was a large open area with a space in one corner where the elevator traveled up and down. At first glance the area seemed empty and there was no obvious way out. Davenport climbed down.

He handed the flashlight back to the man. "I want one of you to stay in this room, in case they return. I want the other two of you to get up there and try to figure out either where they are, or where they've gone."

Davenport returned to the main floor. The dogs were on their way and would arrive shortly. The building was locked down and a guard stood ready at each door just as had been ordered. There was nothing he could do but wait.

The grate next to the elevator flipped open and crashed to the floor. One of the men he had sent to search the area began to crawl from the hole. "Mister Davenport, if they came out, they must have come through here. There is no other way out of the room," said the man.

Davenport stormed through the halls until he came to the surveillance room and crashed through the doors. A man sat at a monitor fast-forwarding through the video footage. "Tell me about the progress you've made."

"I'm still looking at footage from yesterday, sir."

"I want you to skip ahead. Can you start from around midnight?"

The man made adjustments.

"Can't you go any faster?" Davenport blustered.

It was impossible to tell that the technician was fast searching at all. There was no movement in the monitor display except for the occasional shifting of a body in the bed.

Wait. A form rose and speed-waddled to the bathroom.

"Stop. Rewind that," Davenport commanded.

The technician did as he was told. It was Daniel on his way to the bathroom.

"Okay, forward some more."

The clock on the tape fast-forwarded while the image remained unchanged. Twenty-five minutes passed and Daniel did not emerge from the bathroom. Suddenly a second image rose. In fast forward mode, it seemed to race from the sleeping area to the toilet.

"Stop," ordered Davenport. "Rewind that."

The time on the monitor said the footage was from 2:25 a.m. Davenport left the room. As he darted through the halls he pulled a radio up to his face and barked, "Where are those dogs?"

CHAPTER 77

Camille and Daniel stepped out of the entry way and onto the sidewalk, the smell of the nearby ocean filling their nostrils. Avoiding the large pools of light cast by stadium lights which dotted the entire estate, the fugitives raced toward the sound of the surf, stopping abruptly at a cliff's edge. On the surf below the waves lapped at the shore within a few feet of the cliff wall. If the tide was on its way out then great but, if it was on its way in, there was only a short time before it would be beating against the rocks.

"Look. *There*," directed Camille in a harsh whisper.

She was pointing to a concrete path that led toward the precipice. They bolted to it. The path ended at a set of steps that led down to a viewing area facing the ocean. On one side was a small shelter providing cover for a telescope. On the other were several benches. A stone barrier surrounded the entire area except for one small gap in the middle. They ran to the gap. There were steps leading to the shore and they scrambled down them leaving the lights and their prison behind.

At the bottom, the steps disappeared into the sand. Only the fact that the ocean was just slightly lighter in color than the earth bordering it gave them an indication where the two met. Their way to freedom was obvious. They ran along the shoreline staying in the water. The waves erased their passage. Moments later Daniel came to a halt. Camille ran into him. They faced a steep wall of rock that jutted into the ocean creating a private beach.

Camille assessed the situation in a flash. "We'll have to swim."

Even in the near dark she could see the concerns on Daniel's face. She assumed he might be worried that the waves would crash them into the rocks, but he surprised her by saying, "I can't swim. I never learned how."

There was no way out at this end, maybe there was one at the other. She turned and began to race up the beach in the opposite direction. This time Daniel followed. Their window of opportunity was soon slamming shut. There was no way to tell when their absence would be discovered. Camille's lungs were burning, but she raced on. A sense of déjà vu filled her mind. She had seen this before. Impossible.

"I need a rest," Camille said, gasping, with her head between her knees. They had been running for ten minutes. There was no sign that the beach was widening. It was possible that Feldman's beach was entirely private. To top it off they were running away from civilization and not toward it. The only sound in the night was the surf.

They had begun their escape in the near pitch black of the early morning. The sun was beginning to rise now, lending more definition to their surroundings. Now that Camille had recovered a bit, their all out dash resumed with a slow jog. Camille looked back over her shoulder. She could still see the lights from the Feldman estate and it frustrated her that it seemed so dismally close. She turned her face forward again. There were a series of large signs erected at short intervals in front of them. The signs stretched from the rocks to the water. There was enough light to read the bright red letters. "Private Property. Trespassers Will Be Prosecuted. No Access Beyond This Point." Camille sighed in relief. If they were not out of Feldman's clutches, at least they were off his property.

Camille danced in the sand.

"What are you doing," Daniel asked.

"I know where we are! I've been down here before. This place is called White Sands beach." She broke into a jog and Daniel followed.

The shoreline widened significantly but the cliff was still visible on the right. Above them a forested ribbon lined the cliff. Camille ran on.

***

The sky had begun to brighten significantly and the details of the shoreline were beginning to become clear. The main access to the beach was just ahead. Camille left the water's edge and turned toward the parking lot. As far as Daniel could tell, no one was following them. But that didn't mean anything, he knew, and it would be easy to figure where they had gone. It was frightening to think there was no plan for their next move—all it would take to end up enslaved again would be a car waiting in the parking lot ahead. He'd had a lifetime of captivity. The risk was simply not worth it.

"*Camille*," he yelled.

She continued to run.

"Camille!"

She turned and it was bright enough to see the furrow in her brow.

Now that he had her attention he motioned to her.

"What is it," she asked, jogging impatiently in place.

"We need to think about what we're doing. If they're after us, this is the first access to the beach. If they know we're gone, this could be the first place they'd look."

"What time is it?"

"What?"

"What time do you have?" This time it was more of a demand than a question.

"Five thirty," Daniel said.

Three hours had passed since she walked into the bathroom earlier that morning. "If we haven't been followed so far, we should be good for about another half an hour. Breakfast won't come until later and if they didn't catch us on the monitor, there won't be a reason for them to check the tapes until after that. Besides, I don't know of any other way off this beach. Come on. We're wasting time."

"Can we at least be a little more careful?"

Camille nodded and led the way up the beach toward the cliff base.

A set of stairs led to the parking area. As they reached the top they hunkered down and crept up the last few steps on their bellies.

CHAPTER 78

Davenport glanced at his watch periodically as he paced the halls, holding his two-way radio in his hand. After bringing the mic to his mouth uncountable times, only to return it to its position on his belt in exasperation, he decided to take a walk on the grounds. At least it was something he could do.

Fifteen minutes later he had skirted the entire building and checked with each of the posts. Somewhere, someone was crowding dogs into the back of a van to bring them to the estate. There was no way of telling when they'd get here. Hell, it might even be too late already.

Dew was still thick on the grass. The bottoms of Davenport's pants were soaking wet, water seeping into his Guccis. He wandered to the front of the building, estimating there must have been about a quarter mile of groomed lawn and trees in almost every direction. A deer grazed next to the tall rock wall. Its tracks dotted the lawn, appearing light grey-green in the dark grass.

He noticed a large area of disturbed grass. Maybe a deer had bedded there. Curious, he walked closer to examine it. Even before he was on top of the marks he realized the tracks had not been created by wild life. The trail led back toward the mansion in one direction and in the other it continued over to the concrete path that led down to the viewpoint. Davenport's hand flew to his radio.

"Calvin!"

"Yes sir," a voice crackled.

"When the dogs get here take them down to the beach. I'm heading over to White Sands. Let me know if you come up with anything."

"I'm on it, Mister Davenport."

Tom Davenport didn't bother to reply. He was already jogging to the garage. The road wound along the beach. It was a bit of a loop and it would take him at least twenty minutes to get there if he left immediately. He called the front gate.

"Yes, Mister Davenport?"

"I'll be there in less than five minutes. Have the gate open when I arrive."

"Yes sir."

Tom ran to the garage. By the time he was in the car and on his way to the gate he was later than he'd predicted. In the distance he could see the metal gates beginning to swing open. He could not expect this kind of service at the next gate. He raced through the small village knowing he would draw complaints about his speeding. It was the nature of the sort of people who tended to live in these kinds of places and not something he was going to worry about at the moment.

Davenport arrived at the final gate. He punched the numbers into the pad and tapped the steering wheel while the gate took its time swinging out of his way. Before it had finished its arc he sped through, barely clearing the mirror. The road teed. Davenport glanced to the right and cranked the wheel to the left without coming to a full stop. There was a car to the left, but the driver slammed on his brakes. It was enough for Davenport to make the turn. He ignored the angry hand gestures from the other driver and in seconds the trees were flying past him.

Like most oceanfront roads, this one was curvy and slow. He cut the corners and took them as fast as the car would allow. He looked down at his speedometer to see he was traveling sixty-five. He rounded a corner to see the first signpost warning that the parking area of White Sands beach was approaching. He flew by it. Although he was less than quarter of a mile away and could see his turn just ahead, he maintained his speed. He was almost upon the road when he dropped two gears and slammed on the breaks. The RPM on the tachometer jumped and the wheels skipped on the pavement. The car slithered around the corner with wheels squealing. He dropped one more gear and glided into the parking lot, scanning the area ahead.

It was early morning. There were no other vehicles around. He pulled into a nearby parking space. A weathered sign with a blue wheel chair on a white background stood directly in front of him. Ignoring it, he stepped out of the car and proceeded down the steps to the beach.

CHAPTER 79

Camille peeked over the last step into the parking lot. If they got onto the road they had a better chance of getting away. The lot was empty so they walked over to the highway, maintaining a cautious vigil.

The city was down the road to the right. The only way back was to pass by Feldman's estate. As dangerous as it might be, when they got to the winding coast road they began to walk toward town. Camille wondered what might be going on with Faber. The last time they had seen him, he had been working to decipher the images they had given him. Maybe by now he had some answers. She hoped Feldman hadn't found him yet.

Daniel grabbed her arm and hissed in alarm, "*Vehicle.*"

They ducked into the foliage next to the road. The odds were good that it was just an early morning traveler, but nothing was worth risking it. A Jaguar sped by and Daniel recognized the man behind the wheel. Feldman's head goon. They watched as he dropped gears and skidded into the beach's parking area.

"Maybe this wasn't such a good idea," Daniel suggested.

Camille's shrugged her shoulders. "I hope you're wrong. This is the best way back."

"Let's stick to the woods for now."

Dew may have been heavy enough on the grass, but in the woods they were soon soaked from the waist down. "Maybe we should go into the forest a little farther," Camille said. "There's a better chance the undergrowth won't be so deep away from the edge of the road."

Although the bushes did thin out a fair amount, it was clear that early morning travel through a wooded area meant they were going to get wet. They trudged on ignoring the growing discomfort in their feet. The bottom of Daniel's right big toe had begun to sting, but there was nothing he could do about it. He did what he could to ignore the pain.

Their progress came to rude stop when they came to a stone wall rising out of the foliage. It disappeared in both directions for as far as they could see. "Feldman's property line," Daniel surmised.

The ocean lay to the right. They turned left and began to work their way along the fence toward the road.

"Camille," Daniel said. "I'm sorry, I gotta stop."

"What's the matter?"

"I'm not sure." He sat down on a dead log and untied his shoe. His socks were soaking wet. The tip of his right toe was bright red. He slowly peeled back the fabric. His feet were the texture and the color of prunes and looked as though they had never seen sun. He wondered if they would ever recover. Once he got the sock off he rolled his foot over to get a better look at the underside. There was a thick loose flap of skin on the bottom of his toe. The flesh beneath was a rich strawberry color. It was obvious why he had been having trouble walking.

Camille sat next to him, pulled the hem of her tee shirt out of her pants and tore a long strip off the bottom. "Put your foot up here," she said, indicating her lap. She pushed the flap of skin to its original position then wrapped the cloth around the wound and tied it with a small knot. She wrung the water from the sock and worked it onto his foot. "How does that feel?"

"Better."

"I can't believe that you held out so long. Do you think you're going to be able to walk?"

CHAPTER 80

The dogs finally arrived. Their handler was unloading them as Davenport came up the stairs from inspecting the beach. The trained animals nosed around the parking lot until they found the trail and they were off at a baying run. For the first while it had been easy for Davenport and the handler to stay near the edge of the road … until the trail suddenly dipped into the forest. Davenport waded through the underbrush cursing with every step. His suit was soaked within a few strides. Bits of bark, dry leaves and other plant material had already begun to stick to it. He prided himself on presenting himself well. This was simply disgraceful. Why the hell was Feldman trying to hold on to these two kids anyway?

The dogs were getting away from him. Stop allowing yourself to get distracted. You can change clothes later. He picked up his pace, ploughed through the brush and was relieved when it lightened. He had no way to know how far behind them he was. He pressed on fast as he could. After nearly an hour of slashing through the woods the trail came out onto the road again. The dogs turned toward the main gate. Davenport stopped to catch his breath and allow the growing pain in his side to subside a little. Then he broke into a casual jog. It was a good thing the dog handlers were in front of him. They could deal with any situation well enough.

The sound of the howling canines grew fainter as their gap increased. Davenport slowed, but continued a fast walk trying to remember why he hadn't waited in the car for a progress report. It was too late to worry about that now. His suit was an embarrassment: another seven hundred dollars thrown away.

CHAPTER 81

Daniel eased his foot into his shoe. He couldn't remember what Camille had said. He nodded to her, but he was no longer listening. His attention was on the sound of barking dogs far in the distance. He couldn't be sure, but the sound seemed to be getting closer. He retied his laces ignoring the pain and stood up. "Feels good," he said. "Thanks, but I think we need to get going, and fast."

They ran through the thick foliage with only a general idea of where they were going. The dogs were definitely in pursuit and the distance was closing. They broke onto the pavement. What if someone saw them? It was a risk they had to take. They needed a ride.

Daniel foot was in tremendous pain—he couldn't help but limp. He made the best of it as they hurried along. He kept most of his weight on his heel, forcing him to walk with his knee locked. They hugged the edge of the road. The nerve-wracking noise of those hounds seemed farther away for now, but that might be because they were still in the woods. What would happen once they hit the open road? The best thing to do was to increase the distance between them, so the fugitives raced on.

The road curved to the left, leaving the high fence behind and, for the time being anyway, Feldman's estate as well. But there was still the gated community to skirt. The barking continued to fade in the distance.

All at once the main gate appeared. Everything was quiet. They ran across the driveway. Daniel sighed audibly. Was the worst of their plight over? The sound of an approaching vehicle interrupted his thoughts. It was coming around the corner from behind too fast to gain cover before they would be seen.

CHAPTER 82

Davenport kept his pace for a while; then he noticed the yelping of the dogs was growing closer. He rounded a corner in the road to see them mulling about with the trainer close at hand. "What's going on?" he called.

"I'm trying to pick up the scent again." The handler took one of the dogs by the collar and, starting where the pack seemed to have lost the scent, he began to walk in ever increasing circles. When Davenport reached the scene the dog handler spoke to him. "It seems that the trail ends back there. I've tried to get the dogs to pick up the scent, but there's nothing here."

"Damn." Davenport pulled out his radio. "Send two vehicles down here on the double." He barked out his location and returned the two-way radio to its side holster. His impatience mounted as he watched the handlers take the dogs through the laboriously slow paces of trying to pick up the trail. They were being thorough, but Davenport already suspected they would find nothing. The most obvious reason the trail suddenly ended was that the two managed to get a ride from someone. There was no telling where they might be, but probably heading toward town. He'd have to find out what Feldman wanted to do and go from there.

The cars arrived. Davenport took the nicer of the two, a silver Audi, and sent the other two back for the car he'd left at the beach. He turned the vehicle around and headed to the mansion. He flipped his phone open and dialed Feldman's private line. Feldman answered the instant the phone rang, the frustration in his voice apparent. Tom Davenport didn't wait for Feldman to interrogate him. He launched right into his update. "We picked up their trail right away. It was easy to follow and led back around the estate. The dogs lost their scent just beyond the gate. It's likely they got a ride. If they did, they're probably heading into town."

"Get back here and meet me in my office."

Davenport arrived in the office damp and dirty. Feldman gave him a look somewhere between disdain and understanding, but didn't say anything. Davenport wisely stayed off the carpet. Feldman rattled off a number of possible destinations, with a brief explanation of each one.

CHAPTER 83

An old Volkswagen van barreled around the corner making more noise than a giant yellow Twinkie ought to. Years out of place, a young man adorned with dreadlocks, an old leather vest and enough beads to make a curtain, was at the wheel. A woman who couldn't have been much older than Camille rode in the passenger seat next to him. Camille shot her thumb into the air. They followed the van with their eyes in hopeful expectation, but it passed without slowing, dashing Camille's hopes, until ... the brake lights came on. The van slowed, came to a stop and began to back up. Camille and Daniel ran to meet it. It stopped with a halting screech when it reached their side.

"You two look as though you need a lift," said the driver through the open window.

"Oh wow! You have no idea," said Camille.

"How did you manage to get so wet," asked the passenger.

"Our shortcut up from the beach didn't turn out to be such a good short cut after all," said Daniel.

Camille nodded in agreement while the occupants of the van smiled their understanding — their curiosity seemingly satisfied. Daniel opened the rear door and they climbed in. Moments later the van was rattling down the road, a steady flow of conversation ensuing. The Hippies were more than happy to fill the silence with stories about their unconventional lifestyles and adventures. The miles sped by and before long the city loomed ahead.

They approached the first intersection when the driver interrupted one of his own stories. "Where do you wanna get dropped off?"

"We've got a room at the Motel Six just up the road here. Do you know where that is?"

"Be there in a flash," the enthused driver replied.

The van stopped in front of the main office and Daniel and Camille got out. The vehicle puttered off around the corner and disappeared. They waited for a moment until they could no longer hear the old beater and then Camille started walking up the street.

"Camille, where are you going?"

"To the only place we can go ... the museum."

It was true. Faber Smith was the only person who Feldman had not connected to them. The Motel 6 had been the perfect drop off point. Even if the bad guys went looking for them, they wouldn't get any information from here and the museum was only minutes away.

CHAPTER 84

Faber Smith sat at his desk hunkered beneath his lamp in near darkness. He appeared to be sleeping. Not wanting to startle the old man, Daniel cleared his throat. Faber continued to sit slumped over in his chair. Daniel cleared his throat again, this time louder. Still, Faber did not respond.

Camille feared the worst. She raced forward and shook Faber's shoulders. "Mister Smith. *Mister Smith*. Are you all right?"

The old man woke with a start. His hands shot to the vicinity of his heart in a single dramatic motion. His eyes flew open and his pupils rolled back in his head. "Girl, what are you trying to do, scare me to death?" he nearly yelled.

"Oh no, Mister Smith. I'm so sorry. We tried to—"

"Where the hell have you been? I've been worried sick about you two. You disappear without saying a word. *And look at you*. You're both a mess. You better not get anything wet in here or so help me, I'll—"

"Mister Smith!" Daniel said. "We're being chased by some very bad men. We didn't know where else to turn."

Faber's eyes shot wide as he sucked in air, a hand clutching his heart. "Why me? Why here?" "It's all about those pictures we showed you," Daniel said. "Can you help us?"

Faber stood up and grabbed his briefcase from his desk. "Come with me," were the only words he said clearly. The rest were mutterings reminding Camille of her own grandfather. She picked out "damn kids," "worried sick," and something about "catching a cold." He led the way to the parking lot in the rear of the building and pulled his keys out just as he neared an ancient beige Volvo station wagon on the far side of the parking lot. Once inside, he reached across the seat and opened the front passenger door. The back seat was crammed full of unrecognizable debris. Daniel pulled open the door and made space for himself.

"Hey! *Careful back there*. Those are important documents."

Daniel apologized, but whatever damage he did was too late to rectify so he sat back and closed the door.

Faber spun the starter producing an unhealthy whirring sound. He released the key, waited for the noise to disappear and spun the starter again. This time it kicked in, but the old battery sounded as if it wasn't going to turn the engine. The motor finally made one revolution and the old car popped into life. "Not unlike me," Faber noted with a hint of a smile, "a bit slow to get started."

The car sputtered forward. They pulled out of the parking lot and headed out of town, gratified to see that Faber was driving in the opposite direction from where they had just come.

They wound their way out into the countryside for more than twenty minutes. First the city streets gave way to a highway and then the highway became a country road with deep ditches. Those ditches gave way to driveways and mailboxes. Huge trees grew up along the edges of many of the old homes. Daniel envisioned the original young owners planting the saplings, never imagining the result after fifty or sixty years of growth. Faber slowed and turned into one of the driveways. Branches hung close on either side, threatening to tear the paint off the old car. Limbs thumped across the luggage rack as they passed under them.

Faber stopped the vehicle in front of an opened-door garage so full of junk it would have been impossible to get out of the vehicle if he had pulled inside. He led the way through the maze and into the house through the back door. There was a small mudroom with a washer and dryer on the left. From there it opened up into the kitchen. Cigarette smoke had long since transformed the white ceiling into a dull yellow color. Thick cobwebs hung in every corner. Camille was afraid to look in the sink, but she was drawn to it by morbid attraction. Thankfully it only had a few dishes in it and the remaining gunk on them seemed relatively fresh.

"Forgive the mess. I do have things I'd rather do than clean." It was a statement more than an apology.

They passed from the kitchen to the living room, which contained all the normal furnishings one might expect but, unlike other living rooms, every place that Faber could have used as a seat or for decoration, he had piled high with books. There was one exception. Along one wall was a bookshelf. Rather than using it for books, every available space was taken up with some kind of memorabilia. There were photographs, albums, pennants and trophies. The most recent photos looked as though they were from the previous century.

"Wait here a moment. Please don't touch anything."

The one chair that was uncluttered was a recliner in one corner. A coffee table rested before it, covered with a menagerie of magazines. An ancient floor lamp posed in the corner with its flexible head pointed down toward the chair. It was on, brightly illuminating the springs poking through the upholstery. This was clearly Faber's favorite chair and neither of the visitors was about to invade that space.

Faber flashed around the room in a blur, stopping for a couple seconds at the thermostat to change the setting 'seventy-five,' and then he disappeared into the bathroom. Camille could hear him rustling about in there; it sounded like he was opening a creaky cabinet door, pulling things out of it. He returned to the disheveled living room holding several towels, stopped to smell them. "From the bottom of the stack," he said, "but they are some of the better towels I have, and seem fresh still. I'll put them on top of the toilet reservoir." He turned to his task, saying back over his shoulder, "I'll also pull out a fresh roll of toilet paper and put a fresh bar of soap in the tub."

Camille watched the odd little man—a savior in a strange brand—as he padded off, then looked again around the room. She would have preferred if the house were cleaner, but she was grateful for a safe place to be. For the moment it felt like she was a world away from Feldman and she couldn't be happier about that. She could tell Daniel was also satisfied by his grateful expression and more relaxed demeanor. She winked at him, and they shared a knowing smile. Although the old man sounded gruff, he harbored beneath his caustic crust a capacious generous streak.

The heaters had turned on. Camille could detect the smell of burning dust. Apparently the furnace had not run in months. A fan kicked on somewhere making the room soon feel warmer.

Faber returned. "There are extra towels in the bathroom just down the hall if you need them. I threw some clothes you could wear in there, too. Go ahead and clean up and get out of those wet rags."

Camille's shivering was persistent. Daniel insisted that she shower first. Though she knew that Daniel's foot must have been very painful, she was in her own kind of agony. She didn't need a second invitation. The bathroom was less than tidy and—she sniffed--musty, but not disgusting. The towels Faber had left for them were clean, but his idea of 'fresh' was a long ways away from hers—he had obviously not washed them in recent history. There was a nasty black ring around the inside of the tub. Apparently he preferred to take baths, and preferred *not* to scrub the old porcelain fixture clean more than once or twice in a lifetime.

All of this Camille picked up with a glance and a tingling nose, but none of it mattered. She turned on the water, stripped her wet clothes off and hung them on the corner of the medicine cabinet. By the time she was finished undressing, the steam was already rising from the tub. She stepped inside. The sting of the hot water was both excruciating and wonderful. She held herself in the streaming water until her skin became red and she began to acclimate.

***

Daniel sat on a kitchen chair that Faber had brought in and related the events that had occurred since they had last seen each other. It seemed like only moments had passed before Camille emerged from the bathroom wearing a pair of flannel PJ bottoms and an old sleeveless tee shirt. Nothing she wore fit, yet it was somehow sexy at the same time. Daniel looked over at the old man's reaction and it was plainly evident that the sight of Camille had affected him as well. Daniel caught the old man as he swallowed hard and then closed his mouth. Daniel smiled inwardly as he stood and limped toward the bathroom. He held Camille close enough to whisper, after a short kiss, "I've started recounting what's happened. You can tell him the rest. And, ahm … you might want to cover up a little. No bra and a loose fitting tee shirt? He's old, but not dead, honey." He winked and tapped her on her bottom. She giggled in acknowledgment. A moment later he was closing the door to the bathroom and slipping out of his clothes.

CHAPTER 85

At the mansion Feldman paced in front of the lab equipment. He had never taken the time to examine it. If two kids created it then he could surely learn how to operate it. After all, he had paid for the whole thing.

On the console there were readouts for a variety of different measures. One was temperature. Another was a light meter. A third looked like it might be a voltmeter. There were dials that controlled scale and sensitivity. On the left, behind a Plexiglas barrier, was the testing area consisting of two spheres made of some kind of metal with a variety of probes attached to each. Wires fed from one sphere to the other and from there to the control panel. Feldman flipped the clasps that held the first sphere closed. Inside it was a small polished stone, possible quartz or agate. Other than that the sphere was empty.

He moved to the second sphere and opened it. White light blasted out consuming the room with such force and brilliance that even through his closed eyelids he was still staggered by its effulgence. No sooner than it had appeared, the light vanished. Feldman waited while his eyes adjusted. Whatever had been in the crucible had been transformed into a grayish white powder.

Feldman considered himself a worldly man. He liked to think he had a strong knowledge of the elements, but … *this*. What material could possibly be so sensitive that its reaction to light could be that powerful? Clearly this had been a dangerous substance and the kids had used it in some way as part of their experiments. There had to be more of it. Feldman picked up the phone and called for Davenport then waited for him to arrive.

"Bring me every rock sample that you brought back from the apartment. I need them right away."

Davenport returned with several boxes of rocks. Feldman rifled through the stones discarding each as he rejected it until there were no more samples. "None of this is what I'm looking for. Bring me everything that came from his apartment. There must be something else there!"

***

Davenport trudged back to the storage shed. There wasn't a whole lot left to go through. After sifting through the junk one last time the only thing of any interest was an old lunch box. He picked up the old metal tin and took it out into the sunlight for a better look. He placed the lunchbox on the hood of the car and opened it. Inside were several foil-wrapped objects. Davenport picked up the first one and began to unravel the packaging.

***

In his office Feldman paced, glancing occasionally toward the storage building. He couldn't see it from where he stood, but that didn't stop him from looking in that direction just the same. It had been almost an hour since Davenport had left. *What on earth could be keeping him?*

Suddenly a bright light engulfed the entire estate. The building shook and his office window rattled in its frame. When the smoke cleared, the storage building and part of the garage were gone. Although Feldman knew Davenport could not have survived the explosion, the fate of his most trusted employee was not his first concern. The probability that the amazing material no longer existed and the only person who had known of the source of it had gone missing, was … catastrophic. Feldman wasn't looking forward to making the call to Foreman, but it was a situation that would only get worse the longer he put it off.

Several employees had already rushed to the scene. From his vantage point they looked like insects scurrying around. He returned to his desk, punched the intercom button and spoke to the secretary. "Call the fire department and let them know it's a false alarm." He picked up the phone and dialed Foreman's cell.

CHAPTER 86

By the time Daniel was out of the shower he noticed a significant temperature rise in the house. Faber had left him the same selection of clothes he had left for Camille. When he stepped into the living room he was pleased to see that she now sported a dress shirt, buttoned up over the tee shirt.

He limped into the living room keeping his weight on the heel of his sore foot. Camille met him at the sofa and lifted his injured foot. The flap of skin had almost torn off. It was white, dead, and would not reattach itself no matter how much time he gave it.

"Mister Smith," she said, looking his way, "do you happen to have any bandages and a pair of scissors … maybe some disinfectant too?"

"There should be a box of Band-Aids in the medicine cabinet and maybe a tube of Polysporin there as well. I'll see what I can find for scissors."

Faber came with an antique sewing basket made of wicker. Below the top tray was a variety of sewing paraphernalia. He pulled out one thing after another putting each aside until he produced a large pair of equally antiquated scissors and handed them to Camille.

The scissors were large and cumbersome, but Camille worked with careful precision to remove the dead skin while causing Daniel as little pain as she could. She covered the wound with disinfectant and put a piece of gauze over that. Then she wrapped the toe with a bandage. "Good as new," she said and slapped Daniel on the knee. "That's what my mom used to say anyway."

Faber called from the kitchen that lunch was ready.

Daniel stood up expecting the wound to sting, but the new covering protected it well. There was hardly any pain.

Faber had produced a small feast of ham sandwiches, grapes and water. They sat around the table and listened first to Faber tell of his progress and then afterward Faber listened to them retell their story. It was the long version, but Faber listened patiently to the entire saga. It was time that Faber knew everything, so Daniel included the information about the mine and the stones. He explained the work at the university and told Faber of the fact that Millenburg was dead.

Faber had just taken put a last mouthful of ham sandwich to his mouth, but stopped to say, "What about the samples of crystal that you left in the machine?"

"It was still there. It's worse than that, though. I think he has the samples from the lunch box. I know they cleared out my apartment."

"He's going to want to find you." Faber looked over his spectacles in all seriousness.

"We know," Daniel said with wince and a sigh. "I don't know what to do about that. He knows all about Camille's family. He can't know too much about me."

"Do you have some place that you could go?"

Daniel looked first at Camille, then back to Faber. "I think I do."

CHAPTER 87

A few hours later the old car rattled up the Fraser Canyon on its way toward the centre of British Columbia. Camille had spent the first hour looking over her shoulder so often that she had begun to develop a crick in her neck. It was particularly disturbing because ever since they got into the canyon, each car that appeared behind them rapidly caught up and then passed. And each passing car added to the emotional roller coaster of dread followed by sudden relief as it zoomed by. None of the occupants of the passing cars looked familiar.

At times Faber was driving nearly twenty kilometers per hour below the speed limit. It was both painful and stressful, but neither Camille nor Daniel was prepared to offend Faber by mentioning it, especially after all he'd done to help them. The crotchety old man they had first met was long gone … most of the time.

They stopped in a small town. The grass was dry with tumbleweed crowding the barbed wire fences. The city sign, if you could call the place a city, stated that they had arrived in Cache Creek. Graffiti on a large stone beside the highway countered this claim, stating that they were entering Trash Creek. Gas stations and fast-food restaurants lined the main thoroughfare. Faber stopped at one of the gas stations, and Daniel was glad—he needed to pee. The toilet was filthy and reeked of urine. Daniel finished in a hurry and waited in the car for Faber and Camille to return. He watched as car after car passed by, expecting each driver to be Feldman or one of his goons.

They grabbed a quick bite at the local Dairy Queen. After rushing through his meal, Daniel gathered the large pile of garbage that had mysteriously become a mass larger than the whole meal had been. Faber clamored out of the booth and Camille held the door open. Back in the car Faber turned the key and coaxed the reluctant clunker back to life.

The road wound its way out of town. There was little traffic and the meal had drained energy from everyone. Daniel took his shift up front while Camille was more than happy to crawl into the back seat to sleep.

Daniel focused his attention to keeping Faber awake and it wasn't long before Faber grew tired and finally allowed Daniel to drive. They spotted a wide spot in the road and pulled over. Daniel got in the driver's seat just as a black Jaguar sped by.

They arrived in Clinton and Daniel slowed down just enough to avoid a traffic ticket. He knew he was only five or six hours from home and that knowledge seemed to create a constant supply of adrenaline. One Hundred Mile House was the next major town. They had a long uphill drive to get there and it started immediately once they passed the "Come Again" sign leaving Clinton.

The old car had little power and it was no surprise to see a flashy sports car pull up beside them. Daniel looked over in casual curiosity to see what kind of man would drive such a beautiful car.

Feldman!

A menacing glare on his face, Feldman swerved toward him and crashed into the side of the Volvo. Daniel veered away almost hitting the guardrail. Faber woke with a start. Camille jerked upright, screaming. Ahead of them a semi pulling two trailers was coming down the hill. A pickup was taking the opportunity to get by it.

Feldman made another attempt to push Daniel off the road, but this time Daniel wasn't surprised. He met Feldman's car with as much force as he dared—a move Feldman hadn't expected. His car veered into the oncoming traffic. Feldman looked up in time to see the pickup. He slammed on his brakes and pulled into his own lane giving Daniel an opportunity to try to get ahead a little. As old as it was, the Volvo was reliable; but even on its best day it could never have competed with a Jaguar. A moment later Feldman was next to them again, this time pointing to the side of the road.

"Don't do it, Daniel." Smith yelled, "He doesn't want you dead. He wants to know what you know. Keep driving."

It was all Daniel could do to keep the car on the road and the top of the hill was approaching fast. Soon the passing lane would come to an end. The concrete rail was all that was between him and a three hundred foot drop to his right. Daniel inched toward the centre of the road.

Feldman apparently didn't notice the double lane was coming to an end. He was still motioning for Daniel to pull over when a look of dismay came over him. Daniel knew Feldman now realized they were back to a two-lane highway and he was in the wrong lane with a semi bearing down on him. Feldman slammed on the brakes and yanked the vehicle into the lane behind Daniel. The semi clipped Feldman's Jag with a horrendous crunching smash. The Jaguar slammed against the rail and then flipped over it, careening toward the valley floor.

Daniel looked into the rear view mirror, but he could only see the top of the semi. He didn't know what might have happened to Feldman and he didn't care. No one in the car suggested he stop, so he drove on. He was glad Feldman might be dead. His life would be so much simpler if it were true.

From then on the passengers took turns driving and stopped only when absolutely necessary. Six exhausting and worrisome hours later, they pulled into the small town of Vanderhoof. The streets were barren except for an RCMP cruiser that turned a corner and passed them.

Daniel made a right hand turn and crossed a set of railway tracks. The trio made a brief stop at the 7-Eleven to stock up on some snack items. The theatre door was open. Daniel drove by just in time to see William reach out and pull it closed to shut out the winter wind and then they were driving out of town toward Grundpark Road.

Fifteen minutes later, Daniel pulled into William and Phoebe's driveway. He parked in the right hand bay that William reserved for visitors. Faber put a hand on his shoulder, "Are you sure this is going to be okay? I feel a little uncomfortable going into someone's home when they're not around."

"It'll be just fine. They haven't heard from me in awhile and I think they'll be as excited to see me as I am to see them. They're working at the theatre tonight so we have a bit of time before they come home. We could check out the mine."

Being told the cavern was only a few hundred feet away, a giddy Faber didn't wait for a second invitation. Daniel could see the grove of trees that marked the well sight, the only remaining landmark.

At the shaft Daniel produced a flashlight and shone it into the hole. Several feet of snow had accumulated at the bottom. Beneath that was probably a few inches of ice. He handed the light to Camille, dropped the ladder in and began his descent. When he had taken a few steps down Camille handed him the flashlight.

Daniel reached the bottom and called up, "Be careful when you step off the ladder. There's some ice down here."

Daniel offered Faber a helping hand when the old man reached the bottom, but Faber brushed him out of the way. "Unbelievable," he kept repeating.

Once Camille reached the bottom Daniel led the small group down the passage. Faber followed along, slack jawed and amazed. Camille was lost in her own recollections while Daniel relived his time in the cold shaft and shuddered when he passed by Grundpark's shallow burial plot. He felt no need to mention this fact.

It was warmer below ground than above. They entered the large cavern and stood face to face with the ornate door.

Faber ran his hands over the carved wood, marveling, muttering in a sacred whisper about trying to fathom that he was one of the first of only a handful of people who had ever touched it since the original people disappeared.

Daniel produced his key and inserted it into the mechanism. "You're going to be astounded," he said to Faber.

"I already am."

Daniel flipped off the light and turned the key. The familiar clicking sound followed and the door pivoted. Although it was dark, Daniel could sense the chamber in front of him. He wondered if the others could as well.

CHAPTER 88

Camille could sense the crystals. Memories from her last experience in the cave flooded back. She took hesitant steps forward, fearing what would inundate her mind, but ... nothing did. Wisps of ideas came out of the darkness like the sounds of ghosts and she knew none of what she heard had been spoken aloud. She said nothing.

Daniel turned the flashlight on and the crystals jumped to life. He covered his eyes against the brightness and observed his companions. Camille's face looked pained and he went to her. "Are you all right? Do we need to leave?"

"I don't think so. It's not like it was before." She couldn't explain the difference but somehow she felt more capable and in control.

"You will tell me if anything changes?" Daniel said, stepping out of the way allowing Faber to lead.

Camille nodded.

The old man walked as if in a dream. Daniel stopped long enough to show him where the samples had come from and to close the door behind him.

They walked along the bridge until they came to the other side of the expanse where the other door blocked their way. Faber examined it, but when he could see no obvious way to open it he turned to Daniel. "You know the secret?"

Daniel smiled and reached around Faber. His hand glided across the door and found the mechanism. Faber stepped back as the door swung open revealing the passage beyond. Faber stood still, marveled into mute.

It was a moment that neither Camille nor Daniel wanted to take away from him. They allowed him to savor it for as long as he wished.

Faber walked ahead, oblivious to the fact that he was not alone, stopping every now and again to examine something more closely. He knew a little of what lay ahead, but he crept along with no desire to arrive there before he was ready. Eventually he reached the cavern and followed the path around the chamber, stopping to look at each piece of artwork as if he were reading the history for the first time.

While Faber took in his surroundings, Camille and Daniel re-familiarized themselves with the temple. Faber had proven to be their guardian angel, but after seeing his childlike enthusiasm it was evident that he may have come even if it had been Feldman who had invited him.

Daniel glanced at his watch. It was already ten thirty and it wouldn't be long before William and Phoebe returned home. He wanted to be there when they arrived.

"Fascinating, simply fascinating," Faber repeated over and over again.

"What is this place, Faber?" Camille gestured, indicating the chamber.

Faber didn't hesitate at the opportunity to begin his explanation of everything he had learned. "It's so much easier to understand once you are here. This is exactly why archaeologists should work in the field and not be cooped up in some dusty old office. We're in a temple of sorts. The inhabitants of the area would have come through the main doors and worshiped at the altar. They believed that the priests were gods. From what I can gather from the artwork people from all over came here to worship. According to the hieroglyphs this area was immensely populated, but it appears that glaciers from the last ice age have completely obliterated any evidence that this culture ever existed. The gods lived below ground and appeared to the people using this platform."

"Platform?" Daniel's expression was one of fervent inquisitiveness.

Faber pointed to one of the drawings. "Look here. This platform actually lowers even farther. Somewhere there is a mechanism to lower it and I would bet that it is on the altar because only priests would have had access to it."

"Let's check it out," Camille added, excitement in her voice and on her face.

"All in good time my young friend. There is so much to learn first. Look here," he said, pointing to yet another panel. "They would have brought food offerings and other gifts and placed them here," he said, indicating the altar.

Daniel interrupted him. "We really need to be going, Faber. Phoebe and William are due back any time."

"Just a few more minutes?" Faber brought his hands together in petition.

Another hour passed making it likely that William and Phoebe would already be home. "Listen, Faber, we really have to go," said Daniel.

Faber sighed, deep, long, and loud, pulled away from his work and followed Daniel and Camille out of the cavern.

CHAPTER 89

As Daniel had predicted, William and Phoebe were already home when they arrived. What would they think of the beaten up Volvo in the driveway? Perhaps Phoebe had surmised that it belonged to Daniel.

The trio walked into the dark carport. Their movement triggered the motion sensor wired to the porch light—bathing the entire area in light.

"Nifty," whispered Faber. "I've got to get me one of these."

They entered the basement, leaving their shoes with the others piled close by. William and Phoebe were sitting at the kitchen table. They hadn't been in long. They tended to go to bed soon after their return.

William looked up as Daniel came in. "Hey, boy, where did you come from? I thought you were supposed to be in school."

Ever since he had known him, William had always called him 'Boy'. Daniel felt that it was as close to "Son" as he was comfortable saying. It was fine with Daniel, though. He knew what William meant by it.

"Oh, we got here and no one was around, so I thought that I'd show Faber around the farm a bit. We walked out to the barn to check out the cows."

William dipped his head, satisfied with Daniel's explanation and then added, "Aren't you supposed to be in school, though?"

"Oh yeah," Daniel said, his mind racing to come up with believable details. "There was a fire in the wing and our lab was shut down. We're done until they're finished with the cleanup. Sure glad to be home, though."

William's eyebrows elevated. "Anyone hurt?"

"No." Daniel shook his head. "The fire started at night. No one knows what happened yet."

William nodded and Daniel hoped there would be no more pressure.

With pleasantries and introductions out of the way, Daniel elaborated further by explaining that Faber was a good friend who worked in the museum and had always wanted to come north and see what things were like.

"I'm sorry to have barged in," Faber said. "Daniel assured me that everything would be all right. I really hope that I haven't put you out at all."

"Don't worry about it at all, Mister Smith. You're more than welcome," said Phoebe.

Phoebe gave Faber the complete tour of the house, while Camille and Daniel tagged along. It was a ritual for all new guests and it didn't seem to matter how late at night it might be. She always did whatever she could to make everyone feel welcomed. She showed him his room and where he could clean up; making a point of adding that he needn't worry about anything. "Just make yourselves at home," she finished.

Daniel dropped his belongings in the bedroom that had always been his. Some of his clothes were still in the closet. He smiled at the warmth and familiarity of the house. "This is the best place on earth," he said to Camille. "It feels so good to be home."

Phoebe turned to go back downstairs and stopped. "How many should I prepare breakfast for?"

"Oh, don't worry about us. I don't think anyone will be up and moving around before breakfast. We're all pretty tired. I can put something together," Daniel offered.

"Well, get some sleep. I'm sure we'll see you in the morning." Phoebe disappeared into her bedroom.

Daniel heard William ask her something, but the walls muffled her reply. The conversation ended shortly thereafter and the house became quiet.

Daniel found his way to his room and crawled into bed. Camille was already waiting for him there. She wrapped her arms around him. Her skin was clammy and cold to the touch.

"What happened today, Camille—in the cave?" He wondered why Camille's earlier experiences hadn't been repeated. Were the crystals losing their power or had Camille been able to resist? Or was it something else altogether.

"I'm not exactly sure, but something's different. I know that. Do you think that because I've been so close to the crystals for so long that I've developed a kind of immunity to them?"

"It's possible I suppose, but I'm glad I didn't have to haul your limp body out of there while Faber was with us."

Camille laughed. "That would have been hard to explain, wouldn't it."

"When we go back I want to know if you start to react." Daniel cupped her cheek in his hand.

"I'll let you know right away."

"Promise?" he said and kissed her.

"I promise."

Daniel said no more. They cuddled awhile before he rolled onto his back. A few moments later Camille was breathing deeply. Not long after, he followed her into a deep dreamless sleep of his own.

CHAPTER 90

Saturday morning sun rose in a crisp, cloudless blue sky. William and Phoebe had eaten breakfast and had gone about their daily activities. William was outside feeding the cows and Daniel had no idea where Phoebe was. The house was silent.

Faber rippled with excitement. The trek to the well was much easier in the daylight, although once down the shaft it really didn't matter. The walk went faster and soon they were standing inside the geode once more.

A moment later they were on their way down the corridor to the main chamber. Faber didn't delay. He walked directly to the last plaque and continued his examination. Daniel and Camille waited for Faber to include them in whatever new tidbit he might be learning. Hours ticked by while Faber studied the drawings before he finally looked up. "A clan made its way south following the fjords along the coast. They were looking for a new place to live and start a different way of life. They stopped at a river's inlet and followed that inland until they came to this spot. These may have been the first of the Carrier first nation's tribe. They chose this spot and began to excavate for their longhouses. The drawing showed a cavern which ended at a solid rock face that would eventually become the Crystal chamber.

"At some point a second group of people came. They brought with them their stonework skills and joined the first group—eventually becoming one. For a long time the two clans worshiped at the crystal chamber. The village flourished while only the priests and priestesses were allowed into this chamber.

"Then the thousand-year winter struck and the ice moved down from the north. The people stayed to weather the storm and protect their shrine. Eventually, it claimed the lives of everyone who refused to leave and stripped the land of its trees and soil, until ... all evidence of the community was gone. That's it. The story ends there."

Faber went to the altar. "Come down here!" he called.

Camille and Daniel stepped onto the platform with Faber. The old man reached under the edge of the altar. He moved his hand around as if he were searching for something, feeling, groping, and then ... *movement.* The entire platform, except for the raised edge around the room, began to sink slowly into the ground, surprisingly, not into the darkness. On the gigantic elevator, they descended deeper and deeper. Daniel looked up. Already the chamber looked like nothing more than a small, lighted dome high above them.

The platform continued to sink. The ceiling dipped away. They descended twenty, thirty and then forty feet. The ancient elevator came to an abrupt, jarring halt when it reached the bottom. Tendrils of light encircled the room. A single step down surrounded them.

Faber was animated. Speaking as he walked he began to explain. "Somewhere, there should be a burial chamber. Ah, look here," he said, pointing at a slab of rock about knee high and six feet long jutting out of the wall. "This is where the priests would have slept." He pointed out several others flanking the room and chuckled to himself.

"What is it, Faber?" said Camille.

"Oh, nothing. This machinery seems to be working as well as it probably ever did. Fascinating, simply fascinating. Look, there are three more passages."

They turned down the closest corridor and walked for fifty feet or so. The path stopped at a crossing corridor which formed an arc around the centre chamber forming two circles connected by four spokes, like a giant underground wagon wheel.

"I would not be surprised at all to find that this chamber was constructed in the form of a huge medicine wheel," he said, gesturing to the corridors. "May I borrow that," he asked, pointing to Daniel's coat.

Since the temperature was uncomfortably warm Daniel handed him his jacket. Although the warmth in the mineshaft varied little, it was odd to him that it was markedly warmer down here.

Faber took the jacket from him, dropped it with an inelegant toss to the ground in the middle of the path, then turned to the left and began to walk. The passage continued to arc around the central room. They reached the first spoke and Faber stopped to look down the passage. The altar lay directly ahead of them, the face of it being perpendicular. Another opposing passage lay directly beyond it. Excited, Faber picked up his speed and continued his way on the circular pathway. Twice more he looked into the centre of the room and both times he commented the altar was directly ahead of them, identical from every direction. When they reached the fourth spoke, there, resting on the ground was Daniel's jacket.

"If my guess is right, then each of these arms points to the north, east, south and west. And, if that's true, then the altar is also oriented so that each of its sides is facing one of those directions. According to the hieroglyphs this is where the gods—as they were considered—lived."

"Yes, but *how* did they live," asked Camille. Daniel was surprised by the urgent tone in her voice.

"Good question, Camille. I think there must be more down here than meets the eye."

"I don't know how they did it," Daniel said, "but I think there is an underground source of energy that we haven't seen yet. By the feeling in here, I suspect the elevator operates on steam from some geothermal energy source."

"A good guess—and I'll bet it's true. I hadn't really noticed it before, but it's very warm down here." Faber scurried back to the altar. Camille and Daniel were about to follow when Faber stopped them, saying, "Stand back."

Faber was peppy, walking so fast it looked unnatural for a man of his age. He found the button and pressed it. A high-pitched whistling sound followed as He ran to get back to his friends. He managed to step off the platform just as it began to rise.

"What are you doing," Camille demanded. "We could be stuck down here."

"No worries, little miss. I'm sure there must be more chambers below."

"That's all well and good, but we're going to be sealed down here. What then?" Camille screamed. Her distressed wailing was too late and of no avail. The platform had already risen out of reach.

Faber made a 'calm down' gesture, wagging his open palm downward. "Relax, little miss. You have a point, Camille, but just stop and consider: I don't imagine the priests would have designed this place so that an accident of that magnitude could occur." Faber gave her a reassuring smile.

A stone cylinder several feet smaller than the rising disk supported the platform. A set of stairs circled the cylinder, disappearing even further into the earth.

"Shall we?" suggested Faber with a sweep of his short arm.

Daniel looked over at Camille. Her eyes were wide with horror. "Camille, what's the matter?"

"Can't you see it? What if we can't get out of here? What if we're stuck down here? What if we all die?"

Faber was already on his way down the stairs as quickly as his old legs could carry him.

"Stop a moment," Daniel yelled. "Faber come back."

Faber slowed, but did not stop.

Daniel called again. "Faber, I need you to come back. You're going too fast. We need to think about this. You need to come back right now." This last statement was crisp and clear as if he were talking to a young child. Whether it was the tone in his voice or something else, Faber stopped and called back to Daniel. "What's the matter?"

"We need to stay together."

"Hurry up then. I'll wait right here."

"I need you up here right away. It's really important." Daniel said, trying to make the urgency as clear as he could. He had a bad feeling and if he was going to have any chance of bringing the situation under control he was going to have to do something right away.

Grudgingly, Faber began to climb the stairs. "I'm not a spry young fellow like yourself you know," he hollered as he traipsed his way back.

Well, at least he was coming. Daniel turned his attention to Camille. She still wore the hysterical look of a frightened animal. He led her to one of the sleeping benches and helped her to sit.

Faber arrived at the top of the stairs huffing dramatically and clutching his side. "So what's such a big deal that you make an old man hike up and down treacherous stairs? We should get going."

"Faber, why don't you come and sit down for just a minute? Camille's not doing so well."

Faber looked to Camille and then back at the steps. After a long internal struggle he rejoined the group.

As much as Daniel tried, he could not get the old man to sit and relax for even a moment. Daniel spoke calmly and slowly to his two friends. "Camille. Mister Smith. I need you both to simmer down and to think about what's going on. I don't understand very much about it but, as you know, the crystals have many special abilities. Camille, you seem overwhelmed with fear. Think about it. It's unreasonable to feel as fearful as you do. This is not your normal behavior. It's not like you under normal circumstances. Remember how Mister Feldman threatened to kill us both. Were you this afraid then?" Her face appeared to relax a little.

He turned to Faber. "Mister Smith. I know that this is very exciting. I wish I knew you better, but I know that you've spent most of your last few years working in the basement of the museum. You're still holding your side. It hurts, doesn't it? Wouldn't you be resting right now under normal circumstances?"

Faber began to take deep breaths. Even Camille seemed more subdued. Daniel waited a bit and then continued. "I don't think I am immune to the effects of the crystals, but I do think that I have an understanding of them. Maybe that's why they aren't affecting me to such an extreme." In truth, he didn't feel the crystals were having any effect on him. But he didn't want either of them to think he felt superior.

Faber sighed, wagged a hand in submission. "All right, fine already. Just tell me what you want me to know about the crystals."

Daniel took a deep breath. "I'm fairly certain the crystals are able to magnify a person's emotions. I think that's what killed McMaster and Grundpark." Camille still struggled, but at least she wasn't getting any worse. Daniel carried on. "I don't think it affects me the same way that it affects others. Maybe I'm just not as emotional as others are. I try to let my mind do the work and not rely on my feelings. My thinking is that Grundpark and McMaster let the crystals drive them insane. When McMaster locked me in the crystal chamber I was able to figure out how to open the doors from the inside. The crystals seemed to improve my ability to solve problems. It's as if they amplify everything. I bet the crystals helped these people build this place too, but I imagine we may never know for sure."

"But what about getting out of here?" Camille persisted. Although she asked the question with obvious concern, the hysteria was gone from her voice.

"I really don't think that's going to be a problem, Camille. We need to trust the designers. This place has been here for thousands of years. We need to be observant, pay attention, and I'm sure we'll find a way out."

Faber sat, his foot taking up a nervous tapping on the floor. The old geezer must have nearly pushed himself to his physical limits for he was still holding his side. When he recovered enough they went back to the stairs. Camille kicked up some dust with her toe and it landed in a spray ahead of her. Everywhere the particles landed, they created miniature craters.

The stairs wound around the pillar until they came to blunt halt at the bottom. A passage appeared to the right. The farther they went the higher the ambient temperature grew. Daniel noted that it was consistent with his earlier assumption. The corridor opened into a large open area. There were several large stone pools containing water. Daniel dipped a finger in to discover that the water was pleasantly warm.

They passed elaborate chambers that gave the impression of having served as space for an underground community. The group moved along the main corridor until the side chambers and other passages ceased to appear. The passage turned uphill and Daniel could feel a cool breeze. It answered a question that had been plaguing him since they descended. Where was fresh air coming from? Somewhere above, the shaft probably exited into the open air.

CHAPTER 91

Red flashing lights lit up the snow as the ambulance raced down the hill toward the scene of the accident near 100 Mile House. Darkness had already fallen even though it was barely four-thirty in the afternoon. "Deer!" the man in the passenger seat called. The driver swerved toward the centerline, leaving the deer behind in the dark.

They caught up to a slow moving vehicle, hit the siren and sped around the car with ease. When the ambulance arrived at the scene the police were already there. Flares lit up the road where the car had left the highway and more flares identified the semi truck pulled over a short distance down the hill. They moved to the back of the ambulance and took out what they would likely need to bring a victim up from below the embankment. Hopefully he was still alive.

The two paramedics hopped over the concrete barrier, skipped and slid to where the barely recognizable sports car rested on its hood. The first paramedic down the hill could hear the officer talking to the man in the car. "Stay with us, sir. I need you to keep talking to me. Do you have any kids back home?"

"Tom." The victim's voice was weak. "Tom was like my son. They killed him."

The officer handed off his position to the paramedic saying, "He's conscious, but delirious. I didn't want to try to move him."

The paramedic was a pro, and sounded like one. "Thanks for your help."

He crouched down where he could get a better look at the man who hung upside down by his seatbelt. "My name's Norm. Can you tell me your name, sir?"

"What?"

"You're going to be fine. I just thought it'd be nice to know the name of such a fortunate man."

"V … Vance." His voice was growing evermore feeble. "Fel—Feldman."

"Pleased to meet you, Vance. You must be one of the luckiest men alive and I'm very glad to be able to say that."

Norm didn't stop talking as he checked Feldman's vital signs. He didn't see any significant amount of blood. Some dried stuff, but he expected that from an accident that had happened almost an hour earlier.

Feldman was wearing a pair of dress shoes. Norm peeled one off. "Can you move your toes for me Mister Feldman?"

Feldman did.

"We're going to have to get you out of here. You're hung up in your seatbelt. We'll need to cut it, but we'll try not to hurt you. Do you understand what we're going to do?"

Feldman gave a small, slow nod.

The paramedic reached into his pouch and produced a pair of scissors. His partner had clamored around the other side ready to help. They supported Feldman the best they could while Norm cut the strap. The man's body dropped, but Norm was supporting most of his weight. Mike took the legs and moved the injured man so that his feet came almost out of the vehicle.

Norm continued to talk to Feldman. "I want you to stay as still as you can Mister Feldman. We're going to move you onto a backboard and we'll have you out of here in no time."

The paramedics transferred Feldman to the board and immobilized him. His vital signs were decent enough and he maintained consciousness. Once they had him strapped down Norm called to another officer waiting above. The officer scrambled down the embankment to join them. The four men moved Feldman up the hill and into the back of the ambulance.

Norm turned to the officers. "Thanks so much, you guys. See ya later."

Norm's partner rode in the back with the patient for the trip back to town. He radioed ahead and gave the nurse as much information as he had about the patient's condition.

They backed into the emergency entrance of the hospital. The nurse thanked the paramedics and rolled the stretcher toward the emergency room.

CHAPTER 92

Feldman woke in a gown designed to show more than it hid. He sat up to get out of bed. His head swam with dizziness that threatened to overwhelm him and he lay back. He was in a small room with a tiny closet against one wall and a door that could lead to nothing else but a toilet. There was a curtain on one side and beyond that another bed, thankfully empty. He was in a hospital room and some of his memories of the night before started coming back. Though he couldn't recall the transfer to the hospital, he did remember trying to force Daniel off the road.

Feldman made his slow and laborious way to sitting upright. Thankfully, this time darkness did not threaten to overcome him. The movement induced his temples to throb, but he stood, taking care to hold on to the bed with one hand. He tested his legs before staggering in the direction of the bathroom. He stood before the toilet thinking it would have been more convenient if the design of his robe included a slit in the front. He draped it over his shoulder.

He stood in front of the mirror barely recognizing the man in the reflection. The impact had bruised the right side of his face — his eye was almost completely swollen shut. There were bandages on his head holding the gauze in place over a wound that had leaked a little, turning the bandage red in the middle. Feldman lifted the dressing and counted ten stitches. He admired the doctor's work for a moment. It would barely leave a scar, he thought.

Feeling fatigued, he made his way back to his bed. He glanced out of habit at his wrist to check the time, but his watch was gone. The clock on the wall informed him it was eight in the morning. It was beginning to get light outside. His stomach growled. Breakfast would surely be coming around soon.

Feldman eventually dozed off, but movement from his bed wakened him. Disregarding the fact that he was asleep, the nurse had stepped on a pedal at the foot of the bed, moving it into an upright position. Feldman gave the woman a look of disgust.

"I'm sorry, Mister Feldman. The doctor didn't suspect any complications, but he ordered that we wake you every three hours just to be safe. I figured you wouldn't mind quite so much if I brought your breakfast with me. The doctor will be here later this morning to do his rounds."

Feldman ran his hand over his head and a bolt of pain shot across his forehead. "Son-of-a-bitch," he cursed under his breath. The nurse had already pushed his tray into its position and was on her way out of the room. It occurred to him that if he was looking for ruthless employees, he should consider hiring a few nurses.

He poked at his meal a bit, but the sight of it sickened him further. He pulled the tab from the orange juice and drank it. At least with that he knew what to expect. There's no point wasting my time around here, he thought, and wondered where *here* was before pushing the tray out of the way and strolling to the lockers where he expected to find his clothes.

They hung in the closet on hangers that were a part of the fixture. His socks and underwear were in a plastic bag below. They seemed as clean as they were before the accident, he was pleased with that, and pulled them on.

Dressed, he made sure he was respectful enough looking. The facility gave him the impression of a tiny one. There was a main desk at the intersection of several halls and from there Feldman could see the exit and parked cars beyond. In the entry a taxi phone hung on the wall. He lifted the receiver and waited for a receptionist to answer. He ordered his taxi and walked outside to wait for his ride. He unwound his bandages and dabbed at the stitches while he waited. Anyone looking out from inside would not likely see a patient.

The taxi pulled up beside him and he got into the back seat. "Take me to the nearest car dealership."

"You don't look like you're doing so good, mister. Are you okay?" inquired the driver. When Feldman didn't respond the driver said nothing more and pulled away from the curb.

Feldman was pleased to find that his wallet and cell phone were still in his clothes. When the cab stopped outside a Ford dealership, he got out and handed the driver a twenty. Without waiting for change he walked into the showroom. A salesman rushed up. "Can I help you with anything?"

Feldman walked over to a Mustang, bent over and looked inside. "Sell me one of these."

The salesman tried to explain some of the features, but Feldman raised a curt hand. "Just get the paperwork going. I want to get out of here as soon as possible. There's an extra five hundred in it for you if you can make it snappy."

The salesman's eyes lit up on high beams when Feldman handed him his debit card. "Add $500 to the total." He swiped Feldman's card through the machine, entered five digits and some change before handing the machine over. Feldman punched in his personal identification number and waited for approval.

As was customary in the province, an Insurance Corporation of British Columbia representative sat in the corner available to insure new vehicles, the ICBC logo adorned the front of her desk. The salesman escorted him over. Feldman completed the insurance forms while the man bolted the license plates to his car. The salesman may have been about to thank Feldman for his business, but Feldman interrupted him. "What's the easiest way to the highway? I need to get to Vanderhoof."

Feldman got in the vehicle, checked the tank and drove out of 100 Mile House without looking back.

CHAPTER 93

As quick as he could hobble, Faber rushed toward the stone column and mounted the steps. He scanned the area for any kind of switch or lever that would return the platform to their level.

"Have you found anything," Camille asked.

"No."

"What's this?" Camille reached passed him and pointed to an illuminated stone directly in front of him. She twisted the stone and it turned with ease. A grating noise followed. She gave Faber an apologetic shrug and ran to the main chamber missing the look of distain he gave her.

By the time Faber joined her, the platform had reached the bottom. Daniel and Camille gave him the honors of pressing the button that would send them to the surface once more. Camille smiled and said, with a deep sigh, "What a relief," as they rode the stone slab upward.

Daniel looked at his watch. "Eleven in the evening. I'm starving."

Camille felt hungry as well. "We've been in this cavern for nearly twelve hours. No wonder if we're *all* famished—especially after the ordeal we've been through."

They climbed the ladder and made their way back to William and Phoebe's.

Daniel pulled off his boots and ran up the stairs announcing he would raid the refrigerator and fix something for them to eat. Camille liked that about Daniel. A man who likes to cook and doesn't think all the kitchen duties are a woman's relegated chores by virtue of her birthright. After dinner the friends retired to the living room to watch television. Before long Faber and Daniel were snoring loudly. Camille smiled and drifted off to sleep, too.

***

Camille woke with a jolt. Feldman stood over her, banged up, but not so badly that he couldn't press William's small caliber pistol directly on her temple. Daniel sat beside her and beyond him was Faber. She jabbed Daniel with her elbow and he snapped alert.

"You thought I was dead, didn't you," he said to Daniel. "You thought this was all over." Daniel was about to reply, but Feldman spoke over him. "Just *shut up*. I know you did. Well, it's not over. This is just the beginning. I know exactly what you've been up to."

Camille sat wide-eyed in fear, tears welling in her eyes.

Veins popped out on Feldman's forehead threatening to burst. He glared at Daniel. "The car was totaled, but you didn't actually think that I didn't know where you'd be, do you? I always knew where you lived, or at least where you come home to. I know everything there is to know about you, Daniel. It's why I make the big money."

"I don't think you know *everything* about me Mister Feldman," Daniel said, his steel gaze as cold as his voice.

Feldman's finger tightened on the trigger. "I wouldn't be having any attitude at this moment. You're the only one who is crucial to me. Shall I start seeing what kind of a mess I can make in here?" he said, alternating his aim between Camille and Faber. "Now get up."

Feldman forced everyone into the basement. The dog lay on the floor, tied to a post next to the furnace. When he saw Daniel he stood up and pulled his lips back over his gums exposing his teeth. Daniel felt a sudden jerk on his shoulder as Feldman grabbed a hold of him and pulled him in front of the snarling dog.

Daniel explained with contempt thick in his voice. "This is the only dog that I've ever seen that smiles. He's not going to bite anyone. Let go of me." Daniel ripped his shoulder free.

Daniel remembered the story William sometimes told. Apparently, when the dog was a pup and while William was working under the tractor, the dog gave him that same look. Thinking the pup was growling, William threw a crescent wrench at it and it hit him smack dab in the forehead. At first, he thought the dog was dead. It wasn't until later that he realized that the dog had been excited to see him and was just smiling.

Feldman looked at the dog suspiciously and gave him a wide berth.

The four figures stepped out into the snow which was almost a foot deeper since they came in. The trail to the well was now obliterated making trudging back across the field a bigger ordeal than any of them cared to deal with. The snow was now up to their thighs, coming down thick and wet.

Heavy snow subdued the glow coming from the yard light. Daniel led Feldman into the field where the cattle stood idly around the feeders. He stopped just long enough to open the gate held shut by a length of chain and a large nail bent into a hook. The gate swung freely open and he closed it behind them.

Daniel led Feldman toward the barn. He approached the cows and they began to scatter—all except one. The muscles on its shoulders were massive. It looked as though it could pulverize any one of them without any more effort than it would take to move. The bull stood there chewing its cud looking dumbly at them as they passed by. Feldman followed warily with one hand on Camille's shoulder, the fabric of her coat clenched in his fist.

Daniel led the group forward and the animals, having grown accustomed to the intruders, began to return to the feeders. Without warning, Daniel crouched low and ran, putting as many of the cattle between him and Feldman as he could. Camille felt Feldman's grip loosen as he was temporarily distracted. She shook, spun free of her jacket and bolted. Feldman was left holding nothing more than her coat and the pistol.

***

Feldman turned to try and find the fugitives, but already the cattle had once again returned to their normal routine. He scanned the herd until something caught his eye. He ran toward it, but it was only a calf which half kicked at him then bounded away. He turned again and saw a figure, a short man standing with his back to Feldman. He snuck up and put the gun barrel to the back of his neck.

"Are you ready to die, old man?"

Faber said nothing.

Feldman looked all around, searching for but still not seeing Daniel. "Boy! Step out … or this old fart takes a bullet!"

Daniel stood and came out from behind a cow.

"Daniel, what are you doing?" Camille yelled from behind a bale of hay.

Feldman yarded Faber along. "Come out, Camille. There's nothing you can do! Get out here, now," screamed Feldman and his voice cracked. He fired the pistol into the air. Cows scattered.

Camille rose from her hiding place and joined the three men.

"This one is easier to hold on to I'll bet," he said, digging his fingertips into Faber's neck. He released Faber and took hold of Camille again. "The next time you try something like that it'll be the girl laying face down in the snow with blood dripping from her temple. Then I won't have to work so hard. This old man won't be any challenge at all to chase around. Challenge me now, boy. I dare you! Now," he wagged the pistol in the direction of the well, "let's try this again, shall we?"

***

Reluctant, Daniel turned through the gate and into the yard. As he neared the house he found his stride shortening. The well was somewhere off to his right.

Feldman slammed his hand into Daniel's back, rocking his head. "Get moving, kid."

Daniel led them across the fence to the well. He paused in front of the hole and then turned his body to begin his descent.

"Your turn, sweetie," said Feldman, sending Camille into the darkness.

At the bottom of the shaft Camille clung to Daniel. "Why did you give yourself up?"

"I couldn't let him kill Faber and I know he would have. He's already killed Doctor Millenburg."

Somewhere above the clouds, the moon shone brightly, but what did it matter in the dark of the cavern? Camille wept, but she said nothing. Daniel knew that she knew he was right.

Faber clamored down next followed by Feldman. Whatever light there may have been had vanished after the first corner. Feldman pulled a lighter from his pocket and brushed his thumb across the sprocket, sparking a small flame. Daniel led the group onward, oblivious to the darkness he had become so used to. His right hand fluttered along the dirt of the wall and the occasional truss which eventually gave way to stone. He knew instinctively that staying to the right would lead him to the mysterious portal.

He came to a halt when his hand reached the carved surface of the door. Feldman stood with his mouth agape, his nose almost touching the wood. "Open it," he commanded.

Daniel withdrew the key and slid it into the keyhole. The door swung open. In an instant the room was bathed in light as the crystals reacted to the firelight in Feldman's hand.

Clutching Camille, Feldman pulled her through the door and into the blinding light. Daniel could see that Feldman was already falling under the spell of the crystals. He was as shortsighted and pathetic as both McMaster and Grundpark had been before him. Why he had ever feared the man, Daniel would never understand. His fury rose and he reached for Feldman's throat, but as his hands came up, Feldman whirled.

Maintaining his firm grip on Camille, Feldman stepped backward along the platform. His finger tightened on the trigger. The hammer clicked into its firing position. Feldman yelled, "You will tell me everything you know about these stones. Now!"

"Put the gun down, Mister Feldman, and I'll tell you everything."

Feldman waived his gun in circles above his head and rolled his eyes.

Daniel could see the man was growing impatient. "These stones have great power," he said. What could he say to buy a bit more time?

Feldman shrieked, "Tell me something worth knowing."

"These stones have killed everyone who has come in contact with them. They are more powerful than anyone can stand, including you, you pompous asshole. Your greed will kill you, *Mister* Feldman. Believe me; we must leave this place *right now*." He hoped the simple truth would be enough to sway Feldman, but the man was crazed.

Feldman laughed. "Why would I? Why would I ever choose to leave this place? The others were weak. They must have been." Feldman pulled Camille tighter to him. "This young woman is no longer of value, Daniel. Feel free to say your good-byes."

Daniel saw the tendons begin to constrict on Feldman's knuckle and he knew that the man would kill again. The power of the crystals ensured it.

***

Camille was terrified. She could see Feldman's ever tightening trigger finger. But wracked with fear or not, she was not about to die. *Hell, no.* Her eyes darkened and her face became a storm.

Feldman's hand began to shake. Camille knew she had him. She was gaining control. His finger loosened. The gun fell from his hand.

Camille's fury rose. She spun away from Feldman's grasp. His eyes were filled with disbelief. A horrific smile had replaced her mask of fear. She said nothing, staying with her mind's silent, simmering, growing power. He watched, helpless, as she glowered at him, feeding his horrified mind with thoughts of impending doom.

Feeling dumbfounded asshole? Can't control you body, can you … well, you haven't felt anything yet. Her intensity grew.

Feldman's hands flew to his temples. He writhed in pain as blood began to pour from his nose and ears.

Camille's wrath swelled into ubiquitous ferocity.

Feldman dropped to his knees. Crimson tears bled from his eyes. He fell forward, his hands still clasping his head, and crashed face first onto the walkway.

***

Daniel gawked at her in dismay. "Oh my God, Camille … what did you do to him?"

Camille could not take her eyes from the form, twitching in a growing pool of blood. "I wanted him to stop, that's all. I guess I gave him a thought he couldn't refuse." She sounded as if her intent was humor, but the result was wicked.

Daniel's jaw was on his chest. "How is this even possible?"

"All I know is that every part of me wanted him to stop." The casual nature with which she spoke and acted astounded Daniel. "I didn't want him to hurt anyone else. What should we do with him?" She shrugged, nonchalant.

Daniel chewed his lower lip, thinking, still amazed as he watched Feldman's last twitches come to an end. "I guess we'll have to leave him here along with the others and find some place to ditch his car. I don't think there will be any connection with us. He would have made sure of that. I doubt anyone will come looking for us—or him—at this place."

"I'm not worried about that. I'm imagining what it's going to be like the next time we come down here."

"Maybe we should drag the bodies to the side tunnel. We could even bury them. At least that would slow down the stench."

"I can't believe any of this," Faber blurted, his voice a rapid fire staccato, "What-is-wrong-with-you-people?"

Daniel had failed to disclose *everything* to Faber, the least of which and most important now being the changes associated with the crystals. He explained. "The crystals are immensely powerful. They've helped me to learn incredibly fast. I have had dreams that have been of past events and I've developed a photographic memory. I don't know very much about them myself, but I know that all of these men are dead because they were ignorant and greedy. The crystals act as a catalyst with a person's latent abilities. You've seen how they react to light. In direct sunlight they'll explode. McMaster was a greedy man to begin with, but as time went by he became greedier—to the point of egregious. Eventually he lost everything and crawled down here to die. Something similar happened to Grundpark, the man who lived down here fifty or so years ago."

"Yes, but that's not what happened to Feldman," Faber said, directing an accusing look at Camille. "What did you do to him?"

Camille told her story and then described her most recent understanding. "Daniel and I have had constant exposure with a few of the crystals. I now understand that I have adapted and am able control the flow of the thoughts that bombard me. Instead of being flooded with Feldman's evil thoughts, I turned them against him. Imagine if having the *wish to kill* had power—and that a person could increase that power a thousand times. That's what killed Feldman—his own desire to kill me."

Faber had a distant look of awesome consideration. "If this is all true, imagine what we could do with these crystals!"

"I wish I was a wise man," Daniel said, his voice thick with despair. "Then I would know what to do."

"Why do you say that," asked Faber.

"If you give in to your feelings about how powerful man could be if he was able to harness the power of these crystals, I am sure that it would be the beginning of the end for you and maybe everyone else as well. There is no controlling the stones. There is only self-control. I don't know anything about the original inhabitants, but I know about the last six people who have found this place. Three of them are dead and I can't help wondering what will become of us."

Faber took a pensive step back. "And what do you think *will* happen?"

"There's no way to know for sure, but no one is perfect, and ...," Daniel looked down in thought, then lifted his face back to Faber, "... it seems that those imperfections can be deadly."

"We should bury this place." Camille was adamant, her hands planted on her hips.

Faber countered. "No! We can't. Evidence of a lost civilization is down here. This may be the most significant find in recent history."

"Then what do you think we should do," asked Daniel. "How many more Feldmans, McMasters or Grundparks do you think there might be in the world?"

Faber had no response.

It was Camille whose good sense prevailed. "We need to go. There's no way we can think straight in here."

They returned to the house and Daniel started Feldman's car. "I'll let it warm up for a bit and then can you follow me."

Faber nodded and prayed under his breath that the old Volvo would start. The motor turned, painfully slow, and with every revolution the battery lost power. When he had no hope, the engine caught and the car sputtered to life.

Daniel drove to a nearby gravel pit to abandon the car. He stepped into a foot of dry powdery snow. Each footfall left nothing more than a depression, like walking in dry sand. Another snowfall or a little wind would obliterate any trace that he had been there. He followed the tire tracks to the road and to Faber's waiting car. Without a body there would be no evidence of a crime. With any luck Feldman's story would end here.

CHAPTER 94

The return trip to the house was solemn and silent. For each of the occupants, a gnawing dilemma loomed. Faber drove at a dozing snail's pace, struggling with the possibility of having to give up his lifelong dream of making an invaluable contribution to the world. How could he walk away from the one of the most—if not *the* most—significant finds modern mankind would ever know?

Meanwhile, Camille reflected on her first meeting with Daniel. She remembered having been astounded by his ability to read and recall whatever he wanted. She thought then that he could have had whatever riches and success he might desire and, at the time, she could not understand why he wouldn't want to pursue that. Now, faced with the ability to manipulate the mind of another and the subsequent death of Feldman, she understood that it was not a power she wanted the responsibility to wield. How could she be the one to determine the difference between good and evil? And if not her, then who ... who could she trust with such capability? She could think of no one.

Daniel debated the loss of an old friend. More than the crystals, he deliberated the loss of the dark warmth of the cavern which had been his refuge. If they decided the crystals were too dangerous for humanity to handle responsibly, then the only solution would be to bury the mine. In the darkness he had grown strong and, in some sense, he had healed. He remembered reading that children raised in foster care or who live in abusive homes sometimes develop an attachment disorder. These children can lose their ability to feel empathy or even the ability to feel love. He never thought that disorder applied to him, but he could not ignore the fact that when the crystals amplified his feelings, they did not become unmanageable as they did for the others. For him, the crystals seemed to help him feel alive. Without them, would he lose the feelings that he had come to cherish? Would he lose Camille one day? Of all that he had gained, he could give up everything ... except her.

In too short a time, Faber pulled into the driveway. The Bernards were still out. Thankfully, everything had happened in their short absence—confirming how suddenly life can change. Their adventure had turned deadly and, although they had lived through it, Daniel could not escape the feeling that part of them had died with Feldman. None of them would view the world the same and each would always know that there was something more.

Daniel shivered as he lit the fireplace. The three sat, huddled around the flickering light as warmth rose in the house. Faber was the first to speak.

"I see no way around it." He clapped both hands onto his thighs. "I have to purchase this property. We cannot destroy the site and we cannot leave the fate of these crystals to chance."

Camille's eyebrows rose. "Can you afford it?"

Faber laughed. "Of course I can. I've been saving my whole life, and for what?" Both his hands flew up. "I have no family to speak of. If I should leave this world having done nothing to improve it, maybe I can go out having done something to protect it."

Daniel listened intently, but if Faber were to own the property, yes, it might keep the crystals from being exploited, but ... he would lose whatever control he felt he had. "I'm not so sure, I—I mean, wha—"

"I know," Faber said with quick-to- reassure tone, "that you two are just starting out and I could certainly make this purchase on my own whether you agreed or not, but ... this was never my discovery." He looked directly at Daniel. "It is yours, Daniel. I propose that, although I would be backing the project, there are three names that must be on the deed. I have my life's work ahead of me, but the property needs a caretaker. We must proceed carefully, and I think we have all the expertise and skills necessary to do just that. What do you say? Can we be partners?" He looked first to Daniel, then to Camille.

Camille placed a hand on Faber's leg. "I would be honored to be your partner, Faber, but I feel strongly that your investment should be repaid."

"Thanks." He put a hand on top of hers, patted it. "I appreciate your sentiment, but it is unnecessary. I imagine we will want to explore these crystals further and learn more about them. This will take time and a greater investment. We will need to work cautiously to protect each other if we hope to avoid the fate of the others. I think there will be plenty of opportunity to repay me. If you like, you could start working off your share of the debt by taking over the responsibilities of looking after and rebuilding the site."

Daniel felt if he became any more excited he'd explode. "Faber, you won't regret this. I guarantee it. I'm sure I can rebuild what McMaster destroyed. Camille," he took her hand, the three of them now bonded in touch, "What do you say?"

Camille's broad smile and nod were all the response he needed.

"Good. We've settled it, then." Faber stood. "I'll get started on the paperwork first thing in the morning."

They shook hands all around and, after some sighs and laughter, an awkward silence followed.

Daniel broke the quiet. "I'm hungry. Maybe I can make us something to eat."

About the Author

Randy K. Wallace was born in Stayton Oregon. A few years later, his father moved the family of seven to Vanderhoof, a tiny town in central British Columbia, Canada. There was no electricity, water or phone service in their new home and Randy grew up helping his family turn a piece of wilderness into a farm. These meager beginnings shaped Randy's life, his teaching career and later, his writing.

ALL THINGS THAT MATTER PRESS ™

FOR MORE INFORMATION ON TITLES AVAILABLE FROM
ALL THINGS THAT MATTER PRESS, GO TO
http://allthingsthatmatterpress.com
or contact us at
allthingsthatmatterpress@gmail.com

www.ingramcontent.com/pod-product-compliance
Lightning Source LLC
Chambersburg PA
CBHW051530260626
47170CB00003B/873